PIRATE'S KISS

"You are a privateer?" Katelin had almost not dared ask the question. Most people agreed that privateers were much the same as pirates. "Tell me of your adventures," she went on, bolder now. "Have you captured ships filled with gold and caskets of rare jewels?"

"There is little to tell, Kat. Life on the sea is a business like any other . . . only more dangerous." Garrick rose to his feet and, placing his brandy glass aside, reached out and took her hand. "I think it is time for me to show you to your cabin."

But the simple act of touching her proved to be his downfall. The merest touch of her tender flesh sent dangerous flames of passion throughout his body. Without another word spoken, Garrick's head lowered, his mouth tenderly slanting over her rose-petal lips.

Katelin felt herself drowning in a sea of incredible pleasure. Her slender arms rose up to encircle his neck; her fingers entwined in the strands of his ebony hair, and without thinking, she pressed herself against his massive chest. Never had she been kissed so tenderly, so passionately, so hungrily!

At last he drew from his inner strength, and with a sigh of mixed pain and pleasure, he pulled his mouth away from hers.

Katelin stood on tiptoe to bring her lips back to his. "Why did you stop?" she whispered.

WHAT'S LOVE GOT TO DO WITH IT?

Everything . . . Just ask Kathleen Drymon . . . and Zebra Books

KATHLEEN DRYMON

PIRATE MOON

ZEBRA BOOKS
KENSINGTON PUBLISHING CORP.

ZEBRA BOOKS are published by

Kensington Publishing Corp.
475 Park Avenue South
New York, NY 10016

First Printing: August, 1993

Printed in the United States of America

To Ann LaFarge,
A wonderful editor and dear friend:
Thank you for all your support.

Prologue

London, 1814

Peacock blues, brilliant cherry reds, and shades of mauve, pink, and emerald, along with artfully gold-edged crystal, decorated the main saloon — a breathtaking spectacle that brought to mind all manner of erotic suggestions. The early evening hour revealed a bevy of women in various degrees of undress reclining upon plush, fashionable furniture. The glow of candlelight and fragrantly scented oil lamps brightened the lower portion of the establishment at 122 Cockspur Street.

It was a slightly rowdy group of six that entered through the front double doors and were greeted by Amos, the six-foot-six, no-nonsense black man who was known throughout London as the bouncer and butler of the bordello.

"Can I be taking your hats, gentlemen?" Amos remembered very well the last time this same group had visited Rose Bishop's establishment and the disruption their arrival had set into action, caused principally when two of the young men had desired a woman who

7

had already been promised to another customer. A very expensive fight had broken out. Amos frowned only slightly as he also remembered that it had been the fathers of the young men who had paid the bill. His frown gaining little attention, Amos was handed several hats amid the joking and jostling of the sons of the wealthy who had stayed on for the season and were wont to roam the streets of London at any hour, looking for entertainment.

As the group made their way into the lower, open portion of the lavishly appointed three-story building, one of the young men nudged an elbow against the forearm of his companion, and spoke in a low tone. "Do not forget, Kat, the only reason I agreed to bring you along with us tonight was because you promised to keep your eyes lowered and the brim of your hat pulled down. Those green eyes of yours are a dead giveaway!"

It was easy to see that the young man's companion had never been in such an establishment before. He nodded in assent to the other's words of caution. The green eyes peeping from beneath the brim of the black silk hat widened as one of Rose's girls, wearing little more than a sheer black low-cut negligee, boldly left the gilt-edged red velvet couch she had been lounging upon, and with a sultry walk, perfected over the years with the express purpose of capturing the male eye, she approached the group.

"I can see that you gentlemen want to have a good time this evening." She winked knowingly and her generous smile with its chipped top-front tooth included all of the small group. "My name is Milly, and I will let you gents in on a little secret." She leaned closer toward them as though indeed she did have a secret to

8

tell, and at the same time her hands cupped the outside fullness of her partially exposed, abundant bosom. "I have been known upon an occasion or two to be able to curl a gentleman's toes right up in his boots!" And as her wickedly sensual laughter left no doubt to her invitation, with an experienced movement of her hands, her breasts were set free. Capturing the attention of all in the group, the twin mounds of pale flesh with their darkened tips began to move in a circular motion as the rest of her lusty body remained motionless.

All eyes for a full minute held upon the rotating globes of creamy flesh. With a slight clearing of his throat, the first young man who came to his senses murmured in deep tones, "Well, Milly, I am your man. I could use a bit of toe curling this evening!" Milly reached for his hand, not allowing a second to pass in which he could change his mind and choose another, and began to lead him away. Stephen Robards caught the eye of the one called Kat, and as the hand pulled him from the group, he stated rather softly, "God's teeth, Kat, I am but human!"

As the evening progressed, one other departed from the group of six, and as Jeffrey Spencer was led away by a buxom blonde, Robert Newberry, the young man who had originally cautioned Kat about keeping the hat lowered, decided that it was time to call a halt to the evening.

It was just as the group began to make their way toward the main saloon that a darkly handsome gentleman stood upon the second-floor landing of the staircase. Before descending, he bent at the waist to a middle-aged, pale-featured woman at his side. Taking her hand within his own much larger one, he kissed

9

her wrist. "Be sure to tell Prinny I am sorry I did not get to see him while I was in London this time, Rose."

"Oh, I do wish you were not leaving on that dreadful ship so soon. You have only been in the London ports for a scant few days!" The woman made an attractive pout with her rouged lips which gave her a much younger look. "I am sure Prinny and his group will be coming in soon, and when he hears that he missed you by only a few minutes, I do not know what he might do!"

The tall, broad-framed man threw back his head and laughed loudly. "I fear not what our Prince Regent will make me suffer, Rose. Tell Prinny I will be back in London next season and that he still owes me much for forcing me to suffer those three dances with Corrine Applewhite at Lenox's ball the last time I saw him."

Rose Bishop's tinkling laughter trilled down the stairway as she envisioned the dashing Garrick Steele enduring the simperings of the overweight, long-faced Corrine Applewhite for the better part of an evening.

"Are you ready to leave now, Kat? I take it you have seen quite enough to satisfy?" Robert Newberry questioned, but noticed that his words were being cast upon deaf ears as he followed Kat's green gaze, which was focused upon the couple walking down the stairway.

It was at that exact moment that Rose Bishop turned her head away from her companion and looked down into the main saloon, riveted by the brightness of the almond-shaped green eyes that were staring at her and the handsome man at her side. Regaining herself quickly, she took hold of her escort's arm as she waved her orange blossom-scented, lace handkerchief about in the air to gain the attention of her trusted servant, Amos.

As Rose Bishop and Garrick Steele reached the bottom of the stairway, they were met by Amos, and Kat noticed that the man at the woman's side was even bigger than the butler. After Rose whispered a few hurried instructions into Amos's ear, the black man hurried off to do her bidding.

The small group stood off to the side of the stairway, the green eyes not seeming able to break away from the sight of the man and woman. And so it was that the group was caught unaware by the approach of the black man who, in a solitary motion, swept the wide-brimmed hat from Kat's head.

An audible gasp circled the crowded room. Rose Bishop's male patrons as well as her girls were caught by surprise as a cascading wealth of gleaming black curls tumbled from beneath the hat and fell to the waist of the handsomely tailored silk suit, which until this very moment all had believed to be worn by a young man.

Whispers began to circulate about the young woman's identity, even as the man at Rose Bishop's side seemed to have some trouble regaining his composure as he stared upon the vision of incredible beauty at the foot of the stairs. The ebony hair framing the creamy texture of her skin and the sparkling, jade green eyes were impossible to ignore.

It was Kat's companions who first came to their senses. Pulling Kat by the arm, they dragged her toward the front double doors, and severed the spell that had been cast by the possession of the man's steel blue eyes.

One

Word traveled like wildfire throughout London about the incident in Rose Bishop's main saloon. By the following morning, most of the servants at Wessely House were gathered around the scarred kitchen worktable, relating what they had heard about the old mistress's young niece. As though mimicking a gaggle of geese, they were all talking at once.

"Surely it must have been that same group of young rakes that visits Miss Katelin upon occasion here at Wessely House who led her down such an unsavory path!" Bethany, the young and very naive upstairs chambermaid voiced her opinion about the whole affair. "It is certain that Miss Katelin would never have gone to a house of ill-repute without their directing her to take such steps!"

It was Bertha Mallory, the overly plump Wessely cook, who gave the young chambermaid a withering eye. Knowing that Bethany was more than a little in awe of Elizabeth Wessely's beautiful niece, she tried to take charge of the conversation. "This whole affair could well be nothing more than a rumor and false at that, for all we know! Not that I be one to deny that

Miss Katelin can be a bit too carefree upon occasion, mind you, but if I were all of you"—she glanced around the large kitchen with a superior eye, not leaving any of the servants out—"I would not be adding more fuel to the fire, where such rumors are concerned. The mistress will not be pleased if word gets to her ear that the help have been talking about her niece!" Bertha Mallory was not one to look the other way over a bit of gossip, but at this time she thought she would take charge over the servants clamoring around in her kitchen.

"You are wrong there, Bertha Mallory." The butler, Thomas, spoke out just as he was entering the kitchen door. Puffing out his thin chest, he strode farther into the room and, in spite of himself, felt like gloating over the cook, who upon occasion thought herself more important than her position deserved. "The mistress herself received a visitor early this very morning, who brought her full detail of her niece's conduct in Rose Bishop's vice-filled establishment last night."

"A visitor, you say?" Bertha Mallory hated it when Thomas appeared to sneer down his long thin nose at the rest of the Wessely servants as he was doing now, especially when that nose was held in her direction. But in spite of his high-and-mighty attitude, her curiosity was piqued by the news that the mistress had had an early morning visitor. This was very unusual.

"Aye, the Reverend Jonathan Dansmith himself arrived on the front stoop of Wessely House an hour now long past. I showed him immediately to my lady's drawing room, so anxious was he to see her."

Bertha could well imagine Elizabeth Wessely's mood at having to receive a visitor at such an early hour. Her habit was always to rise late, after midmorning.

Hating to press Thomas for more information, but knowing no other of the Wessely servants were brave enough to dare pry out of him the tidbits he might have overheard while he was upstairs, Bertha drew in a deep breath. "And how can you be so sure that it was news of Miss Katelin's conduct last eve that brought the good reverend to our doorstep?" Bertha turned back to kneading her dough for bread, knowing that if she were to find out anything more from Thomas, she would have to appear uninterested, even as the rest of the servants awaited what next would be said by the always prim and overly proper butler.

Thomas straightened an imaginary wrinkle from his dark green velvet jacket as he felt all eyes except Bertha's upon him. "I am not given to gossiping about the mistress's business," he began, wanting to verify the fact that this occasion was most unusual for him. "I did hear the Reverend Dansmith saying that all of London is talking about Miss Katelin being caught unaware in the front room of that notorious house owned by Madam Rose Bishop." He pronounced the name of the lady as though it were loathsome in his mouth.

"And what is it that you be meaning when you say 'caught unaware'?" Again it was Bertha Mallory who questioned Thomas.

"The good reverend said something to the effect that Miss Katelin was dressed like a young man, and was revealed only when her hat was taken from her head by an employee of Rose Bishop's."

"Lud, can ye be believing the truth of all this?" Bessy, the brassy, red-haired parlormaid gasped aloud. "I be guessing that the old lady herself near fell dead away in a faint with such news being brought

15

to her about her precious girl!"

Thomas instantly seemed to realize, with the parlormaid's coarse comment, that he was lowering his usual high standards by gossiping with the servants here in the kitchen. "I am sure that her ladyship was taken by surprise by this news, just as everyone else is, but I see no reason to be standing around the kitchen table discussing Miss Katelin's affairs! Let's be getting back to work now before anything further can be added!" Thomas hoped that his slip of deportment would not be bandied about so that the mistress would hear of it.

That his mistress had been taken by surprise had in truth been an understatement. Elizabeth Wessely at the age of seventy-one stood ramrod straight before her niece, her anger more than apparent in her wrinkled face as two bright flush spots graced each high cheekbone. "My solicitor, Mister Grisewald has been sent for, Katelin. He will be arranging your passage immediately to Saint Kitts!" Looking at her beautiful niece, Elizabeth Wessely felt some of her fury die down. She knew that much of Katelin's conduct had to be laid upon her own head. She had spoiled the girl outrageously over the past ten years.

"You are sending me to Saint Kitts, Aunt Elizabeth? To my father?" The cry from the young woman was one of total disbelief. Katelin had just finished dressing in a lovely lavender, flower-sprigged day dress, when her aunt had entered her chamber without even a knock of warning. This had been unusual in itself, beside the fact that the hour was still early for her aunt to be up and about, but the moment Katelin had looked into her aunt's features and glimpsed the flush of anger plainly visible, she had known that news of last night's escapade had already reached her lady aunt.

The truth was that Katelin had not expected such a strong reaction from her aunt Elizabeth, and at the moment was stunned by her declaration to send her to the island of Saint Kitts.

There had been many other times that Katelin had been caught in pranks over the past ten years. She had been expelled from school for helping another girl sneak out into the stables late one night to meet the head groom's son. It was an exclusive girls' school, which her aunt had sent her to with the hopes of making a young lady out of her. And there had also been the time she had tried to help her friend Myra Livingston run away with her sweetheart, but they had been caught by Myra's father. Her aunt had been angry these times also, but she had never threatened to send her away! Even when it was discovered that Katelin had disguised herself as a boy and been taking fencing lessons with her longtime friends — the same friends she had been out and about with last evening — her aunt had not reacted so drastically.

"Aunt Elizabeth, you cannot be so upset with me that you will not even give me the chance to explain what truly happened last night!" Her green eyes sparkled with unshed tears as she wondered to herself what she could say that would make what had taken place in Rose Bishop's house any easier for her aunt to hear.

The tightly coiffed gray head instantly shook back and forth. "Not this time, my dear. My mind is already made up. You are running wild here in London! You need the strong guidance of a man to take charge of you before you dare anything more outlandish than visiting such an ill-favored place as you did last eve!" As though the girl could do anything more unheard of! Elizabeth Wessely had made up her mind with the guidance of Reverend Dansmith, and she was not going to back down now in the face of her niece's threatened tears.

"But, Aunt Elizabeth, I have not seen my father in ten long years. There has been no word from him since he moved from London to Saint Kitts!" Katelin could not believe that her aunt could be this cruel!

"My solicitor has kept me aware over the years of your father's affairs," Elizabeth confessed. She had not informed Katelin of this in the past for she saw no reason to sadden the girl without cause. Richard Ashford had not taken it upon himself to inform his daughter about the new life he had made for himself on Saint Kitts, and Elizabeth certainly did not think it her place to repeat what her solicitor had told her. "Your father still resides on the plantation on the island of Saint Kitts, which he inherited before your mother's death." She did not mention, for fear Katelin would increase her argument, that Richard Ashford had remarried shortly after his arrival on the island. However, Elizabeth thought that perhaps the marriage would be all to the better. Another woman, one some years younger than herself, could perhaps direct this strong-willed young lady much better than she had been able to.

"I do not even know my father any longer!" Katelin pleaded even as she glimpsed the determined slant of her aunt's firm chin. Fearing the worst, she felt tears trickle slowly down her cheeks.

Elizabeth sighed softly. She had warned herself, before coming to her niece's chambers, to keep herself hardened against the tears she had known would come. She had not come to her decision with the purpose of punishing the young woman; she truly believed that Katelin would benefit from the guidance of a father. "Your father loves you dearly, Katelin. When he left you in my care after your mother's death, he was too overcome with his own grief to tend to your needs. He is a good man, Katelin, I have always told you this, and if I did not believe this myself, I would not send you to him. With the passing of time you will see that I have only your best interest at heart. Mister Grisewald will arrange matters as quickly as possible. I do not want you to leave the house between now and the time you leave London. I fear that the gossipmongers are having a fine time with your latest exploits, and frankly, my dear, the Wessely name has suffered quite enough." With this, Elizabeth walked to the door, but before she turned the knob, some small regret must have touched her. "Dear, try to adjust to life with your father for at least two years. If you still miss London after this period of time, then of course you may return here to me." Opening the chamber door, she walked out of the room.

Katelin Ashford stood watching her aunt's straight back as she left the chamber, and with the soft sound of the door being closed, a soft cry of despair escaped her lips. "Noooo. I cannot be made to leave London and all those I care about, even for only two years!" Brushing away her tears with the backs of her hands, Katelin tried to rally her spirits by telling herself that surely her aunt would relent. She was using these threats only as a means of punishment and would change her mind in a day or two.

Aunt Elizabeth could not be serious about sending her to Saint Kitts.

Two

Standing alone on the wooden deck of the ship called the *Caroline*, Katelin leaned against the railing and wiped away her tears. The docks of London slowly faded amid the damp fog that stretched from sea to land. Wrapped within her own feelings of doom, she wondered, if somewhat belatedly, how the whole situation had ever come to this sad end. Everything had happened so quickly that she could hardly recall the last few days.

From that very morning when her aunt had announced she would be leaving London for Saint Kitts, Kat had been secluded behind the stone walls of Wessely House. Her friends, including several of the young men who had been with her that fate-filled night at Rose Bishop's establishment, had been turned away at the front door by the dour Thomas, under strict orders given out by her aunt Elizabeth. Katelin herself had not been allowed to step one slippered foot outside the house until this very morning, when she, along with numerous trunks and boxes containing her belongings, had been ushered into the Wessely carriage by Elizabeth Wessely. There at the busy London docks, a tearful good-bye was shared between aunt and niece. Katelin had been hurried across the wharf, and stepping across the gangplank, she had boarded the *Caroline*. Taking a position near the railing she had watched as her luggage had been boarded. Her aunt, now barely recognizable through the haze of swirling fog, waved her farewell.

Feeling the motion of the ship beneath her feet and the tang of salt spray mixed with the circling fog, Katelin patted at her swollen eyes with her laced-edged handkerchief. Two long years away from home and friends! The thought played over and over again in her head. How would she ever be able to survive a two-year separation? It was as though she were being banished from everything she held dear.

"Excuse me, Miss Ashford." Her dark thoughts were interrupted. "The captain sent me to see if there is anything that you are in need of." The first mate of the *Caroline* was a tall, slender young man in his middle twenties. He wore his light brown hair short beneath his seaman's cap, his hazel eyes proclaiming his easy manner. He was known as Scotty to his mates, and always having an eye for a beautiful woman, he had been more than pleased to do his captain's bidding on this occasion.

Kat had learned from Mr. Grisewald, who had met her and Aunt Elizabeth on the docks before the ship departed, that the *Caroline* was a merchant ship, carrying a full hull of fine wines and crates packed with bolts of laces and linens. She would be the only female of the four passengers aboard ship; however, Katelin had not expected personal attention from the officers. As the young man with the dark blue seaman's jacket awaited her reply, a smile slowly settled over her bow-

21

shaped lips. Perhaps her voyage to Saint Kitts would not be so very dull after all. Shaking her head, she replied, "Thank you, but I think that I will retire to my cabin for now."

Even with her tear-swollen eyes, her smile sent a radiant burst of light through the first mate's chest; her voice, so liltingly soft, left her words ringing in his head long after her beautiful lips had stilled. It took him a full moment to regain his composure, his hazel eyes looking upon her as though he awaited some small favor to be cast in his direction by her slender outstretched hand. "Tea then?" he at last stammered, and felt his face beginning to flush. What on earth was the matter with him, he berated himself. "I will send a tea tray to your cabin," he hurriedly explained as he tried to recover himself, and feeling more flustered than he had since being a raw youth, he quickly turned to carry out his self-appointed mission.

As he hurried down the upper deck toward the companionway and galley, he looked over his shoulder for one last glimpse of her beauty. He would claim the honor of carrying her tea tray to her cabin, not the cabin boy, Duffy. Perhaps, with any luck at all, he would witness her enchanting smile once more. And he would tell Captain Howard that he'd be delighted to entertain Miss Ashford throughout the voyage to Saint Kitts.

The officer's flattering reaction was certainly nothing new to Katelin. For the past few years, ever since she had changed from an ungainly, long-legged girl into a self-assured young woman, she had had numerous gentlemen paying her suit. A small smile still remained on her lips as she watched the young man hurry across the deck of the ship. Pulling her fur-lined cloak a bit tighter around her shoulders, she began to make her way to her cabin.

Perhaps she had been a bit hasty in her first impression of this sea voyage. After all, there was little she could do to change the fact that she was on her way to her father. What other choice did she have but to make the best of the situation? She certainly was not one to wear a long face and bemoan her fate! With the eternal optimism that is usually granted to youth, she decided then and there that she would put her best foot forward, and look at this whole undertaking as a high adventure! Feeling somewhat better as she entered her cabin, she tried to convince herself that her stay on Saint Kitts would be a holiday of sorts. A two-year holiday, and then she would return to London.

Her cabin was small, since most of the space on the *Caroline* was intended for transporting goods. There was a cot against one wall and a table and wardrobe against another. Unpacking a few items of clothing and setting her toilet articles on the small table, Katelin brushed out her long hair before hanging up her warm cloak in the small wardrobe. With little else to do, having already adjusted somewhat to the easy, gliding motion of the ship, she took up the book she had been reading while still at her aunt's house.

A few minutes later, there was a knock on the cabin door. Setting her book aside, Katelin found the young officer standing with a tea tray in hand. Her generous smile welcomed him. "You returned so soon," she said with some surprise.

The first mate entered the cabin and set the tray down upon the foot of the cot. To his way of thinking, he had not returned soon enough! Katelin Ashford was quite possibly the most beautiful woman he had ever met. Without her cloak, it was even more apparent to him that she had been blessed with an abundance of charm. She wore a stylish walking suit, the black velvet skirt molding her hips and covering long, slim legs; her form-fitting, red short-waist jacket covering a crisp white silk shirtwaist, which boasted a red lacy tie about the throat. With her glistening ebony curls flowing freely down her back, she was utter perfection standing before him. Sparkling green eyes held upon him so warmly that he felt his insides melting.

"The tea will take the chill off, miss," he stammered, at last pulling himself out of his stupor and hoping he did not appear the fool in front of her, for at the moment he felt as though he were little more than a dull-witted lackey.

What Katelin had missed most while under confinement at Wessely House was the company of her male friends. She had learned early on that she could be herself around most men. There was not the competition among men that she felt when she was around other women. Katelin also felt that men knew much better than women how to entertain themselves. The women she had known had considered it an enjoyable afternoon to sit around sewing and gossiping. Men, on the other hand, were much livelier companions. This young man standing before her now she found interesting, if somewhat shy. "The tea is most appreciated, Mister—?" Katelin wished to put him at his ease, and thought that perhaps learning his name would be the start.

"The name is Scott Roberts, miss. Most everyone calls me Scotty. I am the first mate aboard the *Caroline*, and if there is anything you need, do not hesitate to let me know." Scotty lingered in her cabin, wishing

24

he did not have to leave and get back to his duties. If it were up to him, he would stay where he was forever.

"Well, Mister—I mean, Scotty—again I thank you for the tea." Katelin smiled, at the moment enjoying herself immensely. What woman in her right mind would not enjoy being showered with silent praises to her beauty as she was now, for the young man's green-brown-flecked eyes told her all that his stammering lips could not!

For a full minute more the first mate stood staring. Then, turning around at last, he started to the door, but he pulled up short of turning the knob. "Dinner is served in the captain's cabin at seven. The passengers usually dine there with the ship's officers." He said aloud the only thing that came to his mind, the only thing that could prolong his leave-taking.

"Well then, I am sure we shall see each other again at dinnertime, Scotty," Katelin replied. And with nothing else to keep him, Scotty silently pulled the cabin door closed.

Leaning back against the pillow propped against the cabin wall, with a cup of tea and her book, Katelin spent her first day out to sea a little less worried. Determined now to make the best of the situation, she admitted, if only a little bit, that she was anxious to see her father again after all these years.

It had been ten long years since Richard Ashford had delivered her to her mother's eldest sister, Elizabeth Wessely. She could well remember that day when she and her father had arrived at Wessely House, and sitting in the front parlor, her father had wiped away the tears falling from his eyes. She could still remember his words when he had spoken brokenly to her aunt, claiming to only need time to try and deal with the loss of his beloved wife.

Katherine Ashford, Katelin's mother, had died in childbirth, trying to deliver herself of the child she and her husband had desired so much. With her death, some of the life had gone out of Richard Ashford. He blamed himself and, he swore to Elizabeth Wessely, the pain intensified each time he looked upon his daughter, who was the living reminder of her young beautiful mother.

There had been no argument. Katelin's Aunt Elizabeth was more than willing to take over the responsibility of her dear sister's only child. Richard Ashford left England for Saint Kitts two days later, having inherited a plantation called Coral Rose from his cousin, and Katelin herself had not heard from her father again. For a few years he had kept in sparse contact with her aunt, but no letters had ever been sent directly to her.

Over the years Katelin had hardened herself to her father's desertion. She had been more than happy living at her aunt's residence in London, and without question she had been amply spoiled by that great lady, even though her aunt tried upon occasion to hide her softer nature. Katelin knew that her aunt truly believed she was making the right decision by sending her away from London, and upon reflection, she had to admit that even London had been growing rather tiresome of late.

If the truth were told, restlessness had been the reason for Katelin's wilder exploits about London; many she knew her aunt had never found out about. And boredom had certainly been the reason she and her friends had visited Rose Bishop's house of ill-fame. Katelin had been bored to distraction with the round of parties and balls that her small group had been attending; the same faces, the same dance partners, the same mindless chatter. The evening she had overheard Robert Newberry and Jeffrey Spencer talking about the infamous Rose Bishop's house, she had quickly decided to disguise herself as a young gentleman and accompany them.

At first they had refused her plan to go along with them, but as usual, her friends had been unable to resist her charming pleas. It was not long before they, too, were growing excited with the idea. It had been a great lark! Katelin had always wondered what such a house looked like from the inside, and she had not been disappointed as she had viewed the erotic splendor of the place. All had been going so well until the minute she had been found out.

As the tea cooled and the book had long ago quit holding her interest, Katelin lay back against the pillow to rest. If it had not been for that man standing on the stairway talking to the woman, who she had learned later had been Rose Bishop herself, she would never have been caught. Her small group would have left the front door of the establishment just as they had entered, instead of her being dragged out by Robert while every patron in the building, as well as the girls who worked for Rose, stared after her.

Everything that had happened, from the moment she had looked up that staircase and glimpsed the couple until this very moment, was the direct fault of that darkly handsome, blue-eyed devil!

Dinner aboard the *Caroline* was a pleasant affair. Katelin, being the only woman in the small group was, of course, the center of attention. There were three other passengers aboard and all had turned out for dinner in the captain's cabin. Captain John Howard was an agreeable host. A man in his early sixties, with graying hair and a slim frame, he cordially poured his company's wine as he asked after each person's comfort aboard his ship. He paid much attention to Katelin's plate, and each time she sampled the fare, he quickly replaced it with another spoonful.

Sitting to the captain's right, Katelin was the recipient of questions from all the gentlemen in the room, officers and passengers alike. "Have you ever been to the Caribbean before, Miss Ashford, or in fact have you ever taken a voyage aboard a ship?" asked a portly gentleman with twinkling black eyes and graying tufts of hair sticking out over each ear.

"The truth is, Mister Graham, I have been aboard ships in the past, but I have not been far from England. While I was in school, the father of a dear friend of mine owned a shipping line, and one summer her father took us both aboard one of his ships for a couple of days. He taught me much about sailing and I admit that I loved every minute of the experience."

"Ah, then, my dear, you are certainly in for quite a treat. There is nothing in all the world like a warm tropical day on the beaches of Saint Kitts." Austin Graham smiled fondly as though in remembrance of some delightful afternoon spent in his past.

"There are also plenty of reasons to be on guard in the Caribbean, dear lady. Do not let my friend here fool you," a slender, middle-aged man with a long-bearded face countered. Katelin had been told that he was Austin Graham's traveling companion. His man-

28

ner was the opposite of his friend's; he forever looked upon the darker side of everything.

"And pray tell, Mister Parrish, what would you warn me of?" Katelin looked around the table and found several of the captain's guests, including the captain himself, shaking their heads, for they already knew of Joel Parrish's penchant for finding little favor with most topics of discussion.

Mr. Parrish was not unaware of the patronizing looks that were directed his way. But ignoring them, he focused his attention upon the young woman. It was better to be aware of trouble coming your way, then to be taken unaware, he always thought. "Why, the sun for one thing. It can all but dry up a soft complexion like yours. And another thing, these waters in and around the Caribbean are infested with pirates and cutthroats! Why, a young lady like yourself would have little chance in the company of such rogues!"

The captain and Scotty would have both intervened at that moment, believing Mr. Parrish trying to frighten Katelin, but with a generous smile she spoke up before either man could come to her defense. "And, of course, you have met such men in your travels, Mister Parrish?" Katelin like everyone else in the group had heard stories about pirates. But such tales were rare to hear from the lips of anyone who had ever encountered these so-called pirates and cutthroats.

"Why . . . why no, of course I have not had such misfortune myself. But mark my word, there are plenty who have, and even plenty more who did not live to tell their story!" Joel Parrish glimpsed several grins around the table, and dusting at some unseen lint upon the arm of his dark jacket, he straightened his frame in the chair. "Bristol Jack is the worst of the lot. Perhaps you have heard of him?" His gaze included the men. "Why, he has killed and maimed hundreds throughout the Caribbean!" There, he thought to himself, let any one of them rebuke that.

It was Captain Howard who answered, having had enough of such talk. It was one thing for gentlemen to talk about such matters in private, but quite another while in the company of a young lady. "Miss Ashford, I suggest you get yourself a hat to ward off the bright rays of the tropical sun, and as for the other"—here he looked meaningfully at Joel Parrish, as though warning him to remain quiet—"you have nothing to fear while aboard the *Caroline*. My crew would defend your honor to the last breath, as I am sure every man in this cabin would!"

Katelin smiled warmly to those sitting around the table; they nodded in agreement to the captain's words. "Of course I have no fear of pirates." She laughed softly, believing that the world of pirates, blackguards, and cutthroats was far removed from her own life.

"So tell me once again, my dear, the name of your father? I have heard of the Coral Rose plantation, but I am not sure I caught his name," Jason Hamilton, the third passenger aboard the *Caroline*, questioned Katelin.

Katelin felt more at ease talking about pirates than about her own father, but she tried not to allow her inner feelings to show. "My father's name is Richard Ashford."

The gentleman appeared to think hard for a minute before responding, "No, I am afraid I have not had the pleasure of his acquaintance. Perhaps during my

30

stay on Saint Kitts I will meet him."

The rest of the evening passed in the same manner. Joel Parrish said little, but appeared to enjoy the lively company in the captain's cabin. The first mate of the *Caroline* also seemed to enjoy himself immensely, appearing to hang on every word Katelin uttered, and as the evening grew late and she claimed fatigue, he insisted upon seeing her to her cabin.

"One day I will captain my own ship," Scotty stated proudly as he led her down the companionway.

"That will be wonderful, Scotty." Katelin tried to sound excited before a yawn overtook her. The motion of the ship, the good food, and the fact that she had had few restful nights over the past week were all strong inducements to sleep and at the moment Katelin wanted no more than to find her small cot and lie down.

"Miss Ashford, I do hope you did not let Mister Parrish's talk of pirates frighten you. I have often ventured upon the seas of the Caribbean, and have never met up with a pirate ship."

Katelin turned toward the young man as they stopped before her cabin door. It was kind of him to assure her that she was safe, but at the moment Mr. Parrish's words of warning were the last thing on her mind. "Thank you, Scotty, but I assure you I feel safe indeed aboard the *Caroline*. There is no need for you to think upon the matter again."

Not wishing to leave her presence so soon, the first mate reached out for anything that would keep her a moment longer. "I . . . I was wondering, Miss Ashford, that is, I know that you made mention of your father living on Saint Kitts, but I was wondering if there is someone else that you have as yet not mentioned? Perhaps a gentleman, someone you are going to Saint Kitts

31

to meet?" There, he had gotten it out at last.

Katelin's tinkling laughter filled his ears and circled about the companionway. "No indeed, Scotty, there is no gentleman." Indeed, a gentleman friend in her future had not even been considered. Oh, she admitted that she did enjoy the company of men, but in truth she was not ready to settle down.

Scotty seemed to sigh aloud with relief. A smile appeared on his handsome face, and after opening her cabin door for her, he took hold of her hand and kissed the back of her wrist. "Perhaps then we shall see each other upon the morrow, Miss Ashford." His brown eyes held all the warmth that his heart was feeling at the moment.

Katelin knew instantly that she had made a mistake. She should have told him that she was not interested in any kind of dalliance. All she wanted was to get through the next two years of her life and return to London! But before she could say another word, the first mate had left her side and was making his way back down the companionway. For a minute she thought to call him back and explain herself fully, but as she witnessed the jaunty way he walked back to the captain's table, she did not have the heart to dissuade him. There would be plenty of time to set him straight during the voyage to Saint Kitts. Why should she ruin his evening as well as her own? She would just try to avoid him as much as possible in the future.

That first night aboard the *Caroline,* Katelin slept like a baby. Dreams of one day returning to London filling her head as the merchant ship sailed on toward her destination.

Three

After the first evening aboard ship, Katelin found it easy to avoid the first mate. She was careful not to look in his direction and declined any attempts he made to further their acquaintance. She found her own way to her cabin after dining at the captain's table, and after a day or two the cabin boy, Duffy, came to her cabin each afternoon with her tea tray.

Much of her time was spent in her cabin reading, but upon occasion she stood at the railing and watched the beauty of the sea. Often one of the other passengers would also be on deck and would join her for a few moments of pleasant company.

They were now only a few days away from Saint Kitts and the weather had turned foul. Dinner at the captain's table that evening was rather a strained affair as the ship was restlessly tossed upon the waves. Mr. Parrish and Mr. Graham stayed in their cabin, both declaring that their stomachs were much too queasy to partake of the evening meal. Katelin, however, felt fine. Even bad weather did not affect her love of the sea.

"I would ask all passengers to stay in their cabins until this nasty weather runs its course," Captain Howard announced as Duffy cleared away the dinner dishes. "Upon occasion the storms in this area can become rather unsettling, and I would not wish any harm to come to any one of you." As he spoke, he looked toward Katelin. "But have no fear." He had not missed the slight widening of her green eyes. "We shall come through this storm safe and sound just as we have many others. The *Caroline* is a fit vessel!"

Just as Katelin stepped out of the captain's cabin, a huge wave rocked the ship. Katelin grabbed hold of the guard rail that ran the length of the companionway, and as the ship settled, the first mate approached and placed a hand upon her back to ensure she did not fall.

"Miss Ashford, I hope I have done nothing to offend you." He could not figure out what he had done to put her off, but after that first evening, when he thought he had made some headway in her regard, she had all but ignored his existence.

"Of course not, Scotty." The words came out rather sharply, and truly not meaning to be cutting or to hurt the young man, Katelin gave him a small smile to show her goodwill. But another wave dashed the ship about and she had to hold on for all she was worth in order not to fall to the deck and roll down the companionway. She was finding her effort to pacify the first mate a bit more than she could deal with at the moment. "Perhaps tomorrow we will have a minute to talk about this," she shouted over the sound of crashing thunder. "Right now, I only want to get to my cabin." And if tomorrow ever did come for those aboard the *Caroline*, Katelin thought as she worried

34

over the ferocity of the storm, she would simply tell this young man that she held no thought of furthering any kind of intimacy with him or any other man.

Appearing to come quickly to his senses, Scotty realized that this indeed was not the right time to speak to her about his feelings, for the storm appeared to be worsening by the second. He knew he could spare little more time in the companionway; he was needed above deck with the rest of the crew fighting the raging storm. "Of course, I do apologize," he shouted above the commotion of the storm. Taking her hand from the security of the rail, he held her tightly about the waist and led her to her cabin.

Katelin sighed her pent-up relief as she closed her cabin door and hurriedly reached the safety of her cot. Thank God it had been secured to the floor like the rest of the furniture in the cabin. Now all she had to do was keep herself from being thrown from the bed to the floor!

The night seemed endless as Katelin lay fully dressed upon the bed without even a light to lessen her fears as the overhead sounds of the mighty tempest combined with gale-force winds to dash the *Caroline* to and fro about the sea. Sometime during the early hours of the morning, Katelin jumped straight up on the cot as the sound of a gigantic crash assaulted her ears and seemed to rumble throughout the ship. Closely following upon its heels another crash erupted, but this one held lesser intensity.

Katelin's first thoughts were to escape the cabin. Trying to pull herself off the cot, she felt the ship lurch then lunge, throwing her down upon her back. A few minutes later all seemed calm. She could hear running footsteps overhead, and the shouts given out by the crew penetrated even the wooden walls of her small cabin.

Tentatively she placed a foot upon the wood flooring, then another, at any moment expecting the ship to be plunged about once again. With a deep gulp of air, she started to make her way toward the cabin door, prepared to grab hold of a piece of furniture to steady herself if the need arose. But the *Caroline* seemed to be riding the waves calmly for the time being. She opened the door and peered down the companionway.

There was water on the floor—rainwater, seawater, or both—but she ignored the soaking of her slippers as she made her way toward the upper decks. The worst of the storm appeared to be over but Katelin had to be assured that there was not terrible damage caused by the loud crashing sounds that had shaken the ship. She did not want to remain in her cabin, there to be caught unaware if the worst were to happen and the *Caroline* were sinking. She had to find out for herself that all was well.

Katelin stepped out upon the upper deck, and as Duffy ran past her, she followed the direction he was taking. Acrid smoke filled her nostrils as she rounded a corner, and as shouts and calls filled her ears, she was held immobile as she watched the crew frantically fighting off leaping flames where fire had engulfed a great portion of the main mast.

Lightning had split the main mast in two and the bright orange flames were now licking the wood and canvas sail. Katelin could not move as she stared at the crew scurrying around with water buckets, trying to combat the dangerous fire. The rains had stopped as quickly as they had come the day before, and though the sea was now calm, the disaster the storm had caused was still being felt.

"Ship ahoy, astern!" shouted the lookout in the crow's nest, and all eyes were drawn in the direction the crewman indicated.

The *Caroline* was listing now, and the only way the ship could recover from her damages was to be aided to a nearby port. Katelin immediately felt relief fill her as she rushed to the railing along with the other passengers, and watched as a sleek ship quickly approached them.

"We had best all be praying that it's not a pirate ship coming toward us, or even Bristol Jack and his scurvy bunch of cutthroats!" declared a member of the crew who was standing near Katelin, and for emphasis spat out a long stream of tobacco juice over the side railing.

" 'Tain't likely that any of us will be seeing tomorrow shine, if it is!" another crewman stated, his gaze holding on the approaching ship.

Standing not far away from Katelin was Joel Parrish, and drawing her attention with his stern glance, the older man nodded his head as though warning her that she should have paid more attention to him that first night while they shared dinner at the captain's table. He had warned her about pirates who roamed the Caribbean. Now she might be meeting them face to face!

"She sails the British flag, Captain!" the lookout shouted as he peered through his spyglass at the approaching vessel. Each detail of the ship's approach was quickly reported to Captain Howard. "Her name be the *Sea Witch!*"

The crew and passengers let out a collective sigh of

relief. Everyone began talking at once, all overjoyed that the ship flew their country's flag and not the skull and crossbones they had all inwardly feared.

Scotty had asked Katelin to return to her cabin while the crew put out the fire, but she had stood fast, not wanting to miss any of the excitement. She now remained on deck to watch as the crew tried to repair the mast.

It was becoming apparent that the *Caroline* was in serious trouble. Without the main mast, she could make little headway, and where the mast had been broken away there was a large hole which was allowing seawater to enter the bowels of the ship. At this moment men were manning the pumps to drain out the water that was rushing in as quickly as it was pumped out.

The approaching British ship was a godsend. Captain Howard hurriedly ordered the distress flag to be raised, then directed his crew to make ready for the coming vessel.

The *Sea Witch* was a sleek ship with sails dyed a light gray. Seemingly it had appeared out of nowhere and in a short amount of time she was pulling up alongside the *Caroline*. All four of the *Caroline*'s passengers as well as the crew stood on deck and watched as a young man with a trimmed beard and flowing mustache, who sported a dark blue seaman's jacket, appeared on deck and called out to the *Caroline*, "We saw your flag of distress. Can the *Sea Witch* be of any help?" It was apparent that the man was being very cautious for the *Sea Witch* was holding a short distance away while the dark gaze of the sailor appeared to search out the decks of the damaged ship.

Captain Howard did not hesitate to call out a reply.

"Aye, my ship is in bad need of repair. We are on our way to Saint Kitts, but the storm has caused severe damage." He looked over at the crew aboard the other ship, but finding nothing that would worry him, he again thanked his good fortune.

"I am sure my captain will be more than glad to accommodate you. If you would care to come aboard, Captain, you may speak with him in his cabin," the young man shouted back.

Within minutes the two ships were loosely secured together and Captain Howard was boarding the other ship. Crew and passengers aboard both ships shouted back and forth as Captain Howard and the first mate of the *Sea Witch* headed for the other captain's cabin.

Katelin watched expectantly, enjoying the lively conversations around her.

Captain Howard was gone only a short time, and reappearing aboard the *Caroline*, he seemed well satisfied with the time spent with the captain of the *Sea Witch*. "Very personable fellow, that Captain Steele. Yes indeed, he's a good sort. He will be taking us on, all the way to Saint Kitts. It appears it's his destination also." Captain Howard spoke aloud to his first mate, but everyone standing around deck took some interest in what he said.

"Miss Ashford, Captain Steele has graciously agreed to allow you to travel aboard his vessel for the remainder of the voyage. I am sure you will be much more comfortable without the worry that riding aboard a damaged vessel might cause."

"But Captain, I see no reason for me to go aboard the *Sea Witch*. I am fine here aboard the *Caroline*." Katelin balked at the idea of having to go aboard the other ship. There were only a couple more days to the

39

end of the voyage, and the thought of having to get used to another vessel did not at all appeal to her. Besides, she knew she was being singled out because she was a woman. Thus far she had weathered the hard times as well as any man aboard ship, and she saw no reason now why things should change.

Captain Howard, hearing her words and easily sensing her objections as he viewed the straightening of her back, quickly made his way to her side. Taking her hand in his, he stated with a fatherly appeal, "You will have nothing whatsoever to fear, my dear. The *Caroline* will be right behind the *Sea Witch*. I will have Scotty bring a few of your things along for the completion of the voyage." He looked in the first mate's direction as Scotty hurried off to do his captain's bidding.

Not allowing her any more objections, Captain Howard, with a hand upon the small of Katelin's back, led her to the plank that had been stretched from ship to ship. The crew of the *Sea Witch* scurried around the deck securing the *Caroline* with grappling hooks, but as Katelin stepped foot aboard their ship, the lot of them stood still for a full minute staring after her.

Captain Howard escorted her to the first mate, Lucas Bennett, as the rest of the crew aboard the *Sea Witch* stood in awe of her rare beauty. Bennett's gaze stole over her from head to foot, her sparkling green eyes holding upon him and making his heart flutter crazily in his chest.

It was Scotty who brought the first mate back to reality, as he crossed the plank with Katelin's valise. Spying the way the other man was staring at the woman he had fully hoped to win for himself, Scotty stated in a rather cool fashion, "Miss Ashford will

40

need your hospitality for only the two days it will take us to reach Saint Kitts."

"Aye, two days should see us to our destination," Captain Howard added, somewhat surprised at his first mate's tone since he was unaware of Scotty's feelings toward the lone female passenger. Nor did the captain detect the instant dislike that had arisen between the two first mates. "Once we arrive on Saint Kitts, Miss Ashford will join her family and we will make our repairs. Please tell your captain once again of my deep appreciation for his assistance." Captain Howard was rather distracted at the moment, and wanted to return to the *Caroline*. The sky was growing rather cloudy, and he feared another storm would catch them, one perhaps even more disastrous than the first.

"I will see that Miss Ashford is made comfortable, rest assured, Captain." The first mate's words were directed at Captain Howard, but as he spoke them, he looked Scotty directly in the eye as though adding more to their meaning.

"I truly don't think that all of this fuss is necessary, gentlemen." Katelin once again tried to object to her being moved from ship to ship, but instantly she was overruled by all three men. Even though Scotty hated the thought that she would be out of his sight for the next couple of days, he knew she would be far safer aboard the *Sea Witch*.

After Captain Howard and Scotty had left the *Sea Witch*, the first mate led Katelin to his own cabin, and there explained, "I will just get a few things and then I will be out of your way, Miss Ashford."

"Oh no, I cannot possibly take your cabin!" Katelin objected as she watched the young man throwing toilet articles and clothing into a canvas bag.

"I am afraid there is nowhere else for you to go. I will take a hammock down below decks with the rest of the men." Glimpsing the concern on her pretty face for casting him from his bed, he added in a gentle tone, "After all, it will only be a couple of days before we reach Saint Kitts."

"I guess you are right, Mister—?" Katelin tried to remember if she had been told this young man's name.

"Lucas Bennett, at your service." The young man with the neatly trimmed beard and flowing mustache stood in the doorway with his canvas bag tucked under his arm. "Just make yourself comfortable. I will come for you at the dinner hour to dine with Captain Steele. I am afraid until then he will not be available."

Katelin could only smile her thanks. It appeared that everything had been taken out of her hands, so she had no alternative but to adjust to her new surroundings. "Until dinnertime, then," she responded just before he shut the door.

This cabin was somewhat bigger than her room aboard the *Caroline*, but it took Katelin a few minutes to adjust to the fact that she had removed Lucas Bennett from his quarters.

All she wanted was to get this voyage over with! Once she was on Saint Kitts she would begin to pray in earnest for the next two years to pass quickly.

The afternoon slowly waned, and captured in the grasp of utter boredom, Katelin began to prepare for dinner with the captain. The dinner hour aboard the *Caroline* had been a lively affair, with the passengers and officers sitting around Captain Howard's table, so she anticipated another pleasant evening in the captain's cabin aboard the *Sea Witch*.

Dressing in a green velvet gown with a lacy, low-cut, cream-colored décolletage, Katelin brushed out her long, dark tresses and swept the sides up to the top of her head. She pinned the mass together with a diamond hair ornament and allowed the curling length to hang free down her back. Wearing dangling diamond earrings that matched the hair pin, she critically studied her image in the small, chipped glass mirror that hung upon the cabin wall.

Thinking of the evening ahead, she wondered once again about the captain of the *Sea Witch*. She had set in her mind that he would be an older gentleman, who left the running of his ship mostly up to his crew. What had Captain Howard said about him? A personable fellow, a good sort? Well, at least there would be younger officers in attendance, she told herself. The first mate certainly seemed pleasant enough.

Shortly after she put on her matching slippers, there was a knock on her cabin door. Opening it, she was met by Lucas Bennett, who for a full moment seemed to have taken leave of his senses, as he stared at her as though he had never seen a woman before.

After regaining his senses, the first mate cleared his throat. "I . . . I am so sorry for staring, Miss Ashford. Please do not take offense at my ill manners, but in truth you are a vision to behold."

Katelin felt a slight blush grace her cheeks; she enjoyed the courtly game of flirting with an attractive young man. "Surely, Mister Bennett, my ship-worn appearance cannot measure up to such a compliment." Her eyes sparkled like emerald lights, enchanting the young man in front of her and for another moment causing him to forget why he was there.

"I . . . I am afraid Captain Steele is still somewhat busy, but dinner will be served shortly. Once he is away from his desk, the captain is enjoyable company." Lucas forced his thumping heart to settle down somewhat as he tried to focus on his duty, which at that moment was to see this beautiful creature to his captain's cabin.

The first mate's appreciation of her beauty put Katelin in a reckless mood. She had to admit she'd been growing rather bored, on the *Caroline*, with the few passengers and officers competing during dinner to entertain her. If the officers aboard the *Sea Witch* were anything like this young man, the evening would not be dull.

Presenting his arm for her to take, Lucas Bennett led Katelin down the companionway, his chest swelling with pride as he passed two crew members and drew their jealous stares. After a single knock on the outside portal of the captain's cabin, the first mate pushed the door wide and motioned for her to step in front of him.

Katelin's green eyes flashed quickly around the lavishly appointed, masculine cabin. The walls were covered with a rich mahogany paneling. An intricately designed oak and glass bookcase stood against one wall, and a window seat was built on the opposite wall. In a corner of the cabin was a curtained alcove, which she assumed contained the captain's bed. In the center of the cabin rested two comfortable-looking wing chairs with a small table between, and off to the side of the room was a large oak desk littered with charts, ledgers, and maps of every description.

Just as Katelin was about to turn back to the first mate and question him about the whereabouts of his captain and the other officers, a tall form stepped from the curtained alcove, and in that instant Katelin Ashford felt her heart skip a beat, then begin to thump wildely in her breast. "You!" That was the only word Katelin could gasp aloud as the large shape of the man stepped closer and the dim lighting of the cabin slowly revealed his face and form.

Four

"At your service, my lady." The deep, masculine voice seemed to circle the cabin and settle over Katelin in a heated rush, and at the same time left her feeling as though she was going to suffocate.

Turning around to demand that the first mate return her to her own cabin, she found that Lucas Bennett had disappeared and the door had been silently shut behind him. She was entirely alone with this man — the very man who, she believed, had been the cause of her whole life being turned upside down. Drawing a deep breath, Katelin tried to soothe her shattered wits, but her inner voice kept repeating the warning, *It's he! It's he!*

At first sighting of the *Caroline*, Garrick Steele had hurried above decks. Grabbing the eyeglass himself to ensure that the listing ship was not a pirate vessel, he had been caught in utter surprise as he allowed the spyglass to go over each person on deck and it had finally upon the woman now standing before him. Even from a distance, there had been no doubt that the woman aboard the *Caroline* was the same one he had seen in Rose Bishop's bordello. He could never forget that face and those beautiful green eyes! Unsure of his reason at the time, he had returned to his cabin and instructed his first mate to bring the captain of the *Caroline* aboard. It had been easy to suggest to Captain Howard that his female passenger would be more comfortable, and far safer, aboard his ship.

"I must admit that I am as startled as you are," Garrick Steele began, enjoying the total surprise and confusion on the young woman's face. "Who would have believed that any man could be blessed with such good fortune?" He now stood fully within the cast of yellow light given off by the oil lamp glowing on his desk, and without second thought his gaze lingered over her cloud of dark hair and the perfection of her heart-shaped face. He wondered how many times over the past weeks he had seen this face in his dreams.

"Good fortune?" Katelin gasped aloud. The cause of her being sent from her home and friends and all she called dear stood before her and dared to call this unlikely meeting *good fortune!*

Garrick Steele sensed the lady was not pleased to find him the captain of the ship that had come to the *Caroline*'s rescue. For a few lingering seconds, he pondered the cause of her upset, but having never conversed with her he was truly in the dark as to her temper. "Perhaps you would care to sit down and we can discuss this topic of good fortune that we appear to disagree over," he offered. Looking toward the two chairs, he invited her to take a seat.

"On second thought, Captain, I believe I will take my meal in my own cabin." Katelin was determined not to dine with him, and the first thing in the morning, she would demand to be put back on board the *Caroline*! She did not want to stay on the same ship with this man who had caused so much disaster in her life, yet at the same time seemed to be the handsomest man she had ever met.

"I'm afraid that is impossible. Dinner will be served any minute now, and I will not make more work for my crew by forcing one of them to take a tray to your cabin."

Katelin was not lost to the harsh edge that had crept into his voice, and she dared not try to force the issue. She admitted, if only to herself, that she felt her knees trembling before his awesome regard. He was so tall and broad-shouldered, and she could not take her eyes off his handsome face.

Reaching out a strong hand, Garrick tenderly took hold of her elbow and led her to the chairs. "Let us make ourselves comfortable until dinner arrives. I have not had the pleasure of learning your name." The harshness in his tone had left, but Garrick's determination not to let this woman out of his sight had not. He knew that Lucas had put the young woman in his own cabin, and though Garrick would have sought her out that afternoon to ensure she was comfortable, he had been too caught up in his plans to track down the outlaw pirate known as Bristol Jack. He had gained some information the day before from a passing ship that he hoped would aid in his search. He'd been pursuing the pirate for the past two years, and if his information was correct, his search of the Caribbean would not last much longer.

Katelin certainly had no desire to sit there and make simple conversation with this man. "My name is Katelin Ashford, and I tell you this only because I am sure you could easily find out for yourself." Her jade green eyes flashed as he led her to the chair and she had no choice other than to sit down next to him.

Garrick savored the rare name in his mind. God, she was even more beautiful than he had remembered. But then, their first meeting had been brief. A small smile tugged at his lips as he recalled the image of her standing at the foot of Rose Bishop's stairway in her tailored man's suit, staring up at him and Rose, her sparkling green eyes locked with his even as she was pulled to the front door by her companions.

Katelin glimpsed his smile and could not help noticing the way the tilting of his lips helped to soften the hard, handsome lines of his sculpted face. She drew in a ragged breath, remembering the first time she had seen him, and how she had been unable to take her eyes off his dark good looks.

Before either could say another word, there was a light knock on the cabin door, followed by the entrance of the first mate carrying a large covered tray.

"Set that down here, Lucas," Garrick ordered, indicating the table between the two chairs. "That will be all," he added, somewhat surprised that it had been his first mate who had brought the dinner tray and not the cabin boy, whose job it was.

Loath to leave and be forced to take his eyes off the woman sitting in the captain's cabin, Lucas Bennett nevertheless turned his attention to his captain, saluted smartly, turned around, and quietly left. It was well worth carrying out the cabin boy's duty to get a brief view of their passenger, he told himself as he walked down the companionway.

Having fully expected more of a formal dinner party in the captain's cabin, Katelin was somewhat surprised when the first mate departed. With the closing of the cabin door, she questioned, "Is Mister Bennett not joining us for dinner?" Her green eyes watched his large hands as he uncovered the tray and revealed two plates heaped with a steaming variety of food.

"Nay, my men for the most part have already eaten by now down in the galley. It will be just you and I this evening, Kat. Does being alone with me bother you?" He seemed to add this as an afterthought.

Why, of course being alone with this man in his cabin bothered her! As did the fact that he so lightly called her by the pet name, Kat, as did the way he pronounced her name. The husky tremor of his voice seemed to flow over her like a warm caress. "My name is Katelin, Captain. To you, Miss Ashford should do." There, she told herself, she had put him in his place, but as his smile never wavered, she wondered if anyone could possibly put this large man in his place.

"I prefer Kat." Garrick poured dark wine into two goblets and held one out to her.

Katelin was finding this man totally exasperating! She would not argue with him, she told herself, as she reached out stiffly for the offered glass of wine. She would suffer through this meal and then, the first thing in the morning, she would demand to be put back aboard the *Caroline!*

"While we are eating tell me your reasons for being aboard the *Caroline* and bound for Saint Kitts. The last time I saw you, you appeared . . . well occupied in London." Garrick was more than a little interested in this young woman. Their chance meeting at Rose Bishop's had made a lasting impression on him. That night, when she had left with her friends, it had crossed his mind to seek information about her identity, but time had not allowed him the opportunity.

Now, as his cool, silver-blue gaze held her, he desired to know all about her.

Instead of answering him, Katelin took a sip of wine. Why should she tell him anything about herself? He had already acted far too forward for her peace of mind, and as she felt his heated gaze traveling over her from head to satin slippers, she kept her own gaze lowered. She had never met a man quite like this Captain Steele, and if the truth were known, he frightened her for some reason she did not wish to probe too deeply. Men in her past had been easy enough to take or leave as she liked, but this man was not in the least put off by her desire to remain cool toward him.

"Perhaps you will feel more like relaxing and conversing after we finish our dinner."

The man was truly insufferable, Katelin told herself as she began to sample the ship's fare. "I am very tired, Captain, and I would like to be allowed to retire to my cabin as soon as I am finished," she stated between bites, her discomfort at being alone with him intensified.

"Of course, Kat, I understand. I am sure you were able to sleep very little last evening because of the storm. We do, after all, have one more evening to share some time together before we reach Saint Kitts."

Katelin's fork stilled midway to her lips. She had no intention of sharing another evening alone with this man. "I would like very much, Captain, to be allowed to return to the *Caroline* in the morning." She quit pushing her food about on her plate and set it, along with the wine goblet, on the small table between them. This man was not to be taken lightly, and without being told, she knew that she was totally out of her element depending upon her graceful charm to see her through in his company.

"I am afraid that will not be possible, Kat. My first mate reported to me the damage done aboard the *Caroline*, as did Captain Howard. It would not be safe for you to leave the *Sea Witch*, and I myself would not allow such risks taken where you are concerned, even if you would. We will arrive at Saint Kitts the day after tomorrow, that will be soon enough for you to leave my ship." Garrick also set his plate aside, his strong fingers remaining wrapped around the crystal stem of his goblet as he wondered about her mounting anger.

From the moment she'd learned that he was the captain of the *Sea Witch*, she had appeared upset.

"But you cannot hold me aboard your ship against my will!" Katelin rose to her feet, and for the first time, her anger began turning to true fear. Why would he not allow her to reboard the *Caroline*? She knew her thoughts were unreasonable, but she could not halt them. There was something about this Garrick Steele that provoked her hidden fear. Fear that a man, any man, might hold the power to draw her to him against her will. Never had she felt such a fearsome, and at the same time powerful, attraction to any man, and this frightened her more than the risk of being aboard a damaged vessel. She had to get off of this ship, and as quickly as possible.

"Kat, my intention is not to hold you aboard the *Sea Witch* against your will, but to lend my protection, whether you believe you need it or not." Garrick rose to his full height, which was at least a head taller than Katelin, and at the moment he appeared to tower over her, though his words were spoken with the greatest of patience.

Drawing a deep, ragged breath, Katelin knew her

52

anger was blown way out of proportion. She tried to gather her wits and appear calm. All right, she told herself. She would remain aboard this ship! But she certainly did not have to abide this horrible man's presence any longer than she desired. "If you will excuse me then, Captain." She drew her green velvet skirts aside as she stepped around him and headed for the cabin door.

"Until tomorrow then, my lady." Garrick Steele bowed from the waist when she turned back to him for a final nod. What a prize she was, he told himself as he glimpsed the heated flush staining her cheeks and the deep, passionate anger in her shimmering emerald eyes.

Garrick Steele was able to find little relief from the nagging images of the voluptuous black-haired vixen who was now aboard his ship. All morning, as he tried going over the paperwork which littered his desk, he was tormented by visions of sparkling emerald eyes framed by fluttering dark lashes. He threw down his pen. *The woman has cast a spell on me,* he thought as he rose from his desk and left his cabin. He would tire his mind with hard physical labor. And without hesitation, he stripped off his shirt and climbed into the rigging where Jeremy, a crew member, was repairing a piece of torn canvas.

Katelin was not as lucky as Garrick; staying in her cabin throughout the day, she had no way to release her pent-up frustrations. All morning and afternoon, she worried about the handsome captain of the *Sea Witch*. What damnable luck! Of all the vessels on the face of the earth, why did it have to be Garrick Steele's ship that had offered the *Caroline* aid?

As the afternoon progressed, she told herself over and over that she simply would not abide his company in the evening. She would refuse dinner if forced to take it in the captain's cabin! Certainly she could forgo one meal, she told herself. Tomorrow would see her on Saint Kitts and she would be able to share a hearty meal with her father. The thought of having to face the darkly handsome sea captain and to once again feel her inner emotions turned upside down was more than Katelin could bear. But as the afternoon shadows turned into early evening, Katelin slowly prepared herself for the confrontation that was sure to come.

She felt her blood rushing boldly through her veins as anticipation filled her. Garrick Steele was plainly not the type of man who could be put off, and there was bound to be an encounter before the evening was finished. Dressing with minute care in a peach and cream gown boasting a high sheer lace collar and a fashionable tightly cinched waist, she was determined to look her finest when she came face to face with that handsome scoundrel. She allowed her hair to flow loosely down her back and around her shoulders, and the shimmering lights in her jade eyes intensified as she heard a soft knock on the cabin door. Drawing a deep breath to steady her nerves, she hesitated only a moment longer before opening the door. If nothing else, Katelin Ashford enjoyed a good argument.

She was surprised that the captain of the *Sea Witch* himself had not arrived at her door to insist that she join him in his cabin for dinner, and she admitted, if only to herself, that she was a little disappointed as she looked upon the cabin boy, Jeb, who had brought her two trays during the day.

Standing before her now, the young boy blushed brightly as he stammered, "The cap'n sent me to fetch you, miss." The youth was more than a little awed in the presence of this beautiful woman.

"Fetch me for what?" asked Katelin, pretending she had no idea what the young boy was talking about.

The youth seemed even more flustered with her answer. The freckled features screwed up in confusion. "But the cap'n said . . ."

"Perhaps it is your captain who does not understand." Katelin softened her tone to try and put the boy at ease, feeling some sympathy for him for being caught in the middle. "I have already told Captain Steele I do not care to dine with him. Just tell him that I feel unwell this evening and will be dining alone here in my cabin." There, that was final and easy enough, Katelin thought, and before the sandy-haired young boy could say anything further, she gently closed the door.

Something told Katelin that the matter of where she would be dining was still at issue, and that thought filled her breast with a strange excitement. She had time to pace around her small cabin only a few minutes before there was another knock on the outside portal. With her excitement riding high and her temper beginning to flare, she opened the door wide, expecting to find the cabin boy back with a word from his captain. It was not young Jeb standing before her but Garrick Steele himself. Katelin swallowed hard as she braced herself and glimpsed the stern features of the man before her. She would not give in to him, and she boldly tried to bolster her courage. "Captain, I am afraid I do not feel—"

"You will either share dinner with me in my cabin,

55

madam," he stated simply in that husky, masculine tone she now associated with him, "or I shall have the tray brought here to yours."

He started to turn, then added over his shoulder, "I will give you only a few minutes to consider before I take matters into my own hands." With this said, he reached out and pulled her cabin door closed.

For a full minute Katelin's fury threatened to overwhelm her, and pacing around the cabin, she swept her hairbrush and several toilet articles to the floor with a clatter. Who did the man think he was? How dare he treat her so high-handedly! She would not dine with him in his cabin, and he certainly was not welcome in her small chamber! She hurried over to the door and latched the flimsy lock, knowing well that a man of Garrick Steele's size could easily break down such a puny defense.

She expected at any moment to hear him outside her door demanding she comply with his wishes. But as the minutes slowly ticked by and her temper eased somewhat, she began wondering if his threat had been little more than bluster. Picking up her hand mirror, which had landed on the floor with her other things, Katelin glimpsed the high color in her cheeks and knew that her flush was more than a little becoming. *Why are you deliberately trying to provoke the man?* She was surprised by the question in her mind as she looked at her reflection. *You have to admit he has done nothing to cause you to act so trifling where he is concerned! It certainly was not his fault you went to Rose Bishop's establishment. And after all, his ship is helping the* Caroline, *and you have safe passage for the rest of the voyage.*

"But everything is his fault!" she cried aloud to the empty room. If he had not been standing on that

56

stairway looking so damnably good-looking, she would not be on her way to Saint Kitts right now. She would be in London, enjoying herself with her friends!

Are you afraid of him, Katelin?

"Of course not!" she said aloud, scorning the thought that she could fear any man. Yet at the same time she envisioned the crystal-clear blue-silver eyes and his strong masculine features, and a slight chill raced along her spine.

Perhaps she was overreacting to Garrick Steele. She set the mirror down upon the table with a loud thump.

Now you're thinking. Why not share dinner with him? What harm can it do? You survived last night, didn't you? her internal voice argued.

Katelin herself, though, was a little more reluctant than that daring inner nature of hers. But slowly that more venturesome part of herself won out, as memories of the night before in his cabin caused a quickening of her heart. Taking hold of the doorknob and opening the door, she stepped out into the companionway. Before she could change her mind, Katelin made her way to the captain's cabin. Standing outside his door she silently drew in a deep breath to steady her frayed nerves, then raised her hand to knock. The door opened even before her knuckles could touch upon the wood.

"Dinner will be served shortly, Kat. Come in and make yourself comfortable." Captain Steele seemed not in the least surprised to find her standing outside his door. In fact, as his pale eyes went over her, there was a bit of smugness in his features that was not lost upon his dinner guest.

With hesitating slowness, Katelin entered the captain's cabin, at the same time feeling a warmth settle over her with the familiarity of the name he called her. Her chin raised a notch as she stiffly spread out her peach skirts upon one of the chairs.

Garrick silently watched her every movement from where he stood near the cabin door. The scent of her flowery perfume filled the cabin and mingled with the tropical sea breeze which came through the open windows above the window seat. He was content just to stand and watch her fair beauty from afar, but forcing himself to move, he silently made his way over to the desk and poured himself a goblet of brandy. Sipping the potent brew, his silver eyes met hers of jade. "Would you care for something to drink?"

Each night before retiring, Elizabeth Wessely had had a goblet of warmed brandy. She claimed the heady brew was as good as any medicine, and swore her ritual drink prepared her for the day ahead. "Brandy will be fine," Katelin responded. If the drink could fortify her aunt, surely it might lend her the strength she needed to get through this evening!

Filling the extra goblet on his desk half full, Garrick approached her, and Katelin could not help witnessing the powerful, pantherlike strides that brought him across the cabin. Without a will, her glance took in the tight-fitting breeches, which molded every ounce of the bulging leg muscles.

Taking the chair opposite her, Garrick offered her the brandy without comment, content for the moment just to look at her.

As he handed her the goblet, Katelin glimpsed the long, sun-bronzed fingers wrapped around the crystal, and she hesitated before reaching out. *What is wrong with me?* she asked herself, then forced her hand to take the extended goblet. The accidental brushing of his fingers against her own left a fluttering deep within her breast.

"Why don't you tell me something about yourself, Kat?" Garrick suggested, leaning back in his chair and making himself comfortable. He appeared to be in a most amenable mood, and stretching out his long legs in front of him, he smiled warmly. She had refused to talk about herself last evening, but he hoped that she would reconsider tonight.

Katelin would have rebuked him once again about the careless use of her pet name, but she knew without being told that it would do little good. This man seemed intent upon torturing her! Feeling the heat of his steady appraisal she bent her head to her goblet and took a healthy draught. The raw heat of the liquid brought a moment's surprise over her senses. The fire of the brandy left her gasping, as her green eyes enlarged. Slowly the initial shock waned as the liquid made its way down her throat and she felt the warmth of it in her belly. She took another sip, this time more slowly. At last she appeared to remember her host, and looking toward him, she said, "There is little to tell of myself, Captain Steele." She drew the goblet back to her lips, hoping the drink would do its work, and quickly.

A small, indulgent smile had settled over Garrick's full, sensual lips as he had watched her take her first drink of the brandy. The widening of her eyes and the small gasp were not lost upon him. It was obvious she was not used to strong drink; he applauded her spirit. He still wondered at her animosity toward him, for he could sense that this was her reason for sampling the drink so thoroughly. At the moment, though, he was not willing to shatter the spell by warning her to go easy. "Surely you would care to share some small part of your life with me?" He grinned, hoping to put her more at ease.

The grin was boyishly disarming, but instead of replying as Garrick had hoped, Katelin instead looked down into her now empty goblet, and as a slight blush stained her cheeks, she held the glass out to him. "If you do not mind, Captain Steele?" One more glass of brandy and she would be able to handle any situation that came her way, Katelin thought as a warmth spread throughout her limbs.

Garrick was not one to argue with a lady. Getting to his feet, he brought the brandy bottle to his chair and refilled her goblet and his own. "I would give you warning, Kat. This brew can upon occasion catch one unaware." He relented from his first inclination of saying nothing of her overindulgence.

Ignoring his warning, Katelin hastily took another drink, then feeling quite relaxed, she took pity on her host. He seemed so very handsome sitting there across from her, and at the moment her mind could not grasp her earlier reasons for being angry at him. "I am going to Saint Kitts to be reunited with my father, Richard Ashford."

Ah, at last the hard veneer she had built up around herself was cracking. Garrick smiled to himself, knowing full well that this was due mainly to the effects of the brandy. But always a man to take advantage of a situation, he mentally prepared the dozen questions he would like to ask her. He wanted to know every detail of her past. Why was she going to meet her father? Who had she been living with in London? What had been her reason for being in Rose Bishop's establishment that evening when he had first seen her? He wanted to know all her likes and dislikes, her secret desires, and mainly her plans for the future. Was there a man in her life now or had there been one in London? From the first moment he'd set eyes on her, a current of raw energy had drawn him to her. But before he could question her further, a knock sounded on the door and the cabin boy entered with their dinner tray.

Five

Garrick's irritation at being disturbed could be easily heard in his voice as he instructed Jeb, "Set the tray down here, and we'll serve ourselves."

"Aye, Cap'n." Young Jeb quickly did as bid, his eyes going to the beautiful woman; once again he was entranced by her lovely looks. Taking in every minute detail of her dress and hair to report back to Big Mike, the galley cook. Jeb hesitated by her chair.

Garrick was well aware of the boy's glances in Katelin's direction, and as on the night before when Lucas Bennett had stared at her, he again felt a strange tightening in his gut. "That will be all, Jeb. You can go back to your other duties now."

Jeb noted the hardness that had crept into his captain's voice, and quickly obeying, he turned and started toward the door. Glancing around one last time to see if his captain was really angry with him, he found that the man had already forgotten all about him. He watched him smile fondly upon Miss Ashford, then lift the cover of their dinner tray. With a small sigh, Jeb eased the door shut. He, for one, never wanted to have Captain Steele's anger directed at him. He had seen many men come up against the captain and live to tell the tale only because Steele had been merciful to them!

"What happened to that charming first mate, Mister Bennett?" Katelin remembered his name only after searching her mind for it. She had found him very charming the day before and was surprised, now that she thought about it, that she had not seen him again.

"My first mate has other duties, Kat." Garrick sat back in his chair and felt somewhat confused by his own feelings. He had deliberately given his first mate duties that would keep him away from their passenger until they reached Saint Kitts. Lucas had not appeared to mind the orders, but now as Katelin inquired about his first mate, Steele wondered if she had been somehow attracted to the man. With the thought, he swallowed hard. Bringing his fork to his mouth, he tried with some will to keep his temper at bay.

Katelin made no further comment about Lucas Bennett, her thoughts already taking off in a different direction as she began sampling the food on her plate. Throughout the day, she had been nervous about her coming encounter with the captain, so she'd been unable to eat much of the food Jeb had brought to her cabin. With her first bite of dinner, however, her appetite increased, and she began to eat with enjoyment.

For the first time Katelin Ashford appeared to find him bearable company, and Steele's thoughts of a rival slowly disappeared. "My galley cook will be pleased to hear how much you enjoyed dinner." He grinned, then with the same gusto that she was displaying, he also attacked his food.

Katelin laughed aloud some moments later as she looked down at her plate. "I do not think I have eaten so much at one time since I was a young girl. My aunt Elizabeth would be more than a little scandalized if she could see me wolfing down such a great quantity of food!" Her aunt had painstakenly given her lessons in comportment, and under no circumstances would a lady be allowed to partake of so much food! *A true lady is known by her temperance and her table manners while in the company of others, especially in the company of a gentleman.* Her tutor, Mrs. Burnshaw, had also tried to drum appropriate etiquette into Katelin's brain time and again.

Garrick enjoyed the sound of her musical laughter, and with a grin, he offered, "Would you care for some more?" He held out a plate with a piece of lemon tart sitting in the center.

For a single second, Katelin debated over the temptation of dessert, but the lemon tart was far too tempting. "Whoever here would tell my aunt? Surely you would not, would you, Captain Steele?" With an impish grin, she reached out and took the proffered treat.

"Call me Garrick, Kat." The captain was entranced with the young woman sitting next to him. And as she took a bite of the lemon tart and her tongue lightly licked the small crumbs from her pert, pinkened lips, he was more than a little tempted to bend toward her and taste for himself the flavor of those delicate morsels. Firmly he cautioned himself to go easy. For the first time she was enjoying herself in his company. She was laughing and smiling, and he did not want to destroy the slim progress he had made, even though in the back of his mind he knew that her relaxed manner was due to the brandy.

"I shall indeed call you Garrick, if you wish, Captain," she stated as she finished the tart off and daintily licked her fingers. The movement stole Garrick's very breath, and as she set the plate aside, lifted her goblet, and took another sip of brandy, he could not restrain his impulse to stare at that tempting mouth.

"Good, good." Garrick almost choked out the words as he fought for his composure. "I hope we can become friends, Kat." He hoped as well that he was not pressing her too hard, and too soon.

"My very closest friends call me Kat, so I guess you must be my friend." Katelin could not remember ever having felt so good. She was sated with good food and drink, and at the moment a warm haze enveloped her like a cozy shroud.

"Are you comfortable?" Garrick ventured as he watched her stretching like a contented feline in the chair.

"Hmmm," was her response as once again she brought the brandy to her lips. "I appear to need a refill once again, Garrick." She held the goblet out to him, her warm green eyes meeting his of cool blue, and she once again thought how very handsome he was. As he took her glass, she allowed herself a long moment to examine him in detail. She had not yet allowed herself such pleasure, but now she noticed the way his dark brows arched over his steel blue eyes, his lashes appearing long for a man. His aquiline nose above his full, sensual lips held even more fascination for her hungry gaze. Indeed he was the best-looking friend she had ever had, with his midnight black hair hanging loosely about his collar. A small sigh escaped her lips.

A fine dark brow arched as though questioning her thoughts. "Go easy with this one," Garrick warned as he handed her the goblet. "It should be the last." Finally, Garrick decided to take some kind of control where her drinking was concerned. She was already tipsy, and he knew he should escort her back to her cabin so she could sleep off the effects of so much food and alcohol. But he could not bear the thought of being without her so he tried to play the honorable gentleman by limiting her brandy.

"Are friends allowed to do that?" Katelin looked at him with wide, questioning green eyes.

Not understanding, Garrick looked at her with his own question in his gaze.

"You say we are friends now, and I must admit you are by far the best-looking friend I have ever had, but are you allowed to stop me from drinking?" Even in her own reeling mind, Katelin knew the answer to that question, and she knew she should never have complimented his looks—but she just couldn't help herself!

"You were telling me about yourself, before dinner was served, remember?" Garrick ignored her question with one of his own, though he had particularly liked that comment about his looks.

"Was I?" For a minute Katelin tried to remember, but not able to, she took his word. What would such a handsome man be interested in, Katelin wondered as she tried to say something that might capture his interest. With a sigh, she realized that her past life had been rather boring. "My aunt Elizabeth sent me on this voyage. I must stay on my father's plantation for a two-year period, then I will be allowed to return to London." Instead of telling him something interesting, she knew she was bemoaning her own fate once again.

"And why would your aunt make such a decision regarding your future?" Garrick still wondered if there was a man in her past. Perhaps her aunt had sent her away from London to direct her attention elsewhere for several years. The thought of a close gentleman friend made him squirm in his chair.

"Well, surely you of all people know the answer to that question!" Katelin retorted, looking at him in surprise.

Garrick smiled indulgently upon her. "I am afraid I don't know what you mean."

"The episode at Rose Bishop's, of course!"

"Oh, of course." Now Garrick understood. Word must have reached her aunt, who had in turn banished her niece from London until the scandal died down. A grin slowly curved Garrick's lips as he remembered her standing at the bottom of Rose Bishop's stairway dressed in gentleman's garb. "Was it your idea, or your friend's, to take such a daring risk?"

Her green eyes sparkled mischievously. "Why, mine of course! Robert and the others were totally opposed at first. But I guess the boredom of London was also plaguing them, so at last they agreed that it would be a tremendous lark to accompany me to such a wicked house!" Katelin still felt no remorse about the episode. She had seen all she wanted to in the downstairs portion of Rose Bishop's opulent house. Her only regret was that she had been caught, and though the cause of her undoing was now sitting across from her, for some strange reason she was no longer angry at him.

"Oh, so you found Rose's house to be wicked, did you?" Garrick was delighted with every word that left her mouth.

Remembering the bawdy woman who had approached her small group shortly after they arrived, the same woman who had in fact dragged Stephen Robards away, and remembering also the vivid description of what she could do with her bosom, Katelin nodded her head. For a moment she was tempted to tell Garrick Steele, her newfound friend, exactly what the bold woman had said! Her common sense won out, though, over her brandy-sotted brain. Perhaps he was her friend now, she told herself, but surely he was not the type of man with whom one could be so bold.

Straightening up in her chair, she realized that she had indeed drunk too much brandy. She did not answer him, but instead redirected the questioning toward him. "It is your turn, Captain, to tell me of yourself. What cargo does your ship carry, and why are you going to Saint Kitts?" Her eyes lowered to his broad chest, which was covered by a white silk shirt, opened at the throat. The first and second buttons had been carelessly undone and revealed sun-bronzed flesh and curling black hair. Quickly her heated gaze went back to his face.

"At the moment the *Sea Witch* holds no cargo. And

to answer your second question, I often visit Saint Kitts when I am in the Caribbean."

Katelin was somewhat disappointed with his answers. She had hoped he would tell her some exciting secret about himself or his ship. Perhaps he would confess that he was a pirate, or that he was fleeing from the hand of British justice for some daring escapade. "Have you ever met up with any pirates, then?" She hoped for some story of adventure to entertain her. "Perhaps you have even met Bristol Jack?"

"And what do you know of Bristol Jack?"

"Only what I was told aboard the *Caroline* during dinners in the captain's cabin." A slight sigh left her parted lips. "Dinner aboard the *Caroline* was a much more crowded affair than here aboard the *Sea Witch*."

To Katelin, Garrick seemed relaxed in his chair. Apparently she did not notice his attention sharpening with her question about Bristol Jack. "I am afraid I have no stories to tell about this Bristol Jack, Kat." Her disappointment showed instantly upon her lovely features. "But what if I were to tell you that the *Sea Witch* is a privateer ship?" For some strange reason, he wanted to see her eyes gleaming once again with those dancing lights of excitement.

"You are a privateer?" Katelin almost dared not ask the question. "Is that the reason why the *Sea Witch*'s sails are dyed gray?" She had wondered about that when she had boarded the ship, that and the fact that his crew appeared a bit more casual and rougher than those aboard the *Caroline*, but until this moment she had not understood their significance. As she looked at the darkly handsome sea captain, a trace of

69

fear could be read in her green eyes, but it quickly vanished and was replaced by excitement. She had heard about these privateers who roamed the sea with their letters of commission given them by King George. The legend of Jean Laffite and his brothers was well known in London society, and most people agreed that privateers were much the same as pirates! "Tell me of your adventures. Have you captured ships filled with gold and caskets of rare jewels?"

At that moment Garrick wished that he had not gotten carried away with her lovely interest and told so much about himself. In her romantic notions, the life of a privateer was filled with nonstop adventure. But in truth, his life upon the seas was growing rather boring, and if not for this one last mission for the Royal Navy, he would be in England this very night sitting before the great hearth at his country estate. "There is truly little to tell, Kat. It is a lonely life here on the sea for myself and my crew. My profession is just more dangerous than others!"

Katelin stared as though waiting for him to add something. That was it? That was all he was going to tell her after announcing he was a privateer? "But what of—"

Garrick did not wish for her to continue so he rose to his feet, and placing his brandy glass aside, he reached out and took her hand. "It is time for me to show you to your cabin." He had to do something to distract her warm regard, or soon he would be telling her everything, relating to her that his true mission in the Caribbean was to capture Bristol Jack and to also somehow put an end to the killings that were taking place in the town of Basseterre, on the island of Saint Kitts.

But the simple act of touching her proved his downfall! One mere touch of her tender flesh sent dangerous flames of passion licking throughout his soul!

Katelin felt some of the same strange reactions to their touching, and with that contact, she looked into his face as though seeking out some sort of explanation.

Without another word spoken, Garrick's head lowered, his mouth tenderly slanting over her rose petal lips.

Katelin felt herself drowning in a sea of incredible pleasure. Her slender arms wrapped around his neck as though struggling to hold on to something for support. Her fingers entwined in the strands of ebony hair lying against his shoulders, and without thinking, she pressed herself against his massive, unyielding chest. Never had she been kissed so tenderly, so passionately, so hungrily! She felt as though she were melting by degrees as she was held within his heated embrace.

Garrick's feelings were not much different from hers. The taste of her brandy-sweet lips pressing against his own, the feel of her shapely curves as he drew her slim form tightly against his own, and the womanly scent of her intoxicating his senses all left him feeling heady with an overwhelming desire to claim this woman as his own. He wanted to hold her tightly and never let her go. At last he drew from his inner strength, and with a sigh of mixed pain and pleasure, he pulled his mouth away from hers.

Looking up into the dark, compelling features,

Katelin could only ask, "Why did you stop?" Having been deprived of little in her past, she wondered why this man would hold back such wonderful feelings.

Garrick could not answer. His silver-blue eyes looked upon the pouting pink petals that had tempted him all evening, and now that he had tasted them, he could not put their delicious flavor from his mind. Clasping her tightly, he looked into her lovely face and whispered with a husky tremor, "If I do not stop myself now, I will be lost forever!"

His words were a desperate cry, for inside he knew that he was *already* forever lost. Of all his travels to different ports of the world, of all the women he had known in his past, this woman alone had touched some secret part of his soul. Something of her spirit that first night in London had reached inside him and forever seared his heart. Since she did not speak but still stared up at him, he once again lowered his lips to hers, but this time the fusion of their mouths was no tender hold. There was a hungry need in Garrick's kiss that flamed its meaning into Katelin's body.

She rose up on tiptoe to fully mold herself against his powerful length. Her mouth opened as though of its own inner knowledge to receive the heated branding of his searching tongue. A soft moan escaped her lips as she felt a simmering heat in the very depths of her being.

Garrick's ears were filled with the soft sounds coming from deep within her throat, and he held her crushed against him as his lips left her mouth and tasted the softness of her cheek, the fragile curve of her jaw, the slim line of her throat. As he placed moist kisses along the upper edge of her sheer lace collar, he felt the straining fullness of her breasts. His hands left her sides as she leaned toward him. His fingers caressed where his mouth had been seconds before until they rested upon the upper swelling of her bosom, and with a practiced motion, he lightly pushed aside the lacings of her bodice. Then he lowered his lips and placed feathery kisses between the valley of her breasts while his fingers brushed against the hardened tips.

Nothing in Katelin's life had prepared her for such an erotic assault upon her senses. Bethany, the upstairs chambermaid at Wessely House, had told her of her own exploits with the gardener, Sampson, and Aunt Elizabeth had in a roundabout way warned her of the sins the flesh could provoke, but no one had ever told her of the wanton pleasure to be found in the arms of a man such as Captain Garrick Steele! Her breasts pressed against the heat of his searching fingers, wanting to feel all that he was willing to give her! His kisses became more lavish as he scorched a path back up her throat to recapture her lips.

Partaking fully of the sweet ambrosia she appeared willing enough to share, Garrick deftly found the trim line of tiny glass buttons that ran down the length of her back, and quickly finished with the hindrance which blocked his access to her temptingly sweet flesh.

Katelin inhaled sharply as she felt the soft caress of his fingers down her spine. But she released her breath just as quickly as his head lowered once again to her breasts.

Sheer carnal desire flamed throughout her body as

his lips settled over one rose point nipple. And, he suckled the tender tip, her limbs weakened and she felt herself slipping to the floor.

Before she could fall very far, Garrick gathered her up into his arms, his lips leaving her breast and once more covering her mouth. Then he broke off his kisses and, for a moment, simply stared at the rare beauty in his arms. He looked over at the door, but after a moment of indecision, he turned and, pushing the curtain aside, stepped into the alcove that contained his large bed. Gently he laid Katelin down upon the satin coverlet, but his eyes bespoke his willingness, if she so desired, to release her.

Katelin's thoughts at the time were not those of a clear-headed rational woman. The brandy had clouded her senses, while the feelings Garrick had stimulated throughout her body — through his seeking fingertips and moist, heated tongue — had driven her into a mindless, unreasoning place. She, as he, was forever lost to the moment. Reaching up, she drew his dark head toward her with a slight pressure on the back of his neck. She knew only that she wanted to feel those incredible feelings again. And she did not want to wait!

His mouth consumed hers with its searching demand as his tongue pushed forward and, finding no resistance, sought out each tiny crevice, then traced a tempting path down to her breasts. As he drew a rose-crested tip into his mouth, Katelin's body trembled with a deep, wanton desire that left her clutching his head and pressing herself fully against him.

It seemed only seconds later that Katelin lay upon the silken coverlet with nothing covering her body from his flaming regard. Her gown and underthings had been discarded upon the polished wooden floor, and for a breathless moment Garrick stared down at the luscious curves of perfection. The heated flame within his eyes seared every inch of her flesh as he gazed upon the fullness of the twin globes with their dusty rose-colored buds. His eyes roamed down the length of her trim rib cage to the tiny indent of her navel, across the womanly flare of her hips, and down the long, shapely legs. His gaze caressed the delicate ankles and slim feet, and drawing halfway up, his eyes filled with burning desire as he boldly looked upon the junction of her womanhood with the feathering of dark curling hair lending a definite contrast to the creamy, pearl iridescence of her skin.

As his eyes returned to her face, Katelin parted her lips as if to speak. But she glimpsed the unbridled lust on his face and realized that she was too far gone into the game of love to beg off now. His gaze locked with her own, and she felt the escalating rampage of her heartbeat. Seeing the desire in his eyes, she sensed, too, the power of her woman's body—at that moment she knew that this man desired her above anything else in life. This indeed was raw power, and her passion-laced wits welcomed his seduction!

Garrick looked away only long enough to remove his white silk shirt and tight dove gray breeches and toss them to the floor, where they joined Katelin's own discarded clothing. Katelin drew in a deep breath as she beheld the hard, bronzed flesh covering bulging muscle.

For a few lingering seconds Garrick stood beside

the bed, as if giving her the opportunity to view perfection in the opposite sex. And indeed as he stood before her, he was all male! A man in his prime, unequaled by any!

Pure, primeval, muscular strength stood for her viewing. Her flashing jade eyes traveled slowly over the dark hair lying against massive, tanned shoulders. His forearms and chest bulged with unleashed strength. Hard slabs of muscle-rippled flesh covered his ribs and tapered down to a narrow waist and hips. But she only glanced at the tight contours of his buttocks and powerful thighs as her attention was captured by the giant, throbbing lance protruding from his lower body. Like the rest of him, there was no doubting the power of his mighty swollen shaft!

Even as the tropical night breeze filtered through the curtained alcove, a far distant voice of reason whispered in Katelin's mind: *What are you doing in this man's bed? This is no game, Katelin! The stakes are far too real! Get your clothes and run as fast as you can!* But she seemed powerless to respond to her own inner warnings. Her body seemed too weak to move, and as Garrick lay down next to her and drew her to his chest, her thoughts flew far away from reason and common sense. With a will of their own, her slender arms rose up and wound around his neck.

The irresistible pull of pleasure's promise grabbed her body as Garrick's mouth and hands roamed over her. Feathering kisses, licking and nibbling, he ravished her breasts, his straight white teeth caressing the underflesh and driving Katelin mad with desire. A moan escaped from deep within her throat, and at the same time his dark head lowered to her ribs and the tempting curves of her waist and hips.

The taste of her sweet flesh and the feel of her satin-smooth body, combined to seduce Garrick into a physical wanting that knew no bounds. His hands splayed over the firmness of her belly then pressed her closer to his hips. His tongue sent flames shooting throughout the lower portion of her body as he laved the inside of her thighs. As his mouth touched her woman's jewel, Katelin's body bucked in surprise and sweet, forbidden pleasure snaked through her womb and limbs.

Awash upon this tide of new sensations, Katelin clutched out, her hands entwining in his hair as he opened her with his fingers and plunged his tongue into her essence. Casting her head long into a pool of boundless rapture, his tongue filled her again and again with its stroking heat.

Spinning out of control into a vortex of exquisite pleasure, Katelin felt a spark igniting deep within her belly. Hot flames of molten desire spread throughout her body and pulsed within her womanhood. She was on fire! The flames shot higher, then erupted. Her hands clutched his hair, her nails raked his back. Her head and shoulders rose off the bed as a cry of utter pleasure burst from her lips and her body shook with a satisfaction she had never known before.

Without mercy, Garrick kept up his love play, his tongue plunging into her moist, sweet depths and lingering over the sensitive nub as she shuddered again and again. Her cries filled his ears and fueled his desire to pleasure her to the fullest.

As the trembling of her body slowly subsided and the fingers within his hair lessened their tight hold,

Garrick rose from his position between her thighs. His lips seared branding kisses over her body as he pressed his length against her. His silver-blue eyes witnessed the sated passion on her face before he covered her mouth once more with his own.

So this was the secret thing that took place between a man and a woman, Katelin thought as his lips plundered hers with a hunger that seemed even more insatiable than in moments past. Never before had she had such wonderful feelings—the things he'd done to her were incredible! But he was still not finished as he molded himself into her body and his throbbing, blood-engorged shaft was pressed between them, seeming to seek out the place where only a short time ago his mouth had left her trembling with hot desire.

Katelin opened to him, too swept up in the steaming rapture of the moment to do otherwise. As Garrick's tongue filled her mouth, she felt the sculpted, marble head of his love tool pressing at the opening between her thighs.

His buttocks drew upward, and as he entered her just an inch, he felt the tightness of her passage; another inch and he felt the velvet trembling of her inner sanctum. A low rumbling came from deep within his chest and filled the cabin with his animal-like groan.

In that same moment, a small cry pierced the air as Katelin's maidenhead was breached. Garrick stilled, his raging desire stemmed for the moment, caught as he was by total surprise. Not once had he considered that this woman was a virgin. That first moment he had seen her in Rose Bishop's house in the company of her male friends, she had appeared much more worldly than she obviously was. "Kat, Kat." He murmured her name as though in apology. His hand tenderly stroked her smooth cheek.

The sound of her name forced her eyes open, and looking into the tender regard of the man above her, Katelin forgot the momentary pain now past. There in the depths of his crystal blue eyes she was held for a timeless second by the promise of what more lay ahead if she could but trust him. Slowly she moved her body as though adjusting to the weight atop her and the fullness between her legs.

Her movement stoked the passion between them once more to full wakefulness. Garrick's lips descended in a kiss that caught her within a tender budding and slowly grew to a tempting hunger. His body slowed, keeping always in mind to have a care for her virgin's flesh. He moved back and forth, not allowing the full thrust of his massive size to claim her, but instead going slowly deeper, then withdrawing to the lips of her moist opening. Over and over he plied her with his skillful seduction, until she was clutching his back, her head thrown back wildly as the fullness in her loins drove her toward a frenzy of mindless desire. Each time the brand of his lance drove into her depths and stirred her, her body moved toward the fullness. Her legs slowly rose as she sought to capture the entire length of him.

Still holding back somewhat, Garrick caught hold of her buttocks, and with a talent born from past lovemaking, he maintained an inner control. Even as he felt the shuddering begin again within her depths and travel the length of his manhood as her sheath suddenly trembled and tightened, he inhaled deep breaths of air, willing himself not to release the true fury of his passion.

Shudder after rippling shudder coursed through Katelin's body and centered upon the branding flame of his probing shaft. She slipped beyond control as her body thrashed about, her hips jerking convulsively as she was swept into the realm of true satisfaction.

Garrick knew the power of her climax, and for a moment he fought the heated need racing through his own loins. He watched her passion-filled face and heard the climactic moans escaping her throat. Each thrust was now torture-laced as he fought off the aching need for his own fulfillment. Only when he felt her climax receding did he allow himself to give vent to his own desire. His mouth covered hers, and as he plunged just a fraction deeper into her soft velvety depths, wildfire caught within his loins. Scalding pleasure burst from the center of his being and showered upward, racing through his powerful lance and showering into brilliant particles of light. "Kat, Kat!" The cry was torn from him as he showered her lovely face with kisses.

So this was what it was really all about! Katelin dreamily gathered her wits as Garrick's trembling subsided, and though he still held her tightly in his embrace, his heartbeat began returning to normal. An inner voice told her she should be ashamed, that she should leave this man's bed and get as far away from him as she could. But at the moment her bones felt molten, her mind trembling upon the edge of sanity and unreality. It felt simply wonderful lying here within his arms.

It took Garrick several minutes to regain his normal breathing and to conquer the disbelief that filled his brain as he relived what had just occurred between him and this woman. Virgin she had been and more woman than he had ever known. A slight shudder coursed through him and his loins tightened as he realized that he had never before been driven to such powerful feelings of lust. Surely, he thought, she must have felt the same thing. Turning his face so he could gaze into her beautiful face when he spoke to her, he found her eyelids closed, her breathing softly caressing his neck. She slept peacefully in his arms, and a small smile filtered over his lips. Tomorrow would be soon enough for him to declare his feelings to her. Tomorrow they would arrive at Saint Kitts, he would explain to her his mission in the Caribbean, and he would beg her to wait the short time it would take him to complete his job.

Six

At the first break of dawn, the shout of "Land ho!" was carried over the decks of the *Sea Witch* and floated into the open window of the captain's cabin.

Groggily Katelin fought off the clutches of sleep. It was not until she was able to force her eyes open, while trying to pull herself upright, that she found it was more than her tiredness that prevented her from rising up on the bed. Large, muscular arms wrapped around her and held her prisoner. By slow degrees, Katelin's green eyes expanded as horror filled her soul with the realization of where she was and whose body was tightly pressed against her own. Her heartbeat quickened as she raised her head away from the warmth of a naked male chest, and her eyes met those of startling silver blue. Instantly she felt the intense heat of a flush covering not only her face and neck but also her breasts. What on earth had she done, she moaned inwardly. Not daring to say a word, she glimpsed a warm smile settle over the captain's sensual lips.

"Good morning, sweet. I trust you slept well?" Garrick at the moment was delighted to have spent the night holding the lovely Katelin Ashford in his embrace.

"What . . . what am I doing? I mean . . . why am I here in your cabin?" Katelin was at last able to stammer softly. Slowly her thoughts were beginning to gather, she was remembering the vast amount of brandy she had drunk, and God forbid she could not help but remember the feel of those tempting, heated lips pressing down upon her own! Her face reddened even further as everything that had taken place last night began to flood throughout her thoughts. "Oh nooooo," she at last moaned aloud.

Watching her every facial feature, Garrick had to admit that he was somewhat disappointed, but he was determined not to let her actions discourage him. He had found a rare woman in Katelin Ashford. A woman of beauty and sensibilities and also a woman of passion. And he was not about to let her get away from him! "You fell asleep last night before we had a chance to talk. I wanted to thank you for the treasured gift you shared with me." His voice was low, the words a mere husky tremor that held the power even at this moment to cause gooseflesh to travel along Katelin's spine, and set her heart to fluttering wildly in her chest.

"Nay, it was not in truth a gift!" Katelin jerked herself upright, and feeling the breeze from the open window traveling through the opened curtains enclosing the alcove, she realized that she was entirely naked. Crimson flame graced her cheeks as she pulled the sheet away from him and quickly wrapped herself in its length.

Not looking in his direction to see that she had left

him entirely exposed, she hurried across the cabin to retrieve her gown and underthings. "Last night was no more than a terrible mistake!" she declared as, turning her back to him, she tried to pull her gown over her body with the sheet still wrapped around her.

"There was no mistake made last eve, Kat. The woman I held in my arms gave herself willingly enough." Garrick studied her for a moment longer before throwing his long legs over the side of the bed and looking around for his breeches.

"It was the brandy that made me act so!" Katelin at the moment wanted only to get out of his cabin before he could lay a hand on her again. There was no telling how she would react if he took her into his embrace—if his mouth once more settled over her own. As always when confronted by a difficult situation, Katelin wanted to run away. Put the matter from her mind and hope it would not arise again. And at the moment she only wanted him to stay there on the bed and allow her to leave his cabin without making her appear a bigger fool than she felt.

Standing there in his bare feet with his breeches covering the lower half of his body, Garrick slowly began to approach her. "Perhaps it was the brandy which allowed you to loosen up somewhat in my presence, but it was you, Kat, whom I made love to. You, whom I held throughout the night." Still his voice was soft as he tried to force her to acknowledge her part in what had taken place between them.

"Do not call me that again!" Tears now stung her eyes as she turned to face him. It was all his fault, she told herself. The way he pronounced her name, and that damn desirable body of his! Her glance filled with his towering presence and she quickly had to force her eyes to lower before she found herself gushing over him once again! Drawing a deep breath, she forced herself to say the words she was sure he would be saying before long if given the chance. Of course he would try to pacify her with kind words but in the end he would say that last night had been no more than two people sharing a moment's pleasure where they could find it. If he thought for an instant that she was some weak-kneed, simple maid who was going to throw herself at his feet and beg him to take pity on her now that he had sampled what she rightfully should have saved for her husband, he would be sadly mistaken. She was not the kind of woman who would beg a man for anything. She had made a terrible mistake last night and now she would have to live with that fact.

As she turned toward the door, she felt somehow braver now that she could not see him. "Whatever it is that you think, Mister Steele, or whatever you want of me, I am afraid that last night meant nothing! In two years' time I shall be leaving Saint Kitts and returning to London, and nothing is going to change that. Do not worry yourself over my welfare — you owe me nothing!" Turning the knob of the cabin door and stepping out into the companionway, she told herself firmly that she would have lost her maidenhead sooner or later anyway. He had just made it happen sooner than she had anticipated. She would be much more cautious with her favors in the future.

Garrick was more than a little surprised by her actions and words. He had hoped that last night would have softened her hard heart toward him. He had planned last night before falling to sleep to gently lead her into conversation this morning about a future for both of them together. As he stood across the cabin and watched her stiff back as she went through the cabin door, he had the greatest desire to go after her and force her to listen to him. He would beg her to take pity on him, and if that didn't work, he would hold her against her will aboard the *Sea Witch* until she admitted her feelings for him were like his own for her! But all this was wishful thinking. He was on a mission in the Caribbean, and no matter what his own desires were, those of his country came first. He could not afford to keep her with him when his own life could very well be in great danger. He could content himself with the fact that part of his job would be here on Saint Kitts. He would be able to keep an eye on her for himself, if only to make sure that when he had finished his mission, Katelin would be there waiting for him. Whether she agreed to go with him on her own, or whether he had to steal her away from under her father's nose, he would have Katelin Ashford one day for his own — he swore that to himself.

Standing on the deck of the *Sea Witch*, Katelin watched as an island mystically appeared, rising out of the ocean's green-blue depths. Its interior appeared rugged and mountainous. The lowlands and bluffs reached out to hilly jungles and white beaches.

The island itself looked oddly out of place in the vast, glistening ocean.

Saint Kitts — the name of the island had haunted her since childhood. This strange place that her father had fled to after her mother's death had always strangely affected her senses. She had never expected to visit the island herself, and now here she was looking out at all the tropical beauty from the deck of the *Sea Witch* as the sleek ship quickly approached the docks of Basseterre, the island's capital.

Garrick silently watched Katelin from his own position near the ship's railing, and at the moment he wondered at her thoughts. Looking at her now, he could glimpse no trace of the woman he had held in his arms throughout the previous night. Gone was the smiling seductress and in her place stood a coolly composed young woman in a dark blue traveling outfit and a matching hat, which boasted a feather and was angled to the right side of her cheek. He was tempted to approach her, but the firm set of her shoulders held him at bay for the time being.

It was after the *Sea Witch* and the *Caroline* were both anchored at the wharf that Garrick made his way to Katelin's side. "I insist upon the pleasure of arranging for a carriage and seeing you to your father's plantation."

Katelin stiffened at his approach and it was on the tip of her tongue to refuse his offer. But when she saw the hard cast to his features and the firm set of his jaw she knew it would do little good to argue with him. Garrick Steele was used to having his own way and he would in this matter also.

Just a short time later as Katelin stood next to

Garrick on the docks, Captain Howard and Scotty, the first mate, approached. "Captain Steele." Captain Howard stretched out his right arm to Garrick. "I have already seen your first mate and thanked him for the assistance the *Sea Witch* rendered to my ship, but again I wish to thank you personally." Thus saying, Captain Howard then turned his attention warmly upon Katelin. "I do hope you were comfortable aboard the *Sea Witch*, Miss Ashford?"

Still supporting Katelin's elbow after escorting her to the dock, Garrick took it upon himself to answer Captain Howard's question. "It was a pleasure to have been able to aid you in your time of distress, Captain. And as for Miss Ashford, I myself can vouch for her comfort aboard my ship. I personally saw to her every need."

Katelin would have liked nothing better than to be able to slap the smirk off Garrick Steele's too handsome face. But doing so would surely force Captain Howard and Scotty to read more into his assurances over her welfare aboard his ship. It was one thing for her to take his words for what they truly meant, but quite another for anyone else to catch his meaning. So all she could do was stand next to him and smile pleasantly.

Captain Howard was not a man to worry for long about the creature comforts of a woman when his ship was badly in need of repairs. Taking Captain Steele's word that all had gone well for Katelin Ashford aboard his ship, he nodded his graying head, his eyes already scanning the wharf as though searching for someone.

"Perhaps I could assist you, Miss Ashford, in finding your father's plantation?" Scotty offered, feeling somewhat cheated of her company for the past two days. And he was now feeling jealousy stirring within him as he watched the large captain of the *Sea Witch* standing so closely to Katelin's side, his arm remaining so possessively under hers.

Katelin would have gladly accepted his kind offer, if only to get away from Garrick Steele, but as she opened her mouth to thank him, Garrick once again took over and the hold upon her elbow slightly increased in its pressure. "That will not be necessary. I will see that Miss Ashford safely arrives at her father's plantation."

The cool blue eyes that stared at Scotty let him know there would be no arguing on the subject of Katelin's escort to her father's plantation. The first mate did not say another word, but as the captain led Katelin down the dock, his glance followed.

As Garrick led her away from the first mate and Captain Howard, thoughts of harshly rebuking him for his high-handedness toward her entered her head, but upon second reflection Katelin knew that it would do little good. This man would do exactly what he pleased and no one would ever be able to sway him from his purpose. She could content herself only with the fact that once she arrived at her father's home, she would never have to see him again. She remembered vividly what he had told her the night before about his ship being a privateer, and at the moment she held no doubt that he was little more than a pirate! Everything bad that had happened to her lately she could attribute directly to him, and now there was one more thing on that long list of his misdeeds: his forcing his company upon her though she certainly did not welcome it!

The waterfront docks were a rougher portion of Basseterre. Seamen, bold and brassy-appearing women with loose morals seeking to gain coin for their favors, and those of both sexes hung around the area to prey upon any opportunity in which to try and further their lot. It was not until Katelin and Garrick passed several rundown warehouses that the atmosphere tended to change; and the change was dramatic! In this area they walked through, stalls had been set up and much of what came to the island of Saint Kitts from the many ships that frequented the island was to be found in this portion of Basseterre, set up for the viewing of passersby. Tropical fruits and vegetables of every description were displayed from a booth in which the savory aroma of meat pies and fruit-filled tarts could be sampled. Fine laces, bolts of exotic cloth, and jewelry fashioned by the finest workmen could be found here in the port area. Assortments of fine goods as well as every imaginable object from seemingly any port of the world were openly displayed to tempt the viewer to part with his money.

Katelin was amazed at the busy activity that went on in this part of town. In this area, ladies strolled about with lacy parasols to ward off the direct rays of the glaring sun. Gentlemen in tailored suits accompanied their ladies and chatted with friends. It was as though the rough, ill-smelling docks were miles away instead of a mere hundred yards.

Standing next to Garrick on the wood plank sidewalk as he began to lead her in the direction of the livery, Katelin watched the busy traffic for a few minutes before her attention was drawn to an elderly, pinched-face woman in a stylish apple green walking dress, who appeared to be all but dragging a younger version of herself along behind, and in their direction.

"Why, Captain Steele, what a surprise to see you! I was just telling my dear friend, Fern Atworth, you know the dressmaker here in Basseterre, only the day before yesterday that the island offers so few eligible young gentlemen for our young ladies, and now here you are! Returned once again to our fair shores!"

Garrick grinned at the warm reception the woman offered, and looking to Clarice Langston's only daughter, Thelma, his grin widened at that young lady's deep blush. "Why, thank you so much, Mrs. Langston, for including me on the list of eligible gentlemen here on Saint Kitts."

"Oh pooh, Captain Steele, you know you are at the top of every available young woman's list! Why, even my dear, sweet Thelma . . ." Then the older woman pushed her blond tight-lipped daughter forward, and forced her to stand directly beneath Garrick's notice. "Why, she has been counting the days until you returned to Basseterre!"

The young woman called Thelma flushed even brighter and a gasp escaped her pinched lips at her mother's bold comment. And as all eyes focused upon her as though she should make some worthy statement, she could only squeak out, "I . . . I . . ."

Katelin rolled her emerald eyes heavenward. Did neither of these women know what kind of cad Captain Steele really was? Were they so enamored of this

91

handsome pirate that they could not see through to the real man? If this mother did know what a blackguard he was, she would surely be running to the other side of the road. The silly, simpering Thelma would more than likely have to be dragged away from the rogue just as she had been dragged to his side.

Feeling Katelin's impatient movements next to him, Garrick looked down at her, his silver eyes twinkling with good humor. He was clearly enjoying himself. Not the type of man to leave a lady in distress for long, Garrick reached out and drew the trembling Thelma's hand to his lips. "Why, my dear, Thelma, I had no idea." Boldly he winked into her now scarlet features, and though she would have left her hand in his for all eternity, he let it slip back to her side.

Katelin all but choked at this latest remark, then quickly pretended to clear her throat. She had had about all she could take of this gushing and flattering for one morning. If Garrick Steele wanted to stay around all day and be ogled by these two women, he was more than welcome to do so, but she certainly did not have to stand by and watch.

"Oh, please do excuse my ill manners, Miss Ashford." Garrick turned toward Katelin as though sensing she was ready to bolt. "This lady is our good governor's wife, Clarice Langston, and her lovely daughter, Thelma." Turning back to the two women, he stated, "And this, ladies, is Katelin Ashford. She is going to be staying in Saint Kitts for a while."

Both women gave only the slightest notice to the introduction. Their attention was fully focused upon the handsome sea captain at Katelin Ashford's side. Later the couple would discuss the added competition that Katelin Ashford would present to the single women on Saint Kitts, but for the moment their attention did not waver from the dashing Garrick Steele.

"Yes, yes, that is so very nice for you, Miss Ashford." Mrs. Langston felt forced to say something to the young woman out of good manners, but quickly she turned her eyes back to Garrick. "I am so pleased you have arrived in time to attend the ball that is being held in the governor's honor at the end of next week. You know it is Samuel's sixty-first birthday! All the invitations have been sent out already, but rest assured I will have one sent straightaway to your ship. And perhaps Thelma would even honor you with a dance or two!" Clarice Langston was not adverse to arranging a match for her only child. Now that Thelma was approaching the ripe old age of twenty-two, and heading for spinsterhood, Clarice knew it was about time to take matters into her own hands. If left to her own pursuits where the opposite sex was concerned, her darling Thelma would become an old maid and stay under her charge forever!

"Why, of course I would be delighted to place my name on Thelma's dance card, but I fear I will have to stand in a long line with the other gentlemen vying for the hand of such a lovely young woman." Garrick was well aware that flattery would get him everywhere with these two women. Samuel Langston, as the governor of Saint Kitts, held the power to forbid his ship legal access into the ports of Basseterre. And besides the purse filled with gold coins that he sent to the governor each time he was in port, Garrick went out of his way to stay in Clarice Langston's good graces, and that included flattering the shy, blushing Thelma; what harm was there in offering the daughter a few kind words?

Katelin sniffed aloud, then turned her attention to the street before her, which was bustling with the everyday life of a thriving seaport town. Trying as hard as possible to ignore the simpering of both women over Garrick's latest flirtatious remark, she felt an odd prickling of irritation and forced herself not to turn back around and glare at mother and daughter for being so obvious.

Then becoming more serious, Clarice Langston told Garrick their reason for being out that morning along the dock area — that another woman's body had been found floating along the wharf and she was hoping to pick up any gossip or information about it from her friends. While she was relating what she knew, Scotty pulled up along the sidewalk in a one-horse buggy. Katelin's bags from the *Caroline* were piled high in the back of the vehicle.

Katelin gazed at the young first mate as though he was a godsend. Turning back to the group on the sidewalk, and noting that Garrick's attention seemed fixed on the elder woman's every word, she boldly interrupted, "You ladies will surely excuse me, and you also, Captain Steele. It appears that my ride to my father's plantation has finally arrived." With this, she turned away from the group and started to make her way to the buggy, but not before she glimpsed the hard glare of blue fire in Garrick Steele's eyes.

Tempted for a second to follow her and to teach the first mate a lesson he would not soon forget, Garrick forced himself to remain where he stood, and not make a scene in front of the governor's wife and daughter. Drawing a deep breath, he smiled at the pair as he glimpsed Scotty helping Katelin into the buggy. "So you were saying that another woman's body was found here along the wharf? How many does that make now? I seem to recall that the number had been five the last time my ship was here in port."

Neither Clarice nor Thelma took much notice of Katelin Ashford's departure, as all their concentration was focused on the handsome man they had cornered there on the busy sidewalk.

"Why, I do believe this makes the number eight, no mayhap it is nine. But Samuel says, what matter the loss of another bawd!" The only reason Clarice herself cared a wit about the trollops who had been turning up tortured and murdered along the docks was that it made for good gossip and high speculation! And at the moment, if this topic held Garrick Steele's interest, she was more than willing to tell him all she knew!

Settling her skirts upon the buggy seat, Katelin glanced back in Garrick's direction one last time. He seemed not even to notice her leaving, she thought as she watched him. He was still talking to Clarice Langston, still hanging on her every word. She had indeed been right about him—he was no more than a rake! He wanted to gain the attention of any available woman. And to think, she had almost been fooled into believing he might be different! She straightened her shoulders as Scotty started the horse into motion. She would be much more cautious in the future where this man was concerned. One mistake was all she could afford, though that mistake had cost her dearly!

"I got the directions to Coral Rose, your father's plantation, at the livery. I was going to take your luggage there first, but when I saw you standing on the sidewalk, I thought you might wish to arrive at Coral Rose before the lunch hour." Scotty felt the need to explain how he had come upon her with the horse and buggy. He did not wish her to think he had been awaiting such an opportunity, even though he admitted to himself that the moment he had seen her on the sidewalk, his prayers had been answered.

"I truly appreciate your kindness, Scotty. I must confess I was growing rather bored in Captain Steele's company." Katelin sat back against the seat as she gave the young man a warm smile, then forced herself to put Garrick Steele out of her mind.

Leaving the town behind, Scotty directed the mare along an upwardly winding road. Their view of the island at that elevation was magnificent, as the dusty road looked out over the beach and sea. The fresh air and tropical sea breezes helped Katelin to revive her spirits somewhat. "Did you find out how far it was to Coral Rose, Scotty?" she asked rather anxiously.

"The blacksmith said it was several miles outside of town. He said that if we stayed on this road, it should not take too long. And with the sky slightly overcast, it will be a pleasant enough drive." Scotty smiled broadly, appearing pleased with himself at being able to supply her with the information she requested, and with her at his side, he was pleased with life in general.

"Have you been on Saint Kitts before, Scotty?" Katelin tried hard to be good company to this kind young man and tried even harder to put Garrick Steele out of her mind.

"Aye, I have been here several times in the past. It rains upon occasion, but aside from that, I think you will enjoy yourself here. It is a beautiful island."

"Will you be staying long?" Katelin wondered how long it would take for Captain Howard to make the repairs needed on the *Caroline*.

"I heard the captain saying we might be in port two weeks. As long at it will take to repair the main mast." Which, to Scott Roberts, was far too brief a stay. As he looked at Katelin, he dreaded ever having to leave Saint Kitts!

Katelin swiped at a flying insect that seemed determined to settle on her sleeve. The island's heat became more pronounced as they left the coolness of the open beach road and traveled toward the interior of the island. "Perhaps, then, you will be able to visit for tea one afternoon before you leave the island?" She owed the young man at least this small consideration, she told herself. After all the care he had showed her aboard the *Caroline* and now after today's rescue of her from Captain Steele's brutish company, he did indeed deserve some small reward. Besides, Katelin knew she could easily handle this young man and keep him at an entertaining distance. He was just like most of the male friends she'd had back in London, ever ready to present himself before her and willing to snatch out at any small offering she would bestow.

Scotty jumped at the invitation of tea. "I would be more than delighted to pay you a visit, Miss Ashford."

"Good, then let us say tomorrow afternoon. That should give me some time to settle in, but we do not wish to delay our afternoon tea for too long, in case the repairs aboard the *Caroline* are finished in a shorter time than expected." Now that she had invited him, Katelin was already anxious to have the affair over with.

Scotty was more than a little delighted with her answer. Tomorrow would not come soon enough as far as he was concerned.

"I also wish to thank you for bringing my luggage along, Scotty. I had thought that I would have my father send for it, but now that will not be necessary."

The luggage had been the only excuse that Scotty could come up with to go out to Coral Rose. But wisely he kept this to himself.

It was a short time later that Scotty directed the horse down a long lane off the main road. A sign overhead on a thick wooden board read CORAL ROSE. The drive appeared little used, overgrown as it was with the wild jungle foliage that seemed to thrive on the island. Trees shaded overhead, blocking out the bright sunlight, and the scent of tropical flowers hung heavy in the air.

As the carriage passed through the border of trees, directly before them, sitting all by itself, was a large white-framed house. The grounds had probably seen better days — tall grass grew along the drive, and a wild profusion of multicolored tropical flowers encircled the airy-looking, two-story structure.

There was an air of laziness about the place, Katelin thought as Scotty brought the vehicle to a halt and handed her down from the carriage seat. "If you would just set my luggage on the front porch, I will have it tended to later." Katelin indicated the front veranda that ran the entire length of the house and disappeared around the sides.

Scotty was more than willing to do her bidding, hoping to somehow further himself into her favor.

Katelin lingered outside the house until the first mate had set all her bags on the porch. It seemed odd that neither her father nor one of his servants had come out to welcome her, but nevertheless she said farewell to her escort, reassuring him that she would be awaiting him for tea tomorrow afternoon. The buggy pulled slowly away from the house and back down the lane, and she made her way to the front door.

She hoped that the first mate of the *Caroline* had not brought her to the wrong plantation. Setting her hand against the wooden door, she lightly knocked.

Seven

Without resistance, the front door swung wide, and stepping gingerly into the cool interior, Katelin found that the house was well tended after all, and not deserted as she had begun to fear. Light, airy pieces of furniture were placed strategically throughout the open rooms of the lower floor, and large windows had been placed at every angle of the house to catch the lightest of tropical breezes.

Hearing noises coming from the back portion of the house, Katelin quietly approached the kitchen area. Pushing aside a swinging door, she came upon a heavyset black woman who was standing over a large wood-burning stove and softly humming a native song.

Katelin was more than a little nervous about the reception she was going to receive if she had somehow found herself at the wrong house. But even if this was the right house, she was still nervous about the fact that her father had no idea she was coming for a two-year visit. Katelin softly cleared her throat and waited for the black woman across the room to turn from her cooking pot and look in her direction.

As she swung around, the wide grin that had been on the amply endowed black woman's face slowly disappeared. Her dark eyes fixed upon the young woman standing in the doorway of her kitchen. "Can I be a-helping you, missy?" She set her spoon beside the pot she had been stirring and began to wipe her hands on the apron that covered her wide hips.

"Why I hope so." Katelin took a step farther into the cleanly scrubbed, fragrant-smelling room. "I am looking for my father, Richard Ashford."

The woman's mouth dropped open in surprise, her dark eyes enlarging in disbelief. "Why Lordy, child, you surely can't be Miss Katelin?"

"Why, yes I am." Katelin smiled at the woman with as much relief as the woman was showing surprise. "Where is my father? Is he here on the plantation?" The house was so quiet she thought that perhaps her father had gone to town and she had missed him, or perhaps he was out working in the fields somewhere.

"Why, you poor child, didn't you receive word about yer pappy?" But before Katelin could ask who had sent her word about her father, the woman continued in a rush. "The master done gone on to his maker, honey child. Not more than six months ago he passed on to the other side. I thought for sure you knew all about yer pappy and Miss Carol. That nice young man who wrote out yer pappy's last will and testament said he would send you a letter explaining everything."

101

"A letter never arrived. My father is dead?" Katelin fought off the dizziness that threatened to engulf her, hoping that somehow she had misunderstood the woman.

"I'm right sorry to be the one to tell you, honey. Sit yerself down over here at my table and let old Lizzy fix you a cup of good hot tea." The woman went to Katelin's side, and glimpsing the paleness of her features, she led her by the arm over to the scarred, work-worn table.

"There weren't nothing that could be done for the master nor the mistress. They took the fever and inside of a week they both were done in!" Lizzy made sure the young lady was settled in the chair before turning back to her stove and putting on a pot of water for tea.

Katelin shook her head in bewilderment. "You speak of a mistress—did my father have a wife?" She was learning quickly enough how little she knew about her own father.

"I at least thought the master done wrote and told you about the mistress." Shaking her large head, which was wrapped in a bright red turban, Lizzy implied that in the past she had not agreed with everything Richard Ashford had done in his lifetime. Bringing the teapot to the table, she poured a cup of steaming water into the tea leaves. "Now don't be thinking too hard on Master Richard, child. His grief was what made him keep to his strange ways where his little daughter was concerned. He told me years ago, before he ever met Miss Carol, how he lost his heart when yer mammy was called to heaven with the saints. It

102

ain't fitting as how he left you, but he never in a day's passing forgot about you. He carried a miniature of you right close, next to his heart, in his jacket pocket, and I made sure it was right there when he was laid to rest."

Katelin was unsure at the moment how she was supposed to react to this news about her father's death. She could remember him only dimly, his image having faded over the years. The news that he had remarried was rather startling, but she had to grant that it was no more than she could have expected. Richard Ashford had been a handsome, virile man; not one who would languish away forever without the company of a woman at his side.

"Have one of these little sweet cakes, honey. I baked 'em only this morning." Lizzy held out a small plate of iced cakes and Katelin absently picked one up and took a bite. "You surely look plum tuckered out. You had best rest yerself before too long. The heat on this island can do in most anyone, let alone a bit of a thing like you."

Lizzy seemed to try and give the young woman a moment to take everything in before she spoke again. "I reckon as how the master didn't write to you and tell you about the mistress, then he didn't tell you about young Master Joshua either?"

"Joshua?" Katelin questioned, having no idea who Joshua could be.

The turbaned head nodded eagerly now. "The young master ain't here right this minute to meet you, he's more than likely out running wild somewhere along the beach."

"You mean my father had a son? Is that who

103

Joshua is?" Katelin could not believe what she was being told!

The head nodded once again in total agreement. "He be a handful, young Master Joshua be, but inside he has a heart of gold. He be a good boy when he takes a mind."

"How old is he?" Katelin swallowed hard, hungry from not eating any breakfast. She tried to force the bite of sweet cake down her throat as it threatened to tighten on her.

"Why, Joshua be twelve years old now, Miss Katelin. Ain't it something you have a little brother you done never knowed nothing about! Can you be beating that?"

"I have a twelve-year-old brother?" Katelin repeated as though she were in a daze, her green eyes looking about the kitchen expecting to find her father jumping out from a corner or from behind a cabinet and shouting, Surprise! The joke is on you! "This just cannot be possible! Who has been taking care of Joshua? Who is responsible for him now that my father is dead?"

"Why, now that you've come to Saint Kitts, I reckon that it be yer place to tend to yer brother, Miss Katelin. Coral Rose is all that the young master has now as his birthright, and I allow that it be yer place to see that he holds on to it!"

A twelve-year-old brother who at this very moment was running wild somewhere upon the beach! Katelin could only stare at the black woman. Her entire world seemed to be spinning crazily on an axis that held no steady tilt. Her inner defenses shouted out that right this moment a carriage

104

should take her back to Basseterre. She would seek out a ship, any ship, and go straight back to her aunt. Back to London where her life had always held some kind of order. Where she had known pretty much what every day would hold for her. But of course, reason prevailed. She knew that she could not possibly abandon her father's child—even as much as she would like to at the moment. "Did this Carol, whom my father married, have any family?" First off, she should find out if there was some part of the child's mother's family that could foster him until he came of age and could care for himself.

"No, ma'am. Miss Carol didn't have a soul she could claim as family besides the master and her boy, Joshua. Master Richard was a lonely man when he met Miss Carol one day in town. She was working for Mrs. Bates at her boardinghouse, helping the old lady cook and clean and such as that. It weren't a week or two after Master Richard met Miss Carol that they got hitched up, and Miss Carol never talked about her family. One time she told me that they had all passed on and all she had in this world was the master and young Master Joshua."

Well, no help there, Katelin thought to herself. "Didn't they have any friends who could take care of the boy until he comes of age and can run the plantation on his own?" There was a bit more desperation in her voice now.

Lizzy wagged her head back and forth. "Most everyone who be knowing the young master be thinking him a little too much to handle." As Katelin's eyes grew wide with surprise, Lizzy quickly reassured her. "It ain't that the boy is bad, mind you. He just be a little bit set in his own ways. Master Richard allowed him to have his own way much of the time, and Miss Carol, why, she loved the boy so much she saw no wrong in his wild ways!"

There once again was that word *wild,* Katelin thought as she tried to figure out what Lizzy's smiling features were not telling her. A sigh escaped her as she finished with her tea and the cake. She was far too tired to deal with the astonishing news that she now had a brother. Her head began to pound fiercely from the combination of tropical heat and the shock of her family news. "Is there someone who can show me to a room where I will be able to rest for a while?"

"Most of the house servants now spend their time out back in the cabins. Things have grown a little lax around Coral Rose without someone here to give out daily orders. Master Joshua is just too young to care about such things!" Lizzy said in a way of explaining the condition of the plantation. "It won't take me a minute to go out and fetch a couple of the house girls, though. We will be needing more help now that you're here with us."

"For now, just tell me where my father's room is? That will do for the time being." Katelin was feeling wearier by the minute, and wanted to rest at once.

Lizzy seemed more than pleased to direct the young woman to her father's chambers. "The old master's room is the first door up the stairs. You go on up and I'll fetch old Rufuss to see about your bags." Perhaps things would get back to order here at Coral Rose with Miss Katelin in residence! As

106

far as Lizzy was concerned, things at the plantation had been far too lax and there was a need for some straightening out!

Katelin wearily nodded as she rose to her feet, and started out of the kitchen. Her head was in a whirl as she made her way up the stairs, and opened the first door she came to. Her hand still clutching the doorknob, she paused. There, on the wall directly opposite the door, hung a painting of her father, and next to it a painting of a woman with nondescript features.

The Richard Ashford that Katelin remembered from her childhood seemed to come to life for her in the brush strokes of the canvas. He was every bit as handsome as her girlish fantasies had been after that dreadful day when she had been left with her aunt at Wessely House. His green eyes, so like her own, shone with humor and his high brow and firm chin bespoke intelligence. While gazing at her father's dark hair, came the unbidden image in her mind of another man who had midnight hair. Coming to her senses as the vision of the bold, womanizing sea captain came to mind, Katelin hurriedly turned her attention to the woman's portrait hanging next to her father's.

There was little in the woman's features that Katelin could see would have attracted the attentions of her father. The woman's brown hair was severely pulled back. Her chin pointed and her eyes a dull, pale blue, she appeared thin, almost angular, with her hands primly clutched in her lap. What form of comfort could her father have found in the embrace of such a woman, Katelin wondered as she studied the painting, trying to imagine what the portrait hid from view. Surely the artist had left nothing out of the woman he was painting, for he had captured her father to the fullest.

Perhaps this boy, Joshua, was like the mother, Katelin thought as she turned away from the paintings. Still, it was hard to believe her father had a son whom she had never known about and that she was now somehow responsible for him.

The chamber was large and had been decorated in rich, warm colors, which plainly revealed a woman's hand. The furniture was more in keeping with an English manor house than a bedchamber on a tropical island. The large, oak four-poster bed rested in the center of the room. A lovely wine red, rose chintz had been tastefully turned into tied-back draperies and an inviting comforter, which graced the bed. Across the room a curtained alcove boasted curtains made up of the same material in a comfortable-appearing window seat. On the opposite wall was a balcony that looked over the front lawns of the plantation house. There was little evidence of her father or his wife having used the chamber. The closets and bureau had been emptied some time ago.

Kicking off her traveling boots, Katelin sighed aloud as her toes curled into the thick, plush carpet. Pulling off her hat, she placed it atop the bureau and once again her glance sought out the large bed. A couple of hours' sleep would do her a world of good, she told herself. Perhaps upon awakening, she would find that things were not nearly as terrible as they appeared to her now.

Lying down upon the soft coverlet, she tried to forget about her father, his bride, and the brother she had not known even to exist until only a short time ago.

The bold image of Garrick Steele quickly took shape in her mind. Had it only been this morning that she had found herself lying naked in that handsome sea captain's bed? Perhaps if she had found the enfolding comfort of a father's arms when she had arrived at Coral Rose, she would have confessed all to him and let him deal with that dashing rogue. Slowly her eyes began to shut, the fleeting thoughts passed. Without her father here to defend her honor, she would have to stick up for herself. *As if I could put up any defense where that man is concerned,* she thought as she drifted off to sleep.

"Lizzy say you ain't to disturb the missy! Come back here right this minute!" A door slammed, a high-pitched squeal filled the air as something crashed to the floor, and boyish prank-filled laughter settled within the bedchamber.

Katelin jumped to full wakefulness, her green eyes wide, not knowing where she was or what was taking place around her!

"I'm sorry, missy, I'm sorry!" A young black girl stood at the foot of Katelin's bed and wrung her hands in misery. Her black eyes were wide with fear as she stared at the young woman sitting on the coverlet, the green eyes searching out the chamber for the disturbance which had woken her. "I done tried to stop the young master, but he wouldn't pay me no heed!"

Quickly coming to her senses and seeing the fear on the young girl's features, Katelin instantly took stock of the situation, realizing that ready or not, she was about to meet her brother. Searching out the chamber for the twelve-year-old child, she looked back at the trembling black girl. "Did he come in here?" she questioned, wondering if she had missed some event the girl had not yet told her about.

Quickly bobbing her shorn, kinky head, the girl pointed a finger to the curtained partition that contained the window seat. "He be hiding in there, missy!" She spoke softly as though not to give away that she was an informant.

Katelin smiled softly, remembering how shy she herself had been at the age of twelve. Certainly her brother would feel somewhat uncomfortable with their first meeting, she reasoned. "Thank you . . ." She did not know the young black girl's name as yet.

"I be Bessy, missy. Lizzy say I am to tend to your needs from here on out."

"Well, Bessy, I guess you can leave Joshua and me for the time being. We will need some time to get acquainted."

Bessy's eyes widened once again. She was not so sure this was a good idea. "I can be staying if'n you wish, missy. I don't mind none at all."

Having quickly recovered from her sleep, Katelin took in the situation and thought it best that she be alone with the child. If everything that Lizzy had told her was true, the young boy more than likely was in need of a comforting shoulder to cry upon after enduring these past months here on the plantation without the security of family or friends. She could well imagine how afraid he must be after the death of both parents. "That will be all right, Bessy. If you will just see that my luggage is brought upstairs, I would be very grateful."

"If you think it best, missy, all right then." Bessy reluctantly went to the door, still unsure she should leave the new mistress all alone with Joshua Ashford!

As the door closed, Katelin pulled herself from the bed and went to the window seat. Pulling aside the draperies that made up the enclosure, she found the seat empty. Swinging around, she was met with boyish laughter coming from outside the chamber on the balcony. Crossing the chamber, she stepped out onto the balcony. The sight that met her eyes claimed her heartbeat and froze her in her footsteps.

There, walking upon the top portion of the iron grille enclosure of the balcony, which rose up only a little over waist high, was a dark-haired, green-eyed boy wearing only cutoff trousers, no shoes, and no shirt! The afternoon island breezes ruffled the long, unruly strands of his hair, as he watched her standing openmouthed as though any minute she would let out a bloodcurdling scream, fearing for his safety. His devilish laughter once more filled the air.

"Come down from there, at once!" Katelin at last gasped out, afraid that any movement on her part could cause the child to tumble over the edge, and having earlier glimpsed the height of the balcony to

111

the ground, she feared that he would never recover from such a fall.

"Why should I?" The boy's wide, impish grin appeared.

Katelin was to stunned to speak. Wild was right! This was the wildest child she had ever encountered! Recovering somewhat, she tried to sound calm as she said, "Because you will fall, if you do not do as you are told!"

"You mean like this?" His arms had been held out to his sides, and for a fraction of a second, the boy tilted his body toward the opposite side of the balcony as though he were going over the side.

Katelin closed her eyes, not able to watch him go flying through the air to his death, but when she opened her eyes once again, he was still standing there on the balcony railing, with that huge grin upon his mischievous face. Spinning around on her bare feet, she marched back into the chamber. If the boy was intent upon harming himself, there was nothing she could do to stop him. If she tried to pull him down, surely that action could prove disastrous! No, the best thing she could do at the moment was to let him grow bored with his own antics and he would eventually get down from the railing himself.

Once back in the chamber, Katelin sat down and waited in one of the chairs that had been arranged in a corner of the room. Her heartbeat accelerated and took several minutes to calm itself to near normal. Nothing had prepared her for such a first meeting with her only brother. Lizzy had said that the people on the island did not understand the child's ways, and at the moment Katelin held no doubt to the truth of this.

Only a short time passed before Katelin glimpsed a bare foot stepping through the chamber door leading from the balcony, and then shortly another foot as the boy stepped into the room.

His green eyes were hard as they instantly searched out the room and found her sitting on the chair. "So you are my sister?" he questioned when he stood midway into the chamber, his chin tilted firmly as though daring her in some fashion.

"So you are my brother!" was Katelin's only reply.

The pair, resembling their father's handsome looks, stared hard at each other for a few minutes before Joshua spoke once again. "If you think that you are going to take me away from Coral Rose and make me live with you at your aunt's house, I won't go!" The jade green eyes sparkled with challenge. The small fists doubled at both sides as though ready to fight off any attacker.

At the image of her aunt's reaction, if she indeed had brought this wild creature to her home, a smile settled over Katelin's lips. "How do you know about my aunt Elizabeth?" Katelin softly questioned, hoping that somehow she would be able to win over this brother of hers.

"My father told me all about you and your aunt! He said you lived across the ocean and that one day you would come for me and take care of me. But I won't go with you and you can't make me!"

Katelin was truly taken aback by this outburst. "And when did your father tell you all of this?" She tried to use a tone that would not frighten the

113

boy into running away from her.

"When he and mother were sick. Right before he closed his eyes and didn't open them again."

Katelin expelled the breath from her chest. Her father had spoken of her on his death bed. He had thought of her and had told this child that she would come for him and take care of him. Well, how very thoughtful of him! Her father had left her without a word for years to live with her aunt, and upon his death bed he thought he had the right to tell her brother that she would take up responsibility for him! She knew that her anger was misplaced even as the next words left her mouth. "And what makes you think I would wish to take charge of a boy like you?" The minute she said this she wished she were able to take the words back, but the effect they had on Joshua was more than a little surprising.

The hardness in the green eyes left and slowly the chin softened as did the firmness around his lips. "You mean you didn't come to Saint Kitts to take me back to London with you?"

Slowly she shook her head, not trusting herself for the moment to speak. She had to remind herself that she could not take her own hurt out on this child, since he also had suffered greatly over the past few months.

"Then why are you here?" For an instant the eyes, so much like her own, glinted once again with their distrust.

"I was sent here by my aunt for a period of two years." As her brother looked her over and for the first time appeared to be measuring her worth,

Katelin quickly decided that it would be best not to tell him or anyone on the island about any of her past exploits! "My aunt Elizabeth thought it best that I visit my father before I began to make plans to settle down and think about marriage," she quickly added.

"Then you didn't know about my father and mother?" Joshua was still not able to believe that she had come all the way to Saint Kitts without intending to take him away from Coral Rose. From the moment his father had told him about his sister, he had dreaded the day when she would arrive here at the plantation.

"Lizzy told me about my father and your mother, when I arrived. I had no idea that my father had even remarried, or that I had a brother until this very morning."

"My father told me about you."

Katelin was not sure if that was good or bad in this young boy's mind, and she was not about to question him on the subject.

"So what will you do now?" He came right to the point and Katelin found it rather unsettling to be questioned so directly by a twelve-year-old child.

"Well actually, I have not had any time to think upon the matter. What would you suggest that I do, Joshua?"

Her easy manner seemed to lull the boy into trusting her for the moment, though he still kept his distance. "I think you should go back where you come from and leave everything at Coral Rose just like it is."

"You love this plantation, don't you?" Katelin for

some reason had to ask the question, and as she awaited the answer, she knew it would mean much in the decision she would be making soon for both of their futures.

The dark head nodded vigorously, and a glimpse of an unshed tear filled the green eyes. Though Joshua Ashford had been forced to grow old for his twelve years in the short time since his parents' death, at this moment he felt very vulnerable standing before his newfound sister. She held the power within her hands to change his world forever, if she chose to do so!

Katelin certainly could not fault the child for the love he held for his home. Had she not herself felt terrible leaving London? Standing, she tried to make her tone as light as possible as she said, "Then why don't you show me around and let's get something to eat from Lizzy's kitchen?"

For a long minute the young boy stood still, as though not believing she had not said the words he had dreaded hearing from the moment Lizzy had told him his sister had at long last arrived at Coral Rose. Suddenly the caution on his features disappeared. "You mean you might just let me stay here?"

"Why don't we take one thing at a time, Joshua. First you and I need to get something to eat, and we do need to get to know one another. After all, we are brother and sister." She avoided answering his questions for the time being, for she did not know what she would do with him. She knew she would have to make some decisions sooner or later, but right now she wasn't sure what they would be.

She would need more time to think this matter over, she told herself as she looked down at the boy standing before her and reminding her so much of herself.

The warning lights seemed to instantly flash once again in the boy's eyes. The shield of distrust that he so often put up around himself was quickly being erected once again as he wondered why she would wish to get to know him. After all, no one seemed to care anything about him, except for Lizzy. Slowly he nodded his head as he felt her green eyes studying him. Perhaps if he showed her the plantation and she got something to eat, she would decide that he could stay, and everything could remain as it always had!

Eight

By that evening Katelin still had no idea what she was going to do about her newfound brother or the plantation. She had found out through Lizzy that the servants had all grown lazy in the absence of a master or mistress at Coral Rose. There was no overseer to handle the workers in the fields and there was a large problem with available money. It appeared that her father had not been wise in his investment of the profits he had made from his sugar cane and cotton fields. He had sunk a great deal of money into outfitting a ship and filling its hold with wines from France and laces from Brussels. The captain of the ship had had one disaster after another, and in the end the vessel had sunk somewhere near Portugal. The plantation had never recovered its losses.

At least there was no mortgage on Coral Rose, Katelin told herself as she leaned back against the brass tub, and in the relaxing depths of warm water she tried to sort out her options. Lathering a slender foot and shapely leg with the fragrant-smelling jasmine soap that Bessy had set out for her use with an assortment of bath oils, she smiled as she thought about her young brother. He was a prankish hellion—he delighted in tormenting the servants in good-natured fun and he certainly was more active than any child she had ever met.

The boy was determined to stay at Coral Rose. She washed the inside of her thighs slowly as she reflected over everything they had spoken about during the afternoon. She knew he would be a problem if she decided to take him back to London with her. It could take some time before the plantation could be sold, and in the meantime he as well as she would be totally dependent upon her aunt's good charity.

The thought of Joshua Ashford living at Wessely House and tormenting the straitlaced servants, as he did those here at Coral Rose, all but sent Katelin into peals of laughter. It would be no laughing matter, though, in reality—of that, she was well aware. Aunt Elizabeth would more than likely have to increase her libation to two glasses of warmed brandy every evening!

Leaning her head back once again, she allowed the water to do its work, her body feeling more relaxed than it had in weeks. The hour was late, the house servants having gone off to bed after heating water for her bath and carrying it up the stairs. Joshua was in bed after having jumped out at her one last time from the curtained alcove in her chamber, and she now had the time she de-

119

sired to herself. It appeared that, willingly or not, she was no longer the same young woman she had been days ago when she had left London.

Her face acquired a rosy hue, as much from the water as from the thoughts that assaulted her as she remembered the last night she had spent aboard the *Sea Witch*. Those long hours spent in the arms of that handsome, virile pirate had surely changed her for all time, but her reception at Coral Rose, and learning that she was now responsible for her brother and a plantation and its people, had brought home the full extent of her adulthood. She could no longer depend upon her aunt to make decisions for her. Right or wrong, she would have to take charge of her future and also the future of her brother.

Some slight noise intruded upon her thoughts. It came from across the room, away from the corner where the small bathing chamber had been set up. Could Joshua have sneaked back in her room and this moment be out on the balcony? "I have had about all the pranks I can abide for one day, Joshua! Come out of there now!" She tried to make her voice sound firm, knowing the boy would listen to her only if he truly wanted to anyway.

Having left the balcony double doors open to catch any night breezes, Katelin gasped aloud as not her brother, but Garrick Steele stepped into the chamber.

"And pray tell, madam, who is this Joshua whom you think is in your chamber while you are at your bath?" The silver-blue eyes held chips of ice in their depths as without a second thought he strode purposefully toward the corner of the chamber where Katelin sat in her bath.

"You! How dare you enter my chamber unbidden? How dare you come to Coral Rose at all!" Katelin would have shouted at him, but for some strange reason her words touched his ears in low tones.

"You should be the one to answer my questions first! Who is this Joshua whom you believed hiding out on your balcony?" Garrick felt fine pricklings of jealousy coursing over his entire length as he awaited her answer with some impatience. He had been a damn fool! He had believed her when she had told him that she had come to Saint Kitts to be reunited with her father, but now he found that she had come only to meet some man called Joshua! The fact that he had found her to be a virgin only the night before never entered his head as he was consumed with but one thought — to find out who this Joshua was and tear him limb from limb.

"I will thank you to leave my presence and Coral Rose right this minute!" Katelin's shimmering green eyes shot daggers of retribution at him if he did not do as she commanded and do so immediately. "I do not have to answer you! I am no longer aboard your dreadful pirate ship, and you can force nothing more from me!" she added as a last insult.

Within seconds Garrick was at her side, and bending down, he reached into the warm depths as

121

he lightly grasped hold of her forearms. "Perhaps your memory plays you falsely, madam. There was no force that I can remember while you were aboard my ship!" Holding her tightly without hurting her, he demanded, "Answer me. Who is this Joshua?" Within the depths of his pale eyes, dancing flames of scorching fire clashed with hers of glimmering green.

What did it matter if he knew about her brother? All Katelin wanted at the moment was to be free of him! Trying in vain to shrug out of his grasp without revealing too much of her upper torso, she at last relented to his demands. "Joshua is my brother, if you must know!" Drawing a ragged breath, she glared, "If that is what you want of me, take your hands off and leave my chamber, now!" In the back of Katelin's mind she wondered why she was not shouting the house down around his head. She was sure that old Rufuss, the black man who acted as butler and handyman, would come running to her rescue if she let out a call for help. And with the call downstairs, she was sure he could have brought several of the Coral Rose workers running also to her defense.

Garrick stared down at her, his gaze appearing to judge if she was telling the truth. "You never mentioned you had a brother, Kat." His tone was no longer hard, but had the husky tremor that Katelin remembered held the power to steal the very breath from her body.

"I did not know then that I had a brother!" *As though I have to explain anything to this brute,* she told

122

herself. But while he still held her by the arms, there was little she could do but try to convince him to release her.

"Oh, now I understand." At last Garrick did take his hands from her arms, but remaining at the foot of her tub, he was still formidable-appearing as his heated gaze seemed to seek out something that she was not willing at the moment to give.

Sinking lower into the depths of her bubble bath, Katelin pulled her wash rag over her breasts, trying even with her nervousness to shield their fullness from his hungry gaze. "You understand what? You know nothing of me, Captain!" Her anger seemed to rage somewhat out of control as she was forced to endure those pale silver eyes upon her. "Do you understand that I have been forced to leave all that I love, both family and friends, only to find that my father is no longer alive and that I now have a brother to care for and a rundown plantation to try and get back to some order? Do you understand that I have taken about enough? You are but one more added torment to the long list!" Her own eyes now shot out sparkling heat as she glared up into his handsome face.

At that moment Garrick looked upon her with admiration for her unusual beauty, mingled with sympathy for all she had been forced to endure. "If only you would allow me, Kat, I would willingly give you the comfort you are in need of!" His words were so tenderly spoken as he looked down at her, and it was clear they'd come straight from his heart.

Whenever Katelin was near this man, however, some inner force spurned his attempts at kindness toward her. "I have already tasted of your comfort, sir, and it was not to my liking!"

Garrick could have easily disputed this caustic remark, but he thought better of the idea. At the moment his spitting tigress appeared more the wounded kitten, and he could glimpse the inner pain which she was suffering. "Do you truly want to know what has brought me out to Coral Rose at this ungodly hour, Kat?"

"If in the telling you will at last leave me in peace, then get on with it!" Katelin spat out, still feeling blistered from his high-handedness with her about Joshua.

"I think I should wait until you finish your bath." Garrick smiled warmly, and bending down, he felt the water temperature. "You will take a chill if you stay in there much longer, Kat. The temperature is dropping by the minute." With this, he turned his back to her and strode across the room. Standing before the double paintings hanging on the chamber wall, he silently appraised the couple.

Katelin could easily have screamed aloud her frustration! Who did this man think he was? Barging into her chamber and treating her in such a bold manner? With his back to her, she quickly took the opportunity to wrap her body in the soft, thick towel that Bessy had set out for her. Securing the corner of the towel between her breasts, she drew in a deep breath, trying to gather her wits for another confrontation with this devil of a sea captain!

Garrick heard the soft padding of her bare feet upon the carpet and turned around. Suddenly a warm, admiring smile settled over his sensual lips. The entire day he'd been remembering her rare beauty. Over and over he had told himself that she was little different from a hundred other women he had known in his past. But standing now before her, he knew that was a lie! Her beauty was incomparable! She was the finest jewel, awaiting only to be put in the perfect setting—which he knew was right in his arms!

"Your reason for being here, Captain?" Katelin coolly questioned, wanting only for him to say whatever he had come for and then to leave by the same way he had entered her chamber.

The sound of her voice pulled him from his mind's wanderings. "Aye, the reason for my presence in your chamber." His hand eased into the inside pocket of his dark seaman's jacket, and slowly he withdrew an envelope with a scrawling handwriting on the front. "I came with the express purpose of delivering this." He held the letter out at arm's length for her viewing.

"What is it? Who is it from?" Katelin's curiosity was well pricked. Who would be sending her a message through Captain Garrick Steele?

"Come and see for yourself." He tried to lure her closer to his side.

Eyeing him cautiously, she took a step and then another, her hand tightly pressed to the knot of the towel.

Garrick would not budge an inch, but allowed her to approach him. He could read the caution in her features and for a second he was tempted to grin, but thinking better of further antagonizing her, he kept his face innocent of any teasing insinuations.

Having had firsthand knowledge of the power this man seemed to have over her senses when she was near him, Katelin nevertheless was drawn by her curiosity toward him — to the letter which he was holding out for her. She expelled a drawn breath just as she reached out and took the envelope from his large hand. As though for self-protection, she took a quick step and then another backward, putting several feet of distance between them before her finger broke the wax seal and she pulled out an ivory card from the envelope. For a few seconds she stared transfixed upon the card in her hand, and then slowly her eyes rose back to him. "It is an invitation to the governor's ball?" She glanced back down at the card not in the least believing that this was his only reason for coming out to Coral Rose.

In that split second it took for her to look back at the hand holding the invitation, Garrick with pantherlike strides was at her side. "Both yours and mine arrived at the *Sea Witch* this afternoon, and I took it upon myself to hand-deliver your invitation."

Feeling his warming breath against her cheek, Katelin knew that she had not reacted quickly

126

enough. She should have put more distance between herself and him! She should have run while she had the chance, instead of being seduced into playing into his hands with the temptation of a letter, which proved only to be an invitation to the governor's ball, and instantly she thought of the governor's wife and his simpering daughter. There was little time for such thoughts though as she felt her cheeks flush and the slight quivering of her flesh at his nearness. She tried to put on a brave face and appear as though his closeness did not affect her in the least. "You have certainly done your good deed then, Captain. I thank you most kindly, and now you can be gone!"

Garrick's sensual lips drew back in a smile as he looked down at the top of her head. The fragrance of the curls piled atop her crown assaulted him even as he sensed her reluctance to look up into his face. "Do you not think that this deed at least deserves some small reward?" A long, tanned finger drew her chin upward until he could look down into the turbulent sea of her emerald eyes.

Katelin wanted to run from him. She wanted also to hit out at the hand that was forcing her chin back so that she had to look up into his handsome face. But at the moment she was powerless to respond to her own good senses. She was hypnotized by his consuming gaze, and as his head slowly began to lower, her own mouth silently opened as though it would indulge him, whether her mind willed it or not!

The kiss was a carnal flame that seared her to

the very depths of her soul. She no longer thought of the knot of the towel above her breasts. Her hands encircled his powerful neck as her body molded itself against his long, muscular torso. Everything she had suffered at this man's hands was forgotten in that instant. His actions aboard his ship, the fact that she believed him to be a womanizing cad, and the numerous times she had told herself that she would never again allow herself to be swept away by his handsome maleness did not at this time enter into her thoughts. She was consumed totally by the seduction of his mouth over her own, and as his hands reached down and lifted her legs within the crook of his arms, she did not make the slightest objection.

The reward that Garrick was receiving for delivering the invitation was even greater than he had expected. The moment his mouth had coveted hers, he had succumbed to everything but the taste and feel of the woman in his arms. Her lips were the most potent elixir he had ever known. The soft, satin feel of her flesh beneath his hands was a heady aphrodisiac. Lifting her with ease into his embrace, he carried her over to the corner of the room where two chairs and a small table were arranged with a vase of fragrantly scented, tropical flowers sitting on the table top. The temptation of going directly to the large bed in the center of the chamber was a hard one for Garrick to fight off as he sat down with her in his lap.

Still their lips had not parted. The kiss lasted for some time longer before both broke off with a large sigh. Katelin could not look him fully in the face—she felt some inner betrayal, which she had inflicted upon herself, but felt powerless to fight off his attraction. Garrick gently pressed her head against his broad chest as though sensing her feelings. "Tell me of your father, Kat." He spoke softly, his heartbeat filling her ears as his fingers lightly traced a silken pattern over the soft flesh of her upper arms.

Katelin knew that she should rebuke him while the power of his lips was some distance from her own. She should jump from his lap and insist that he leave her chamber, this very moment! But something in his tone, the gentle concern she heard in the husky depths, held her where she sat. So much had happened to her in so little time and it seemed that she had been totally alone to deal with all of life's problems. Tears stung her jade eyes and sparkled throughout her thick, dark lashes as she wondered what she would tell him of her father, and in a rush all her memories of a father now gone forever came back to her: the times Richard Ashford had held her tenderly in his lap before she went to bed each night when she had been no more than a child; how his strong voice would chase away all her childish fears and bring a smile to her lips. Until now, she had not allowed herself a single moment to grieve for the man she had known as a child, and as the tears broke through, great, trembling sobs shook her slight frame.

Sensing the magnitude of her grief, Garrick allowed her all the time she needed to cry against his chest. He tenderly soothed her, cradling her in his arms, his lips plying soft kisses against the crown of her head as his own heart experienced the pain of her bereavement.

The candles around her bath had burnt low, the one near her bedside glittering in its dish. The chamber was dimly aglow with the moonlight which entered through the balcony double doors. It was some time before Katelin's sobbing turned to soft gasps and her body's trembling subsided. It was even a longer time before her soft words touched his ears. "My father was my hero." She sniffed loudly before telling him of her childhood, the death of her mother, and how she had come to live with her aunt in London.

She finished her story with the events that had taken place at Coral Rose today. She told him how she had come to Coral Rose only to find her father had remarried, that he and his wife had died of the fever, and now it was up to her to take care of her brother and the plantation. She seemed exhausted at the end of her tale, lying limp within Garrick's arms, all the fight and emotion drained from her as for once she allowed her more vulnerable side to be viewed.

Garrick had not once interrupted her. He sensed rightly that she needed to get all these emotions out. He doubted she had ever opened herself up to any other person; even her aunt had more than likely not been privy to the inner feelings of her crying soul over the loss of her mother and father in such a short period of time. She was like a wounded animal and needed this small reprieve from the hardness which she had built around herself over the years, to lick her wounds, and then once again she would be able to go on and face the world. He knew much of this for he had upon occasion had his own wounds to lick and to allow time to heal. Raised by a father who loved him but a stepmother who did not, he had thought there were many instances in his own childhood that were better off buried forever, until he had dug them up and reviewed them for his own inner peace of mind.

Lending her strength within the comfort of his embrace, Garrick sat in the chair for sometime longer, even as her words quieted and her breathing returned to normal.

Slowly her head pulled away from his chest, and looking into his face, Katelin's green eyes sought out each feature as though trying to understand something of this man who was holding her so tenderly.

It seemed quite natural for Garrick to reach up and unclasp the hairpins that held the dark tresses atop her head, and unleash the shiny mass of silky curls about her shoulders. Without thought, his hands twined within the strands. With a small groan, he dipped his head and kissed her tenderly.

A long shudder coursed over her entire body. She felt her bones melting, as he filled the kiss with all the bittersweet intensity she so desperately needed. Eagerly, she kissed him back, hungrily, passionately, her lips opening as she matched the pressure of his mouth. His heated tongue slowly tantalized the inside of her mouth, drawing her own tongue out and playing a dueling game of sensuality, which left them both trembling with desire.

Garrick suddenly rose to his feet with her held in his embrace. Her slender arms entwined around his neck, her fingers tangling with his hair. Her cheek was pressed against his chest as he carried her across the space of the chamber. She could hear his heart thundering, smell his masculine cologne mixed with tobacco and the faint scent of the sea; the combination induced her senses to spiraling heights of awareness.

With a light, fluid motion he set her to her feet, the bed brushing the backs of her knees, the towel that had covered her body somehow having disappeared. At that moment she ached with her wanting of him, and as he once again took her in his arms, she knew that his want was as great as hers. The hardened length of his manhood between their touching bodies betrayed his greet need, as did the aching buds of her strutted nipples pressed tightly against his rib cage betray her longing to be filled, to be satisfied.

As his mouth covered hers once again, Katelin no longer knew him as her enemy. He had helped her to allow herself to vent her great sorrow at her father's death, and this, too, she told herself, was a part of the healing which she was in need of. Held within the tight embrace of his strong arms, feeling the searing flame of his lips over hers lent her a heady feeling of rightness to the moment.

As his lips drew back and his face looked down into her own with a searching regard, the silver-blue fire of his gaze locked with that of precious jade, and the smoldering ardor that raged between them shook Katelin to the very depths of her soul.

Glimpsing the exotic, sparkling green eyes, the creamy complexion, the delicate cloud of sable hair, left Garrick aching with his desire for her. His belly tightened. His shaft strained with a pulsing fullness against his breeches. His groin ached with heated desire. With an inward groan of restrained passion, he wondered if she knew how desirable she truly was. Had she any idea of the incredible havoc she stirred within him by the simple fluttering of her thick lashes against her pale cheeks, the way she tilted her head to a certain angle or the movement of her small pink tongue wetting her lush red lips? His hand reached up and a long, sun-bronzed finger traced a line from her collarbone upward, over her slender throat to her chin. "Lord God, Kat, you're beautiful!" he whispered in that husky tremor of his that held the strange power to send Katelin's pulses fluttering wildly out of control.

"Kiss me," were his next words, and mindless but to obey, she stood on tiptoe, her body pressing lushly against his as she tilted her head up to him to comply. Tasting the sweet, vulnerable softness of her pink lips, their slightly parted shape allowing her ragged breathing to escape, sent an overwhelming rush of desire flooding throughout Garrick's every limb and organ. She was just too damn delicious for further delay, he told himself.

The kiss drew them together as they fell upon the coverlet of the large bed. Garrick plied her every facial feature with tiny kisses, leaving her breathlessly clutching to him and groaning aloud. The feel of his hands roaming over her naked body made her dizzy with wave after wave of steaming desire. Sensations of velvet heat rushed into her breasts, engorging her already aching nipples to unimagined hardness. A swirling sensation of spinning pleasure streaked through her, centering its pressure low at the quivering need of her woman's desire. Against his exploring mouth, she moaned deeply, the sound coming out as a soft purr as he once again covered her lips with his own.

Garrick stepped back from the bed, eyes sparkling with dancing blue lights of consuming fire as he looked upon the glorious body of the woman whom he desired above all others. His hands quickly divested himself of his clothing, freeing his throbbing lance stirring as though searching with a mind of its own for the sweet bounty of flesh that lay in wait. Its power manifested greatly as it rose up from between the muscular strength of Garrick's thighs.

Katelin's tongue streaked out to wet her lips as she viewed him, her green eyes twin, limpid pools of swirling desire.

He lowered himself downward toward her, the caress of his body barely touching as he braced himself. His mouth lightly rested against her own. The kiss was a brush of fire leaving her lips and stealing over her chin and down her slender throat to the tempting hollow of her collarbone, and at the same time his manhood lightly brushed along the curve of her belly, against a hip, and against the treasure of her womanhood.

Katelin would have opened to him. Her thighs parted and her body pressed toward him, but Garrick would have none of that. He desired to prolong the rage of their desire and in so doing stir their rapture to its fullest!

He suckled each breast, his lips raining heated kisses between the valley of soft, full flesh. Slowly he inched himself lower, his mouth and tongue creating a scorching pattern of heat, lovingly, temptingly down her midriff, his tongue lingering over her ribs to the indent of her navel.

In the agony of her desire, Katelin knew that she should call out to him to stop. Once before they had gone too far and now here again she was a willing participant to his forbidden love play. But the words would not come. She could only lie still beneath the force of the sensations he evoked as his lips traveled ever lower.

Caressing and tasting the essence of her woman's flesh, his tongue swirled in a leisurely pattern over her abdomen, and with an unbidden cry coming from her lips and circling the chamber, she entwined her fingers in the rich mat of his ebony hair. She was not strong enough to stop him or to bring about a halt to her own desires, which were now towering out of control!

The brand of his lips swept over a hip, then glided back to her navel, causing scorching flames to spring forth from the very deepest, most intimate recesses of her woman's passion. Slowly the warm, moist stroke of his tongue moved lower, his kisses temptingly running a path through the scented forest of her womanhood as his hands caressed the inside of her thighs and ran lightly along the outline of soft flesh covering her buttocks.

Sweet, warm anticipation bubbled up within Katelin as her lower body pressed toward him and at the same time his hands captured the fullness of her buttocks and welcomed her with the pleasurable assault of his mouth.

A cry of unbridled passion escaped her lips as golden streaks of shooting fire gloriously coursed through her entire body. She was aflame, his plunging tongue spiraling her toward the boundaries of fulfillment. But keeping her just short of that goal, Garrick drew his length over her, his hot, searching manhood pushing through the velvet petals of her womanhood. His pulsing length filled her trembling sheath and the sensation it sent throughout her body drove Katelin mindlessly across the threshold of spinning ecstasy.

Her body trembled, the tightness of her contractions in the lower portion of her body causing a surging tremor to ignite in the pit of Garrick's being, and with another contraction, brilliant, scorching flame took hold and erupted. The thick, pearllike essence of his seed gushed out and upward into the trembling valley that opened into her womb.

They were clutched together in the arms of ecstasy until the bonds of passion slowly played out, and still Garrick would not release her. He held her tightly to his chest, not saying a word, knowing at the moment there was no need.

Sometime later before sleep claimed them, the rapture that had so swiftly flared between them stole over them once again, and within the dark confines of Katelin's bedchamber her pirate lover acquainted her more fully to the pleasure that could be had in the arms of a man!

Nine

Katelin awoke with a smile on her lips as her shapely body stretched in feline grace. She was entirely alone, she found as her hand reached out and caressed the opposite pillow. Still the soft smile lingered as she kept her eyes closed and relived the moments spent in the arms of the dashing sea captain. Never had she allowed herself to be so wild and carefree. Not for a second had she thought of consequences, or even reality for that matter. Only the moments spent in his arms had mattered and certainly that had been enough!

It was some minutes later before Katelin pulled herself from the bed. Glancing around the chamber, she realized that there was little sign that could prove that last night had ever taken place. Only the balcony's double doors standing open and the envelope with its bold script with her name, resting upon the chair across the room, attested to the fact that Garrick Steele had ever been in her room. The invitation to the governor's ball had been Garrick's reason for coming out to Coral Rose, and as she slowly began to dress, she wondered when he would return. The thought brought a high flush over her cheeks and down her neck, as once more she thought of all that had taken place on that large bed only hours previously.

Dressing with some care with the hopes that Garrick would return to Coral Rose, and remembering her afternoon date for tea with the first mate of the *Caroline*, Katelin brushed out her long dark curls and allowed them to flow freely down her back. Her cheeks held a rosy flush, her spirits high as she made her way downstairs and to the kitchen, where she found Lizzy puttering about the stove.

Shortly after one in the afternoon Scott Roberts arrived at the plantation, and Katelin having worried that Garrick would pay her a visit while the young first mate was there, instructed Lizzy early in the day that as soon as he arrived, she was to serve tea in the front parlor. She would have the affair over with quickly and send the young man on his way.

Scotty was far too captivated by the beautiful Katelin as she poured a cup of tea and handed it to him, and pleasantly asked about the health of Captain Howard, to notice that he was being delicately rushed through tea.

"Captain Howard is well, and the repairs to the *Caroline* began yesterday afternoon." He appeared to hold some regret as he added, "We will not be in Basseterre as long as I had hoped. The captain believes the damage done to the ship was not as bad as first expected."

"Well, I am sure Captain Howard is anxious to

go on about his business." Katelin offered him a small sweet cake resting in the center of a fragile, bone china saucer. "You must pay me a visit though when the *Caroline* returns to Saint Kitts." She smiled as he took the plate and balanced it on his knee as he sipped at his tea.

"It will be my pleasure, Miss Ashford," Scotty quickly replied, already anticipating the return trip of the *Caroline* to Basseterre.

In less than an hour Katelin was standing at the front door and seeing the young man off. With the pretext of a slight headache coming upon her and reminding Scotty that she had only arrived at Coral Rose the day before, it was easy enough for her to lead him through the front door, and manage a farewell with him still smiling and declaring his heartfelt hope that she would soon be feeling better.

Two hours later Garrick Steele had still not arrived at Coral Rose, and feeling somewhat disappointed, Katelin wandered about the stables out behind the main house. There were several horses in the stables as well as a pair of mules. Katelin decided to take one of the horses for a ride, instead of sitting and waiting for a man who it appeared was not going to show up. The animals were a shabby lot, used mostly for working the plantation and drawing the carriage. She selected a sorrel mare, who it appeared had seen far better days.

Finding a pair of lads behind the stable, sitting on wooden crates with their backs against the stone stable wall, Katelin interrupted their conversation as she asked if one of them could saddle the mare for her.

Both young black boys had been told about the new mistress at Coral Rose, and at the same time they jumped to their feet and started into the stable. "It be a fine day for a ride, missy." The taller of the two nodded as he pulled a saddle out of the tack shed and his friend gathered up the reins.

The job was finished within minutes and both boys stood watching Katelin as she approached the animal. The old mistress never rode except in the carriage so there had been no need for a sidesaddle. This fact did not in the least bother Katelin. With a wide grin at the two boys, she winked boldly as she put a foot in the stirrup and with little effort pulled herself atop the horse. Settling the light cotton dress she wore so that only a small amount of leg showed, she took up the reins and started out of the stable.

The two boys watched until she disappeared out of sight, both wearing smiles as they left the stables and resumed their interrupted talk.

Katelin was unsure which direction she should take, the island appearing dense with trees and undergrowth. Fearing she might get lost, she made her way down the lane that had yesterday brought her to Coral Rose, and then for a time she held the mare on a steady path down the same dirt road that she had traveled with Scotty from Basseterre.

She was not far from the road that turned off to the plantation, when she spied a path leading off the main road. Deciding to take the path and investigate its reason, Katelin found that only several feet off the main road the path became somewhat wilder with tropical growth. Determined to continue on for some strange reason, Katelin was surprised to find, as her mount broke through some thick foliage, a small pond glistening in the sun's bright afternoon rays. About the pond's edge, lush green grass grew so thickly it was apparent that one could easily sink within its depths.

The pond looked as if it received few visitors, and with that thought, Katelin climbed down from her mount. The water looked cool and refreshing on the hot afternoon, and with little hesitation, Katelin tied the horse where she would be able to feed on the grass.

The water was just too inviting to resist any longer. Pulling off her clothes and leaving them in a pile at the pond's edge, Katelin dove into the sparkling depths.

Garrick Steele had been unable to leave the *Sea Witch* until much later in the afternoon than he would have liked. All through the day, his thoughts had centered around the lovely Katelin Ashford, and what the two of them had shared last night in her bedchamber. Having left Coral Rose in the early hours of the morning in order to leave undetected, Garrick couldn't shake the memory of Katelin's lush body pressed tightly against his own, her dark, glistening curls spread out over her pillow and entangled with his arm as he had rose from the bed. Looking down at her softly pouting lips and creamy complexion, he had been all but tempted to remain at her side, but in the end good sense had won out.

Now with his day's business complete, he left Basseterre behind as he rode toward Coral Rose. There had been no promises made last night, nor talk of tomorrow, but as the horse brought him closer to the plantation, anticipation filled him as he imagined Katelin's green eyes sparkling with invitation at his arrival.

Some distance down the dirt road, Garrick glimpsed the figure of a woman and horse leaving the main road, the long black hair in wild disarray even at this distance plainly revealing to him her identity. Without a second thought he turned his mount down the same overgrown path. As he drew on the reins and halted his horse, his breath caught in his chest.

The view before him was beautiful—a large, shimmering pond was spread out and was circled by deep, lush green grass. As he cast his eyes about the area, he saw the sorrel mare, which was tied to a tree and lazily munching on the thick grass. A slow grin spread across his face as he also caught a glimpse of the small pile of clothing along the pond's edge, and looking farther, he caught sight of a creamy-skinned sea nymph, floating upon the depths of the crystal blue water, not far from the bank.

It was Katelin and she lay upon her back with

143

her eyes shut, drinking in the sun's warm rays.

Garrick silently walked his mount back toward the trail. Tying his horse, he began to shed his clothes. He would also take a swim, he decided with a wide grin, his thoughts of Katelin Ashford already turning to swift desire.

With silent footsteps Garrick neared the water's edge. He stood, bold and bronzed, his desire apparent as he took in the beauty of the woman lying in seeming repose upon the water's surface.

Katelin, who had swum for a few minutes, had rolled over and lay floating on her back, letting the cool water soothe her and the sun's rays soak into her naked flesh. She felt no fear in this secluded spot, but as she lay with her eyes shut, for some reason she felt a presence nearby. Cautiously, she opened her blue eyes a crack and tried to see about her, and there, directly in front of her, was Garrick Steele. The sun glaring off his back held him in a bronzed-gold cast, and as her green eyes filled with the sight of his naked magnificence, she swallowed hard as her gaze lowered to the powerful size of his thrusting shaft. "What . . . what are you doing here? How did you know I was here?" Katelin had instantly shifted her body so that now only her head appeared over the water.

The moment she had hidden her body from him, Garrick felt instant disappointment, the thought filling his mind that it was a shame to hide such perfection. "I was on my way to Coral Rose, when I saw you from a distance turning off the road." There was no need for him to say anything else. He noticed the blush staining her cheeks, and his grin never wavered as he took a step closer to the water.

"What are you going to do?"

Was there a touch of fear in her voice, Garrick questioned himself, or could it have been anticipation? "Well, madam, I have every intention of joining you there in the water."

Katelin knew she should do the ladylike thing and turn around and not keep staring at him, but she was powerless as he stood before her waiting for her to voice any objections. What could she say? After last night and what they had shared in her bed, could she ignore the swiftly coursing desire that was sweeping over her? Could she accuse him of misleading her, as she had claimed aboard the *Sea Witch*? She knew she could not! What had happened last night had been out of the control of voicing objections, just as this minute was.

Seeming to take her silence as an invitation, Garrick dove into the cool, swirling depths and shot back to the surface with his dark hair flying as he shook his head and droplets rained the air. A deep chuckle vibrated the silence. "I see well the reason you stole away to this secluded spot, my sweet." The cool water was a relaxing interval to the heat of the day.

Not quite sure how she should act, or what she should say to the naked man now standing only a few feet away, Katelin simply nodded her head. She still felt uncomfortable while in his presence and not shielding herself with her anger. There was a fear of the unknown where this man was concerned. She had never felt these stirring emotions for any other man and she was afraid of giving too much of herself.

Within the depths of her enchanting eyes, Garrick must surely have read all her thoughts, for in the next minute, he was standing before her, his strong arms wrapping around her and bringing her body up closely to his own. The refreshingly cool circling water encased them and parted with velvet smoothness as her belly pressed against his, her slender arms feeling weightless as they automatically wrapped around his neck, and at the same time, his large hands cupped the fullness of her rounded buttocks.

A timeless moment passed as Garrick stared into her gleaming jade eyes, the raging passion flickering like quicksilver in his own regard as his head slowly lowered and his mouth slanted over hers.

Katelin clung to him as though he were her only lifeline. No words were needed, their bodies molding in an ageless joining that spoke of itself.

Gently Garrick brought up her legs and wrapped them around his hips, his legs braced a step or two apart to carry the full burden of their passion as he drew her downward, her womanhood opening to the brush of his manhood, and as he slowly eased into her tight opening, he felt her body shudder as a gasp filled his ears.

The water seemed to intensify Katelin's sensitivity. She felt each curve and muscle of Garrick's body; her breasts pressing against the crisp curl matting of his chest stirred the dusty rosebuds to hard nubs.

The contact of his hands caressing her buttocks, then gathering her legs and setting them against his hips drew her breath away as she felt his hands remaining upon her thighs and gently easing her downward. As she felt the velvet smoothness of his lance touch the heart of her passion, her breath clutched in her chest, and with the feel of him sliding into her, her breath expelled in a gasp as an uncontrollable shudder traveled over her length. She could feel the cool water circling her and filling her, a small amount of the coolness traveling before the heat of Garrick's powerful shaft and showering within the depths of Katelin's womb. The feeling set off a trembling that left Katelin rocking back and forth upon the hardness of his man root. She was on fire and being quenched both at the same time. With each thrust of his body, she felt the cooling brand of his passion stirring deep within her.

Garrick himself was lost upon the tide of their raging passion. Like the woman he held in his arms, he felt every caress, every movement of her body as she moved against him. The tightness of her sheath moving back and forth upon his love tool became the center of his existence. He felt the flaming cauldron of white-hot passion stirring within the depths of his loins and racing upward and at the very moment when Katelin cried out his name, her body coursing with trembling shudders, her head thrown back and her eyes tightly closed, Garrick met her release with his own storming climax, his seed expelling as he clutched her tightly against his chest.

For a time the couple could not move, or dare even to breathe, as their joining bodies slowly calmed, the fire-laced passion that had claimed them waning by tepid degrees as their lips finally joined in a tender kiss.

Katelin slowly seemed to stir to reality as her shuddering body began to regain strength. Her feet left Garrick's hips, her body still pressed against him, her lips still joined to his. But slowly with reality, her consciousness stirred. The feelings he had caused her to feel had been all-consuming, stealing even her very thoughts. A slight shudder traveled over her with the reminder of all she had experienced, and a portion of her brain whispered out, *You are not supposed to let this happen! He is stealing more than your thoughts while you are in his arms. He is posing a threat to your heart! That cold spot in your chest where you have promised never to allow yourself to be hurt again as your father hurt you. Don't forget, you will go back to London one day and resume your life without this Garrick Steele. You will return to your family and friends perhaps wiser because of this man, but don't let yourself go back broken because you have let down your guard.* With such thoughts, Katelin automatically stiffened in his embrace. "I must go." She broke away from his lips, and as he stared down at her, she mumbled, "It is getting late, the servants . . . I mean my brother will worry about me." She said the first thing to come to her mind.

Garrick let out a sigh as he watched her back as she hurried out of the water and to the side of the pond where her clothes were lying in the grass. He had hoped that last night would have broken down her defenses completely but he could see now that only a small portion of the wall she had erected around herself had been scaled. A small smile settled about his lips as the thought struck him that he would never give up. Today he had made just another small crack in her defenses, but one day he would demolish the imaginary shield she had cloaked herself with.

He stood where he was in the water and watched on as she mounted her mare. For a single moment she looked across the space between them. The smile was now gone from his face as he stared back at her, his silver-blue eyes caressing her through the dampness of her gown and lingering over the wet hair flowing down her back.

Katelin jerked the reins about, and with a kick upon the mare's flanks, she set her in motion down the path, the physical touch of his gaze still following her long after she had left the area and was shrouded by the denseness of the island forest.

During the next few days life at Coral Rose became much of a challenge to Katelin, who busied herself with the workings of the plantation. She assigned Kip, the hardest-working, and according to Lizzy, the most trustworthy black man on the plantation, the position of overseer. He took care of the people in the fields and also the cabins behind the main house. Daily she gave out instructions to Kip for the day's routine. There were crops that had to be tended, and the lawns around the house had to be cropped, for the wildness of the island threatened relentlessly to take back what was once its own domain. And the house itself needed cleaning from top to bottom.

Each day after breakfast, Joshua disappeared. Katelin assumed that he was running wild somewhere entertaining himself as Lizzy had laughingly told her. For her part, she was thankful that her brother was able to occupy himself. It was tedious work trying to balance books, keep ledgers, and see that the plantation ran smoothly. She was tired by the end of each day, and with barely time for her dinner and bath, she would fall into bed in total exhaustion. She was thankful she did not have to worry about entertaining Joshua on top of everything else!

By the end of the first week Katelin began to see Coral Rosé coming to life. There was much activity about the house; the servants were cooking and cleaning and appeared to go out of their way to please their new mistress. Yard boys were assigned by Kip to make their rounds about the grounds daily, and the fields were slowly taking on some kind of order. The hard work seemed somehow to strengthen Katelin, and as each day passed and she pondered over what decision should be made about Coral Rose and Joshua's future, she threw more of her energies into trying to make the plantation run smoothly.

"If only there was more money to be had here at Coral Rose!" Katelin slammed down her fist atop the desk in the study as she shoved the accounts ledger away from her. She could not believe that her father had been so careless with his plantation records. There were entries of money that had no mention of where they had come from, and withdrawals that were meaningless, for they were just penned in without explanations of their use or replacement. The only positive proof she had of the plantation's worth was in the cash box that was locked in the third drawer of the desk, and there was little enough of that. There was perhaps enough to see them through another few months, but then what would they do?

"Did you call me, Miss Katelin?" Lizzy stuck her head into the study, her one hand carrying a lunch tray for her mistress.

"No, Lizzy." Katelin sighed as she ignored the ledger completely and took the tray the other woman held in her direction. At the moment she was eager for anything that took her thoughts away from her nagging problems. "I just don't know where I am going to get the money to keep Coral Rose going, Lizzy." Over the past few days the black woman had become a confidante of sorts for Katelin, and though she tried to put her full attention upon her lunch, Katelin could not help letting her fears show as she spoke freely about the problems she was facing because of a lack of money.

"I just be knowing that you be thinking of something, honey child. You can't be letting young Master Joshua's inheritance be getting away from him. He ain't got no one else! Why, child, you already got Coral Rose back on the right track. It looking better than when your pappy was alive! The people all be talking about the beautiful mistress that done come to Saint Kitts. They's all got their faith in you, missy!"

Oh, this was just what Katelin had truly wanted to hear! Not only did she have a brother to worry about, but all the people on Coral Rose were counting on her to see them through. "I just don't know, Lizzy. There simply doesn't seem to be too much more that I can do without any money."

"You can always be thinking of getting yourself a rich husband, honey child." The surprised look that Katelin gave her caused a rumble of rich laughter to escape Lizzy's mouth and fill the study. "Why, I thought that's what most white ladies do. Get themselves a rich husband and let the rest handle itself."

"Maybe some of them do, but not me!" Katelin sounded scandalized. Marriage had in the past been the farthest thing from her mind, but as she began to sample the lunch, over and over Lizzy's words came back to her. The woman had struck a spark that would not easily be extinguished.

Later that same afternoon while still going over the books, Katelin once more sneered at the idea of finding herself a rich husband. She had no intention of remaining on this island, she told herself as she slammed the ledger closed and rose to her feet. All she wanted to do was ensure that Joshua kept his birthright, not to take a husband! Why, she held every intention of returning to London just as soon as possible.

But as the long afternoon drew on, the idea would not leave her thoughts. *Would it not be the easiest solution to all our problems?* the more conservative side of her nature questioned. After all, one day she would take a husband—what matter if she did the deed sooner than expected? Perhaps she could even find someone who would be willing to allow her to reside part-time in London. She owed it to herself to at least consider the idea a little more thoughtfully, she argued with herself each time she tried to cast the thought of marriage from her mind.

As she lay in bed that evening, her sleep was hard won. Thoughts of trying to save Coral Rose would not give her a moment's peace. Tomorrow evening was the governor's ball, and though she had not planned to attend, she now thought she should at least reconsider the invitation; perhaps by attending, she would get some idea of the available men on the island.

She told herself that there was one thing for certain, Captain Garrick Steele would never be on her list as a possible husband! Her features flamed with the reminder of the man who had so boldly stormed into her life, and it appeared he had as boldly stormed out! The cad had never returned to Coral Rose, nor had he sent her a message since that afternoon at the pond. He was no more than the loathsome rake she had believed him to be upon their first meeting aboard the *Sea Witch!* He was a womanizing blackguard, and she swore to herself that she would never again be misled by his handsome appeal. He had caught her at a low point in her life and had taken advantage of her need for comfort. She would not allow such a thing to happen again!

Ten

"Why won't you let me go, too?" Sitting crossed-legged in the middle of her bed as Bessy pinned tiny ringlets atop her head with twinkling diamond hairpins, Katelin listened once more to Joshua's plea.

"But I've already told you, Joshua, there will be no children at the governor's ball; the affair is only for adults. Lizzy and Bessy will be here with you." He had been nagging all afternoon to be allowed to go with her. She had not announced until that morning that she had received an invitation, and of course she did not mention how she had received it, but from the moment of her announcement, Joshua had been tagging at her heels, begging to be allowed to attend.

"But how about the story you always tell me at bedtime? And who will I be able to sword-fight with, if you're not here?" Joshua hated the thought that Katelin was going to leave Coral Rose. He was surprised that he had grown used to her so quickly, her being a girl and all, but he had learned that she could tell the most marvelous stories about pirates and robbers. The one she told him upon occasion about the man called Robin Hood was one of his very favorites! He wanted to grow up just like the outlaw who stole from the rich and gave to the poor! But how could he do that if she did not teach him all that she knew about sword play, he asked himself as he watched her preparing for the ball.

"I will ask Rufuss to tell you a story, Joshua. I am sure he knows many exciting ones, and can't you just skip your fencing lesson for one evening? I promise you that tomorrow afternoon we will have an extra lesson." One evening while Katelin was in her brother's chamber, she had noticed the twin wooden swords in the corner of his room. He had told her rather forlornly that their father would occasionally play at sword fighting with him, and feeling rather saddened by his tone of voice, she quickly volunteered her own services. At first he had seemed rather disinterested in her as his sword mate, but after she revealed that she had taken lessons from a famous fencing instructor in London, he seemed to take more interest in her proposal.

"Rufuss won't be half as good as you at telling a story!" Joshua pouted. "But if you promise me that you will tell me two tomorrow evening, and even though we have a sword fight in the afternoon, we can have another before bedtime, I might consider."

Katelin laughed with glee as she turned from the mirror and away from Bessy, and approached the bed. "You are a rascal, Joshua, but an endearing one!" She grinned as she rumpled his dark hair with her fingers. "You are also very handsome, dear brother," she stated truthfully as she looked down

156

into his features, which were so much like her father's.

"And so are you, dear sister!" Joshua stood up on the bed and began to jump up and down, trying to see just how high he could go, but not before his gaze took in Katelin's perfect form dressed in an ice pink gown and matching slippers. "Maybe one day soon I'll take you with me to my secret place, and you can meet my friends. But you can't wear anything like that!" He pointed a finger at the billowing ball gown with its low-cut bodice.

"That would certainly be quite an honor to be allowed to go along with you one day." Katelin laughed, knowing how much her brother enjoyed his privacy during the daylight hours away from the plantation. "For now, though, I must be on my way. How about a kiss on the cheek?" She could see that with each passing day she was winning more and more of her brother's trust. All he needed was a lot of love and understanding for his youthful antics.

Screwing up his face, Joshua cried aloud, "I don't kiss girls, even sisters!"

Katelin would have tackled him down upon the bed then and there and forced a kiss upon him, if she were not dressed for the ball. "Then you do not know what you are missing, little brother, but one day you will!" she warned with a wink just before turning to the door, and missed entirely the sour face that Joshua pulled at her words.

Dressed in his best plantation clothes, Kip awaited Katelin outside in front of the veranda. He would drive her to the governor's house this evening. He had spent the best part of the afternoon grooming the pair of matching mares, and he had also polished and shined the carriage inside and out. He sat straight and proud with the reins in hand as he awaited his mistress, and after Rufuss helped her to climb into the interior and she had settled her full skirts, he set the team into motion.

Katelin smiled fondly to herself at Joshua's antics, and as a tropical island breeze came through the carriage windows, she absently raised her gloved hand to her lips. She had spoken to him as though she had held some great knowledge about a kiss. The slight pressure of her hand against her lips reminded her of the times she had shared kisses with Garrick Steele! There was no denying that the rogue had a genius for making a woman forget everything else while he plied her with his attentions. It surely must have been a talent given him by the very devil himself! She forced her hand away from her mouth and tried to shut out his image from her mind, which had been provoked by thoughts of kissing.

The governor's house was a sweeping mansion in the center of Basseterre. The circle drive was lighted by oil torches, and as the Ashford carriage pulled up to the stone carriage steps, one of several footmen standing on the porch hurried to the vehicle door before Kip could climb down from the driver's seat. "Now watch your step, missy," the smiling man cautioned as her slippered foot touched upon the top stone.

The sprawling, whitewashed house was alight inside and out, doors and windows were opened wide to catch the slightest island breeze, and music circled the interior as well as the well-tended grounds. After being led up the steps of the house by the footman, Katelin started toward the front double doors, which had been left open in welcome. She felt her first moment's nervousness at arriving unescorted to such an affair. Perhaps she should not have come, the thought struck, but she knew that it was too late to back out now.

Numerous other guests were arriving at the same time as she, and Katelin was pulled along in the crush. Taking a deep breath, she could only put on a smile of courage as she went through the doors. Governor Samuel Langston and his wife, Clarice, stood greeting their guests in the marble-tiled foyer, directly before the stairway, with its circular iron-worked banister. When it was her turn, Katelin approached the pair, and Clarice gave a thin smile of recognition.

"Why, Samuel, this is the young lady I was telling you about. The one who Captain Steele introduced Thelma and me to. I think her name is Miss Ashford and she comes from Coral Rose plantation, if I am not mistaken. I am so pleased you were able to attend, my dear." Clarice seemed to pass Katelin right on to her husband standing at her side as she breathed a sigh of relief that the young woman had not showed up on the arm of the captain of the *Sea Witch!* She had been reluctant even to send her an invitation, and but for Garrick's insistence, she would not have. Her Thelma needed little more competition let alone in her own home. She could relax now, for she had earlier instructed Thelma about holding the captain's attention the entire evening. She would signal her the minute he arrived.

"Why, you must be Richard's daughter, then. He spoke to me of you. Mentioned something about your living in London with a relative." Samuel Langston was a portly, good-natured fellow with a partly balding pate and a pot belly that moved up and down as he spoke.

Katelin smiled warmly as she nodded her head. Samuel Langston appeared reluctant to turn her hand loose.

"I was very sorry to hear about Richard and his wife. He was a good man. I guess it is up to you now to take care of the lad—what is his name?"

"Joshua," Katelin automatically responded. She felt rather strange standing there and talking about her father and family as beautifully gowned and be-jeweled women and their escorts passed by.

"Yes, he's a handful, that one. I saw him one day throw a rock and hit Nelly Benson's little pony, Sheba. I don't remember ever seeing that carriage of hers move so fast!" The governor chuckled aloud and the girth of his belly seemed to roll with his amusement.

"Dear, here are Allen and Abigail Henderson; they want to wish you a happy birthday." Clarice frowned at her husband's antics, and tried to bring him back to her attention. In her ever-efficient manner she attempted to hurry Katelin on her way, and out of the foyer.

Katelin's smile was genuine as she offered the governor a happy birthday, and she quickly started to move away from the reception line.

Before relinquishing her hand, Samuel Langston said, "My dear, I just cannot stand to see a lady as

beautiful as yourself enter a ballroom all alone."
Turning in the direction of a nice-looking gentleman
standing not far away from the staircase, he called
him to his side. "This is Nathan Baldwin, my dear.
Nathan, this is Miss Ashford of Coral Rose plantation."

Nathan Baldwin had an eye for a beautiful
woman, and having seen Katelin enter the foyer unescorted, he had only been hanging around the reception line with the hopes of an introduction. "Miss
Ashford, it is my pleasure." He bowed at the waist in
a courtly fashion. "It would be an honor if you
would allow me to escort you into the ballroom."

Katelin smiled sweetly upon the gentleman. "Indeed, Mister Baldwin, your company would be most
welcomed." Having learned the perfection of flirting
in the surroundings of fashionable London, Katelin's
smile and the lowering of her lush dark lashes held
the power to knock the breath from the young
planter's son.

Nathan Baldwin could not believe his good fortune; the woman placing her slender gloved hand
upon his arm was stunning. She was the loveliest
creature he had ever seen! Surely she was the most
beautiful woman on the island, and every man here
tonight at the governor's would be green with envy
when he stepped onto the dance floor with her upon
his arm. "May I have this first dance, Miss
Ashford?" As they started through the ballroom
doors, he knew in that instant, as her sparkling emerald eyes gazed upon him, that he would willingly
fall to his knees and beg her for the honor of the
dance if he read the slightest hesitation upon her

161

lovely face.

Of course, such dire measures would not be necessary. Katelin would be more than glad to honor the young man with her first dance of the evening. He had been a lifesaver by escorting her into the group of dancing couples, and being nice enough in his manners and pleasant to look at with his pale blond curls hanging over his collar and eyes the color of a clear blue sky, she quickly assured him, "I would be delighted to dance with you, Mister Baldwin."

"Please call me Nathan." His most reverent wish at the moment was that she would consider him worthy of her friendship, as he led her upon the dance floor and thought her an angel as her pink-slippered feet glided easily to the steps of the music.

Katelin's tinkling laughter filled his ears and had the power to turn several male heads in their direction. "Then surely you must call me Katelin," she insisted as well. This was one of the things she had missed most since leaving London—the companionship of her friends. True, most of her friends had been male, but her association with the opposite sex had always made her feel more at ease. When women were around her, they tended to feel her a threat, and there was always that tedious air of competition.

"What a beautiful name!" Nathan Baldwin declared as he swung her around and she once again gained his side. "Katelin, how unusual!" Much like the young woman herself, he thought. He would have to be sure and find a worthy gift to bring to the governor for signaling him out to introduce to this gorgeous woman.

His boyish manner and smiling handsomeness kept Katelin smiling throughout the dance. As the music ended and his hand lightly rested at the small of her back as he led her from the floor, she was quick to notice that several young men were making their way to her escort's side.

"Introduce us, Nathan," a tall, slender young man with a topping of fire red hair and sandy-colored freckles over the bridge of his nose declared as though he were the spokesman of his group.

At first Nathan appeared loath to do so. If he could have his own way, he would keep Katelin Ashford all to himself for the rest of the evening — dancing every dance with her, and banishing any other gentlemen from coming forth. As it was, though, he knew that manners insisted that he do the introductions. Stiffly, he stated, "Gentlemen, this is Miss Ashford, of Coral Rose plantation." He certainly would not tell them her first name. That was one concession he kept for himself.

"Katelin, gentlemen," Katelin supplied and missed the crestfallen look that came over Nathan Baldwin's face as she was instantly bombarded with questions from the gathering of young men. Where had she come from? What was she doing on Saint Kitts? How long would she be staying on the island? Everyone had known her father and had been saddened by his death, but in the minds of these young gallants, Katelin Ashford had arrived on their fair shores, and little more was said about Richard Ashford or his wife.

The music struck up once again from the small alcove in the farthest corner of the ballroom, and instantly one invitation to dance after another was extended to Katelin, until at last she relented and stretched out her hand in the direction of one of the gentlemen. Kenneth Stratler was the lucky young man, and as the dancing became a lively romp across the dance floor, Katelin was swung about in his strong arms with breathless abandon.

Nearing the finish, she laughed aloud as the young man was returning her to her group and she noticed that it had increased by three more young men. "I would never have thought to find so many handsome young men here on Saint Kitts!" The group around her appeared to strut before her compliments, and quickly another requested that she allow him to escort her to the dance floor.

It was sometime later as Katelin was standing before the open French double doors leading out into the governor's gardens, trying to cool herself, that she glimpsed Garrick Steele. With that first glance, she felt the instant racing of her heart. He was by far the handsomest man at the ball. The cut of his dark suit with his snow white shirt boasting a small line of ruffles at the sleeves and throat accented to the eye the power that was leashed within the restraint of cloth. His dark hair carelessly combed back over his collar added to his daring appearance.

Nathan Baldwin and two other gentlemen acquaintances stood close, and Katelin with a strong will forced her head from the direction where Garrick stood with the clinging Thelma Langston holding on to his arm, her too skinny face looking up into his as though she could easily eat him alive. Katelin tried to pay attention to what was being said around her, but the sound of the blood rushing in her ears helped to increase her light-headedness. What was Nathan saying—was it something about a carriage ride and picnic at the end of the week? It was the governor who at last helped her to gather her wits as he approached with a middle-aged gentleman at his side.

"Miss Ashford, I would like you to meet your closest neighbor, Alex Blackthorn. He told me earlier that he had been admiring you from afar, and claimed not to have had the pleasure of your acquaintance. He is the owner of Shadow Mere, the plantation next to Coral Rose."

For a few seconds Katelin forced herself to forget about Garrick Steele as she was drawn by the dark, piercing gaze of the tall, slender man before her. "It is my pleasure, Mister Blackthorn." She held out her gloved hand, and he took it most willingly within his own.

"I hope you are enjoying your stay on our island, Miss Ashford," the gentleman murmured in a deep, masculine voice that was not unpleasant to the ears.

"Oh, yes indeed. Saint Kitts is quite beautiful. Much different from London." Katelin smiled, and again she felt herself being searched out by his dark regard.

"Would you care to dance?" Alex Blackthorn appeared to ignore everyone else standing around them, including the governor, who had hoped to have further conversation with the owner of Shadow Mere.

Katelin nodded her head, the diamond hairpins twinkling brightly as did the strand of diamonds

165

around her neck.

As Blackthorn took her hand, she turned her gaze one last time across the room where she had seen Garrick with Thelma Langston. Instantly she felt a bright flush upon her cheeks as she was met by his glance. She felt her heart tremble, but Alex Blackthorn appeared not to notice as he led her through the steps of the dance.

There was no conversation shared during the dance, but at the finish the gentleman started to lead Katelin back to the French double doors, and said, "I wish to extend my condolences, Miss Ashford. I knew your father, Richard." The dark eyes appeared to watch her every facial expression, and at the moment they appeared to enjoy what they were seeing. The high flush upon her cheeks and her emerald eyes held quite an attraction. "I do hope that if there is anything you are in need of out at Coral Rose, you will not hesitate to let me know."

Forcing herself to forget that Garrick Steele was standing across the room, Katelin tried to direct her full attention to the man at her side. "Thank you, sir, I do appreciate your kind offer, but I am sure that I will be able to take care of everything." What a lie that was, she told herself, as she was once more reminded of the state of affairs at the plantation.

"A woman alone, running a plantation the size of Coral Rose, can run into many problems. What say you, that I come over tomorrow afternoon, and if there is anything you need advice about, I would be more than willing to try and help out the situation."

Katelin at that moment took a second look at the attractive man with his courtly manners and search-

166

ing black eyes. His hair was dark brown with just the slightest featherings of gray at the temples. He appeared to be in his middle forties — not old, but certainly not as young as those she usually associated with. A man of the world, was Katelin's first impression of him, and as his neatly manicured hand lightly held her elbow and led her across the room, she debated with herself about taking up his offer.

"Perhaps you would care to take a ride about the island tomorrow? I have some very fine horses in my stables, that I fear are terribly neglected." Alex Blackthorn added his final inducement for her to spend some time with him.

Katelin hesitated only a moment. From the corner of her eye she glimpsed Garrick Steele making his way across the room in her direction, and remembering the last time she had gone for a ride on the island, she was determined that she would not allow herself to be caught up in that dashing rogue's silvery web of seduction again. She looked back to Alex Blackthorn and nodded her head. "A ride across the island certainly sounds inviting, Mister Blackthorn."

"Shall we say about two, then?" Alex questioned before leaving her to be once again surrounded by her admirers.

She could but nod her head, for in the next second Garrick Steele was standing before her. "May I have the next dance?" His blue eyes seemed to travel over her features with far too much familiarity.

Why didn't the cad just keep himself across the room in the clutches of Thelma Langston, she seethed inwardly, but as he reached out a hand and

167

pulled her along with him toward the dance floor, she knew better than to try and pull away. She certainly did not wish to make a scene right here in the governor's ballroom. She would never be able to live down such a scandal! *As though a scandal has ever bothered you before,* her conscience chided her.

As he pulled her into his embrace and drew her body along with his to the motion of the dance, it was all that Katelin could do not to lean into him, to feel once again the hard planes of his powerful body held tightly against her own. But she hardened herself not to make such a show. In her mind this man was the worst sort of rake! He had not returned to Coral Rose, or even sent word after that day at the pond. Straightening her spine, she resolved to show him that she was not his plaything. She would not be so used again! Twice now — she discounted the night aboard the *Sea Witch* because of her tipsy state — she had given way to some baser need which had been lying dormant beneath the surface of her being, but not again would she be enticed by this handsome devil.

"I am sorry I have not been out to see you, Kat." Garrick could easily sense that she was angry with him.

"There is no need for an apology, Captain. I can see that you have been very busy with the likes of your earlier partner." And at that moment as Garrick led Katelin around the dance floor, the couple passed Thelma Langston standing with one of her girlfriends, and neither young woman was able to hide her devouring gazes for the tall sea captain. Katelin stiffened even further in his embrace.

168

"Why, Kat, don't tell me that your jealous?" Garrick grinned down into her lovely face, and he also felt the racing of his heartbeat.

"No, Captain, I am not in the least jealous of such a scoundrel as yourself!" Her small nose turned upward in the air as she sniffed aloud. "I simply want nothing else to do with you!" And that was the truth, she told herself.

"Then I don't suppose you would be interested to know that I left the island shortly after my return to Basseterre from the pond near Coral Rose. I have just this evening returned." His searching eyes watched her features for any softening.

For a second Katelin felt her heart leap, but as quickly her inner mind's workings told her that if he had truly cared, he would have sent her some word. He would not have left her to wonder at his desertion of her. No, it was better that she break off with this man, whatever he believed they had between them. She now had too many responsibilities in her life to be the object of some man's game. She had to try and save her brother's inheritance, and Garrick Steele didn't seem to be the type of man to be held within the bonds of matrimony. "No, Captain Steele, you are absolutely correct in believing that I would not wish to hear your excuses. I simply do not care!" And thus saying, she jerked herself from his embrace and determinedly strode away from the dance floor.

Garrick slowly followed, his blue eyes twinkling warmly as he admired the delicate swing of her shapely back.

Nathan Baldwin met her at the side of the dance floor and graciously offered her a moment's respite by escorting her to the banquet tables. Katelin accepted willingly, feeling the heat of her flushed face and hoping that a drink might well cool her temper.

The tables had been set up in long lines directly outside the ballroom doors, and as Nathan hurriedly fixed a plate with an assortment of tempting morsels and gathered two glasses of champagne, Katelin once more was assaulted with the image of Thelma Langston clinging to the arm of Garrick Steele, as the couple also approached the banqueting tables.

The evening was forever ruined for Katelin. After sampling the food that Nathan had brought her and drinking thirstily from her glass of champagne, she danced one more dance before claiming a raging headache and begging leave of her partner. Each time she heard female laughter, her head turned and she looked about for the dark head of the man she professed to despise, as though she had no willpower but to torture herself with the viewing of that rakish sea captain surrounded by a score of other women.

Shortly, she found the governor and his wife and made her goodbyes. Without looking across the ballroom again, she claimed her cloak with its fur collar and made her way out to her carriage and Kip.

From across the ballroom Garrick saw Katelin leave. Following at a distance, he watched her put on her cloak and leave through the front double doors. As she climbed into her vehicle and the carriage pulled away from the mansion and down the circle drive, he leaned against one of the marble pillars before the front steps.

Lighting up a cheroot, he inhaled deeply and the fragrant smoke circled his head. For a moment he allowed himself the pleasure of envisioning Katelin as he had seen her earlier. Dressed in her shimmering, ice pink ball gown, Katelin Ashford had indeed been a sight to behold. The diamonds that had sparkled about her throat, on her ears, and in the tiny curls of her dark hair had enhanced the picture in his mind of her startling perfection. It had certainly been all that Garrick could do not to scatter the group of young men that had clamored around her all evening. The one dance he'd had with her had been torture. He had promised himself after that afternoon at the pond that he would go slowly where she was concerned, but he was finding such a resolve a hard one to keep.

Throwing the cheroot away from him, he told himself once more that he had a job to do here on Saint Kitts. When his work was finished, he would be able to go to Katelin and make his feelings known to her, but not until then. The type of people he was dealing with were far too dangerous to get wind that Katelin Ashford could be the one way to get to him. He could never place her in any kind of danger!

Eleven

Dark clouds scuttled over the quarter moon and the island was held in shadowed darkness. A sharp, piercing cry sounded upon the still night, but no one heard. The wild tangle of jungle vines and thick tropical foliage abounded and took over as though a living thing around the old stone-walled rectory. A dim candle had been lit within, but shed its light no farther than the interior of the small, damp room. The bare windows had long ago been taken over by the thick growth of plant life.

Shadows danced across the decaying ceiling like eerie specters of morbid demons, their arms reaching out with ghostly delight. Once more a scream, like that of an animal in pain, punctuated the quiet night, and at the finish a low moan was expelled and lingered within the corners of the chamber.

Death was so close, but at the same time so far. "Please . . ." The woman who had once been known on the island of Saint Kitts for having some beauty tried to plead, but her body with its breasts now sagging with age, was too pain-laced for her to force any more words out of her mouth.

"And can you ever remember a time when you were denied your pleasure, Madeline? Or perhaps you would have me call you Jasmine, as all your many lovers do? I promise, I will please you again and again before this night is over!" The voice held a deathly promise, as it spoke in low, menacing tones. The gleaming blade, held in a tight fist, slithered over the woman's upper body, leaving a fine trail of red.

"I am not this Madeline, who you think me!" The woman fought against the excruciating pain he was inflicting, hoping beyond hope that somehow a mistake had been made, and that she should not be the woman tied hand and foot, spread-eagle upon the dark, bloodstained table. "My name is Sally!" The last was a cry as the knife circled the hardened point of one blood-veined breast, and cut deeply into the strutted bud.

"I know you, Mother! You can no longer deceive me with your lies! I watched you each night from my hiding place. I saw the men who you seduced with your evil body! The sight of your pale flesh sickened me as you writhed upon your whore's bed! Sickened me, yes, and in some unnatural way also tempted me! Me, your own son was tempted by the sight of those thrusting breasts, and that high-pitched laugh that always held the power to drive men wild with want! I can tell you all of these horrible confessions now, which I never could before. Now, because at last you must pay for all the confusion and loneliness you forced upon your only son!" The sharp, serrated knife was forgotten as the madman who was dressed entirely in black wrapped both hands around the prostitute's throat, and as she struggled against her bindings, his thumbs pressed hard, her eyes bulging as her air was cut off.

Sally's last thoughts were that this was a mistake, she was not this insane man's mother, she was Sally Harper, a simple bawd, who had been paid in gold by the man who had brought her to her death!

By midafternoon following the day of the governor's ball, Katelin had sworn off all handsome men — especially one dashing, roguish sea captain. She had not been able to fall asleep until the early hours of the morning as her thoughts of Garrick Steele would not leave her in peace. Upon arriving back at Coral Rose and going straight to her chambers, she had hurriedly reminded herself to shut and lock her balcony doors. Not again would that cad catch her so unaware. But in so doing, the evening heat seemed to intensify within the chamber and added to her discomfort. She did not know which one she cursed more throughout the night — the tropical heat or Garrick Steele.

Being awakened in the morning by Bessy puttering around her chamber as the black girl straightened and hung up the clothes that she had discarded the evening before, Katelin felt as though she had barely slept a wink. "Damn all good-looking men to the pits of hell fire!" she swore under her breath as she dragged herself from the bed, and after dashing water upon her face, she started to dress for the day ahead.

"What you say, missy? You be saying something to Bessy?" Bessy turned just as she was leaving the chamber with an armload of clothes for the wash.

"Oh nothing, Bessy, I was just talking to myself." Katelin began to brush out her sleep-tangled curls.

"My mammy always say that talking to yo'self is a bad sign. The devil can be hearing you and set a trap! Is you ailing this morning, missy?"

Ailing surely, but only for some peace of mind, Katelin thought to herself, then she shook her head, so that the black girl would go on about her business and allow her some privacy with her plaguing thoughts. Looking into the dressing table mirror and glimpsing the puffiness around her eyes, she threw the hair brush down just as Bessy shut the chamber door. Garrick Steele and her father, Richard Ashford, at this moment were linked as one in her mind. Both men too handsome for their own good, and both no more than rakish cads in their dealing with the opposite sex! She did not allow herself to consider that she had been little more than a child when she had been deposited at her aunt's house by her father, and in fact she had little knowledge of his dealings with women. The wound inflicted by Richard Ashford had been deeply ingrained over the years and now with all she had endured at the hands of Garrick Steele, Katelin brought forth all the defenses she had built up around herself as a child. She had learned to harden herself, to distrust men of their ilk, and at the same time she believed herself stronger and better able to deal with the inner hurt that was inflicted upon her.

After breakfast Katelin busied herself with Coral Rose's books once again, knowing this was one surefire way of forgetting about Garrick Steele! By the appointed hour for Alex Blackthorn's arrival she had her emotions well hidden. Having had years of prac-

175

tice, not the slightest flicker of her raging turmoil could be seen within the sparkling jade green eyes.

Katelin herself answered the front door promptly at two, and was greeted by a distinguished-appearing Alex Blackthorn. "I hope you do not mind that I have brought along my manservant, Jubel." Alex indicated the hulking giant who stood outside the veranda steps holding the reins of his own large horse and those of a dark stallion and a beautiful, dappled mare. "There have been occasions on the island when I have run into some trouble. Jubel is usually not far from me. I believe he worries more about my safety than I do myself."

Of course she assured him that she did not care. If this polite, nicely dressed man thought it necessary for the larger man to accompany them on an afternoon ride, she surely would voice no objections; after all she was the newcomer to Saint Kitts.

"May I say, Miss Ashford, that you are every bit as beautiful this afternoon as I remember from last evening." Alex Blackthorn's dark eyes roamed over her in a quick assessment as he stood in the entryway and waited for her to pull on her kid gloves.

Katelin had dressed very carefully for this afternoon's appointment with Alex Blackthorn. Not only was this her first engagement with a man since her arrival on the island (she did not count what had taken place between herself and that blackguard, Garrick Steele) but all morning through she had been confronted with the financial problems that gripped Coral Rose. She had finally come to terms with the fact that she either would have to leave Saint Kitts with Joshua in tow and return to England and the charity of her aunt, or she would have to make do with the best that was available here on the island, and that meant leaving herself open to the option of marrying. After talking to Lizzy this morning about their neighbor and owner of the plantation called Shadow Mere, she had learned that he was one of the wealthiest, if not *the* wealthiest man on Saint Kitts. Shadow Mere was a thriving plantation, but Lizzy had been unable to tell Katelin much about Alex Blackthorn himself. It appeared that his people kept totally to themselves and very little gossip was ever heard about their master.

Katelin's emerald green velvet riding habit with matching little hat showed off her dark tresses and green eyes to perfection. The bit of white ruffle blouse at her throat lent her a modest appeal to the otherwise tailored outfit that showed off every curve, from shapely hip to full, high breasts. Even the gleaming-black, calf-high boots with their emerald heels and the emerald crest on their points attracted careful attention. As she pulled on her matching kid gloves, Katelin turned somewhat as though in a distracted manner in order to allow the gentleman a full glance, then looking up into his face as though only awaiting his pleasure, she softly murmured, "I guess I am ready, Mister Blackthorn."

Alex Blackthorn was more than a little taken with the young woman standing before him. Her beauty was without flaw, her manners all innocent. Taking her small gloved hand and tenderly tucking it into the crook of his arm, he replied, "Please call me Alex." Then noticing the slight flush that touched her cheeks, he thought he had been too bold too quickly, and hurriedly tried to make amends. "We are neighbors, after all. I see no harm in the use of first names in such a case."

Katelin was not lost to the fact that she was enchanting her neighbor, and by the time they had reached the horses and his manservant, she softly replied, "If you are sure that it would be proper, then of course I will call you Alex."

From that moment on, throughout the rest of the afternoon, Alex Blackthorn was totally captivated by Katelin Ashford! She sat a horse as though she had been born to a saddle, her dark green skirts flowing over the dappled mare's hind flanks and capturing a picture of ladylike beauty within his dark eyes. After about an hour's riding, with Jubel staying far behind, the couple stopped along a rugged incline that looked out and over the ocean.

"I never dreamed that my father's property was so vast or so beautiful! Thank you so much for inviting me to go riding today." Katelin meant every word she said as she looked out upon the blue-green depths of the sea with its surging tide breaking in foaming waves against the rocks below. The sight was absolutely magnificent, and the sea gulls flying overhead and crying their shrill song added a certain calm to the otherwise turbulent scenery.

The everyday beauty of the island had never meant as much to Alex Blackthorn as it did at this moment. This woman was the essence of everything pure and good in this dark and trembling world. Standing along the cliff, she was captured in the picture that he now believed should be imprinted in his heart forever when he envisioned the island; the sea and even the blue clouds overhead were but mere illusions created only for this moment in time. "And I have never viewed Saint Kitts in the way that I am

178

now seeing it, while standing next to you," he stated, uneasy at revealing this much of himself to any woman.

"Have you always lived on the island?" Katelin for some reason felt somewhat uncomfortable with his declaration, even though this had been her aim from the beginning. Quickly she thought to say something that would distract him from his thoughts which were centered around her, and also aid her in finding out something more about him.

"No," he answered hesitantly. "I have lived here for many years, but I was born on the island of Martinique." Alex felt somewhat uncomfortable talking about himself, and quickly asked his own questions. "And do you find Saint Kitts to your liking after the life you led in London?"

"I admit Saint Kitts is far different from London. There is an air of wildness and beauty here that I find much to my liking. Besides, here I can do such things as take an afternoon ride with a charming gentleman. My aunt Elizabeth would have been more than a little scandalized at such an idea as my going about unchaperoned for an afternoon ride through the park in London." She was not lying, she told herself as her lashes fluttered and then lowered against her pinkened cheeks. Elizabeth Wessely would have been very upset if word reached her that her niece had gone riding without proper escort — she was just not confessing to this gentleman that she had done so often and that her aunt had taken her to task on more than one occasion for similar circumstances!

Alex Blackthorn seemed pleased with her answer, and believing her flush to be one from maidenly innocence, he steered the conversation in another direction. "I know that your father was having some financial problems before he was taken with the fever. I would hope that if there is ever any need, you will consider turning to me for help. I do not boast when I say that I am a very wealthy man, and Shadow Mere is the largest plantation on the island."

The flush upon Katelin's cheeks deepened to a bright pink. He did not know how close he spoke of what was prominent on Katelin's mind day and night. Her worry over her brother's future lent her the ability to graciously thank him, but she was wise enough to know that she could not accept his offer of help at this time. "I do thank you, Alex, but I am trying to get Coral Rose running as it should, by myself. I fear that since my father's death everything has been let go, but I hope that things will start to pick up soon."

The sound of his name leaving her lips filled his ears with its gentle melody. He had never before known such a woman! Her words told him of her determination to make a go of Coral Rose, but her beauty bespoke her womanly inexperience. Most of the other women whom he had known in his past would not have hesitated to jump at such an offer of financial help. "Perhaps it would be better if we talk of this matter at a later time," he offered kindly, and at that moment his intentions were those of a man who would do whatever it would take to ensure that there would indeed be another opportunity to offer her his help. "Perhaps we should ride back to the house now; I would not wish you to overtire."

Katelin nodded her head, not in the least tired, but willing for now to portray the kind of woman he wanted her to be. "It has been a glorious afternoon, Alex. I hope we will be able to do it again very soon."

Helping her to remount, Alex Blackthorn was more than willing to agree to another afternoon ride, or in fact any other engagement that she would agree to. "There is a dinner party that I must attend at the end of the week; I wonder if it would not be too much of an imposition, to ask you to be my companion?" He remembered the dinner party that he had promised to attend, and took advantage of the moment.

Katelin was taken by surprise at the suddenness of his invitation, and taking her silence as a sign that he had been far too bold, he hastily tried to soften her impression of him. "If you are disinclined to accept, Katelin, I will understand. It is only that I have attended so many of these dinners at other planters' houses in and around Basseterre. It would be a pleasure to have your enjoyable company at my side."

"Put in such an inviting way, Alex, how can I refuse? I would love to accompany you to this dinner party." She smiled down at him from where she sat atop her mount.

Her beauty outshone even that image he always held in the back of his mind of his beautiful mother, and for a second Alex felt his body tremble. Turning away as though the very sight of her filled him with a strange feeling of pleasure-pain, he mounted his own horse, and under the ever-watchful eye of Jubel, they left the sea behind and started off in the direction of the Ashford plantation.

That evening after dinner Rufuss reported that

181

while he was in town picking up supplies, he had heard that another woman's body had been found along the dock area, floating in the water.

"I can't be believing that someone would hate them women so much!" Lizzy declared as she was clearing away the supper dishes from the small wood table in the kitchen where Joshua and Katelin usually took their meals, to help from having to make so much work for Lizzy.

Rufuss was sharpening the kitchen knives with a whetstone, and eagerly nodded his gray head. "I swear if that ain't the truth! It appears to me that there's a madman loose on Saint Kitts!"

Katelin as well nodded her head. Since her arrival on the island, this was the second such killing that she had heard of. Thank God they lived far enough out of town not to have to worry about who was going to be the killer's next victim.

"But they were only whores!" Joshua declared right after shoving the rest of his lemon tart into his mouth, his declaration drawing the attention of everyone in the kitchen.

"Joshua, whoever told you such a thing?" Katelin was shocked that a word such as *whore* would come from the lips of a twelve-year-old child.

"What's the big deal?" Joshua looked around and found both Lizzy and Rufuss shaking their heads, and his sister looking at him rather sternly. "Abe told me all about the killings. He said that the dirty whores were asking for it." Joshua omitted that he had overheard the one called Abe talking to another man when neither adults had seen him standing nearby, nor did he say that the other man had gotten angry from the statement and had walked away, leaving Abe murmuring behind his back.

"Who is this Abe?" Katelin felt her anger flare that anyone would dare to say such a thing in front of her brother.

For the first time Joshua realized that he had said too much. His face turned an off-shade of red as he reached out for another tart and stuffed it into his mouth. Mumbling through the food, he would only reveal, "He's a friend." And then would say no more.

"Well, he is your friend no longer, young man! No woman deserves to be murdered, no matter what her trade!" And if I ever hear you say such a thing again, I swear, I will . . . will turn you over my knee!" For an instant, Katelin was unsure what she would do, but with her brother's eyes holding on her, she knew she could not back down. He must be taught some kind of respect, and if she ever came face to face with this boy named Abe, why, she would give him a firm piece of her mind!

For a split second Joshua had thought to retort that no woman would ever turn him over her knee, but seeing Katelin's sparkling, angry eyes and the stern tilt of her chin, he thought better of making such a hasty declaration. He knew that she had a lot of strength in her slim form, and he was not of a mind to test that strength on himself. Instead he hung his head downward as though he were sorry for his bad manners.

Looking upon her brother's dark head, Katelin realized how much he had been neglected lately. She had been so busy trying to get Coral Rose back into shape she had left him to run wild, and now she was realizing that his friends were not the ones whom she would desire for him. She would have to start taking more of an interest in the boy, she told herself. "Joshua, why don't we go up to your chamber and have our fencing lesson now?"

That seemed to perk him up, for instantly his head snapped up and a grin appeared on his boyish face. "I'll go and get the swords ready, sis." He jumped from the chair, and started from the kitchen. "Don't be too long!" he called to her before leaving the kitchen.

Letting out a soft sigh, Katelin stood up from the table. "I'm sorry for his rudeness, Lizzy, Rufuss." Somehow Katelin felt herself responsible for her brother's behavior.

"Honey child, you're doing the best you can. Master Joshua gots a lot of growing up to do. But he be little more than a young'un, so don't you go on taking the blame! He'll be just fine, just you wait and see!" Lizzy cleared away the last of the supper dishes and gave Katelin one of her encouraging smiles.

Their sword play that evening, as those in the past, turned into a rough-and-tumble wrestling match, as brother and sister rolled and frolicked over Joshua's bedchamber floor. Their laughter could be heard throughout the house and more than once Lizzy grinned to herself as she lingered downstairs in the kitchen putting away the dishes. "This old house ain't never known so much laughter!" she murmured softly.

Twelve

Over the course of the next two weeks, Katelin saw Alex Blackthorn several more times. Twice they took afternoon rides over Coral Rose property, and she had even gone to Shadow Mere one afternoon for tea. At one dinner party she had attended with Alex, Katelin had learned that Garrick Steele had sailed away from Saint Kitts the morning after the governor's birthday ball, and as far as she knew he had not returned. But Katelin was determined that she did not care in the least if the privateer captain ever returned to the island. When his handsome visage filled her mind, she pushed it out by finding hard work for her energies. Preoccupied with Coral Rose, her brother, and her efforts to entice Alex Blackthorn, Katelin vowed she could care less if she ever saw Garrick Steele again.

Each day as more money was needed to keep the plantation running, and no funds were forthcoming, the need for a husband was made clearer in Katelin's mind. And thus far she had not found a man to offer her and her brother more security than Alex Blackthorn. Perhaps at times she was made a little uncomfortable by the look of absolute possessiveness in his dark eyes when he was with her, and though she had found his home, Shadow Mere, oddly quiet, even with all its servants roaming about, and had been glad to return to Coral Rose, still Katelin realized she had little choice in the matter. It was either Alex Blackthorn or try and sell Coral Rose for any kind of money she could gain, and she and Joshua return to London. Each day it seemed to grow more impossible for her to consider the latter decision. She and Joshua had grown much closer and she now took her responsibility as his guardian without complaint, but she could sense that her wild sibling could never be happy with the confinement of everyday life in London. She remembered her times of lashing out at the system that tried to keep a woman in her place and could not imagine her brother constrained in the trappings of a gentleman! No, there was just no other way that she could see out of this than for her to wed, and if not Alex Blackthorn, then some other gentleman here on Saint Kitts. Perhaps Nathan Baldwin would be suitable, she told herself as once more the handsome image of Garrick Steele filled her mind, and finding herself having to use much more effort to dislodge him from her thoughts, she tried hard to think of the young man she had met at the ball.

Once again this afternoon Katelin was waiting for Alex Blackthorn's arrival. She had invited him for tea at one, and after seeing that Lizzy had everything readied, she went out and sat in a wicker rocker on the front porch. It was a warm day, and after a morning rain, everything smelled fresh and clean. A group of black boys were playing chase and rolling around on the dampened grass, and Katelin smiled fondly as she watched them at their play. For the first time in her life she felt as though she was doing something meaningful. By fighting to keep Coral Rose going, she was not only securing her brother's future, but also assuring that the people on the plantation were kept healthy and happy. Lizzy, Rufuss, Bessy, and Kip had already found a place in her heart, and she knew if she were to leave the island, she would miss them terribly.

Alex Blackthorn sitting his horse straight and proudly arrogant appeared coming down the drive of Coral Rose, followed closely by his manservant, Jubel. There was no wild racing of her heartbeat at the sight, Katelin admitted to herself, as she had felt on more than one occasion when she had seen Garrick Steele. But there was instead the knowledge that this man was not the roving cad that the captain of the *Sea Witch* was. In her thoughts she imagined Garrick roaming the seas and chasing any lightskirt that came in his sight at every port he visited. Stepping away from the chair she had been sitting in, Katelin forced such thoughts out of her mind as she made her way to the veranda steps. Shading her eyes from the bright glare of the afternoon sun, she awaited her company.

As his dark eyes went over Katelin's lovely figure dressed in a violet flower-sprigged day dress, her hair flowing down her back and her one hand loosely clutching a straw bonnet with a violet band and ribbon tie, Alex dismounted his horse and handed his reins over to his manservant. It was just at that moment that a large rock sailed through the air out of nowhere and hit the hulking Jubel.

Katelin watched from where she stood in speechless amazement as a large grunt escaped the giant's lips, and then with speed which was surprising for a man of

187

such size, he sprinted off into the foliage that ran along the side of the drive.

Reaching into the underbrush and dragging his victim out of the greenery by the scruff of the neck, Jubel shook his captive with a vicious hand which produced a loud cry of pain.

Without a thought, Katelin was running across the yard, her delicate violet slippers being ruined from the damp grass, but at that moment this fact was the farthest thing from her mind. "Let him go! Take your hands off him this minute!" she demanded as she neared the brute holding her brother by the back of the collar.

Joshua's green eyes were twin saucers of fear as they looked up to his approaching sister for help. He would have shouted aloud for her to have a care for her own safety against the beast who had taken hold of him, but at the moment his shirtfront was choking off his air, and being shaken as he was, he could not utter the strangled word of warning.

"Take your hands off him!" Katelin shouted once again, herself ready to do battle to defend her younger sibling. Reaching out, she grabbed the hand holding Joshua, and at that moment as the dark brown eyes glared down at her, she felt the unleashed strength in the wrist that still shook Joshua as though he were no more than a bothersome pest. She was privy to the raw power and fury that consumed the large man.

"Jubel, do as the lady says, this minute!" The order was sharp and commanding, and Katelin in that second turned to glimpse Alex Blackthorn now standing beside them.

Instantly the hand clutching Joshua's collar was taken away and the boy fell to the ground coughing and gasping for his breath.

"I am so sorry this happened, Katelin," Alex said as she bent to her brother. "At times Jubel does not realize his own great strength."

Katelin did not even spare him a glance so worried was she about her brother. *Not know his own strength indeed! The hulking brute could have easily snapped Joshua's neck!* At that moment Joshua's throwing of the rock, the entire reason for this whole episode to have taken place, was entirely forgotten in her mind. "Are you all right, Joshua?" she soothed as she held his shoulders. Kissing his forehead and cheek, she waited for him to be able to breathe regularly once again.

Nodding his dark, curly head, Joshua at that moment did not care that his sister was kissing him; in his mind she had saved him from the giant. "I'm all right, sis." He used the name for her that over the course of the past few weeks was becoming his habit.

Assured that there had not been any irreparable damage done him, Katelin at last could breathe easy, but as quickly her anger turned upon her little brother. "How could you have been so malicious, Joshua? You could have hurt someone very badly with that rock!"

"Yeah, that was what I was aiming to do! Only I hit the giant's hat instead!" Joshua got out just as Alex Blackthorn turned toward his manservant with instructions for him to return to Shadow Mere without him.

"Joshua, that is not nice!" Katelin was surprised at his bad behavior, but kept her own voice low so that the two men could not hear their conversation.

"I don't like him, sis! And I don't like his fancy friend either!" His green eyes glared at Alex Blackthorn's back.

"Joshua!" Katelin warned in a sterner voice. "Alex is

189

our neighbor and a good friend." She tried to make the boy understand that he could not go around sailing rocks in the air at people, and certainly not at a guest who possibly could be their only means for saving Coral Rose!

Jutting his chin out defiantly, Joshua stated righteously as he reached his hand around and rubbed his sore neck, "I don't care what you say! I don't like either of em!"

As Alex turned back toward the pair, Joshua sitting and Katelin still bending over him, Katelin pulled her brother to his feet. "Go on up to the house and let Lizzy look at your neck. We will finish our conversation about this later."

Joshua sensed that there was to be no arguing about this with his sister. With a last glare in Jubel's direction where the large man was mounting his horse, the young boy stomped toward the house, kicking up bits of damp grass and dirt on his way.

"I hope this incident can be overlooked, Katelin. At times Jubel does not think before he reacts. He is so used to doing his job of watching over me, he takes any threat a bit too seriously." Alex tried to soothe over the entire ordeal, as he hoped that the happenings here this afternoon would not in any way turn Katelin Ashford's feelings against him.

"And does he take even the threat made by a child so seriously?" Katelin did not blame Alex for his man's actions, of course, but she did believe that perhaps Alex himself should have more control over his employee. "My brother could have been really hurt, Alex. I know that in truth Joshua was at fault, but still, he is only a young boy, and Jubel is a very large man!"

"I agree with you entirely, my dear. I would never

have wished for such an incident to have happened, and I assure you I will do anything I can to make it up to you and your brother." Alex tried to make amends as he viewed her agitation and the flame of temper that still spotted her cheeks. He admitted silently to himself that he had been quite taken by surprise at the vehemence of her protection toward her newfound brother. As he had watched her standing up to Jubel while his manservant had held tightly to the little ragamuffin's shirt collar, he had felt even more affection, if possible, toward her. She appeared so vulnerable, so innocent of the world, at that moment, he had wanted to strike out at his man himself. And he swore then and there that he would never let anything else hurt her! And if that meant protecting this misfit brother of hers, he would make every effort to play the part of their protector. Never before in his forty-five years had Alex Blackthorn ever felt this overwhelming desire to protect another person. His life had been filled with darkness and distrust until now, and for the first time he wanted to open his life to someone else.

Forcing herself to calm down, Katelin attempted to straighten out her skirts. "I certainly did not mean that any of this was your fault, Alex." She softened her tone. "I know that my brother was fully to blame. It is just the fact that Jubel is so large, and when I saw him handling Joshua so roughly . . ." She could not finish for she feared that she had already said far too much. She would not blame this man if he left Coral Rose now and never returned.

Taking her hand and placing it upon the arm of his jacket, Alex patted the slender fingers affectionately. "Do not worry yourself any further over the matter, my dear. It will never happen again, you can be sure." He could at least assure her this much, for the moment that he returned to Shadow Mere, he would have a serious talk with Jubel. No matter his manservant's feelings toward the boy, the larger man would have to adjust himself to having Joshua Ashford around him for a long time. "I think it would be best for now if I return to Shadow Mere. Perhaps another afternoon would be better suited for tea."

Katelin wondered if Joshua had ruined her chances of gaining Alex Blackthorn's help in keeping Coral Rose running. Though she knew that his help would have to come in the form of a marriage proposal, she did not allow herself to think in those terms at this moment. Whatever she did, she told herself, was in order to save the plantation and her brother's birthright! "Please, Alex, let us not let this scene spoil our afternoon together." She fluttered her thick, dark lashes over her cheeks in a manner she knew would be hard for him to resist. "We can take our tea out here on the veranda where there is a slight afternoon breeze."

How could he resist her? Alex Blackthorn was lost as he gazed upon her innocent appeal. "Of course I shall stay for tea, my dear. I had just thought not to tire you, but if you are sure? There is something which I would like to speak to you about." His thin lips pulled back into a smile that for a few strange seconds caught Katelin with an unsettled feeling that the smile did not match his eyes. There was much about this man that she did not know, she reminded herself.

Leading her up the veranda steps, Alex waited for Katelin to be seated before he pulled a wicker chair up near hers. "I fear that you will think I am trying to rush you, Katelin, but I . . ."

Lizzy stepped through the front door with the tea

tray and interrupted the conversation at that moment. "I don't know for sure what happened out here, Miss Katelin, but one thing for sure is that young Master Joshua got himself a nasty scratch on the back of his neck." The black woman set the tray on a small wicker table, and as she filled the twin china cups with the steaming tea, her dark eyes drifted over the man sitting beside her mistress. Taking a good long look at Alex Blackthorn, she could not help remembering everything that Joshua had said earlier about him and the large man who always accompanied him when he came to visit Miss Katelin. "I made these little icing cakes this morning for you, Miss Katelin. I'm hoping you like them well enough." She told herself that young Joshua was of a temperament that could easily not wish for his sister to entertain a gentleman. Lizzy saw the closeness that was growing between brother and sister, and reasoned that much of what Joshua had said about Alex Blackthorn was more than likely said in jealousy. Especially that part about the man being in league with the devil himself!

"Yes, yes, thank you, Lizzy," Katelin replied. She was impatient for the woman to leave her and her guest alone. She had sensed that Alex had been about to ask her something very important, and the only thing she could think of that would be so important was a marriage proposal! "Just leave that, Lizzy. I will take care of it." She tried to shoo the woman back into the house as she placed one of the cakes on a plate and handed it to Alex.

Katelin would have ignored the tea tray and Lizzy's little cakes completely and allowed Alex to continue from where they had been interrupted earlier, but at the moment he appeared relaxed in his chair and looking from her to the tea tray, she hurriedly handed him the cup that Lizzy had already poured out for him.

Sampling the warm, fragrant-smelling tea as though needing to fortify himself, he asked, just as Katelin took up her own cup, "Katelin, my dear, I would never wish to rush you in such a matter, but I wonder if you would consider doing me the honor of becoming my wife?"

Though this was the question Katelin had been waiting to hear from this man, it was still odd to hear the words from his lips. Fleeting images of the dashing sea captain known as Garrick Steele crossed her mind, as did reflections of the chilled feeling she had had the entire time she had been at Shadow Mere that afternoon for tea, but both thoughts she quickly pushed to the back of her mind. Garrick Steele had certainly been nowhere in sight when she needed him, she rebuked her subconscious as it would have reminded her of the nights she had lain in his arms. Ignoring any reminders of Garrick Steele, she told herself she had already thought all of this out. She needed no more time to make her decision. It was either marry Alex or call it quits here on Saint Kitts and return to her aunt with her brother in tow; and some inner resolve forced her not to do the latter! "Yes, Alex. Yes!"

One more time this afternoon Alex Blackthorn displayed one of his rare smiles. "You will consider my offer of marriage, then?" He was rather surprised, but happily so, by her quick response.

"I need no further time to consider, Alex. My answer is yes! I will marry you, I would love to marry you!" Once the words were out of her mouth, the full consequences of their meaning hit Katelin. She had to admit that she enjoyed his company, he was always attentive to her needs or wants, and at all times a gentleman. *But you certainly do not love him,* that side of her nature that always tried to reason out everything warned her. There was no quickening of her heart while in his presence. There was no indrawn breath with his slightest look. Suddenly she wondered what it would be like to lie upon a bed with this man. His tall, slender build did not hold the masculine power that Garrick Steele's did, nor did the sound of his voice send tingles of gooseflesh dancing along her spine. Rebuking the inner workings of her active mind once again, Katelin told herself that she could not compare every man with that rake of a sea captain. She would learn in time to love Alex Blackthorn. She would spend every day with but that sole purpose — to find some great affection for her husband.

Alex knew none of her thoughts as he sat across from her and dared to believe his own good fortune. She was so lovely, so pure, untarnished by the world or man. She was the essence of womanhood itself, her very name carrying the meaning of the word, and she had consented to become his wife! Gazing upon her, he was entranced with the sheer pleasure of his good fortune. Rising from the chair, he bent to her side, not daring to touch his lips to hers, not daring to disrupt that quality of chastity he associated with her. Instead, he lifted her hand from her lap and pressed a light kiss on the wrist, and as he did, his dark regard held upon the virtuous perfection of her beauty. "I will endeavor always to be worthy of you, Katelin," he murmured softly.

His pledge left Katelin feeling slightly at odds with herself. Holding her hand as he was, she felt none of the anxious emotions that were typical of any other young woman who had just consented to become a bride. In fact, Alex Blackthorn left her feeling somewhat empty at the moment. It was the way he held her with his dark eyes. In the center of their depths there was a frightening coldness.

"I will leave it up to you to set the date of the ceremony, my dear. Only be sure that it is a reasonable engagement period. I wish for everyone to know that you will be my wife. You will be my greatest treasure, and I hate the thought of waiting too long."

This last remark did not aid Katelin in her feelings toward him; instead of making her feel cherished as she assumed he had meant, they somehow left her feeling even more chilled. Slowly she nodded her head. "It shall not be too long, Alex." And indeed, she told herself, she could not afford to wait much longer. If Coral Rose were to survive, she would be needing the funds that would see the plantation and its people through.

Alex felt jubilant, knowing that Katelin would be his bride. Gazing into her face, he straightened, and with a smile still curving his thin lips, he stated, "You look a little pale, my dear. Perhaps we should call our tea to a halt for now, to allow you time to rest. I would not wish to overtire you and you have already been through much this day." His words reminded him about the talk he planned to have with Jubel as soon as he returned to Shadow Mere. No matter what, he never wished to witness another scene such as had taken place at Coral Rose. As soon as he and Katelin were wed, he would then deal with her brother. Perhaps a boarding school would suit, or a tour of Europe for a couple of years, at least until he was old enough to remain at Coral Rose and take charge of the plantation for himself.

"But you can't marry him, sis! Haven't you looked

196

into his eyes?" Joshua cried aloud after Katelin informed him that she intended to wed Alex Blackthorn.

She had been arguing with him ever since they had retired to his chamber after dinner for their usual story and sword play. She had thought it a good time to broach the subject of Alex, and get her brother used to the idea that he would soon have a brother-in-law. His words brought a frown over her soft brow, for she could not deny that Alex Blackthorn's dark eyes held no soft, welcoming look. "Look, Joshua, I wasn't going to mention this to you, but marrying Alex is the only way I can think of to save Coral Rose. There is no money, and other than selling the plantation, I can think of nothing else to do!" She was sitting on the bed with him and wished even at this moment that she did not have to burden him with the state of the affairs of the plantation. A child his age should have no worries; he should be able to live in his childish fantasy world for at least a little longer!

"If it is the money, I know how we can get some! You don't have to marry that awful man! And besides, sis, that big brute would be hanging around all the time. We would never have any more fun!" Joshua's features were quite serious and for all his twelve years he looked much older at the moment.

"And where will we get the money to keep the plantation going, Joshua? I have done everything I can think of, but there is just no money to be had at Coral Rose. I hate to say this but our father did not manage things very well." She entirely ignored his remark about Alex's manservant. She would deal with that problem when the time came, she told herself. If in the future things did not work out with the giant called Jubel, she would certainly expect Alex to replace him with someone more suitable.

"But that's what I have been trying to tell you, sis. We can get money the same way Papa did!"

Katelin looked at him wearily. She had gone through all the accounting books—her father had had no money! "What are you talking about, Joshua? How did Father get his money?"

"I can't tell you now, sis. I will have to show you, but I can't do that until tomorrow."

Katelin sighed at her brother's overactive imagination. "All right, Joshua, you can show me tomorrow, but you have to promise that if we can find no means to save Coral Rose other than my wedding Alex Blackthorn, you will do your best to get along with the idea."

"It's a deal, sis!" His green eyes widened as a grin spread over his face. "You'll see, you won't have to marry old cold eyes!"

"Joshua!" Katelin warned, but could not help the small smile that settled over her lips. "You are a little scamp!" she declared right before bidding him good night and leaving his bedchamber.

That night Joshua's words haunted her sleep. Alex Blackthorn's cold, seeking regard pursued her relentlessly. Within the boundaries of her sleep she was running toward the prize that Joshua claimed she would find if only she would not marry Alex Blackthorn. She halted, out of breath, along the cliff that overlooked the sea. Joshua was slowly approaching her, his boyish grin wide as he waved her forward. Katelin could feel her heart pounding as she drew closer. The prize was close, she could sense it. They would be able to save Coral Rose. Joshua would keep his birthright.

From seemingly out of nowhere, Garrick Steele appeared. His arms wide, his silver-blue eyes seeming to devour her.

She turned to flee him, but her legs felt heavy, leaden. She could not force herself to move!

Joshua was laughing wildly as he called to her that this pirate would save them all.

"No!" The cry tore from her lips and before her gaze Alex Blackthorn's form took the place of Garrick Steele's.

"I will never let you leave me, Katelin! You will be my greatest treasure!" The dark eyes had a chilling intensity that left her trembling and terrified.

"No." She tried to break free of the invisible grip that bound her to the spot, and as he approached, she felt herself falling into an abyss of darkness. "Garrick!" The name burst from her lips as Katelin was jerked upright, awake in her bed. Her heart pounded with her fear as she clutched the coverlet to her chest and looked around the darkened room as though fully expecting Alex Blackthorn to step forward and claim her for whatever unholy purposes she had imagined.

It had been a dream, she told herself. It had only been a dream!

But why was she still so frightened? And why was it when she had been in the grips of such terrible danger, she had called out Garrick Steele's name?

Thirteen

Just before daybreak Katelin felt something clutching her arm and softly calling her name. Believing another nightmare coming on, she fought off the hand that tried to drag her from the peaceful enclosure of her sleep, and tried to snuggle deeper beneath her coverlet.

"Sis, wake up. We should be leaving the house soon, while it is still early."

"What?" Katelin groggily began to realize that it was her brother standing at her bedside and trying to pull her awake. "Why are you not in bed, Joshua? What is wrong?" She tried to pull her senses together as she wiped at her eyes. Feeling the full force of her tiredness, she worried that something was the matter with Joshua. Perhaps he had awoken feeling ill.

"Remember, you said you would go with me today."

"But why so early?" She felt as though she had hardly slept a wink throughout the night, and would have gladly ignored her brother now that she knew there was nothing wrong with him or the plantation, and shut her eyes once again.

"Come on, sis." He gave her arm another tug. "Tad and the others will be waiting for us."

With the mention of one of his friend's names, a bell rang within Katelin's sleep-hazed mind. Perhaps she should go and have a talk with the boy called Abe who had told Joshua those horrible things about the murdered women. "Oh, all right." She at last relented, knowing that her brother would not leave her alone anyway until she got out of bed. "We'll need something to eat, Joshua, and Lizzy has probably not even gotten up yet at such an early hour." Katelin was not about to go away from the house all day with Joshua without something to eat. Some days her brother left the house and didn't reappear until just before the dinner hour!

"I already got us some biscuits and lemon tarts that were left over from supper last night. That will do us until we get where we're going."

Katelin could make little sense out of that statement, but fully awake now, she thought to humor him. "All right, Joshua. Just give me a few minutes to get dressed." She covered a large yawn with her hand.

"It's too bad you don't have some cutoff pants like mine, sis. I bet they are a lot more comfortable than your dresses." Joshua threw this statement over his shoulder as he started out of the chamber.

Cutoff trousers indeed, Katelin thought as she pulled herself from bed and began to dress. Knowing her brother, he would probably drag her across half of the island, she thought as she selected a cool silk blouse and thin cotton skirt from the wardrobe. Pulling on a pair of sturdy, calf-high boots, she surveyed her appearance in the dressing table mirror. Gathering her hair back with a ribbon, she told herself that she looked suitable enough to confront the likes of this boy called Abe!

Joshua was eagerly awaiting her when she got downstairs. There was a high flush on his cheeks and his eyes sparkled with excitement. "Come on, sis. We can go the back way." He led her through the kitchen and out the back door, past the stables and down the path often used by the people of Coral Rose as they made their way into the fields each morning. Barefoot and clutching a sack in his hand that bore their breakfast, Joshua ran circles around her as he kept up a steady stream of conversation.

"Wherever are we going, Joshua?" Katelin at last questioned as he rambled on and on about the litter of puppies that had been born in the stables two days ago. She had never ventured off in this direction from the main house, and as he led her into a large thicket which was overgrown with jungle foliage, she was reluctant to follow.

"It's not too far now, sis. This is the easiest way to go, unless you want to take a couple of hours getting there, going across the island."

"A couple of hours?" Katelin swatted at an insect as it buzzed near her head. Already she was beginning to perspire, and the sun had just come out. Besides, she was belatedly learning that her boots had not been made for the rigors of a tropical island!

Pushing away at plant life, Joshua disappeared from sight. Katelin anxiously followed behind, and to her utter surprise found that they were within a small forest, and through the center of the trees and undergrowth, a wide inlet of water ran onto Coral Rose property and, Katelin assumed, ran back to the ocean.

"Over here, sis," Joshua called, and she watched as he threw aside palm fronds and other large leaves that had been thrown over a small boat. "I'll row. You can take your boots off and eat your breakfast, if you like."

His grin was wide as he waited for her to take a seat in the craft.

"And just how did you know that my feet were already aching?" she joked, and wondered how anyone could resist this brother of hers.

"I saw you limping a little while ago. That's why I don't usually wear shoes. These rocks can make your heels blister something fierce if you're not careful."

Not knowing what was to happen next or where he was going to take her in his little boat, Katelin complied with her brother's wishes—in fact, she had no argument at all with taking her boots off. "Is it far from here, where we're going, Joshua?" she questioned after taking a biscuit out of his sack.

Shaking his head, he would only mumble, "Not too far, sis."

"Why don't you call me Kat instead of sis?"

For a moment Joshua seemed to turn this over in his head. "Kat. I like it."

Katelin smiled at him as she finished the biscuit and started on a lemon tart. "Why don't you just tell me where you are taking me? It can't be that much of a secret." She was rather enjoying this secretive side to her little brother, though she would not tell him so.

"I can't tell you. I promised I would never tell anyone. You wouldn't believe me anyway. I'll have to show you." Joshua kept up a steady pace of rowing.

Allowing him his childish dramatics, Katelin for a moment was tempted to dangle her feet over the side of the boat, but the low-hanging branches that reached out and over the inlet made the water dark and dangerous-appearing, and as the images of snakes and other water creatures filled her mind, she restrained her desire to cool her feet.

A short time passed in which Katelin was surprised at the strength Joshua had in his arms, which enabled the twelve-year-old boy to row her and the craft with such apparent ease. With his dark hair lying in disarray around his ears and down his neck, and shirtless as ever with only his cutoff trousers on, he looked like some backwoods waif, not the owner of a large plantation. As his emerald eyes looked down upon her, Katelin could plainly view the enjoyment he was having, and with his mood, her own spirits lightened. Relaxing against the seat of the small craft, she then and there decided to enjoy this day with her brother. It had been some time since she had given herself over to a day of fun.

It was only a short time later that the inlet appeared to widen, and as Joshua pushed their way through an entranceway of overhanging branches and jungle vines, they were instantly plunged into daylight as the craft was rowed into a natural bay that was surrounded on four sides by the mountainous hills of Saint Kitts and opened out into the ocean.

Katelin's loud gasp of utter astonishment was heard even as Joshua rowed on, toward the opposite side of the lagoon. Her eyes were held wide with disbelief as they traveled over a large, four-masted ship which rode upon the top of the crystal-clear water as though an eerie phantomlike illusion. "Joshua, whose ship is that?" she finally gasped as her eyes went from the ship to the surrounding shore bank, then she noticed the crude, houselike shelters which had been constructed only several hundred feet from the beach line. Her jade green eyes stared as though she were not at that moment believing her own vision.

Joshua looked back at his sister, and for a few seconds, he appeared to be thinking over her question about the ship. "I guess she's ours now, Kat." He stated this with some pride as his head turned once again and he looked at the ship.

"Ours? What do you mean, ours, Joshua? How can that ship be ours? Where did she come from?"

"That's what I have been trying to tell you, only I couldn't tell you, because I promised. I could only show you!" To himself, Joshua thought he was making a lot of sense. "This is how Papa made money, Kat. It's a smuggling ship. Papa was in the smuggling business!"

Katelin had little time to react to his words. As they drew closer to shore, a group of roughly dressed men began to emerge from the inside of the shacks and seemed to be standing along the shore awaiting the small boat and its passengers. "Who are those men, Joshua?" Fear swept over her as they drew closer. Fear not only for herself but also for her brother. These men looked much meaner and more dangerous than they had appeared from a distance. In all, there must have been about fifteen of them. Some were bearded, or having a couple of days' stubble, some boasted mustaches, only one or two appeared clean-shaven, but almost all wore their hair long and held back by pieces of leather. Their clothing a mix match of shirts, trousers, and cutoffs similar to that of her brother's. But all had the appearance of hard-core seamen, and Katelin was not sure that either she or her young brother should be associating with such a group!

"Oh, that's Tad and Dirk, and the others. They live here in the secret cove. They were Papa's friends and helped him with the smuggling. They are my friends now."

This group of ruffians were her brother's friends! For a moment she was tempted to instruct Joshua to turn the small boat around and head back the way they had come. She would keep Joshua locked up at Coral Rose until the first available ship could be had that would take them back to England. But too late, the tiny craft hit shore and the men began to surround them. Up close they looked even worse than Katelin had at first feared.

Dirty, work-worn hands reached out to her as Joshua jumped to the bank. Ignoring the help offered her, Katelin did as her brother. With a quick movement, she jumped to the sandy beach.

"This is my sister. You can call her Kat!" Joshua proudly introduced her, and as the eyes of the men traveled over her from head to toe, Katelin found herself blushing profusely.

"Why, she ain't but a little snap of a thing!" responded one burly-looking man with a hoop earring in one ear and a gold cross dangling from the other.

"Be giving the lass a chance, Slade. The lad said she has what it takes and that's good enough for me." The one speaking was by far one of the biggest men of the group, and wearing an open vest without a shirt beneath, which revealed the strength of muscle of his upper torso, he frightened Katelin as he took a step closer to her. "I'm called Tad, Kat. Your brother here has been telling us all about you."

"He has, has he?" that was all that Katelin could say as she tilted her head up to look the middle-aged, bearded man full in the face. So this was one of her brother's friends whom she had thought to give a piece of her mind to if ever she got a chance. Well, upon meeting this group, she quickly decided she would put off the tongue-lashing until another time, if ever! Perhaps it would do for her just to mention that he and Abe and the rest should watch what they say in front of a young boy like Joshua, but even that she could not say at the moment.

He nodded his dark, curly head, and as he did, the rest of the men all began at once to speak. "I'm Ben, and this here lad with the bushy, red locks is John, and that be Simon standing next to him. And I'm Dirk, and this here is Pete." Another punched the man standing at his side in the ribs good-naturedly.

Joshua also jumped in with the introductions, not leaving any out as Katelin's head fairly swam with the names of the men standing around her. "What do you think, Kat? Aren't they the greatest?" her brother questioned after all had been introduced, and as all eyes seemed to hold on her as the men appeared to await her answer as expectantly as Joshua, she had little choice but to nod her head in total agreement.

"The greatest," she mumbled softly, still wishing she could drag her brother back to the small boat and leave the cove. But at the moment she saw no way out of the situation they were in.

The group seemed more than satisfied with her response. "You and Josh, come on over here and try some of my ole lady's stew. She's had it simmering throughout the morning, so I reckon as how it should be done by now," the first man, the one called Slade, offered as he nodded his head toward the stretch of beach, where there was some kind of makeshift encampment set up.

"There are women living here in this cove?" Katelin questioned. With the mention of another woman, she had instantly lost some of her fear. These brigands certainly would not set upon her with other women around to watch!

Tad spoke up. "Aye, some of us have families. It's not too bad living here in the cove. The only time it gets rough is during a storm. Some of the huts leak, but other than that, it's right nice here." Grinning wide, he led them toward the offered stew, the others eagerly agreeing with his every word.

"But how are you taking care of your families? Are you still smuggling?" Katelin questioned as they drew closer to the shanties. She heard a baby crying and glimpsed a woman standing in the doorway of one of the huts.

"We have gone out a few times, mostly just to Nevis-Anguilla. The island ain't far, about fifty miles away from Saint Kitts. There's a man there who helps us get a load of cargo and sends us a buyer. But your father had more connections, and things have been a little slow of late."

"A little? Hell, they have been more than a little slow, Kat. Don't let Slade fool ya!" Tad declared, and after each man had filled a bowl with stew and had drawn himself a mug of ale, they all sat down on one of the crates that had been formed in an open circle around the cookfire. The bubbling pot of stew hung from iron tongs above the glowing coals.

"You probably would do better if you became pirates, than to keep on smuggling for a living." Katelin laughed as she finished her stew and listened to their problems. Now that she knew these men were not the thieves, murderers, rapists and blackguards she had first imagined—that they appeared to wish only to make their living and feed their families—she felt much of her earlier tension leaving her.

208

Pouring her another mug of ale, Tad nodded his dark, curly head. "I've been telling them all that same thing, Kat. Why waste our time smuggling when there are plenty of ships with their hulls full of gold and jewels, riding high upon the sea and ready for the taking! Men are getting rich and making names for themselves under the name of piracy. I, for one, think we should turn the old *Rose* into a ship that can help us all make our fortunes!"

One thing for sure was that this fellow called Tad had a lot of drive, Katelin thought to herself, and for a minute she wished she was not a female and hence could join in with them. It was no wonder her brother spent his days among this company of men who had such a thriving lust for life!

"And what do you think, Kat?" It was Slade who questioned her, and she felt the eyes of all upon her; even her brother had halted shoveling the stew into his mouth. Taking another swallow of ale, she finally said, "I guess I would have to agree with Tad. You probably can make some money at smuggling, but if that is what my father did, you sure can't prove a profit by the books at Coral Rose. Perhaps if he had been a pirate, he would have had more to show for his efforts." She knew that she was speaking out of turn, for she had no idea what kind of money her father had made at smuggling, nor did she have a clue as to what he had done with it. It was that old resentment deep within her that made her speak so hard.

Tad slapped his knee loudly, and Joshua grinned wide. "That's it, boyos, just like I been telling ya! The lass here agrees, what more can be said?"

Katelin would have spoken up, and told them that they should not listen to her opinion. After all, what did she know of their lives, or this trade of smuggling? But as heads began to nod in agreement and more talk was thrown about as they discussed the business of piracy, she seemed to enjoy being included among them.

"Do you want to see the ship now, Kat?" Joshua questioned when there was a lull in the conversation.

"Aye, that should be the right start of it," Tad declared as he stepped away from the crate he had been sitting on and the rest of the group followed suit.

The large ship had been named the *Rose,* and Katelin imagined that her father had probably named it after his plantation. She learned that upon the tide the ship could easily be sailed in and out of the secret cove, and a long wood dock had been erected from shore to ship to allow easy access for her crew to load and unload.

Katelin was carried along by the enthusiasm of the group that encircled her as Joshua ran along next to her and seemed to abound with boyish excitement. "Will we really turn her into a pirate ship, Kat? I hope you like her! Do you like to sail, Kat? I love to, but Father would never let me go along with him."

Her head was swimming with his many questions. She would answer them all later, she told herself, and once again made a mental note that she and her brother had to have a very long talk after they left this secret cove.

Stepping aboard the *Rose,* Katelin glanced up at the upper deck. There were crates strewn about, she could see several places where sails needed mending, the wooden decks looked as though they had not seen a good scrubbing in some time, and all in all, the ship appeared cluttered and unkept. Downstairs through the companionway, things were not much better. The galley was in disorder, the hold contained crates and barrels, with debris scattered about, and a dank, musty smell filled the air.

The captain's cabin was little better. As she studied the dirty and foul-smelling room, with furniture scattered about, she wondered how much time her father had spent in there. She herself wasted little time as she followed the men back out on deck.

"I know she's looking a bit rundown at the moment, lass, but in truth the *Rose* is a sound vessel." Tad stepped forward and offered Katelin an explanation for the state of the ship, and at the same time he could have kicked himself for not having the men try and clean her up just a bit for Katelin's visit to the cove.

Katelin knew very little about the running of such a large ship, but she did know from the summer spent with her girlfriend, and recently being aboard the *Caroline* and the *Sea Witch*, that the *Rose* was in a shabby state. "I think she should be scrubbed from hold to deck, if you want the truth. If you and your crew don't keep your ship in shape, I don't know how you expect to succeed in any type of business, be it smuggling or piracy!" Katelin thoughtfully shook her head, not in the least able to imagine this band of men setting out on such a goal as piracy. There seemed to be no leadership among them. They just did whatever came to mind! Perhaps they should remain smugglers, she told herself, but did not feel it her place to suggest this to them.

"She's right, lads. And this very day we will get to work!" Tad again voiced and Slade standing next to him appeared to back him up.

"I have been saying the same thing, Kat, but since your father passed away, there hasn't been much enthusiasm in taking care of old *Rose* here." Slade added to what his friend had said, and none in the group seemed to disagree.

Katelin was very surprised that these men even considered her opinion worthy for their consideration. "I know it is really none of my business, but . . ."

Tad didn't let her finish. "What do you mean, lass, that it is none of your business? Didn't Josh here tell you, that you now own the *Rose?*"

The thought of owning such a large vessel did not stir any great joy within Katelin's breast. The ship needed a lot of work, and besides, what would she ever do with a ship? "Well, perhaps if you ever do capture some rich Spanish ship, you will think kindly on Joshua and myself. Things have been a little tight at Coral Rose of late."

"We know that, lass. Josh has been telling us about all you've done on the plantation since you arrived and how hard it's been, but you have been determined."

"He has?" Katelin was surprised that her brother had even noticed what was taking place on the plantation. She had believed him running wild with his friends somewhere and not giving a second thought to Coral Rose and her state of financial difficulties.

"I told them everything, Kat," Joshua boasted, his thin chest puffing out with importance. "I even told them about our sword fights and that you took lessons in London from a great swordsman!" His green eyes went around the group of men who were his friends as he added, "I don't think some of them believed me!" But they would now, he told himself as he stood proud before this group of smugglers. Proud of his sister and the fact that she was not like any other woman!

At the moment Katelin did not know if she should

strangle her brother or not. What had these men expected of her? she questioned herself. Joshua's bragging had surely created the illusion in their minds that
she was much more than she truly was.

Tad must have seen her discomfort because he
quickly stated, "As owner of the *Rose*, we thought that
you might consider becoming her captain."

Katelin stood thunderstruck. "Your captain? Captain of that ship?" She could not believe her ears! What
group of hardened seadogs such as these would want
her to be their captain? She could but stand with her
mouth gaping wide.

"Sure she will agree!" Joshua offered for her, but her
dark glare thrown in his direction stopped him from
making any more such declarations. "Well, you might,
Kat, won't you?" He seemed to plead with her with his
large, green eyes.

"But I know little about running a ship," she confessed as her eyes traveled around the group of
men.

"We know all what there is to be knowing about running her, Kat," Slade supplied.

"But why me? Why would you want a woman captain?" Katelin still could not believe they willingly
wanted her for their captain. There had to be something here they weren't telling her!

"Because you own the *Rose*, and you know how to
give out orders. And you need the gold we can gain if
we turn the *Rose* into a pirate ship, and you also know
how to fight!" Tad spoke up and his words attested to
the fact that they had all talked this matter over at some
great length.

"But I might not be what you expected." Her eyes
went to her brother once again. Joshua and his boast-

ing about her had put her in this unlikely position, she told herself.

"And we might not be what you expect either, lass. All we can do is give it a try." Tad tousled Joshua's head before he added, "Don't be too hard on the lad, Kat. He thought he was helping out."

Katelin knew that Joshua had meant no harm by his bragging, she only wondered what he had gotten her into. There was no way she could give these men her answer at this minute. She would have to think the matter over carefully. She explained this to the men, then she and Joshua left the cove and set out once again for Coral Rose. During the trip back, she could not push aside how strangely excited she felt over being asked to be the captain of a pirate ship!

Fourteen

By the time Katelin and Joshua arrived back at Coral Rose, she was still just as undecided as she had been earlier about the offer she had been made to become the captain of the *Rose*. The sensible thing, she knew, would be to reject the offer and act as though she had never gone to the secret cove or met the band of smugglers, but Katelin Ashford did not always allow herself to make what seemed to be sensible decisions. The thought of standing upon the deck of a ship with her hair flowing behind her and salt spray showering her face filled her with an unholy exhilaration. Even the thought of piracy seemed a romantic notion, and what was more, she could not put aside the fact that Coral Rose was in such dire straits.

Did she have the nerve to say yes to that rough-looking group of men who lived in the secret cove? She knew she would have to consider much much more than the riches that might be gained by such a venture. Piracy was a dangerous business — she might well be killed, or even imprisoned! Then where would her brother be? Who would take care of Joshua and Coral Rose, if not her?

Unwilling to retire for the night with so much on her mind, Katelin roamed about her father's study, trying to find a book that would hold her interest. The house was quiet, Joshua having gone to bed sometime earlier, and Lizzy and Rufuss had already retired. Feeling her emotions wound tight as again she relived the moments she had shared that day with her brother at the cove, Katelin silently stepped through the study double doors that led out into the gardens behind the house.

There was a full moon riding high in the velvet night sky and the fragrant scent of flowers filled the night air. It was a night made for lovers, or a night any sailor would love, be he a pirate or not, Katelin thought, and with it again she wondered what it would be like not to have the restrictions that the title "female" imposed. This band of outcast smugglers was offering her just such a chance, she marveled as she sat down upon a cool stone bench off to the side of the tiled patio. All she had to do was say yes to their offer and she would be able to be her own person! She would not even have to marry Alex Blackthorn! For the first time her thoughts went to the man she had told only yesterday that she would become his bride. If she became captain of a pirate ship, she could break off her engagement. Some relief came with the thought.

So involved with her own thoughts was she that Katelin did not notice the shadow that moved from a group of surrounding trees. She did not notice the figure of a man standing only a few feet away until she heard his deep, masculine voice.

"I was hoping you would venture out of the house, Kat." The husky tremor of his voice seemed to fill the night breeze and surround her with its masculine pulse.

"You!" Katelin instantly jumped to her feet, her green eyes aflame, then her heart skipped a beat as his tall frame stepped before her. "What are you doing at Coral Rose, out here lurking in the dark?" She tried to make her words hold a cutting edge to let him know that she thought of him as little more than a skulking intruder.

"I see you have not lost your claws since last we saw each other." Garrick's tone held a touch of humor as he rather enjoyed her fiery temper.

Katelin was quickly reminded where indeed they had seen each other last. "As I recall, Captain, the last time I saw you Thelma Langston was purring in your ear!"

"Kat, there is no reason to be jealous of Thelma." Garrick was serious but his words seemed to taunt her.

"Jealous? Of you? I can assure you, Captain, jealousy is the last thing I feel where you are concerned!"

"Then tell me what you do feel, Kat." Without warning Garrick took a step closer.

Katelin would have backed away but the bench pressed against the back of her legs. She had nowhere to go, but to stand her ground. Beneath the bright moonlight she could glimpse the sparkle in his silver-blue gaze, and drawing a deep breath she questioned herself about what she felt for this man, before she answered him. She had hoped never to see him again, she told herself. She had prayed nightly that his ship would never again dock in Basseterre,

217

and as well she had prayed that her feverish dreams of lying in his arms would also vanish!

She was not quick enough to tell him her feelings. Without warning his hands reached out and pulled her up against his broad chest, his lips descending even as she tried to turn her face away. As one arm encircled her waist, the other hand drew her chin upward, his lips covering her own in such a breathtaking manner, he felt her body beginning to tremble. "What do you feel, Kat? Tell me now!"

She could but moan aloud. She didn't want this, she told herself. She wanted him to leave her alone, wanted him to quit coming in and out of her life and making her let go of all her defenses. But with his arms around her, her breasts pressed against his chest, and his hard frame molding itself so familiarly to her body, she was powerless to reveal her feelings to him.

"Admit it, Kat, you feel the same drawing, the same breathless anticipation each time you are near me, that I feel when I am near you! Your body trembles with the need for my arms to hold you, to claim you, to love you!" God, he had missed her these past few weeks! Her green eyes and witch's locks had haunted him day and night. "Tell me you feel the same, Kat. Tell me that nothing else matters but this thing that is between us. That we were made to be together." Before she could say anything, again his mouth covered hers, the kiss drawing them both out and leaving their emotions open. The swirling heat of his tongue consumed the depths of her mouth, ravishing her very senses with its power to seduce and arouse.

In those seconds nothing else did matter but this

218

man holding her and plying her with such tantalizing kisses. Had he truly said that they had been made to be together? Somewhere in the darkest corner of her mind a small voice questioned, *But what of your brother? What of Coral Rose, and what about the man you have already promised yourself to?* With a gasp, she broke away from his arms, her lips yearning for his even as she cried aloud the one word, "No!"

Garrick had come to realize over the course of the past few weeks exactly how much he cared for this woman and how unfair he had been in not telling her his true feelings. He should have made her hear him out that morning after they had made love aboard the *Sea Witch*. If he had told her then how he felt about her and that as soon as his work in the Caribbean was finished, they would then be together forever, he knew that she would feel differently about him.

"I can't do this again. You have to leave me alone!" Katelin stepped to the side of the bench as though putting some distance between them.

"Kat, this is all my fault. I should have told you my feelings for you while we were aboard the *Sea Witch*."

Katelin did not want to hear this. It was too late! If ever there had been a time for them, it was gone now. She had promised to marry Alex Blackthorn, and she had to save Coral Rose for Joshua. She had to forget the emotions that welled within her every time she set eyes upon this man. She and Joshua needed security; they both needed more than this sea captain coming in and out of their lives whenever the mood struck him. Perhaps she would never experience the fire in Alex's touch as she did Garrick's, but at least Coral Rose and Joshua's future would be secure. "It's too late, Captain Steele." She at last forced the words out of her mouth.

"What do you mean, it's too late, Kat. Surely what we have shared means something." Garrick would have stepped once again to her side and pulled her back into his embrace, but her hands rose as though to ward him off.

"I am going to marry Alex Blackthorn, Captain, so you see we cannot possibly. . . ."

He did not allow her the time to finish. "You are going to marry Alex Blackthorn?" For a minute Garrick thought he had heard her wrong. Why would she agree to wed a man like Blackthorn? The question repeated itself within his brain. "When did this happen, Kat?" He tried to calm himself and allow her to explain.

"While you were off doing whatever it is you do when you leave Saint Kitts, Captain." She brought all her defenses around her and armed herself with the image of Thelma Langston rubbing her bosom against Garrick's arm at the governor's ball, when the woman had clutched him to her as though fearing he would leave her side. Again she fortified herself with the thought that this man was no different than her father had been.

"But I didn't even know that you knew Alex Blackthorn, Kat." How could this have happened so soon? Garrick questioned himself. He had believed that he had plenty of time before making his declaration of love to her, but all this time she had been seeing Alex Blackthorn!

"I met him at the governor's ball," she admitted.

"And you are engaged to him already? Why, you

don't even know the man, Kat." Garrick had met Blackthorn on more than one occasion on the island, and there was something about the man that had made Garrick ill at ease. And this fact alone made him question Katelin's reasons for agreeing to wed the owner of Shadow Mere. "Why did you agree to wed him, Kat? Have you told him about us? Does he know what took place aboard the *Sea Witch*, and what we shared in your chamber? And how about the day at the pond?" Garrick's voice was beginning to hold a hard edge to it as he slowly moved toward her.

"There is nothing between us!" she declared heatedly, then realized that she had really not told Alex anything about her and Garrick. In fact, as she envisioned his dark eyes staring at her, she shuddered at the thought of ever telling him that another man had taken what only a husband had the right to take.

"Oh but you are wrong there, Kat. There is this between us." Garrick pulled her back into his arms and his lips sealed over hers in an intoxicating kiss that left her clutching his shoulders to keep upright. "There shall always be this!" He stepped away as easily as he had caught her to him.

Katelin stood panting, her jade green eyes holding smoky depths of unbridled passion.

"You will not wed him, Kat. I will not let you."

His words were a husky promise that settled over Katelin and once again stoked her anger to flames. "Perhaps I won't, Captain, but it will not be because of you. Never because of you."

Garrick's deep-throated laughter filled her ears and raked over her body. "You will never be able to forget what we have shared, Kat, and what we will once again claim. You and I were meant to be." Thus say-

221

ing, Garrick turned away from her, and without a backward glance thrown in her direction, he disappeared among the trees.

Katelin would have shouted after him that he was wrong, they were not meant to be together, but she could not force the words from her mouth. She could only stand and stare after him.

It was only a few minutes before she rallied her spirits. Who did this man think he was? Her father had dictated the early part of her life by placing her in her aunt's home, and now this arrogant sea captain thought he could take charge of her life while she was on Saint Kitts. No, she would not allow anyone to tell her what to do, ever again! She was determined that from this night forth she would be her own woman. And with that thought she pushed aside the appeal she had heard in his tone, and the fact that he had claimed that they were destined for each other. In order for Katelin to guard against being hurt, she had to remind herself that Garrick Steele was just a womanizing cad, and if she did not fall under his handsome spell, then some other unlikely female surely would!

That encounter with Garrick Steele in the gardens at Coral Rose more than anything else helped Katelin to make up her mind about the answer she would give to the men who lived in the secret cove. She did not tell Joshua what her answer would be, because she feared that at the last moment she would change her mind, but she instructed him, when he questioned her, that she would go to the cove with him the following week and announce her decision.

During that week Katelin tried to keep herself busy

222

running Coral Rose. Alex Blackthorn paid two visits, but with each she was finding herself more uncomfortable in his presence, and this she blamed on Garrick Steele. Each time she looked at Alex, she wondered what his reaction would be if she told him about those hours of passion she had shared with the handsome sea captain, but the way Alex had of appearing to cherish her in his gaze prevented her from coming out and saying what she knew he had every right to hear. He seemed to hold her above other women, always telling her how beautiful and innocent she appeared to him, and for some strange reason Katelin could not bring herself to destroy these illusions, even though she knew them to be false. She told herself each time he left Coral Rose, that she would tell him soon, and if in the telling he wished to call off their engagement, she would make no objections. In fact the thought of not marrying Alex Blackthorn strangely filled her with relief.

Arriving at the secret cove, Joshua heard Katelin's gasp of surprise as he rowed them through the entrance to the inlet and into the bay where the ship rode atop the water. His chest puffed out with pride as he glanced at her and watched her green eyes enlarge as she looked at the vessel that only a week prior had been in such a shabby state.

Every day from sunup until just before dusk Joshua had stayed in the cove and helped the men with their repairs of the ship. They had scraped and repainted the hull, removed rotting planking and replaced it, mended canvas, and replaced cordage. They had cleaned and polished, every piece of brass shining as well did the decks, and as the couple in the small boat approached the opposite bank where the huts had been constructed, the ship seemed to sparkle with new life.

"They have changed her name." Katelin noticed that where previously she had seen the name *Rose* on the side of the ship, it now read, *Kat's Eye*.

"They named her after you, Kat." Joshua declared proudly, his own gaze seeming reluctant to be taking off the ship.

Katelin could not help the grin that came over her lips. From where she sat in the small boat, the *Kat's Eye* appeared fit and sleek, and once again that feeling of exhilaration, mixed with a strange excitement, filled her. She could not wait to go aboard to inspect the ship.

"What do you think, Kat? Do you like her? Do you think you want to be her captain now?" Joshua anxiously questioned. He had been hard-pressed over this past week not to badger her to death about her decision, and now that she had seen the *Kat's Eye*, he could control himself no longer.

"She's beautiful, Joshua," was all she would say.

This seemed enough for the young boy for the moment as he beached the boat and jumped out, waiting for Katelin to do likewise. "Tad and the others knew we were coming; they must be aboard ship. Usually a lookout lets them know if anyone enters the cove." Joshua spied Ben standing lookout and waving from his position high on a ledge that overlooked the cove and far out to sea. Joshua waved back and excitedly grabbed Katelin's hand. "They must be waiting for us aboard the *Kat's Eye!*"

Katelin felt some of her brother's excitement—who

224

4 FREE BOOKS

TO GET YOUR 4 FREE BOOKS WORTH $18.00 — MAIL IN THE FREE BOOK CERTIFICATE T O D A Y

Fill in the Free Book Certificate below, and we'll send your FREE BOOKS to you as soon as we receive it.

If the certificate is missing below, write to: Zebra Home Subscription Service, Inc., P.O. Box 5214, 120 Brighton Road, Clifton, New Jersey 07015-5214.

FREE BOOK CERTIFICATE

4 FREE BOOKS

ZEBRA HOME SUBSCRIPTION SERVICE, INC.

YES! Please start my subscription to Zebra Historical Romances and send me my first 4 books absolutely FREE. I understand that each month I may preview four new Zebra Historical Romances free for 10 days. If I'm not satisfied with them, I may return the four books within 10 days and owe nothing. Otherwise, I will pay the low preferred subscriber's price of just $3.75 each; a total of $15.00, *a savings off the publisher's price of $3.00.* I may return any shipment and I may cancel this subscription at any time. There is no obligation to buy any shipment and there are no shipping, handling or other hidden charges. Regardless of what I decide, the four free books are mine to keep.

NAME

ADDRESS   APT

CITY   STATE   ZIP

(   )
TELEPHONE

SIGNATURE   (if under 18, parent or guardian must sign)

Terms, offer and prices subject to change without notice. Subscription subject to acceptance by Zebra Books. Zebra Books reserves the right to reject any order or cancel any subscription.   ZB0893

GET
FOUR
FREE
BOOKS
(AN $18.00 VALUE)

ZEBRA HOME SUBSCRIPTION
SERVICE, INC.
120 BRIGHTON ROAD
P.O. Box 5214
CLIFTON, NEW JERSEY 07015-5214

would not? This whole affair was like some incredible fantasy! More like a story that would have come out of a wonderful novel of adventure, pirates, and smugglers. Hurrying along with him, Katelin found her excitement growing the closer they came to the dock that would lead them aboard the ship.

Tad, Dirk, Slade, and the rest of the men all stood proudly on the upper deck of the *Kat's Eye*, and awaited Joshua and Katelin. As they stepped aboard, a loud cheer rose up.

"And what do you be thinking of her now, Captain?" Tad stepped forward with a smart salute.

The rest of the men wore proud grins as Katelin's green eyes traveled over the upper deck, and noticed the clean, fresh appearance the ship now had. "She's beautiful!" she stated as she had earlier to Joshua.

The grins widened as Tad said, "We be not wishing to push ya, lass, so go about with yer own inspection. If'n ya see anything that needs to be done, just tell someone, and it will be tended to right quickly."

Katelin nodded her head, knowing that they all were anxious to hear her decision, and to know if their hard work had been enough to win her over. She began to make her inspection, with the entire band of men following closely behind. The galley sparkled with copper pots and pans. Pewter plates and mugs were lined against one wall, and barrels of food supplies along another. "Who does the cooking while you are out to sea?" she questioned Slade, who was the closest to her.

Simon, the smallest man of the group, who bore an elfish grin and wore a tightly knitted cap, stepped forward. "I be the cook, ma'am, and I promise you won't be finding none better!"

Heads nodded in agreement with the little man's words — whether they agreed with him or not, no smart sailor would ever tell the cook of a ship that he was not up to par. "I'm sure you're right," Katelin responded.

The ship's hold held none of the disorder of debris, ropes, crates, and barrels that it had only a few days past. Everything had been cleaned and polished, those things remaining having been neatly stacked against the sides of the ship. Even the dank, musty smell no longer remained; instead Katelin could detect the faintest odor of incense.

"She be ready to be filled," Tad stated aloud, for the hold appeared strangely empty.

Katelin did not comment, but instead she started from the hold, back to the companionway and toward the captain's cabin. She would not verbally make her answer known until she had seen the rest of the ship. Thus far she could not deny that these men had put many hours of hard work into getting the ship in order, but if she agreed to cast her lot in with theirs, she had to know that each and every one of them was fully committed to this venture. There was too much at stake to find out later that the group of them were little more than laggards, who went from one venture to the next!

The captain's cabin door was closed, and before Katelin could open it, Tad stepped before her. "Now, lass, me and the men here took care of the rest of the ship, but much inside here was fixed up by the women."

Katelin was rather surprised that the women had helped with the renovations aboard ship. She would have imagined that they would not in the least approve that their men were wanting a woman to become the captain of this band of smugglers.

Tad opened the door, and Katelin stepped in. She could hardly believe her eyes as they passed about the interior of the cabin. The room smelled of new varnish and polish, the dark oak furniture sparsely placed about the room had a fresh appeal. A large desk was placed in one corner and upon it rested several books, maps, charts, and a stack of new ledgers. A lantern swung from a beam overhead. A hand-carved oak table with six matching chairs sat to the side of the desk, but what caught Katelin's eye was the large bed across the room. The bed had been built into the far side of the ship's wall, and lengths of red silk material had been fashioned into draperies that tied back at each corner, the same material also having been used for sheets and inviting pillows.

A door was positioned a few feet from the foot of the bed, its panes made from leaded glass. Katelin had not noticed this door the first time she looked in this cabin, but now she saw that it opened onto a small balcony, which would be an inviting temptation during a sea voyage, especially at night.

Turning back toward the men, she said, "Your wives did all of this?" Her gaze swept around the cabin once again, and she knew that she would feel very much at home in this room.

"Aye, lass. They found some bolts of cloth in the hold and with a little sewing and cleaning they did a right fine job!" Tad proudly declared.

"They certainly did, but I am rather surprised that they would want me to become the captain of this ship." Katelin spoke truthfully, wanting to know now if there were going to be any problems with their women in the future.

"Our women are as tired as the men of this life we've been living here in the cove. They want something better for themselves and our children, and the only way we're going to have it is if you agree to become the captain of the *Kat's Eye* and she becomes a pirate ship," Dirk replied, and the rest quickly agreed.

Looking at the group of men standing around her with Joshua anxiously waiting to see what she would do or say next, Katelin did not know how she could reject their offer, and in truth, she did not wish to turn them down. She had never imagined that she would have the opportunity to rule her own fate, but at this moment she felt the full power of control over her life. Her head began to nod, her smile widening. "All right, men, you have yourselves a new captain."

Fifteen

A keg of ale was opened above deck, and some of the women who lived in the cove came aboard ship to join in the celebration. Katelin was introduced to one and all as the captain of the *Kat's Eye*. Though appearing shy at first, the women soon were speaking as freely as their men. Slade's wife, Patsy, and Wanda, Pete's wife, indicated that they had been the ones to make the draperies and sheets for the captain's bed, and when Katelin expressed her appreciation, the women seemed to glow with pride. The rest of the women told in detail their own contribution to the captain's cabin, and in a short time, Katelin felt as though she had made several new friends.

"We should leave the cove tomorrow with the tide, lass." Tad approached Katelin in the early afternoon. She sat upon deck with Slade and a couple of other men, Joshua as ever not far away.

"Tomorrow?" Katelin had not expected this. Taking another sip of her ale, she looked at Tad with questioning eyes.

"Aye, lass. Ben and Pete went into Basseterre last night to nose around a bit. In one of the taverns along the docks, they overheard some sailors talking about a Spanish ship which should be sailing through the Caribbean in a day or two. It appears as how these sailors' own captain plans to attack the ship. Slade and I figured that the *Kat's Eye* should beat them at their own game!"

Katelin couldn't fault them with their plans, but even as her dark head nodded in agreement, she began to realize that this game of piracy was not some high adventure lacking danger. If they were not careful, they could all easily pay dearly for their efforts. "I'll be here then," she stated after drawing a deep breath and taking another drink from her mug.

"We'll set sail with the morning tide. The men will retire early, so have no fear that any will be lacking in his ability to work hard, lass. You have but to give the order and it will be carried out."

The only problem with that was that Katelin was unsure of herself and her own abilities at the moment. Who was she to give these hardened men orders, she questioned herself as she looked around at the group of roughly garbed, celebrating men. She had given her word that she would become their captain, and she would not back down now. "Well, I guess that Joshua and I should be on our way, too." She stood to her feet and her brother followed her lead. "I'll see you in the morning."

"Aye, lass, in the morning, and in a day or two the *Kat's Eye*'s hold will be full of gold and silver!" Slade grinned, holding his mug high in the air, and the group of men around him shouted aloud with their own agreement and also raised their mugs to toast the future.

Joshua had oddly seemed silent while they had been aboard the *Kat's Eye* celebrating with the men. As he started to row them out of the cove, Katelin looked at him and wondered what was bothering him. "Are you disappointed that I agreed to become the captain of the *Kat's Eye*?"

"Oh no, Kat. I'm glad that you agreed to become her captain!" His eyes sparkled as though the notion was as exciting to him as it had been earlier to Katelin.

"Then why have you been so quiet, Joshua?"

"Papa never allowed me to go with him and the men when they went out smuggling. Are you going to let me go with you, Kat?" Joshua had been waiting for the right moment to ask his sister this question, and he guessed that now was as good a time as any. She did seem concerned about him.

Katelin had not even thought about her brother wanting to go along with her when the *Kat's Eye* left the cove, and looking at him now with so much hope on his features, she hated to spoil his mood. But she knew that she could not allow him to go along. Piracy was a dangerous business, and she could not possibly risk his life along with her own! Slowly she began to shake her head. "Listen, Joshua, it is just too risky for you to go along. I can't jeopardize you by allowing you to be aboard a pirate ship."

"I'm not afraid, Kat. I can help, I know I can!" Joshua pleaded, and never missing a stroke, his green eyes pleaded silently to be allowed to go along with her.

231

"I just can't let you, Joshua. If anything were to happen to you, I would never forgive myself." Katelin glimpsed the tears that filled his eyes and the way his chin quivered ever so slightly, but she told herself it couldn't be helped. She could not chance something happening to him no matter how much he pleaded!

As the day progressed, Katelin found that she had more than her brother to worry about. Tad had said that the Spanish galleon would be in the Caribbean in a day or two—what would happen if it was longer? How could she explain to Lizzy and the people at Coral Rose where she had been? And Alex, he was supposed to pay her a visit and have tea tomorrow afternoon—what would he think of her absence? Joshua alone would not be able to cover for her. She would have to explain her plans to Lizzy and enlist her assistance in the matter.

After supper Katelin broached the subject to Lizzy. "I am going to have to be gone from Coral Rose for a few days, Lizzy."

The round, sable eyes looked at Katelin with a measure of curiosity. "Where you be going to, Miss Katelin? Will Master Joshua be going with you?"

"This is one of the things I need to talk to you about, Lizzy." Feeling somewhat nervous about talking to Lizzy about the subject of piracy, for a minute she played with the food on her plate. Joshua and Rufuss had already finished their meal and left the kitchen. "Why don't you sit down for a few minutes, Lizzy?" Perhaps she would feel more at ease if the other woman were not towering over her.

Lizzy nodded her head in a quick manner, but

before sitting down, she went to the stove and poured herself a cup of tea. "I think I be needing something to help me get through whatever it is you be going to tell me, and since I don't cotton to hard liquor, this will have to do!"

Katelin smiled fondly upon the loyal woman as she waited for her to sit across from her. Trying to pick her words carefully, she began, "Lizzy, I have not kept hidden from you the fact that Coral Rose has serious money problems." She waited for the other woman to acknowledge her statement. "Well, I have come up with an idea that should help us out, but I am going to need your help."

"What is this plan you gots, Miss Katelin? I thought you was going to marry Master Blackthorn from Shadow Mere," Lizzy questioned her suspiciously.

"All I need is for you to tell anyone who asks about me for the next couple of days, that I am not feeling well and staying in my bedchamber. Mister Blackthorn may also pay a visit, and you can tell him the same thing."

"Why I be telling folks this lie? Where you going off to? How's a lady like you going to be making money enough to save Coral Rose?" Lizzy was not about to let her off easy.

Katelin would have trusted Lizzy with her very life, but she hedged about telling her she was going to become a pirate. She was sure Lizzy would wonder what decent woman would dare stoop to such measures in order to save her brother's inheritance. But if she wanted her help, she knew she would have to take her into her confidence. Drawing a deep breath, she said, "I have met some people who father had dealings with in the past, and they have invited me to join them in their business." There, perhaps that would satisfy her, Katelin thought, but she soon enough saw that the older woman was much too sharp for that.

"And is these people you talking about them smugglers that live in the cove?"

"How do you know about them?" Katelin gasped out in surprise. Lizzy was the last person Katelin would have suspected to know about the secret cove and the band of smugglers.

"Yer pappy told me years ago, honey. You see, one night he and them smugglers were set upon and yer pappy got himself shot in the shoulder. Miss Carol went all to pieces after Master Richard was brought back to the house, and it were then up to me to tend him. He come right out and told me what he had been up to all those days and nights when he had been away from Coral Rose, because he feared the authorities might have figured out who they were and who the ship belonged to."

"And did the authorities ever come out to Coral Rose, Lizzy?" Katelin was more than a little surprised by this story that the black woman was telling her. Why had she not been told this before now? "Did Joshua know about father getting shot?"

"Master Joshua was too young then to notice that his pappy was ailing. The authorities never did come out here, and for a while Master Richard laid off of his unlawful ways, but then he started up again. I thought them people in the cove would have moved out after yer pappy passed on, but I reckon now I

234

was wrong." Her dark eyes looked rather accusingly across the table at Katelin.

"I can assure you, Lizzy, I didn't even know they were living there until last week."

"I don't cotton with all that smuggling, Miss Katelin. It be right dangerous, as yer pappy would be telling you if he were here today. He laid in that bed and almost went on to his maker, short of his rightful time."

"I won't be smuggling, Lizzy," Katelin confessed.

Lizzy's sharp glance held upon her mistress as she came right out and questioned, "Then what you be up to with that group of no-accounts?" Lizzy would never forget the group of rough-looking men who had brought Richard Ashford back to Coral Rose, bleeding and pale as death.

For a moment Katelin thought to make up some other excuse for going away and now she wished that she had never approached Lizzy, but even though she was held beneath that stern gaze, she knew she couldn't lie to this woman. She would see right through her if she tried! "My father's ship has been turned into a pirate ship, Lizzy," she came right out and admitted.

"You ain't thinking to become one of them pirates now, honey child?" The large head shook back and forth and at the same time the dark eyes enlarged.

"Well, the truth is, Lizzy, I am to be the captain of the *Kat's Eye*. That is what the men have named the ship." Katelin could not help sounding somewhat proud of the fact that a ship had been named after her and she was to become its captain.

"Their captain? You? Why Lordy, child, what's

235

you know about being a captain of a ship? I thought that only menfolk did such as that!"

An instant spark of anger swept over Katelin. Why did even other women try so hard to keep females in their so-called place? "Besides the fact that I don't know a great deal about the running of a ship, why should I not be the captain of the *Kat's Eye*? I am her owner, after all, and I am well able to organize and give out orders, as I have proved to everyone here on Coral Rose. And setting all of this aside, Lizzy, the fact remains that Coral Rose is in need of money and fast if she is to keep running!"

There was little that Lizzy could argue with; besides, the large woman was not lost to the glitter of anger that had filled her mistress's gaze. "I only be thinking about your safety, Miss Katelin. You gots to promise that you're going to be careful."

"I'll be careful all right." She could well imagine that Slade, Tad, and the others would make sure of that. "I need you to watch out for Joshua for me while I'm away, Lizzy. He might be upset for the first day or so, but he'll soon snap out of it."

At least the mistress was using some good sense, Lizzy told herself. She would not let young Master Joshua go along on this dangerous venture, and that was for the well and good of the matter. "I be watching him just as I always have, Miss Katelin," she promised.

Feeling somewhat relieved with the assurance that Lizzy would watch after Joshua and become the buffer between her and whoever asked after her while she was away from Coral Rose, Katelin shortly retired to her chamber, but it was some time before she could sleep.

The fact that the *Kat's Eye* would leave Saint Kitts with the early morning tide, and she would be making the boldest move of her life, was not the only thing that disturbed Katelin's slumber. Each time she shut her eyes, she was visited by the image of Garrick Steele. The vision of the handsome rogue would not let her be, and in the back of her mind the thought persisted, *What if the* Kat's Eye *came across the* Sea Witch *while out to sea?* She could only imagine the surprised look that would cross Captain Garrick Steele's face when she and her band of pirates boarded his ship!

Sitting in a darkened corner of the Salty Dog tavern, which was located along the wharf at Basseterre, Garrick Steele gazed around the dim interior of the bar once again, as he had several times since he had entered the establishment only a quarter of an hour past.

The tavern girl, Mercy, saw his look from where she stood near the bar, and once again she wondered what such a good-looking fellow was doing in a place like the Salty Dog, and all alone. Tugging on her blouse, so that it rode even lower over her shoulders and above her bosom, she stepped away from the bar and avoided a grab in her direction from a drunken sailor. Swaying provocatively, with one hand holding her skirt above her knee as though to control her skirts as she made her way through the tables and chairs, and the other hand holding a tankard of ale, she approached the large, dark-haired man sitting all alone in the corner of the room. "You be wanting anything else, Cap'n?" Earlier she had noticed his dark blue seaman's coat and cap and had quickly ascertained that he was no ordinary sailor.

Garrick finished his mug of ale and nodded his head toward her. "If you please." He smiled and his white teeth flashed within his bronzed, tan face and set the wench's heart to fluttering.

Bending low from the waist as though using some effort to fill the mug with the pitcher of ale in her hand, Mercy fully displayed her full, generous bosom for the eye of the man sitting directly before her. "And how about later, Cap'n? Is there an itch that you might not be able to scratch all by yourself?" she boldly propositioned, and in the back of her mind, she told herself she would be even willing to forgo the usual charge with this virile-looking man!

Garrick looked the young woman over with a critical eye. He knew that she was barely out of her teens, for there was still a look of youth about her, but it was quickly fading. With shimmering blond hair and full-rouged lips, she was an inviting picture leaning over him and displaying her charms. Slowly he shook his head. She needn't waste her efforts on him. There was only one woman for Garrick Steele, and since that first taste of her ripened flesh, he had not been able to imagine himself in the arms of another. But he did not immediately turn the wench down. "Are you not afraid that I might be the man who is doing all the killings here on Saint Kitts?"

"A girl's got to make a living, Cap'n." Mercy

smiled widely and for the first time she showed that several of her bottom teeth were missing.

A hazard of her profession, Garrick assumed as he smiled back at her, and nodded his head. "I guess you're right, but still it's dangerous to be approaching men in this area along the docks. It might prove safer if you stick with those you have entertained in the past." It had been a few weeks now since the last prostitute had been found floating along the wharf of Basseterre, and it would certainly be a shame if this young woman was the killer's next victim.

"If I had myself a fine gent like yourself, Cap'n, to see to my needs, I mightn't need to be working overtime from serving tables." Mercy pulled a corner of her skirt up over her knee to show him a sample of what he was in for if he accepted her offer.

"Perhaps my friend, who will shortly be joining me, will be interested," Garrick said not unkindly. He had never been one to put down another because of his or her profession, and perhaps if things were different, he would have taken the young woman up on her offer of a night's romp. But his thoughts of Katelin Ashford prevented him from reaching out and pulling this woman upon his lap as he would have only a few short months ago. Katelin was the only woman he wanted and he knew no other could satisfy him.

Mercy would have felt the sharp rejection of his words if she had been anyone else, but she had been turned down before, and she knew this would not be the last time. She chided herself for thinking that she could capture the attentions of such a gentleman anyway. Her mother had been a prostitute and hers before her. Mercy was merely carrying on the tradition, and before the evening was over, she knew if not this man's friend then another man would take her up on her offer. And with that thought, she was also reminded of the killer who was roaming about the docks of Basseterre, but she forced herself to push the thought to the back of her mind. Few coins could be made by a wench who was unwilling to take a chance! "I'll be back then, Cap'n, in a bit. Perhaps after a few more mugs of ale, you might even change your mind." She winked boldly before leaving his table and approaching another table where two seamen sat.

Garrick's long, tanned fingers wrapped around the handle of the mug as he brought it to his lips and his eyes went to the tavern door, which had just opened.

The man who entered walked with a slight limp. His back hunched a bit about the shoulders and caused his height to appear somewhat shorter than it truly was. Pushing the brim of his seaman's cap back on his forehead, he looked about the pub until his eyes sought out the one he had come to the Salty Dog to meet.

Garrick had never seen the man he was supposed to meet this evening, but as the man approached his table, tossed a gold coin carelessly in the air, and caught it in his palm, Garrick knew that this was his man. This was the signal he had been given which would allow him to know that he wasn't being set up. "Have a seat, and let me buy you a mug of ale." He kicked back the chair opposite him in an easy manner, as though welcoming an old and dear friend.

"I don't mind if I do, Captain, I don't mind if I do." The man smiled and took the seat offered.

Up close he appeared younger than he had to Garrick across the room, and his bent figure belied the strength in his limbs that were visible to the eye up close. It was no wonder the fellow was so good at his job of gaining information, as Garrick had been told—none would take such an inconspicuous-appearing man for a spy!

Mercy hurried back to the captain's table the moment she glimpsed that the man he had been waiting for had arrived. The tavern was getting busy at this late hour, so for the moment she had only the time to pour a mug of ale for the newcomer and promise to return to their table shortly.

The man across from Garrick smiled his appreciation at the young woman when she bent before him as she had done earlier to Garrick, and allowed the seaman a full view of her swollen breasts.

Garrick smiled toward the man after the girl had left their table. "She's available later, if you have a mind."

"Aye, a mind I do have for one such as that." The man winked at Garrick before adding, "I have been aboard ship for the past eight weeks, if you know what I mean?"

Garrick nodded, assuring the man he knew exactly what he meant. After allowing the man a drink of his ale, he questioned now that the pleasantries were over, "Have you gotten me the information that I need?"

The man nodded his head. "The man you're looking for, Bristol Jack, will be on the island of Grande Terre in about six weeks."

"Six weeks?" Garrick had hoped he would be finished with this job before six weeks were over. But nothing thus far had been working out the way he had hoped, so why should this, he asked himself. "Why is Jack going to be on Grande Terre in six weeks?" he questioned, not wanting to be sent on any more wild-goose chases as he had been on in the past few weeks.

"I don't know where you got your information from in the past, but there is going to be some kind of carnival day on the island. They call it that, but in the past it usually lasted a couple of days and nights. The entire island joins in and those like Bristol Jack and the Laffite brothers are among the hardest party-goers! He'll be there, I'll bet my life on it!"

Garrick had made port on Grande Terre on more than one occasion. It was an island that housed some of the most notorious pirates in the Caribbean. If what this man was saying about a carnival day was correct, Bristol Jack more than likely would be on the island just as he thought. And this might well be Garrick's chance to capture him. The man appeared assured of the information he was giving out, and Garrick had no reason to doubt him. "How about the other matter you were apprised of? Have you found out anything yet?"

The man silently shook his head, and for a moment seemed to think about what he was going to say. "Finding out where Bristol Jack is going to show up next seems to be easier than finding out anything about this madman who is killing the women here in Basseterre. No one knows anything, or they're just keeping quiet. I was told by one sailor that the evening the last whore was murdered, he had seen her talking to a large, brutish-looking fellow, but that was about all that I could come up with so far."

Garrick had already been told this same thing, and surmised that they had probably talked to the same sailor. "Well, see if you can find out anything else. You can get word to me by sending a note to the *Sea Witch*. If I don't hear from you before, I'll meet you here at the Salty Dog in ten days." Garrick finished his ale and stood, anxious to return to his ship and begin making some plans. He only hoped that another woman was not murdered before the killer was caught. He had posted several of his own crewmen about the docks, to report back anything that looked suspicious, but with only one piece of information about the possible killer, Garrick had his doubts that they would apprehend him very soon. Throwing down some coins on the table for the ale, he threw a gold piece toward the man, which was easily caught in midair. "The wench is on me, I'll see you in ten days if not before."

The informant grinned widely as Mercy approached their table and began to refill his mug. "I guess your friend had better things to occupy himself with this night." Her glance followed Garrick across the room and through the tavern door.

"I reckon he does, but I'm free for the taking." The man still wore the grin.

"Well, it ain't never been said that Mercy Hawks

243

ever turned a gent down, but"—and here she winked down upon him—"there ain't a thing free about what I have on my mind!"

Garrick left the Salty Dog and confidently strode along the dimly lit wharf area. He passed several reeling-drunk sailors and a few women. One woman approached him, but with his closed look, she quickly realized that she was wasting her time, and Garrick went on his way toward the *Sea Witch*.

Once in his cabin he worked at his desk, going over some charts and writing things down in his ledger. As he readied himself for bed, his mind as usual went to the woman who filled his thoughts night and day. "Kat." The name escaped his lips as he laid his head upon his pillow. Closing his eyes, he could see the sparkling warmth within her emerald eyes and he remembered how her lush dark curls had draped over his forearm the last time he had held her in his embrace. She had bewitched him, he knew, but he was powerless to fight off the golden webs that drew him ever to her. She had claimed that she was to wed another, but he told himself he would change her mind. As soon as he finished his work in the Caribbean, he would convince her that she belonged at his side, and if he could not convince her, he would just steal her away. He would hold her aboard the *Sea Witch* until she was willing to admit her love for him!

Sixteen

By the chiming of the French porcelain clock on Katelin's dressing table, she knew that daylight was only a couple of hours away. Pulling herself from the bed, she began to dress in the dark. Last night she had laid out the clothes she would need along with her black, thigh-high boots. At least her legs would have some protection from the elements, she told herself after pulling them on beneath her skirt and picking up the valise she had packed for her days at sea.

Quietly so as not to awaken anyone else, she left her chamber and made her way out of the house.

Joshua was waiting for her outside the back door.

"What on earth are you doing out here at this hour, Joshua? I have already told you that you cannot go along with me." Katelin was in no mood to argue with her brother. She had gotten little sleep during the night and she did not relish a confrontation this morning!

"I'll row you to the cove, Kat."

Katelin tried to see his face, but the darkness around them held him in shadow. "You don't have to do that, Joshua. You could stay here and get some more sleep."

"I know, sis, but I want to at least watch the *Kat's Eye* leave the cove. If I can't go along, at least I can do that much!"

She could tell by his tone that he was still angry that he was not allowed to go along on the *Kat's Eye*'s first venture as a pirate ship, but with his words she knew that he had at least come to grips with the fact that he would be staying at Coral Rose. "Oh, all right, Joshua. You can go with me as far as the cove, but don't think you're going to talk me into taking you with me!" She wanted him to know right from the start that there would be no chance of that happening.

Taking her valise from her hand, he grinned. "I still think you should get yourself some cutoffs!"

Katelin could not help the wide grin that came across her face. She had to admit that she was going to miss this little brother of hers even for the few days she would be away from Coral Rose. "Maybe you're right, Joshua," she was forced to confess as she once again realized how hindering her skirts were.

"Well, don't worry, Kat. Maybe Tad or one of the guys will lend you a pair of their breeches."

Katelin had to laugh at this as the image of herself wearing anything that belonged to any one of the men in the cove came to mind, and with it, she saw herself swallowed up in a lot of material. "I think not!" She laughed aloud.

After a minute passed, Katelin remembered what

246

had been plaguing her since she had met the group of men in the cove. "Joshua, why have I not met this friend of yours called Abe?" She still wished to give the fellow a piece of her mind.

"Oh, he didn't fit in too well, Tad said. He left the cove and signed on with some ship bound for China."

"Good for him," Katelin murmured, thinking it just as well that the man was no longer living in the cove. She doubted she would have gotten along with someone who talked so carelessly about women.

By the time the pair entered the cove, they could see that lanterns had been lit aboard the *Kat's Eye*, and much activity was taking place. "Come on board, Captain, we've been waiting for you." Slade was the first to see her and Joshua as they started across the wooden dock to the ship.

"I hope I'm not late." Katelin worried that she was late for her first day as captain of the *Kat's Eye*. What would the men think of her if she could not even make it on time her first morning?

"It will still be a few minutes before the tide will be just right to sail out of the cove. You got here in plenty of time." Slade must have picked up on her anxiousness and strove to make her more at ease.

Katelin and Joshua stepped aboard ship, and turning to her brother, Katelin hugged him closely to her side. "Listen to what Lizzy tells you, Joshua. I hope to be back in just a few days, so try to stay out of trouble."

He nodded his dark head as though agreeing to her every word, and after she released him, he said his goodbyes and left the ship.

"It's a shame the lad ain't a bit older. We could

247

sure use him as a cabin boy here aboard the *Kat's Eye*." Tad watched Joshua leaving the ship, and remembered himself at the boy's age, knowing he would have given anything to sail upon a pirate ship.

Katelin was reminded once again of the influence these men had on her brother, and she told herself that the first opportunity she had, she would speak to Tad and the others about their conduct around the boy. She had no desire for Joshua to become a pirate or a smuggler. He was the owner of Coral Rose and would one day be a planter — she would see to that! All they needed was enough money to see them through until they could keep the plantation going from its own crops. Once she had the money needed, she would abandon this life of a pirate once and for all. "I think that I will take my valise to my cabin," she murmured, not wishing to watch her brother leave the ship, for she also knew how much he wanted to be a part of this adventure.

"All right, lass, we'll call you when we pull anchor."

Katelin turned away from the men and started down the companionway and toward the captain's cabin. Joshua would be all right; she told herself to quit worrying about him. Setting the valise down at the foot of the bed, Katelin noticed that the lantern that swung over the desk had been lit, and looking about the cabin, she was once again impressed by all the work the women had done. Gazing upon the scarlet-draped bed with a more leisurely eye while she was alone in the cabin, she noticed that someone had laid out some clothes across the red sheets.

Thinking them to belong to a member of the

crew, she picked them up with the thought of returning them to Tad or Slade, but as she held the white silk shirt in her hand, she could not help noticing the small size. The black pants also were far too small for any of the smugglers. They almost looked as though they would fit Joshua, but she knew that to be impossible, because her brother only wore cutoffs. Beneath the pants and shirt, lying upon the sheet was a head scarf made from the same red silk material as the bedding. Could it be possible that the women had also made these clothes? she asked herself as she held the shirt up against her chest.

Without a second thought she quickly pulled off her blouse and skirt, and pulling the black breeches and white silk shirt on, she found them a perfect fit. The pants molded against her every curve, and allowed her freedom she had never known, the shirt was tied beneath her breasts, and pulling her black, shiny boots back on over the pant legs, she strode about the cabin for a few minutes, her head turning this way and that in order to view herself in this foreign attire.

At last the delightful sound of her laughter filled the cabin. Holding her arms straight out at her sides, Katelin swung about in carefree abandonment. Never had she felt so unrestrained! It was marvelous! Hurrying to the bed she caught up the red head scarf, and standing before the mirror that resided over the washstand, she tied it across the crown of her head, leaving her ebony curls flowing over her shoulders and down her back.

Her emerald eyes flashed with delight as she looked upon her image. She looked the role of a woman pirate! A large grin swept over her lovely

249

features as she pulled the small sword down from the peg on the cabin wall where it had been hanging. Strapping the scabbard about her waist, she adjusted the sword to her hip.

Turning one last time, she looked into the mirror. Again the laughter bubbled up within her throat but this time she restrained the impulse to let it loose. After all, she was the captain of the *Kat's Eye*, and for the first time she felt the part.

Stepping out on deck, at first she felt rather self-conscious standing before her men, but as their admiring glances were filled with respect, she soon forgot about her clothing. Minutes later the anchor was hoisted and the ship slowly began to move out of the secret cove.

Standing near the railing, Katelin searched the shoreline for her brother. Patsy, Slade's wife, was standing there alone with two other women, waving their farewells, but Joshua was nowhere to be seen. Waving back to the women, Katelin reasoned that Joshua had probably started home. There was nothing now to keep him in the cove, until the *Kat's Eye* returned once more to her home berth.

Katelin's excitement grew as the large ship sailed out of the cove, and with her sails filled with a tropical breeze, she made her way out into the Caribbean. There was no turning back now, Katelin told herself. She had boldly cast her lot with these rough and worthy men, and come what may, she would prosper or go down the same as they!

She felt sheer exhilaration as the wind caught up her dark curls, and as the *Kat's Eye* was swept along with full sail, salt spray was carried to the deck and showered her face lightly. This was truly living, she told herself, and with each mile that was put between the *Kat's Eye* and Saint Kitts, the more her excitement grew.

Tad had been silently standing by and watching the woman who he and the men had chosen to be their captain. He, like the rest of the men, admired her beauty, and felt some pride in the figure she made dressed in the clothes the men's wives had made for her, but Tad at this moment was seeing much much more. As her hand clutched the rail, her head thrown back and the sprinkling of ocean spray showering her, he could see that she was not like other women. The boy had been right when he had claimed that his sister was unafraid. He could see in her stance that she welcomed adventure and would meet trouble head on. And in that moment he promised himself that he would watch over her with his very life if the need arose.

Katelin caught some glimpse of the man standing not far from her. Turning, she welcomed him with a smile. "I wish to learn all there is to know about the running of the *Kat's Eye*, Tad. And if you have some time later this afternoon, perhaps you would practice your sword play with me. It's been some time since I have wielded a real weapon." Her grin widened as she remembered her nights with Joshua and his wooden swords.

Tad was unable to resist her. Eagerly he began to tell her everything about the ship that he believed she should know. Perhaps he and the men had thought that they would be getting themselves a captain in name only, but he now knew different. Kat would prove herself more than able, he had no doubt!

By that first evening Katelin fell across the scarlet-draped bed in sheer exhaustion. She had worked the day through beside her men; in the afternoon she and Tad had spent the rest of the day practicing with their swords. He also had shown her how to attack with a knife, believing a cutlass too heavy for her to wield. He made sure that if the need arose, she would not stand with only sword in hand.

Tad and Slade, whom she now viewed as the *Kat's Eye*'s senior officers, joined her in her cabin for supper at the oak table. They discussed their plans of searching the Caribbean for the Spanish ship, and when the meal was finished, they went over the maps that were rolled up and lying on Katelin's desk. By the time they left her to her sleep, she had only time to pull off her clothes and draw the sheet across her body before her eyes closed in slumber.

Upon waking early the following morning to the rocking motion of the ship, Katelin stretched, ignoring her sore muscles. Yesterday had more than likely been the hardest day of her life, but she could remember none as exciting! Dressing, she hurried to the galley to find something to break the fast before starting a new day aboard the *Kat's Eye*.

This day passed much like the day before, finding Katelin exhausted with the lowering of the sun. The only good thing about being so tired, she told herself, was the fact that she was too weary to be plagued with thoughts of Garrick Steele! Her fatigue allowed her no slumbering dreams of handsome sea captains or dark-eyed planters—the minute her head hit her pillow, her eyes shut and she was instantly asleep.

The following morning she was awakened to the call, "Sail ho." Not wasting a minute, she hurriedly dressed and was out on deck with her men. With her sword secured to her hip and her large bladed knife tucked in the waistband of her breeches, she stood against the railing of the *Kat's Eye* and looked far off in the distance to where a ship could barely be discerned. "Do you think it's her, Tad?" she called without looking for the large man. She just knew he was close by.

"We won't be knowing until we get a little closer, lass." His voice held excitement, but it also held something else.

Was he trying to give her an easy way out if she was not ready to attack the other ship? Katelin wondered as she looked at him. "Then by all means, order more sail! Let's see what we are coming up against. Slade," she called to the man who stood near the railing and looking out to sea. "Have the men ready the cannons. If it's the Spanish galleon, we will show her that we are ready to fight, and shall not be swayed!"

"Aye, aye, Captain," Slade called, already running and shouting out his captain's orders.

As the *Kat's Eye* drew closer and Ben in the crow's nest shouted that he could make out the flag of Spain flying from her mast, Katelin gave the order to overtake her.

Dirk and John manned the guns, and when the order was given, they let the cannons fire. A resounding boom filled the air, acrid smoke for a moment settling over the upper deck of the *Kat's Eye*.

Katelin's plan was a simple one. She had guessed that the Spanish galleon would carry no cannons. The ship appeared to ride heavy in the water, and this fact told Katelin that her value aboard was great. The *Kat's Eye* would fire only one round of cannon fire, purposely not hitting or damaging the other ship. The men would be ready to board her as soon as they pulled abreast of the other vessel.

Everything after this seemed to happen so quickly that later when Katelin tried to go over everything in her mind, she found that she was unsure of all the events that had taken place around her. Her emerald eyes sparkled with challenge and daring as the ships neared each other. Compared to the smooth-sailing *Kat's Eye*, the Spanish ship seemed sluggish and heavy, and for a moment Katelin wondered if her cargo was gold and expensive spices and silks. But this thought only had time to linger for a few seconds, for she had to keep her mind on the game at hand. Her men depended on her, she told herself over and over. "Ready your cutlasses, men! Secure her tightly now, that's it." she called as her crew began to throw grappling hooks across to the other ship to secure the two together.

It was right at that moment as she shouted "Move, men, move!" that she glimpsed Joshua standing alone near the stern railing. "Joshua," she shouted, and as his green eyes, filled with the excitement of the moment, turned in her direction, the look that crossed his face clearly told that he knew he had been found out. "Get in my cabin and await me there!" Katelin did not give him the chance to argue, nor did she have the time to make sure that her willful brother did as told; in the next instant she was jumping along with her men the short distance to the Spanish ship, her sword drawn and her other hand clutching her knife. Tad and Slade were only steps behind her.

The Spanish crew had been preparing for the attack of the other ship from the moment it had been first sighted. They were not seasoned, hardened pirates as were the vicious-appearing men boarding them, but they had been promised an ample reward by their captain if they defeated the enemy and saved the Spanish galleon; they were determined to fight and to win!

The crew of the *Kat's Eye* swarmed over the deck of the Spanish ship, their cries fierce as each man swung a gleaming cutlass overhead, and wielded a knife in his fist. Their fury provoked even the most stouthearted sailor aboard the ship to hesitate as they slashed and fought their way across the upper decks.

Pushing all thoughts of her brother to the back of her mind as the life and death game of piracy was being quickly brought home, Katelin did not hesitate, but attacked along with her crew. The first man to approach her seemed stunned motionless as he came up against the beautiful woman with a small sword clenched in her hand. With her black hair caught at the top of her head by the red scarf, and the silken tresses flowing freely over the white silk shirt, she appeared as brave as an avenging goddess, but the moment he felt the clank of her sword against his own, the sailor quickly came to his senses. He fought her toe to toe, no longer thinking about her sex but only of his survival, for the woman he faced had a sword arm that more than

255

surpassed his own.

Taking advantage of his motion as he lunged toward her, Katelin pierced his shoulder, and with a quick movement, she rapped him sharply against the side of the head. The next thing the sailor felt was the cold deck of the ship pressed against his cheek.

There was total chaos aboard the Spanish ship now, and easily glimpsing victory ahead, Katelin, with Tad at her side, hurried toward the companionway. Stepping out of a shadowed corner off from the companionway, a tall, dark man with a flowing mustache and trimmed beard blocked her path.

"I am the captain of this vessel, and I demand an explanation for your actions!" He spoke in an arrogant tone of voice.

"Well, Captain, as you can plainly see, your ship is in the process of being captured by my crew." Katelin grinned wide, already feeling the first flush of victory as she heard more and more steel being thrown down upon the deck.

"Your crew? Why, you are but a woman!" the Spanish captain sneered, not believing for a moment that his ship had been overtaken by a band of savages who were led by a woman, a beautiful one at that, he thought as his dark eyes went over the form-fitting clothes she wore; but all the same she was only a woman!

By this time Katelin's men had captured most of the Spanish crew, and Katelin, feeling more than a little piqued at the Spanish captain, bowed low from the waist before him, and swept her scarf from atop her head. "A woman without doubt, and a ship's captain, sir, and I now have control of your ship!"

Not wishing to so easily surrender this ship that

he had been in command of for the past two years, and especially to give over his authority to a woman, the captain reached for the pistol that was tucked into the top of his breeches.

But Katelin was much quicker. With a wave of her slender arm, she placed the blade of her sword against the hand at his waistband. "Whatever cargo you have aboard this ship, Captain, will mean very little to a dead man, which will prove the case if you persist in such folly," she remarked with a wide grin as though daring him to pull the gun any farther.

For a full moment the Spanish captain's black eyes locked with those eyes of incredible jade green, and seeing in their depths the hard reality of her words, he lowered his hand to his side and at the same time he bent her a small bow. "Quite right, señorita, by no means will I or my men prove foolhardy." Looking about the deck of his ship, he saw plainly that his entire crew had been taken prisoner.

"We care for nothing but your goods, Captain, so have no fear for your life, as long as you and your crew do as you are told," Katelin explained, as Tad and Slade continued on down the companionway and into the captain's cabin.

"Am I at least to know your name, señorita? Your vessel is called the *Kat's Eye,* but I have no clue to your identity." Now that the Spaniard knew that the events taking place aboard his ship were fully out of his control, he was more amenable. The least he could do, though, he told himself, was to be able to tell those in higher authority than himself the name of this female pirate captain who had overtaken them!

"My ship is named after myself, Captain. I am

known as Kat," Katelin told him proudly.

"Kat. A most fitting name for such a lovely señorita," the Spanish captain conceded, as his dark eyes once again lingered over her tightly clad figure. Her dark, streaming curls and sparkling green eyes seemed to fit perfectly the name she had given him.

It was Slade who returned to the upper deck with a huge grin on his face and sacks of jewels and gold in his hands. The crew of the *Kat's Eye* broke out in loud cheers, knowing that their own share of the Spanish treasure would be great, as Slade shouted that there was more where this had come from.

Katelin relished the sense of excitement she felt as she helped to transfer the goods from one ship to the other. Knowing that their time was valuable, for the *Kat's Eye* was not the only ship that had been searching for the Spanish galleon, they took the most valuable of the cargo, then as quickly as they had set upon the other ship, the *Kat's Eye* sailed away, and Katelin returned to her cabin to confront her wayward brother.

As soon as the cabin door opened, Joshua turned from where he had been standing a few feet in the room. His eyes enlarged as he glimpsed the hard set to his sister's chin, then he quickly lowered his gaze to the polished cabin floor. He had been watching the action aboard the Spanish ship and had even seen the cargo when it had been carried aboard the *Kat's Eye*. He had only done as Katelin had ordered him when he had caught a glimpse of her talking with Slade and Thomas, then he had hurried to the captain's cabin to await the fate that she would soon be handing out to him.

For a full moment Katelin did not speak, just

stood there near the door and looked at her brother. Her heart beat a bit faster as she thought of what could have happened had she and her crew not overtaken the Spanish galleon. Surely Joshua would have suffered as harshly as the rest of them for being aboard the *Kat's Eye*. "Why did you not obey me, Joshua?" she said at last and had to restrain herself from shouting out at him that he had no business aboard the *Kat's Eye*, and that he could this minute have been aboard the Spanish vessel, below deck in irons, along with her and the rest of her crew! But using all the control that she could, she reminded herself that Joshua was a young boy and by his very nature he was prone not to think before he acted.

"But I did do what you said, Kat." The bright green eyes once again went to her face but this time there was hope in their depths that he would be able to weather this storm better than he had earlier anticipated. "I'm here in your cabin just like you told me."

"That's not what I mean, and you know it, Joshua!"

Again the dark head bent, but Katelin knew that the submission was not truly felt. "I told you that you could not come on this voyage! You were supposed to return to Coral Rose after the *Kat's Eye* set sail and stay there until my return. Don't you understand that it is too dangerous for you to be aboard the *Kat's Eye*?" The last was a cry that carried fully her exasperation with her little brother.

"But nothing happened, Kat. You and Tad and the others licked that other ship easy enough. I saw you standing up to that Spaniard when he would have pulled his pistol and I saw you beat that one

259

with your sword. No one will ever whip you, Kat!" Admiration shone from his eyes as he looked at his sister and once again thought her the bravest, most wonderful woman in the whole wide world.

"Joshua, the point is, you did not do as I told you!" Katelin left the door, and pulling her knife from her pants and her sword from its scabbard, she put them down on her desk before turning back around to face her brother.

"But if I had stayed at Coral Rose, I would have missed everything. I had to come, Kat! Don't you see, I had to!"

His pleading tone was not lost to her, and once again Katelin realized that the little scamp was getting around her anger. He had to come indeed, she told herself, but searching her mind for what she could do to control him, she did not have a clue. "Where have you been hiding for the past couple of days?" She tried to make her voice still hold a hard edge, for she did not wish him to know so soon that he had won her over.

"I was hiding in the back of the pantry," Joshua admitted, and for a second longer he appeared repentant as he declared, "I'm sorry, Kat, I didn't mean to make you mad."

She did not know what she was going to do with this little hellion! He was just too mischievous and appealing for her to stay angry with. "Well then, I don't guess that you're very hungry? The men are going to have a victory celebration this evening. There will be feasting and bragging the night through, I'm sure."

"Can I join them, Kat? Can I? You're not still mad at me, are you?"

Katelin couldn't help smiling, and for the life of her she couldn't understand how he did it. He had an enchanting way about him, that even in the face of her anger, she could not help being swayed to see his side of things. She knew that she was spoiling him terribly but, at that moment, told herself that she would start disciplining him once they arrived back at Coral Rose.

This day's work of piracy had been quickly and cleanly brought to an end and Katelin with her brother at her side now had the time to revel in the company of her crew and friends. Late into the night she sat with her legs crossed on the wood-planked deck listening to the stories that were bandied back and forth and participating fully with these rough, seafaring men in their victory celebration.

It was Dirk who during the evening came to her side and questioned her about their returning to Saint Kitts; the helmsman, Thomas, needed to know their destination. After a few minutes of conferring with Tad and Slade, and with Joshua always in her thoughts, the decision was at last made that the *Kat's Eye* would not hurry straight home. The excitement flowing through their veins was too heady to bring under control at the moment, the temptation of another ship lying in wait was too much of an allure to be set aside. They would spend a couple of days sailing about the Caribbean.

"We will try out our luck on one more unsuspecting ship, boys, and then the *Kat's Eye* will head for home," Katelin shouted as she raised her mug of ale and sampled fully the heady brew. Always in the back of her mind, and this night was no different, was that the next ship the *Kat's Eye* came across might well be the *Sea Witch*, and after this day's work, Katelin felt herself in fine spirits to come face to face with Garrick Steele!

Seventeen

Over the course of the next several weeks the mild, gentle breezes of the Caribbean swept the *Kat's Eye* on a course of piracy that left few ships from their attention. Regularly the crew of the now notorious pirate ship found a defenseless ship crossing their path, and without warning, they would swoop down and easily make off with its treasure. In a short span of time the *Kat's Eye* and her beautiful lady captain had become well known in the Caribbean, and many a male captain had the pleasure of boasting to his friends and strangers alike that the green-eyed, male-clad sea siren herself had taken his cargo.

To some, it was a delightful sport to have this lovely creature board their ship and graciously relieve them of their valuables. To others, it became a lesson in skill as they tried with sword in hand to overcome the lady pirate.

Katelin relished these fights that tested her skill, swinging her sword in the manner in which she had been taught and delighting in the fear which she saw on her opponents' faces; she drank fully of the cup of life.

Spending more and more time among the men in the secret cove or upon the *Kat's Eye*, Katelin knew that it was becoming increasingly difficult for Lizzy to make up excuses for her. And Joshua had become sullen of late, because after that first sea voyage and the encounter with the Spanish galleon, Katelin had made sure that her brother was not aboard the *Kat's Eye* when it sailed out of the cove. She kept telling herself that after the next venture, she would retire from this life of piracy. She already had enough gold to see Coral Rose through the rest of the year, but the song of the sea was too tempting to resist, and Katelin was powerless to prevail against its attraction for the time being.

The need for a husband was no longer necessary, and daily Katelin told herself that she had no alternative except to break off her engagement to Alex Blackthorn. After all, she did not love him, and she knew that it had been unfair of her from the beginning to allow things to go so far. She had been desperate, she admitted, but now she owed Alex some sort of explanation, but for the life of her she did not know what she would say to gain her freedom from their engagement.

Arriving back at Coral Rose shortly before noon, Katelin found Joshua sitting on the steps of the front veranda and swirling his big toe in the dirt. His glance at first was filled with excitement for his sister's homecoming, but as quickly the bright eyes dimmed with disillusionment.

Katelin's own heart twinged with the hurt that

she knew her brother was feeling over her supposed desertion of him. Pulling something out of the seaman's bag she carried thrown over her shoulder, she approached him. "I brought you a gift, Joshua. I got it from a Portuguese captain who claimed to have purchased it from a Brazilian merchant." She held out a dagger encrusted with precious jewels, the rubies sparkling beneath the late-afternoon sunlight.

"That's nice," Joshua responded dully.

This was not the reception that Katelin had been hoping for. Setting the canvas bag down upon the top step of the porch, she sat down next to her brother on the bottom. "Has everything been going all right here at Coral Rose, Joshua?"

"Yeah," he murmured without much enthusiasm. "Old cold eyes was here yesterday and the day before. He said he would be back today and he hoped that you were feeling better."

Katelin had dreaded hearing this but she knew she would have to face Alex sooner or later. The last time she had seen him had been two weeks ago, and she had been so distracted about her plans to leave that night on the *Kat's Eye* that she had paid him little attention. "I guess I should go change and ride over to Shadow Mere," she thought aloud. Perhaps she would have the nerve to speak with him honestly if she were at his plantation. The one time she had visited Shadow Mere she had felt very uncomfortable, and maybe this would aid her in telling him the truth about her feelings.

"Then I guess you're still upset that I didn't take you along on the *Kat's Eye*?" she came right out and asked Joshua as she set the dagger in his open hand.

Silently he nodded his dark head, his eyes lowered and set upon the weapon in his palm.

"I wasn't going to tell you this until this evening but I guess it's all right if I tell you now."

Still he did not appear interested.

"At the end of the week the *Kat's Eye* will leave the cove, bound for the island of Grande Terre. There is going to be some kind of celebration on the island and the men and I have decided that we need a few days' relaxation. I thought you might like to come along." Her eyes twinkled as she watched his features beginning to light up.

"You mean it, Kat? I can come along?" Joshua could no longer sit still but jumped to his feet in front of her.

"I think you deserve some fun just like the rest of us." She told herself that later she would caution him about the infamous island that they were going to travel to, and also let him know without argument that he would not be allowed to travel around the island without Pete or Simon at his side.

"I do deserve to go, Kat! I've been sitting here day after day waiting for you to return."

"I know, Joshua, and I'm sorry. But it won't be long and then I will be staying here at Coral Rose with you. I think we should begin to make some plans about your education." That was another reason she gave herself for not giving up being the captain of the *Kat's Eye* immediately. It would cost plenty to hire a tutor to come out to Coral Rose for Joshua, and then it would take a large amount of money in a few years for him to do some traveling before he took up his position as a gentleman planter at Coral Rose. Perhaps after a few more ships, she would have all the money they needed.

"Are you going to quit being the captain then, Kat?" Joshua ignored what she had said about his education. His father had hired tutors in the past and he thought he knew as much as he needed at the moment. He would try to sway her about this subject at another time.

"Well, Joshua, you have to know that I can't keep on being a pirate forever. Thus far the *Kat's Eye* has been lucky, but one day I fear that luck will run out. I will play the game out a bit further, then I will retire and leave the *Kat's Eye* to Tad and Slade."

Joshua looked somewhat disappointed with her answer. He had hoped that she would remain the captain of the *Kat's Eye* until he was old enough to sail with her without being ordered about. "Well, Kat, as long as you are the captain of the *Kat's Eye*, I think that you should use this." He held the dagger back out to her. "I think it will go great with your pirate outfit."

"But I brought it home to you." But even as she said this, she knew that from the first moment she had seen the dagger, she had wanted it. She had only thought that such a gift would appease her brother's anger toward her. Reaching out her hand, she smiled fully upon him. "You're right, little brother, it will look fabulous upon my hip."

For Joshua the weapon was far too decorative; in his mind's eye, though, he could see the brilliance of diamonds and rubies standing out against Katelin's tightly fitted breeches and white silk shirt. "Rufuss went into town yesterday to pick up supplies and he said that he heard a lot of talk along the waterfront about the female pirate who is being called the Kat."

Katelin's attention was now fully drawn to her brother. She had hoped that her actions and that of her crew would not have been brought back so quickly to Saint Kitts. At least no one as yet knew that she was the one they called the Kat. Again she was reminded that she had almost played the game too long. Well, perhaps after this trip to Grande Terre, she would call it quits, she told herself as she stood and took up her bag. "I guess I will go inside and change. I think I will take a ride to Shadow Mere. There are some things that I should try and explain to Alex."

"You're not going to tell him that you're the Kat, are you?" Joshua looked at her with frightened eyes. He could only imagine what Old Cold Eyes would do with such information. He would probably go straight to the governor and try to have her arrested.

"No, Joshua, no one is to know that. It is just time that I tell him that I won't be able to become his wife."

A large grin covered the young boy's face with her words. "Good, Kat. I still don't like him."

Katelin hurried changing her clothes in order to arrive at Shadow Mere before Alex paid his afternoon visit to Coral Rose. As instructed, Joshua had told Kip to have a horse readied for her use, so after changing into an attractive riding habit and speaking with Lizzy, Katelin began to make her way to the neighboring plantation.

Like the last time Katelin went to the plantation, she felt ill at ease as she stood before the intricately carved, oak double doors. It was silent at Shadow Mere compared to all the activity and laughter that took place at Coral Rose. There were no servants in sight and from her last visit she knew that those she had seen had appeared to move about with tentative steps, their eyes at all times remaining at a respectful, downward glance.

It took only a few minutes before an aged black man wearing a starched white shirt and dark gray livery opened the door. His dark eyes were wide with question as he looked at the young woman standing on the front step.

Before he could say anything, Katelin smiled in a friendly manner. "I would like to speak with Mister Blackthorn, please."

"The master is in the study with another visitor, missy." He did not open the door wide in invitation, but stuck his head and a portion of his body out of the opening as though guarding against any unwelcomed guests.

"Well, I am sure that he will wish to see me. If you would just be so kind as to tell him that Miss Ashford is at the front door." Katelin was beginning to feel somewhat uncomfortable as she stood there looking at the small-framed black man.

Slowly the servant opened the door a bit wider, as though realizing that he could not very well leave her standing on the doorstep, then he said, "Would you care to wait inside, missy? I be telling the master right away that you be here." Old Jacob remembered the woman from a previous visit she had made to Shadow Mere and how pleased his master had seemed for several hours after.

Perhaps it was not bad manners that made the little man hesitate about opening the door, but something else, Katelin told herself. Could it be fear that she read in his dark gaze? But what on earth would he have to fear from her? she questioned as she stepped into the front foyer. The servant hurriedly left her and went down the long hallway off the foyer, which she assumed led to Alex's study.

Several more minutes passed and with them Katelin's irritation also grew apace. Perhaps she had made a mistake in coming here. She should have waited for Alex to come to Coral Rose to tell him her decision about breaking off their engagement. It had been an insane idea to think that the surroundings at Shadow Mere would give her the courage to tell him that she could not be his bride.

When Katelin at last heard voices down the hall, she was in the process of pulling her gloves back on. She had all but made up her mind to leave the house and return to Coral Rose.

"The master say for you to join him in his study, missy," Jacob said as he returned to where he had left the young woman standing.

"I thought he had a visitor in his study," Katelin replied, and wondered if she was going to meet whoever it was that Alex was visiting with.

"He done gone out the back way, missy."

Katelin was surprised by this, but kept her silence as she followed the man back down the hallway and into Shadow Mere's study. This room appeared the most used of those Katelin had thus far seen in the plantation house. As the central portion of the house, the study was immaculate, but the papers scattered across the teakwood desk attested to the fact that Alex Blackthorn spent much time in his study.

Looking up from where he sat behind the desk, Alex gazed at the woman standing in the doorway. There was not the usual thin-lipped smile, but instead the black eyes coolly appraised her features before traveling over her riding attire. Nodding his dark head, he invited her into his sanctuary.

Had she truly expected a warm reception? Katelin asked herself. After all, Alex had been out to Coral Rose twice in the past week and had been turned away both times.

"I trust that you feel well, madam?"

Nervously she nodded her head. This was not at all as she had planned. Even his tone was chilled. "I am fine now, Alex. I am sorry that you came all the way to Coral Rose to find me retired to my chambers. I did not mean—"

Before she had a chance to finish, he stepped away from his desk and stood before her. There was something threatening in his manner, the way the dark eyes held her, that warned Katelin that he was not at all pleased that she had come out to Shadow Mere. "If you are busy this afternoon, Alex, perhaps it is best if I come at another time."

"And is there ever a time suitable for a whore to pay a visit to my home?"

Katelin could but gasp aloud at his crudity.

"You seem surprised, madam, that I have found you out!" He stepped closer, the dark eyes holding her face without kindness.

"I don't know what . . ." Garrick Steele, somehow he had found out about Garrick!

In the next instant her arm was clutched in a tight hold. "You deny then that you were seen in a whorehouse in London? Before you answer, let me inform you that my sources are always correct." Alex Blackthorn paid handsomely for the information he gained from numerous agents around the world, and the information he had been seeking about Katelin Ashford had only arrived this morning. A gentleman had called at Shadow Mere with a packet that had come directly from his man in London; the same gentleman had left his study only moments before and had been shown out the back door of the house.

Katelin's jaw dropped open. What on earth was he . . . Oh my God, she told herself, he had found out about her visit to Rose Bishop's house of ill-repute. In that moment she would have explained to him what had taken place that evening in London, but there was something about Alex, perhaps it was the violence that she felt in his grip, or the cold stare that peered down into her face, that would not allow her to confess that indeed she had gone to a whorehouse, even if only in fun. Instead she shook her head in denial. "It was not I who went to that dreadful place, Alex." She tried to pull away from the hand that was biting into her flesh.

"You cannot deceive me, Katelin. There upon

my desk is information about your entire life from the time your father left you at Elizabeth Wessely's house."

"What?" Katelin could not believe that he had sought out information about her!

The betrayal that Alex was feeling at the moment surpassed all he had ever known in the past. He had believed this woman different from all the others. She had been the pureness that his life had been missing, and up until the moment when he had opened the packet and her sordid past had been revealed to him, he had held her upon a pedestal in his heart that no other had ever come near. But she was like all the others! Deceit was a part of her woman's game. But no more! He would treat her like the rest of the lying whores he had known in his past. His hand tightened upon her, the other one taking hold of her other arm.

"Alex, you must listen to me. You have made a mistake," Katelin cried out with alarm.

"A mistake?" he sneered. "The reports do not lie!"

"No, but that wasn't me. It was my cousin!" She could think of nothing else to say, and his grip upon her was biting in its cruelty.

Instantly his hold upon her lessened. "Your cousin?" A dark brow rose over one jet-colored eye. "There is nothing about a cousin in the report that I was brought."

"Few people know about her; her name is Kat." Katelin grabbed at anything that would make him release her. There was something very strange in the way he was looking at her and all she wanted to

273

do was gain her release and leave Shadow Mere, and if the only way to do that was to lie, then she was not averse to doing just that.

"Kat?" Alex looked upon the woman beneath his hands skeptically. He wanted with every fiber of his being to believe her. All of his dreams were wrapped up in her, and knowing that all those dreams had been a meaningless sham was beyond what he could bear.

"Kat looks much like me in appearance, Alex. That is why people in London mistook her for me!" Katelin felt the pressure on her arms slacken, and she inwardly thanked God that he was believing her.

"I have been hearing about a pirate captain that uses this same name. Kat, could it be that this cousin of yours followed you to the Caribbean?"

"Yes, Alex, yes!" Katelin declared. Let him believe anything he wants, she told herself. Just let her get out of here!

Instantly his manner changed toward her. His hands gentled upon her forearms, his dark eyes warming somewhat as the hardness around his mouth and chin appeared to soften. "I am so sorry, Katelin, please forgive my harsh treatment of you. But when I read that you had been seen in a house of disfavor, naturally I assumed that you . . ." He could not finish the words that he would have said. Now that he once again believed Katelin the woman he had built her up to be in his mind, he could not say the foul words in her presence that he now held in his thoughts for her cousin. This cousin of hers called Kat was as bad as he believed

Katelin to be good.

"That's all right, Alex." Katelin breathed with much relief, not truly knowing what he would have done to her, but having absolutely no desire to find out.

"Now why don't we sit down and you can tell me why you came to Shadow Mere. Did your servant not tell you that I had planned to pay you a visit this afternoon?"

Katelin was far too upset to sit down and converse with him as though none of the past few minutes had taken place. Shaking her head as though trying to clear her thoughts, she responded, "I . . . I am not sure." There was no way she was going to tell him that she had come here today to break off their engagement! There was no telling what his reaction to this would be and she did not want to test his cruelty a second time.

"You are looking somewhat pale, my dear. I do hope that you are not coming down with a relapse from your illness of the past few days." Alex was all concern for her at the moment, none of his previous conduct showing in the gentle way he hovered over her.

"Perhaps I do feel somewhat fatigued. It was a mistake for me to come here this afternoon. I'm sorry I disturbed you." The best course of action for Katelin at the moment was to get away from him, she told herself. She needed time to think, and to sort out what had just taken place in his study. He had appeared a totally different man from the one she had been courted by.

"Oh, my dear, you did not disturb me in the

275

least." He acted as though the information he had acquired about her and the subsequent abuse he had handed out had never taken place. "Why do you not rest here in my study for a few minutes while I go out to the stables and have my horse saddled. I will see you back to Coral Rose, and perhaps in the future you will send word that you plan to visit. It would be my pleasure to send an escort to ensure your safety."

Katelin certainly did not need an escort, nor did she wish for him to follow her back to Coral Rose. She needed time to think! "That won't be necessary, Alex. I think I should leave now. I'm sure that I can make it back to Coral Rose without any problems." She started toward the study door, and subconsciously she clutched her breath within her breast as though fearing he would lay hold of her once again and insist that he accompany her.

"I will call on you then in a few days. I have some important business to take care of so I shall be away from Shadow Mere for a couple of days, but upon my return, have no fear, I will come straightaway to Coral Rose." He stopped her at the open door, and before allowing her to leave him, he took her hand within his own and pressed his lips to the back of her wrist. His dark, piercing eyes looked upward into her face as he murmured, "Do not trouble yourself with thoughts about this wayward cousin of yours, my dear. I promise you that this subject will not be brought up again by me."

Katelin felt a chill race along her spine with his words. All she could do was nod. If she had felt somewhat uncomfortable when she had entered this house, she now felt her knees wobbling as she left. What on earth had she gotten herself into? she asked herself as she mounted her horse. Not only was she still involved with this man, but she had boldly told him outrageous lies. And the worst part of it all was she had admitted to having knowledge of the pirate captain known as Kat!

Eighteen

The hour was late. The activity in the Salty Dog
tavern was lively and the front common room filled
to capacity. Most available tables were being used,
and sailors and dock workers alike stood with mugs
in hand against the long bar running against the
wall. In a dark corner of the pub two men sat in
deep conversation, their attention broken only when
Mercy or one of the other barmaids refilled their
mugs and tried to tempt one of the men into parting with extra money for their favors in an upstairs
chamber.

Both men at the moment appeared uninterested in
the barmaids. The larger of the pair, the one who
wore seaman's garb, sported a full, unkempt beard,
and had a gold hoop earring dangling from one ear,
occasionally darted a furtive glance around the bar,
wishing to have his presence kept concealed. "I be
having me own ideas about taking me ship and
turning her into a slaver," he said in low tones.
"Black ivory is where the money be! I be hearing
that the Mississippi delta area in America is begging
for slaves, and that the going rate for a ship's hold

full of Negroes is a dollar a pound of man! Ye can't be beating that, now can ya?"

The man sitting opposite him pulled the collar of his dark cloak up tightly about his shoulders. "I don't give a damn what you plan to do with your future when I am through with you! You owe me and I mean to collect. I want that woman pirate captain called the Kat, and you are going to find her and bring her to me!"

"This will be the last of it then! The price on me head is getting too high. Even at this moment I am being hunted down by a man I ain't never met. They say he's a big fellow and that his silver gaze challenges everyone he meets. I know when me time is up, and I tell you it be now!" The man drank the last dregs of ale left in his mug before slamming the pewter container down on the table.

The dark eyes of the other held him with a piercing quality that seemed to scorch his very soul. "We will be finished with our business together when and if I say we are finished! Don't forget who set you up with that ship and crew, and who gets word to you about the richest vessels passing through the Caribbean. From that first day years ago when you approached me with your ideas of piracy, you sold your soul to the highest bidder! If someone is searching for you, deal with the problem. Do not sit and tell me that you are going to cut your losses and run. I need you, Jack, so do not disappoint me. Find the woman and bring her to me!"

Not another man in all of the Caribbean did the pirate called Bristol Jack fear as much as this man sitting across from him. He had good reason to fear him, he told himself. He had seen what he could do with that sharp-bladed knife that no one realized he carried until it was too late, and had also seen the power that his money wielded in the Caribbean. He had the means to employ a full line of ships to track him down if he so desired, and Jack had no doubt that if he did not do what the man wanted, he would do exactly that! Slowly he nodded his greasy, dark head. "I'll find the Kat for ya, have no fear on that score."

"That's more like it, Jack. You bring her to me and I will reward you generously. Maybe I'll even leave you to your adventure of becoming a slaver."

Bristol Jack once again nodded his head, and when Mercy refilled his mug, he downed the contents in a single, long drink.

"Why you're a big one, ain't ya, Cap'n?" She winked at Jack, and turning her head to the other man, she smiled upon him also. "Business is not as good as usual, gents, so if you're both of a mind, I'm setting a deal of a price. Two for one gold piece, but that price stands good only for tonight."

Jack pushed his chair back and mumbled something about needing to get back to his ship. The man draped in the black cloak also moved from the table, but his dark eyes lingered upon the serving girl before he made his way to the side door of the tavern. As he left the pub, he nodded his dark head in the direction of the young woman as a large, hulking man stepped to his side. That one seemed to understand him well enough without a word spoken between them and went back into the tavern. Finding Mercy, he whispered something in her ear that brought a wide grin to her lips and a nod from her head.

The cloaked man disappeared from sight as the other man made the arrangements.

Grande Terre, known to all as a notorious pirates' haven, rose up jewellike from the tropical sea of the Caribbean. Standing upon the deck of the *Kat's Eye*, Katelin watched the island with anticipation. For the first time since she had become the captain of this ship, she would stand before her peers as one of their kind. Knowing that her reputation and that of her ship had spread like wildfire throughout the Caribbean islands, she knew that she had made more than a few enemies, and would not in the least be surprised if she were forced to defend herself in this tropical hotbed of dangerous men and women. Feeling the blood flowing daringly within her veins, she knew that she was more than ready to meet any challenge; she yearned for the adventure that Grande Terre offered!

"What say you, Tad? Do you think we shall be able to find ourselves a clean inn here on the island, or shall we stay aboard ship?"

Standing not far from her side, Tad also scanned the shore of the island. "I be thinking the right of the thing, lass. We will be staying aboard the *Kat's Eye* of an evening. Everything that I have been told about the island from those of our crew that have been here before assures that mostly those living here are outcasts and criminals of one sort or another. Not a soul can be trusted hereabouts. Even the women are out but for one thing, and that be all the coins and trinkets they can gather."

"Be sure then that guards are posted round the

281

hour aboard ship. We all deserve some fun, but we don't want to take any chances that our ship is plundered."

"Aye, lass, you can't be a-telling with the likes of those we will be meeting up with here on Grande Terre. I'll see to assigning guards for first duty before we anchor."

"Is that her, Kat?" Joshua excitedly questioned. Coming up from the galley and standing at the rail, he peered across the ocean to the shore of the island.

"That's Grande Terre, all right, Joshua. Now don't forget everything we talked about. Either Pete or Simon will be with you at all times while we're on the island. I don't want to have to worry about you."

Joshua eagerly nodded his head. He liked both men whom she mentioned, and didn't mind in the least having them at his side. "Do you think we will see many pirates, sis?" His green eyes went over the island with an excited mixture of anticipation and wonder. "Do you think that we will even see Jean Laffite?" From all the tales that Joshua had heard about the pirate, he was a dashing and romantic figure in his young mind.

Katelin did not want to spoil her brother's fun while on Grand Terre, so she just smiled upon his boyish enthusiasm. She did not have the heart to tell him that this more than likely would be the last time either one of them would sail aboard the *Kat's Eye*. She had all but made up her mind over the past couple of days to give up her life of piracy. She told herself more than once that the game was much too dangerous. She had enough money to last them for a while, and was also determined that she would not wed Alex Blackthorn. She contented herself with the fact that all indications pointed to a good crop of sugar and cotton this year for Coral Rose. She and Joshua would make do, but for the time being they would enjoy themselves while on Grande Terre!

"Has the carnival on the island started yet? I haven't ever been to a carnival, have you, Tad?" Joshua as usual was full of questions.

While Tad patiently answered the questions put to him, Katelin watched as the *Kat's Eye* was anchored offshore and a pair of small boats were lowered from their berth aboard ship. The carnival would not start until tomorrow evening, and as she heard Tad talking to her brother, she knew that her own excitement over the event was as high as his.

A short time later Katelin and Joshua and all but those of the crew who would stay aboard for the first watch were being rowed toward the shoreline, a short distance away.

On the island itself the call had gone out that the *Kat's Eye* had anchored offshore. Most of the population of Grande Terre now stood outside the wooden buildings that made up the houses and shops. All eyes were fixed upon the pirate ship which they had heard so many rumors about over the past couple of months. As the small boats were rowed toward shore, the inhabitants gathered along the water's edge, with much laughing, shoving, and speculation as they awaited the captain and crew of the *Kat's Eye*.

Katelin immediately noticed that those standing ashore were a hardened lot. The women were mostly worn and haggard-looking, their tattered clothes dirty and hanging about them in rags. The men were little better with their hair and beards rough

283

and shaggy, their bodies too long unbathed. But with a toss of her jet black curls, Katelin allowed all of them to take a good look at her as she held her head high and gave back look for look. She would not be intimidated by a group such as this! She was Kat, the captain of a fine ship, and she had already made her name and mark in these islands. Her green eyes shimmered with high spirit as she set foot upon land.

"Well, if yon ship be named the *Kat's Eye*, you must be the Kat that we be hearing so much about of late." A burly-looking man with a red and white-striped shirt and dirty, baggy trousers, stepped forward and toward the small boat that Katelin had just vacated. He appeared braver than most as his surly gaze traveled over the newcomers to the island.

In a single motion, Slade, Tad, and Dirk were standing beside Katelin's side, their hands resting easily upon the hilts of their weapons, which were plainly visible.

"I am known as Kat," Katelin declared, her own gaze circling the group as she wondered even if somewhat belatedly what she and her crew had gotten themselves into. For a second her glance went to Joshua as though to assure herself that he was still safely sitting between Pete and Simon. She knew as she saw the hardness in the features peering at her that she had best make good her show of courage. These were not the type who would welcome any show of weakness. Drawing a deep breath, she stated, "Relax, men, there's not a man here who would be stupid enough to challenge us." Her stare went back to the man who had stepped forward, and instantly she saw him take a step backward.

284

This show of bravery appeared to break the tension that had suddenly built up in the group circling the two small boats. People started talking back and forth, the women appraising the crew of the *Kat's Eye*, the men asking questions of Kat and the large men standing at her side, and all appearing to hold a pirate's respect for the lady captain.

The group did not linger too long on the beach. Slade had been on the island on more than one occasion, and he quickly set about directing them to the inner portion of town.

To Katelin, Grande Terre did not appear overly large. The village seemed to be made up of little more than hastily constructed wooden structures scattered across the white sand before it met dense undergrowth. It was the lush foliage beyond these buildings that exhibited the true beauty of the island.

As Slade led the way for the group through the main portion of the village, people looked up from whatever it was they were doing to watch the procession of unfamiliar men and the beautiful woman wearing breeches and boots and sporting a sparkling-jeweled dagger on her hip. At the end of the dusty street the group halted before a tall building that appeared to be a house of some sort. "Let's be getting ourselves something to eat and drink in here, Captain. It be the best the island has to offer," Slade suggested.

Katelin looked over the men who made up her crew. Some appeared to be interested in the promised food and drink and others had an eye for what more the island offered. Joshua appeared to join the latter group and soon was walking away from her with several of her men, but Pete and Simon stayed close at his side as ordered. Katelin nodded her head to Slade. "I do admit that I am thirsty, and could use some food." She would not state aloud that the ship's fare was usually rather bland and unappealing. She would hate for word to get back to Simon that she found disfavor with his cooking, but the fact was that his talent as a cook held something to be desired.

Entering the building with Tad and Slade, Katelin squinted her eyes as she tried to adjust them to the dim interior. For a minute the group stood just past the doorway. It was Dirk who took Katelin by the arm and led her to a corner table where the four of them sat down companionably.

It only took a moment for the large man behind the bar to step to their table. All at the table appeared somewhat disgusted as he stood before them, his ponderous stomach hanging over the top of his breeches, his shirt being far too small to cover the enormous girth, and his jowls sagging in rolls of pale flesh. Yet he asked in an unusually friendly tone, "Are you here for the island's carnival, mates? You'll be finding Grande Terre a right friendly place, you can take the word of Sammy Bates on that. Why, by this evening I expect there won't be room in my tavern but for standing."

Tad nodded his head, indicating to the large man that indeed the carnival was their reason for being on the island. "For now, lad, me and the boys here will be having a mug of ale. The lass would be liking a cup of hot tea."

The fat man could not hold back his laughter, and as his large belly jumped up and down, those in the tavern looked upon the newcomers with interest. "You would more than likely find yourself a cup of mother's milk before you would be finding tea here on the island." Again he laughed.

"A mug of ale will be fine." Katelin felt her face flush with the man's taunting words, and not wishing to cause more of a scene, she hurriedly tried to take his mind away from her desire for tea. "What have you to eat? My crew and I could do with something hot."

The tavern owner's glance instantly became sharper. "I heard tell that the captain of the *Kat's Eye* was more than pleasing to the eye. I admit the stories do you little justice, Captain." He attempted some sort of ungainly bow, but with his immense form, his maneuver appeared a bit ridiculous. "My woman, Moll, cooked up a stew and a few loaves of brown bread this morning, but perhaps for some added coins she could prepare you something special, if you're a mind?"

The greed in his deep-set eyes was not lost upon Katelin. Apparently Sammy Bates made a better living than most on the island by catering to the wishes of the captains of the pirate ships that frequented the place. "The stew and bread will be sufficient for now."

"Well, maybe another time then, Captain. We also rent out rooms, if you're a mind to stay on land while you're on the island?"

There was no way that Katelin nor her men were going to spend the night under this cagey man's roof. At a glance it was plain to see that he would not be averse to stealing them blind if given half the chance. "We'll be returning to our ship for the night, thanks just the same," Katelin answered for herself and her men.

"Suit yourself, but if you change your mind, you can let old Moll know. She'll ready you up a room in no time." With this the large man left them to return to the bar and fill them mugs of ale.

It was only a matter of minutes before the tavern owner's woman, Moll, approached their table with a tray ladened with food. Moll was as skinny as Sammy Bates was fat, and unlike her mate, Moll was quiet and sullen.

By the end of the meal, the tavern had grown lively and louder. Several more men and women began to straggle through the front door, and amid the jovial calls and shouts, Katelin pushed her plate away. Relaxing back in her chair, she slowly sipped at her mug of ale.

It appeared that sooner or later throughout the course of a day and evening on Grande Terre the seamen, mostly pirates or smugglers, and their coarse women, which made up most of the populace of the island, made their way to Sammy Bates's tavern. As her glance went around the large room in leisure, she spied Joshua and several of her crew members entering the front door, another group of men following behind them. But what caught Katelin's attention was the woman who came in with the latter group. She was tall for a woman and broad shouldered. Her bosom full, her hips flaring, she also wore men's attire, but what made her stand out so strikingly from everyone else in the tavern was her long, flame red hair!

Her gaze also went around the interior of the tavern as soon as she stepped a foot within. "Where is she?" she shouted across the room to Sammy. "Where is the one called the Kat?"

A sly grin crossed Sammy's face. He had known that if the lady captain called the Kat stayed in here long enough, she would be called out. There were too many hotheads on the island for her to remain long unchallenged! With a nod of his head in the direction of Katelin's table, his eyes told the woman all she needed to know.

Without a break in her long-legged stride, the woman crossed the room and halted before the table where the dark-haired woman sat with three men. "Are you the Kat?" Her crystal-clear blue eyes fixed upon Katelin; not for a second did she give a glance to the men sitting at the table with the lady captain.

Katelin slowly nodded her dark head, her hand beneath the table easing toward the hilt of the sword which was still in its scabbard at her hip.

"I've been waiting for some time to meet up with the captain of the *Kat's Eye*," she stated without warmth. "A couple of months back your ship attacked a Spanish galleon?"

Katelin again nodded her head.

"You stole her cargo from me!"

"I believe the creed that a pirate ship sails under is that first come first take!" Slade stepped to his feet, and as several men who had also entered the tavern with the woman took a defensive step toward the table, Slade kicked his chair aside and sent it in a clatter to the dirt floor.

With this interference, the woman's gaze shifted from Katelin to the man who had been sitting at the table with her, but at this moment he was towering a full head over her own tall height. Slowly her comely features took on a look of disbelief mixed with surprise. "Slade? Is it truly you?" The woman's blue eyes opened wide, and in the next instant, she was throwing herself into his arms. "I just knew you couldn't stay away forever!"

Slade grinned wide as he pressed the woman tightly against his chest. "Sonja, you are as irresistible as ever, I see!"

"And you, you old tomcat, you haven't changed in the least!"

"Now there you're wrong, Sonja. A lot has changed in the three years since last I saw you." Slade laughed with enjoyment at seeing this fun-loving creature once again.

"Well, you can tell me everything. Are you here for carnival? Why are you sitting here with the crew of the *Kat's Eye*?" Her blue eyes went over him with something akin to lust in her gaze—from the top of his brass-colored, shoulder-length hair, his earrings dangling as she remembered them, down the length of his large, strapping body. She could not wait to get him alone!

"Tell your men to fetch themselves a drink and I will introduce you proper to my captain." The men at Sonja's side still appeared ready to attack or defend whatever the occasion required.

"Your captain? You mean, you helped her to steal my cargo?" Turning to her men, she slowly nodded her red head, an indication that she could handle herself from here on out.

Slade set his chair straight and waited for her to sit down. "Come on, Sonja, you know as well as I that the Spanish galleon was up for the taker. You're just sore that it was the *Kat's Eye* that found her irst." Slade grinned as he took the seat next to her.

By this time Joshua had made his way to Katelin's ide, and glanced at him standing there, Sonja questioned, "Who's the kid?"

"This is Joshua, Kat's brother. And this is Tad and Dirk, they are also members of the crew aboard the *Kat's Eye*."

For a long moment the red-haired vixen settled her gaze upon Tad and then Dirk. Slowly the blue eyes drew back to take a longer look at Tad. "So what is it, family day or something? What's with the kid hanging around?"

"Joshua is part owner of the *Kat's Eye* and has every right to be here." Katelin felt her anger flaring higher with the woman's lack in manners.

Pulling a gold coin from her breeches pocket, the woman tossed it high in the air toward Joshua. She grinned as he deftly caught it in midair. "Scat. Find yourself some trouble to get into!"

Joshua looked from the woman to the gold coin in his palm. "Thanks," he cried and dashed toward the bar where Pete and Simon were drinking a mug of ale. Within moments the three were leaving the tavern, Joshua anxious to see what he could spend the coin on.

"Now for you." The woman known as Sonja turned her attention directly upon Katelin. "Well, lady, I'll give you this: You're as fair to look upon as I've been told, but are you any good as the captain of a pirate ship?"

Katelin had opened her mouth to set the other woman straight, but before she could say the heated words that had instantly leaped to her tongue, Slade spoke up. "Kat can fight harder than most men I

291

know, Sonja, and she can give out orders with the best of them."

With these words coming from such a man as Slade, Sonja took a better look at the woman she had believed over the past few months to be her competition. "I admit that that Spaniard who sang praise to your beauty when he called to my ship that he had already been attacked and boarded did not endear me toward another woman pirate roaming the Caribbean."

"You mean you are the captain of a pirate ship also?" Katelin questioned, and was now finding this whole affair rather entertaining. As long as the woman did not threaten her or her brother, she had no qualms about her. Katelin was more than confident that she could handle herself where this woman called Sonja was concerned; she knew quite well the strength of her sword arm.

For the first time Sonja smiled at Katelin. "My ship is known as the *Lynx*. Have you heard of her?"

Katelin had to admit that she hadn't heard of the other ship, but was quick to add, "My brother and I usually stay to ourselves. This is the first time we have come to Grande Terre, or any other island that allows pirates to roam freely about, so I guess we hear little of what goes on around the Caribbean."

"Well, Kat, you should be changing that as soon as possible. With your looks, you could have any man in the whole of the Caribbean, including Jean Laffite himself, and that's saying a lot, because at the moment he is very interested in his latest mistress, Belinda." Sonja took her words not for what Katelin had intended, but instead believed the other woman to be lacking in male companionship. As ever, Sonja's thoughts revolved around the opposite sex.

"That's not exactly what I had in mind when I came to Grande Terre. We are here for a few days of relaxation."

Sonja threw back her head, her flaming hair cascading backward as she did so. "Relaxation? You'll find none of that on this island!" she declared loudly. "Carnival is the time when the whole island turns out to let themselves enjoy life, to drink, eat, and forget what yesterday held and expect the best of the coming days!"

Tad's laughter joined Sonja's. "You be of high spirit, lass. You be a woman of my liking."

With a bold wink, Sonja responded in kind, "And you're a man who I might like to spend some time with. I surely like a man with a full beard. Perhaps later you might like to see my cabin aboard the *Lynx*."

Never before had Katelin met such a bold woman, but the men at the table appeared to be amply appreciative of her forward manner. Tad was grinning from ear to ear and Dirk appeared to be waiting for his own invitation to her ship's cabin.

Sonja laughed aloud as she witnessed Katelin's shocked look. "Relax, Kat. You'll find that I'm a woman who makes no bones about having a healthy appetite when it comes to men. In fact, that is one of the reasons I made a point of coming this year to carnival. There is a silver-eyed devil of a ship's captain who I'm meeting tomorrow evening."

A ship's captain who had silver eyes? Could it be possible that this woman was talking about Garrick Steele? Katelin questioned herself, but quickly disregarded the notion as being nonsense. The fact that Garrick Steele was never far from her thoughts had brought about this instant assumption. Though she had not seen him in weeks, since that night in the gardens at Coral Rose, Katelin nightly held his handsome visage in her dreams, and with the other woman's words, his silver-blue eyes which in the past had held the power to melt her from within instantly came to the forefront of her mind.

"Me and the boys are going to go over there and join in on the arm-wrestling. We'll leave you ladies to get better acquainted." Slade nodded his head toward the action that was taking place across the tavern where two men sat arm-wrestling and who were circled by a group of rowdy enthusiasts.

"Another round over here, Sammy, for me and Kat," Sonja shouted to the fat bartender as the men left their table. "Perhaps after a few more drinks I'll tell you all about this lusty pirate I have set my eyes on, Kat. It's been some time since I have had another woman to confide in."

Katelin in no fashion desired to be this coarse woman's confidant, but not one given to a rude nature, she smiled and nodded her dark head.

Sammy Bates set two more mugs of ale on the scarred table, and with a sly grin in Sonja's direction, he stated, "The offer still holds. Say the word and I'll be sending old Moll off on the next ship leaving Grande Terre."

"You old horny dog!" Sonja grinned back. "If I were Moll, I would slice you from throat to liver!"

"She ain't got near the spunk you do, Sonja, so I don't have a fear in the world."

"Have you heard word yet about that ship I told

you last night to keep a lookout for?" Sonja questioned with a little more seriousness.

"Naw, all I know is what I told you last night. The ship's crew the last time they were on the island said that they would be here for carnival. I don't reckon that the *Sea Witch* or her captain would have the nerve to disappoint you, Sonja."

"The *Sea Witch!*" Katelin gasped aloud. The "silver-eyed devil of a ship's captain" *was* Garrick Steele! Katelin inwardly froze even as Sammy Bates for a lingering few seconds looked down at her and Sonja took up her mug in her hand, but not before her blue eyes held her in question. Garrick Steele would be here on Grande Terre for carnival; Katelin did not know whether to laugh or to cry.

Nineteen

By midnight Katelin and her crew were rowing back to the *Kat's Eye* in the pair of small boats. Sammy Bates's tavern had proven to be the center of action on the island, and by the end of the evening Katelin's eyes were drooping as she held Joshua upright in the small boat.

"I like her, Kat." Her brother's sleepy voice intruded on her thoughts when the small craft came alongside the larger vessel.

"Who do you like, Joshua?"

"That red-haired lady pirate."

"That figures," Katelin replied as those closest to the rope ladder began to climb upward and aboard ship.

"She seems awful nice to me. With that gold piece she gave me, I bought a new pocket knife. I bet she can do just about anything!"

"I would not be surprised," Katelin responded right before Joshua started up the ladder.

Katelin felt a pounding growing in the back of her head, and rubbing a finger between her brows as though to relieve it, she told herself that she had drunk far too much ale. Sonja had insisted upon buying her several more mugs, and after she had learned that the other woman was on the island with the hopes of meeting Garrick Steele, Katelin had forced a measure of calm over her wildly beating heart by steeping herself in the pleasure of her anger the rest of the evening. The woman pirate with the flaming red locks who her brother thought was so wonderful was just another one of Garrick Steele's many conquests!

Following Joshua up the ladder as easily as any agile sailor, Katelin did not linger long on deck but went straight to her cabin. Once alone, she pulled off her calf-high black boots and removed her weapons. Roaming about the cabin in her bare feet, she stood before the wardrobe that held the costume she would wear tomorrow night for carnival. Shortly her steps led her out onto the balcony that overlooked the sea. For a few seconds her green eyes swept over the moonlit sea and appraised the distant outline of ships lying offshore. Her gaze eventually went to the island, and as a shiver of bold anticipation touched her body, her thoughts went to Garrick Steele.

She told herself, as she had several times this evening, that she should make up any excuse she could think of to her crew and leave Grande Terre. She should turn and flee and never look back, a small voice inside warned. She imagined the incredible pleasure which she had known in the arms of the rakish sea captain, and a small moan of desire escaped her lips. At the same time her hands reached out and clutched the railing that encircled the balcony as though for support.

The man of her dreams, not the man she was engaged to marry, would be on the island tomorrow night! And even though Katelin knew his reason was to meet another woman, she could not help the race of excitement coursing through her veins with the thought.

Why should she leave the island? she questioned the voice. No one knew that the Kat and Katelin Ashford were one and the same. With her costume on, no one would recognize her, and with the half-mask covering her features, even Garrick Steele himself would not know who she was. She could watch for herself as he attracted and seduced another female, and then when he returned to her once again as he had that night in the gardens at Coral Rose, she would have the ammunition to arm herself with — the memory of the red-haired lady pirate known as Sonja clinging to his chest!

A small smile holding a mixture of excitement and anger settled over her lips. She would rid her thoughts of the deceitful privateer for once and all tomorrow night. Once she saw the proof that he was no more than a womanizing cad, just as she had thought him all along, she would be able to forget those nights of heated passion in his arms. She would be able to lock away those memories for once and all and no longer be plagued by that silver-blue-eyed sea captain!

Leaving her cabin, where for two hours Katelin had been readying herself for carnival, Katelin was met with whistles and catcalls the moment she stepped her red-heeled foot upon the upper deck.

"Golly, sis, you look great!" Joshua's green eyes stared wide as he looked at his sister standing before him in a scarlet red costume with layers and layers of black sheer lace showing beneath her skirts, and a black lace headdress resting atop her dark curls.

Katelin had spied the flamenco dress in the hold of a Spanish ship that the *Kat's Eye* had overtaken a month before. She had been unsure why she had held on to the costume at the time, but standing before the admiring glances of her crew, she was now pleased that she had. The red sleeves draped low over her upper arms, the bodice tightly fitting and low-cut. The sheer black bodice and petticoats felt like satin against her skin. Clutching her red-sequined half-mask with its black feathers on each side, she smiled fondly at her brother, who himself was dressed much like the rest of her crew, as pirates. "You look splendid yourself, Joshua."

"You'll be knocking 'em dead on the island, Captain. Me and a couple of the boys will be keeping an eye out for you, don't be worrying." Dirk stepped forward, his own gaze filled with his captain's astonishing beauty in the Spanish outfit.

"That won't be necessary, Dirk. I have my dagger at my side." Her hand lightly rested on the hilt of the jeweled weapon, which so easily blended with her costume that at first it was not apparent. "We came here to enjoy ourselves and I don't want any of you men to worry yourselves over my safety. I will be fine." The fewer people she had around her, the less likely it would be that Garrick Steele would recognize her, she told herself.

The men could see by the tilt to her jaw that there would be no arguing with her. Tad and Slade later told each other in a moment of privacy that, no matter what her instructions, they would keep an eye out for her.

"And what time did you return to the *Kat's Eye* this

morning?" Katelin changed the subject as her gaze was directed upon Tad.

"It wasn't long ago, sis. I saw him being rowed in the small boat from the *Lynx*," Joshua supplied before Tad could say anything.

The laughter of the crew followed the boy's statement, and Tad felt his features turning a shade of red. "The lass wanted to show me about the ship, and there were a few things in her cabin of interest."

"What is the *Lynx* like?" Joshua took his words as truth. "Is she fit as the *Kat's Eye?* Does the captain have a brace of weapons in her cabin and did she swordfight with you?"

"Well, boyo, you might say that me and the captain of the *Lynx* went for a round of sword play." He winked in the direction of the other men as he pulled Joshua along to the side of the ship where some of the crew were already starting to climb down to the waiting small boats.

"I imagine you had a swell time, then."

"That I did, lad, that I did." Tad grinned widely before giving the young boy a hand down to the rope ladder.

"You need to be careful how you talk around him, Tad." Katelin again was reminded of how impressionable her young brother was.

"Don't be worrying yourself none about the lad, lass. All he sees in yon captain of the *Lynx* is a woman captain who is stronger and bolder than most men."

"Then you did enjoy your time with Sonja?" Katelin was somewhat surprised that Tad seemed so high of spirit. She would not have thought that such a bold and

300

brassy woman could hold such an attraction over a man like Tad.

"Like I told the lad, lass, I had meself a swell time. The lass is a lady at heart."

Katelin had her doubts about the captain of the *Lynx* being a lady, but she kept her thoughts to herself. "Will Sonja be on the island early then this evening?" It was already early evening, dusk was just settling over the ocean, but Katelin wondered how soon she would see the other woman, and perhaps how soon she would see Garrick Steele.

"She has plans to meet some captain, but if I have me way about it, I'll be returning to the *Lynx* this night also." Tad grinned in anticipation of what the evening ahead might hold for him.

The populace of Grande Terre for the most part were already celebrating carnival by the time Katelin and her crew arrived on the island. The revelry along the streets was deafening to Katelin's ears, as all about her there were loud voices and throaty laughter.

For a time Katelin's group stayed together, going up one street and down another, following one group of party seekers and then joining up with another. At every house or building where they stopped they were served wine or ale and plenty of food.

It was not long, though, before the crew of the *Kat's Eye* began to disperse, seeking out their own means of entertainment. Joshua along with Pete and Simon left Katelin's side when she was pulled along with Tad and Slade toward Sammy Bates's tavern.

"Come along, lass. Let's see if Sonja is in the tavern. The lass might want to join us with our merrymaking."

301

"You go ahead, Tad, and you, too, Slade. I'll be in the tavern in a few minutes. But don't forget, my identity is to be kept secret." Katelin adjusted her half-mask, once more making sure that it was secure before going into the noisy tavern with her friends.

Fully wrapped up in the enthusiasm of partying, neither Tad nor Slade held any objection to Katelin wishing to keep her identity secret. Leaving her for a few minutes outside the tavern, they went in and were instantly greeted by Sammy Bates's patrons.

Katelin did not linger overly long outside the tavern as several rowdy men dressed as pirates started toward the front door. Spying her, they began to whistle loudly, so she turned about and hurried into the tavern.

The men inside the pub and many of the women halted whatever it was they were doing when the woman wearing the flaming red outfit of a flamenco dancer stepped into their midst. Her red high heels clicked against the wooden section of flooring that ran from the front door and along the front part of the bar. With her ebony curls hanging freely down her back and the red sequined half-mask obscuring her features, there was much whispering and speculation about the identity of the newcomer.

Several men stepped away from the tables they had been drinking at with friends, intent upon approaching the woman. Offers of drinks were called in her direction, and as one man made as though to reach out to her, a fight broke out as another man pulled that one's hand back and made to touch her himself.

With her head high, her chin tilted, Katelin glanced across the space of the room. She hardly heard those around her, not noticing what a disturbance she had caused within Sammy Bates's tavern. *He's here,* her mind repeated over and over. Garrick Steele was there in the tavern and sitting across the room at a table with Tad and Slade. Sonja was draped across his lap.

Even in his costume, Katelin knew that no other could look quite so handsome. Her green gaze fixed upon the dashing appeal of a black-haired, silver-blue-eyed sultan. His costume, including turban and half-mask, were of the whitest satin. His features were a dark, rich-leathered tan with which his steel eyes contrasted dramatically, making him even more handsome than she remembered!

Garrick had entered the tavern only moments before Tad and Slade. The moment he had sat down at the vacant table, Sonja had greeted him by throwing herself into his lap and placing a dampened kiss full upon his lips. Garrick had been attempting to control the overexuberant Sonja when the two men had approached his table. He had quickly invited them to join him when he learned that they were friends of Sonja's, with the hopes that they would be able to offer her a more lively diversion. His entire body had stilled when he, as every other man in the tavern, had turned to watch the gorgeous woman enter the bar. His hands had halted their movements of trying to dislodge Sonja from his lap, his pale stare not able to turn away from the creature that appeared to be making her way directly toward his table.

"What is the matter with you, Garrick?" Sonja questioned as she felt the man beneath her grow still. Turning her head in the direction that he was looking, she quickly saw his reason for appearing so entranced. "Well, who the hell is she to stir up such a commotion?"

An instant spark of jealousy flared in the redhead's tone and manner.

"It be carnival, lass. That's what the costumes be for. We aren't supposed to be knowing who everyone is." Tad quickly attempted to appease Sonja's igniting temper. "You be knowing anyway, lass, that you be the prettiest lass here on the whole of Grande Terre."

Sonja appeared pacified with his words for the time being, but in the next instant when Tad waved to the stunning woman in red, and motioned her toward their table, she could have strangled the sweet-talking Irish bloke with her own bare hands!

Even without Tad's invitation, Katelin would have shortly been standing before their table. She was drawn by the regard of the sultan, as though a bee to honey.

Garrick all but spilled Sonja to the floor in his haste to stand before this vision of beauty. The half-mask covered the upper portion of her face but her lips appeared temptingly pinkened, her cloud of dark hair framing her smooth, alabaster shoulders, and the deep red of the costume standing out starkly against the black sheer lace of her petticoats and the fluff of black that barely covered the tips of her full bosom in the bodice of the gown. In that instant his gaze drew downward over the shortened gown which rose up in the front and exposed a wealth of petticoat, to the tantalizing long length of legs encased in black silken hose, and to the red high heels. At last he was able to dispel his breath, his gaze rising once again to the green eyes that were almond-shaped behind the red-sequined mask.

"You're gaping, Garrick!" Sonja murmured as she steadied herself, and took the chair next to Garrick and

Tad. "You would think you men had never seen a woman before," she swore before reaching for her mug of ale. Her blue eyes glared her fury at the woman who was standing at their table. There was something kind of familiar about this woman, she thought after studying her for a few seconds longer. And as her glance went over her outfit and she glimpsed the jeweled dagger upon her hip, slowly a small smile settled over Sonja's full lips. Wiping the foam away with the back of her hand, Sonja herself was the first to speak to the other woman. "Take yourself a seat. I'll call Sammy with a mug of ale."

"Wine would be more preferable, if you don't mind." Katelin's voice was a feline purr that was invitingly mysterious, and she hoped it disguised her real tone.

"Is Sammy's ale too much for you?" Sonja grinned, remembering last eve and the vast amount of ale she and Kat had consumed.

Katelin was remembering also and a small grimace settled over her lips with the reminder of the headache she had carried back to the *Kat's Eye*. Ignoring the other woman's remark, Katelin looked around the table, her eyes holding for a second longer than necessary upon the sultan. "Let me see, since it is carnival, and we may not reveal our true names, you may all call me . . ." She searched her mind for an appropriate name for the occasion.

"The mysterious lady in red," Garrick offered, and the tone of his husky masculine voice sent fingers of electric energy dancing along Katelin's spine.

"Exactly," she whispered, only because at the moment she was unable to speak as his pale gaze held upon her. She thanked heaven that she wore the half-

305

mask and it covered the blush she knew must surely be staining her cheeks.

"I'll just call you Red." Sonja laughed aloud, seeming to enjoy the game of pretend. "You can call me Sonja, this here big fellow is Tad, and next to him is Slade." Sonja had found to her disappointment last night that her old friend, Slade, was happily married. "And this is the captain of the *Sea Witch*." With this she gave Katelin a wink as though to say she had not been exaggerating in the least about all the things she had said about the sea captain the night before. "His name is Garrick Steele."

"It is a pleasure, gentlemen, and you also, Sonja." Katelin tried to keep her voice low and hoped that the noise in the tavern would drown out much of her tone.

"Why don't we finish here and go out into the streets?" It was Garrick who made the suggestion. "After all, we all came to Grande Terre for carnival. We should at least see what the island has to offer." He lifted his mug, his pale gaze upon the woman in red even as the cup was turned up and drained of its content.

Everyone at the table appeared more than eager to leave the noisy tavern, and Katelin, abiding by her plan to watch Garrick Steele flirt and seduce another woman, was not about to stay behind.

It was as the group was nearing the tavern door that three men stepped into the pub. The tallest, handsomest man of the group instantly fixed his dark eyes on Katelin. With a flourishing bow, he halted the group before they could leave Sammy Bates's establishment. His thin lips drew back in a becoming smile as he murmured, "Mademoiselle, you fairly take my breath from

306

my body. You are the most beautiful woman who has ever stepped foot upon our lowly island!"

Katelin smiled with pleasure at the compliment. "But, sir, surely you cannot discern this with my face half covered."

"Ah, but I can." The man smiled even wider, believing her voice held the most feminine charm. "Why do you not leave this group you are with and join me and my companions?"

Standing next to Katelin, Sonja whispered, "Didn't I tell you, Kat? That's Jean Laffite. I knew he would be taken with you if he ever caught a glimpse."

"The lady is with us." Garrick stepped forward, and taking hold of Katelin's arm, he pulled her to his side.

"Ah, the gallant one, Captain Steele." Jean Laffite had previously met the captain of the *Sea Witch* and by rumor he had heard of his daring nature and abundant strength. "You cannot blame a gentleman for trying when it comes to such a beautiful lady now, can you?"

Garrick shook his head, having to admit that he could not blame any man for desiring the company of this woman in red. "I don't blame you, Jean. If I were in your place, I would attempt the same."

"And Captain, if I were in your shoes this evening, I would consider myself one very lucky man."

Stepping forward, Sonja took hold of Garrick's free arm, once again feeling sparks of jealousy.

"A lucky man indeed." Jean Laffite grinned with her movement before he stepped away from the group and joined his own.

Tad and Slade both sighed with relief as the tall, slender man stepped away. They had not known what the outcome would be between the silver-eyed captain

307

and the man known as Jean Laffite—they had only known that they would have protected Katelin with their lives if necessary. They left the tavern and followed behind Captain Steele who still had his hand upon their captain's arm. Within minutes, the pair of crewmen had maneuvered Sonja between them and put forth their best effort to entertain the lady pirate.

Again Katelin, with Garrick Steele at her side, and Tad and Slade and Sonja closely following, was pulled along with the crush of the island revelers. It was late and as the wine and ale continued to flow, several fights broke out along the streets, and as the group paused to watch a fight between two women over a large man who stood back and grinned over all the attention, they spied another man in a dark cloak breaking the pair apart and wrapping the younger woman fighter within the folds of his cloak. He laughed uproariously as he swept her up into his arms and made off with her down the dark road, amid her laughing protests.

At the next house Katelin was handed a glass of wine, and feeling somewhat light-headed, she would have refused, but her companions all partook, and feeling Garrick Steele's gaze upon her, she hurriedly gulped down the strong brew.

As the group started toward the next house, Katelin was shoved slightly from behind by a drunken pirate and all but fell upon Garrick Steele's broad chest. "Oh, I am sorry," she murmured and tried to pull herself out of his strong arms.

"I'm not." His deep-throated voice filled her every pore and the heat from his fingers upon her arms seemed to penetrate her flesh and char the depths of her very soul.

"Come along, you two," Sonja shouted over her shoulder as Tad and Slade escorted her through a mass of party seekers.

Soon the two were laughing and shouting with the revelers about them — tasting more wine and nibbling at the various foods brought out for their sampling. Katelin could almost forget with the help of the alcohol her reason for being here at Garrick Steele's side. For a time she allowed herself to enjoy the fun taking place around her.

As the sultan and the woman in red followed Sonja and her escorts down the streets, Katelin did not notice the strong arm that encircled her waist upon occasion as Garrick pulled her to him in order for her not to be trampled by another group of people, nor did she notice when Sonja and her crew members disappeared from sight.

It was at this time that, without forewarning, a large gust of wind swept through the streets, followed by a pelting rain shower.

The streets cleared instantly, everyone running for the nearest shelter. Katelin, laughing along with the rest of the partygoers and getting soaked to the skin, was pulled along by her sultan into the nearest doorway of a vacant house.

Katelin's laughter died in her throat as she felt Garrick's heated steel blue eyes appraising her body through the sodden gown.

His strong fingers, which were long and neatly manicured, reached up and slowly unpinned the hairpins that held the black lace headdress in place. Without a thought he allowed it to drop to the ground in a sodden pile, and in the next moment, his white silk half-mask followed. He would have reached up to take off Katelin's mask, but her hands stilled his in midair.

"Let us leave something a secret," she whispered.

With a simple nod of his dark head, he tilted her head back, and for the briefest minute time seemed to stand still while reason fled as his lips descended upon hers; warm, sweet lips, filled with the promise of tenderness, her mind thought as she gave her mouth over completely to this man of her dreams.

Twenty

Responding to the awakening response of her passions, Garrick pulled her tighter against his chest. "Come with me to the *Sea Witch*, my lady. Come with me and allow me to love you as you deserve." His husky whispered words evoked a strange feeling of anticipated desire from Katelin's body and Garrick easily felt her trembling within his embrace.

The rain shower had stopped as quickly as it had started, and gathering her in his arms, Garrick whispered, "Say you will come with me, say you feel the same as I, and will not tempt the moment by saying nay to me."

How could she refuse him? She felt as though she were wrapped within a warm haze of tenderness as she looked into his warm silver eyes. In her mind she had thought he would seduce Sonja, the lady pirate, but instead he was directing his overpowering attentions upon her. In the back of her mind, she asked herself what matter that it was her instead of Sonja? He still did not know her identity—he believed her to be just the woman in red! With that thought, she wrapped her hands around his powerful neck, and once again his lips slanted over hers.

Garrick had his answer. The woman in his arms was willing. With no resistance, he placed an arm beneath her knees and lifted her into his arms. Placing kisses over her chin and along the slender path of her neck, it seemed only seconds before the couple was standing along the beach and soon were being rowed by two crew members out to the *Sea Witch*.

For the life of her, Katelin could not remember later the small craft taking them to the larger ship, nor Garrick carrying her to his cabin. All that she was aware of was the feel of his strength beneath her hands, and the pleasure his sensual lips brought over her.

Dazedly she shook her dark head, barely able to stand without his support. She supposed that she had already drunk far too much, and at the moment the wild rapture pounding in her heart signified that she was drunk not only on the wine she had consumed throughout the evening, but on the steamy passion that had flamed between them.

"Then perhaps you would care to make yourself more comfortable? We should rid ourselves of our damp clothes." The very air seemed to be alive with a sensual current as with slow, pantherlike strides he came to her. Reaching out, he drew her to him. Then with a slight motion, he turned her around and began to unbutton the long row of black glass buttons down the length of her back.

Katelin felt chills coursing over her entire body as his strong hands brushed against the nape of her neck, and as his fingers worked the buttons loose and caressed the tender flesh along her backbone, she all but melted against him. Katelin was lost; beyond the point of being called back, or of actually wanting to be. She had spent so many restless nights dreaming of this moment, when she would once again be in his arms. She shut her green eyes at that moment as he slipped the gown from her shoulders and allowed it to fall in a crimson puddle at her feet. Her petticoats and chemise were next, and as she stood with only her red high heels and her half-mask covering the upper portion of her face, she heard Garrick draw in a long, ragged breath.

"Perfection," he murmured aloud, his warm eyes roaming over every inch of her voluptuous body. "I cannot say the words that pay fair justice to your incredible beauty." He felt the searing song of lust running rampant through his loins and the pulsing thickness of his manhood swelling to aching proportions.

His strong, tanned hands gently turned her to him, and as though taming a wild mare, they roamed over Katelin's body softly. He filled the cups of his palms with her swelling breasts, the rose-colored tips strutting for his caresses. With a soft moan of pent-up passion, his dark head with the silken hair lying against his shoulders bent, his lips and tongue traveling the same path as his hands. The heated streak of his tongue flicked back and forth over the hardened bud and Katelin was forced to grasp on to his shoulders in order to keep herself held upright.

In the next instant Garrick's strong, capable arms were lifting Katelin up against his chest and carrying her to his bed behind the curtained alcove, his mouth greedily tasting the soft, sweet taste that was hers alone.

He laid her upon the satin sheets, spreading her dark, silken curls out over the pillows before he stood

313

back and allowed his warm gaze to roam freely over her every curve. Gently he reached down and pulled off her red shoes, and he would have again attempted to take the half-mask from her face but her hand upon his wrist stayed him.

"Douse the light and I will take off the mask."

A soft smile settled over his lips. "Perhaps such secrecy does lend a certain spell of seduction over the evening," he murmured as though speaking to himself.

As he began to remove his own costume, Katelin, with her senses fully aroused to his every movement, leaned upon one elbow and watched with hazy, dreaming eyes as he removed one piece of clothing, then another.

His turban was first unwound, and dropped to the floor. Then he removed his shirt; this had been open to the waist already but as it was taken from his body she inhaled deeply, noticing the thick short dark hairs on his chest and his bronzed, muscle-rippled back and chest. As he lowered his white pants and let them drop to the floor with his other clothing, Katelin felt her heart all but stop its beating, as her glance filled with the throbbing magnificence of his engorged manhood. His whole presence was raw, powerful man! And remembering the feel of his body pressed tightly to her own, Katelin totally forgot the reason for being on the *Sea Witch* and in his cabin. All thoughts of gaining the evidence that would condemn him as a womanizer were now forgotten. All that mattered was the aching longing that burned within her womanhood. She wanted him more than she had ever wanted anything in her life!

Garrick seemed to sense her need, and standing before her only a few seconds longer, he turned and boldly strode over to his desk, his hand reaching up to extinguish the lantern.

As her glance roamed over his muscular back, tight buttocks, and hard, well-proportioned legs, her desire for him was heightened. It felt like an eternity before he was once more at the side of the bed and she felt the heaviness of his weight beside her.

Dim lighting was cast over the cabin by the moonlight that stole through the sea window, the bedding alcove held in darkness because of the drapes forming the enclosure. Earlier that evening Garrick had whispered against Katelin's ear that there was a pirate moon out this night. A bright full moon that a pirate could sail beneath without fear of running aground. Nervously Katelin reached up and unsecured the pins that held the half-mask in place. Her exotically slanted green eyes searched the small space of the bed for him, and instantly her mouth was covered by the pressure of his.

"You taste as sweet as honey ambrosia, your skin is of the softest satin. I have waited all night for this moment." His hand caressed her face, his lips raining kisses over her cheeks, her eyelids, her forehead.

Katelin was lost to the tantalizing taste of him, the touch of his hands upon her flesh, the heat of his large body pressing against her. Perhaps this was the reason she had become a pirate, she told herself, even the reason she had come to Grande Terre. In the back of her mind perhaps she had been searching for this man, desiring to reacquaint herself to these incredible feelings she had discovered nowhere else but in Garrick Steele's arms. That night in the gardens at Coral Rose when she had confessed to him that she was to wed another, and he had left her side, deep within she had feared never to see him again. But now that she was in his arms, none of that mattered any longer.

Strong, probing, and plundering fingers roamed freely over Katelin's body, and at the same time Garrick's lips seared a path from her lips down to her breasts. He worshipped the twin globes of pale flesh, taking one by one the rosy-hued nipples into his mouth to suckle.

Katelin seemed not to be able to get enough of the taste of his body as her hands reached out and caressed any part of him she could reach, and her body writhed beneath the onslaught of his wild seduction. As he leaned over her and feasted upon her breasts, her own mouth met his muscular shoulder and her lips made a bold pattern of tiny kisses down toward the upper portion of his chest. At the same time her hands glided over the strong planes of his muscled body, outlining the broadness of his sculpted back, down to his narrow hips, and over his firm buttocks. An indrawn breath caught and held for a breathless time as one hand brushed against the pulsing length of his hard shaft.

With the slight touch of her hand, the size of him seemed to enlarge, expanding to mighty proportions as the blood rushed through his loins, and a deep groan started in the depths of his chest and rumbled upward.

Feeling the woman's power she held at this moment, Katelin wrapped her slim fingers around his swollen member and slowly drew them up the length until she touched the heart-shaped head, then slowly, tantalizingly, she traveled back down the thick, throbbing measure of him, inch by inch.

"Ah, my beauty . . ." Garrick reached out and stilled her hand. "If you proceed with much more of this, the act will be finished before it ever starts." His words were whispered against her ear and from there his moist tongue scorched a trail over the delicate contours of her face, down her slender throat, across the fullness of her swollen breasts, gliding over her ribs and scorching a trail over a rounded hip. At the same time his hand boldly touched the crest of her woman's jewel, rioting sensations shot throughout her body. His touch was so intense as he made contact with the nub of her very essence, Katelin had to clamp her teeth tightly together to keep from crying aloud to the dark room.

But with the heated contact of his lips, she could not help the cry torn from her lips as she rose up and clutched Garrick's dark hair. She was consumed with igniting flame, becoming a mass of trembling desire. She rode out this incredible journey of pure ecstasy, her mind void of all but the rippling waves of hot passion that filled her body and erupted into scalding pleasure. As shudder after shudder left her trembling and writhing, fulfillment came . . . and with it, Katelin's cries turned to gasping purrs of contentment.

Katelin's green eyes were passion-filled as he rose above her, spreading her thighs gently, his vein-ridged, throbbing manhood pressed into the entrance of her moist sheath. Feeling the quivering velvet warmth welcoming him, pulling him farther within the tight, quaking folds of her womanhood, Garrick groaned as blinding pleasure filled his very being.

He was an explosive charge ready to be ignited and she, with her satin feel and softly molded curves, was the single flaming torch that could spark the fuse. And as Garrick's body slowly developed a sensuous, luring rhythm, Katelin wound her sleek arms around his neck. Her soft, petal pink lips parted as small shivers of sweet rapture set her entire body to trembling in his arms. Her body moved against his with a silken grace, turning their joining end over end in a whirling, raging tide as each strove to reach their fulfillment.

From somewhere above deck on the *Sea Witch* a sailor sang a love song to the velvet, starlit night. The words had a soft, languorous quality which traveled on the tropical island breeze and reached the lovers upon the captain's bed, heightening their passions and inflaming them ever on.

Garrick wrapped Katelin's satin legs about his waist, striving deeper and deeper into her nether regions; making her body one large unquenchable force striving for the earth-shattering pleasure that was so near.

And when that moment came, Katelin gloried in the feeling of rapture flaming through her body, wrapping her senses in sheer, pulsating pleasure.

Out of a sense of knowing women, Garrick knew the instant she reached the peak to which he had striven to bring her, and at that moment as his lips found hers, he felt his whole being swell with an unreasoning pride. His own body for a few short moments longer drank of her body, and then he also felt that feeling of sheer brilliant delight start at the center of his being and expand in a mighty, plunging storm of rapture.

His body slowly stilled and his breathing was ragged, but his lips roamed over Katelin's face and throat, not seeming to be able to get enough of her passion-drenched body. "You inflame me beyond all reason, my sweet. I would that you would stay here within my arms forever."

As Katelin's heartbeat began to calm, her senses somewhat returned, and with his words she was reminded that she believed him the worst sort of cad. "And do you say this to all your women, sir?"

"Sir? I would think that after what we just shared we

318

could at least speak on a first-name basis." There was a slight tremor to his husky voice that bespoke laughter, and as his lips tenderly kissed her cheek and his hand made tiny circular patterns along the side of her neck, he held his large body around her as though loath to ever let her go. "Would you believe me if I told you that I find you irresistible, and have found my heart totally ensnared?"

Katelin felt a shiver course over her body, but for some reason his words only saddened her. To know that he spoke thus to a woman he believed himself to know only a few short hours only intensified her distrust of him. Her body stiffened in his arms. *You found out all that you wanted to know,* her inner thoughts told her. *You should now get yourself dressed and leave his ship, and if he ever crosses your path again, you will be armed with the knowledge that all women are the same to him. You or a woman wearing a half-mask or one in any number of other women, it does not matter to such a rake! His sweet words were spoken only to ensnare a woman's heart, not spoken with true meaning!* "I should leave," she announced and tried to pull herself out of his arms.

"But you did not answer my question." Garrick's arms tightened around her. "What if instead of answering, I told you that I love you, Kat?"

Katelin stilled in her struggle to free herself. Had she heard him correctly? Had he called her by name? She tried to peer into his face, but could only glimpse the glimmer of his pale eyes. "I think you mistake me for another." She kept her voice low. "One woman must sound and feel much like all the rest of your many conquests, so if you will just release me, I will return to the island." Her heart hammered wildly in her chest.

Husky masculine laughter filled the space of the al-

319

cove and traveled throughout the cabin. "Does a man not remember the scent of the woman who fills his every thought? Does her form, her satin-smooth flesh, delude him into thinking her another. Her walk, the tilt of her head, even the perfect shape of her hands as she holds a goblet of wine and brings it to her sweet, tempting lips, all these things a man in love knows even without being told that the woman beneath the half-mask is his own heart."

"You knew it was me from the start?" Katelin's heart skipped a beat as she dared to believe his words.

"From the moment you stepped foot in Sammy Bates's tavern, Kat, I knew it was you in the red dress. I admit that I had to use some great restraint not to hurry to your side at that moment with the fear that every man in the bar would be stirred to try and claim you for their own. That outfit was most revealing, Kat." He bent with a grin and gave her a lusty kiss full upon the lips.

Some inner trembling within her heart leaped with joy over his words. "But what about Sonja?" The joy began to vanish again with thoughts of the red-haired woman pirate and the bold lust for life she did not try to hide from anyone.

"What of Sonja?" Garrick absently questioned as his hands roamed over her naked back and the feel of her satin flesh once more began to stir his manhood to life.

Taking him by surprise, Katelin sat straight up in the bed. "You know what I mean, Garrick Steele. That brazen woman told me that she was here on Grande Terre to meet you." Katelin would not be easily put off by the feel of his heated lips and his strong hands upon her body. She had to know if she had misjudged him, or if he had only been lucky in guessing her identity.

Garrick let out a long sigh, and piling the numerous pillows on the bed behind his back, he also sat up, but he did not speak until he pulled her back into his arms. "I met Sonja a few months ago, and no, we have never been lovers. Though she made it plain that she would not be averse to my attentions, I'm afraid that my heart had already been stolen, and I knew that there was no substituting the green-eyed, black-haired vixen that was always in my thoughts."

"Truly?" Katelin at last relaxed against his broad chest. She wanted to believe him; she was tired of the distrust she held for him and all men. "Then why were you meeting her here for carnival?"

"She knows a man who I have been searching for." Sonja had told Garrick sometime back that she knew Bristol Jack and that she would set up a meeting for him with the outlaw pirate. That had been Garrick's reason for being on Grande Terre, and now as he held this woman of his heart closely in his embrace, he thanked the good fortune that was watching over him, that he had been in Sammy Bates's tavern when she had walked in the front door.

"What man?"

"No one that you should worry yourself about." Garrick once again lowered his dark head to her and slanted his mouth over her lips.

Katelin felt herself wrapped within the warm sedation of contented bliss as he removed his mouth. "Did you mean what you said earlier?" she questioned softly, her hands lying upon the crisp dark matting of hair on his chest.

"And what was that, sweet?" Garrick's hands wrapped within the satin curls of her hair as he gloried in the feel of her flesh tightly held against his own. "Did

I mean it when I said that you inflame me beyond all reason? Or that I wish you would stay in my arms forever?"

Katelin did not answer him. She admitted that those words had all gone straight to her heart, but they were not the ones she now questioned him about.

"Or do I mean it when I say that your beauty holds perfection, or your slight smile sets my heart to trembling, your delicate scent inflames me, or that I love you with each and every fiber of my being?" His mouth covered hers and the kiss shared between them was a gentle joining of their souls.

"Yes . . ." That was all Katelin could get out on a single breath after her lips were released.

Garrick smiled adoringly upon her. "From that first moment when I saw you standing at the foot of the stairs in Rose Bishop's house, I loved you, Kat. From that very night on, you have plagued my dreams with those enchanting green eyes and your long, beautiful witch's locks. I would have spoken these words from my heart sooner, but it seems as though each time we are together we cannot talk of such things because our tempers clash and what follows is not always pleasant. Our bodies seem to be able to say those things that we feel far better than our lips."

Katelin was well aware that he was right, and she also knew that much of their fighting in the past had been due to her own feelings of insecurity, stemming from her childhood and her desertion at the hands of her father. It was hard for her to believe even at this minute while lying in Garrick's arms that he could love her so completely that he would wish to keep her at his side forever. The hard shell she had imposed around herself as a child, in order to keep herself from being so cruelly hurt ever again as her father had hurt her, was not a shield that could be easily set aside. And though she longed to forget everything bad that had happened between the two of them in the past and accept the love and comfort that he now offered, she was still so used to taking the offensive, it was hard for her to get used to the idea of admitting that she had been wrong about him all this time.

Garrick somehow must have sensed her inner thoughts for his next words gave her permission to let the past lie and start anew the relationship that had been born this night. "Let us not dwell upon yesterday, my heart. Let us think to the future. A future for you and I together." He caressed the tender flesh of her upper arms, enjoying the sounds of the words he had just said. A future with this woman at his side was all he asked out of life.

"Can it be that easy?" Katelin whispered, and now for the first time that evening she remembered Alex Blackthorn, her brother, and her obligations to the people at Coral Rose. She had responsibilities that she could not just set aside. Even the *Kat's Eye* was a matter she could not easily turn away from. She would have to be assured that her crew was able to carry on without her if she decided to grasp on to a future with this man who set her soul afire.

"You and I together can work out any problems, Kat," Garrick quickly assured her, sensing that she was suddenly withdrawing somewhat from him as she thought of her everyday life. "Why don't we start by your telling me how you came to be on Grande Terre for carnival? Who did you come to the island with?" He expected the worst; in fact, he suspected that she had come to the island with Alex Blackthorn and had somehow gotten lost from her party.

Katelin was not sure how she should begin. How on earth was she going to tell this man that she had come to the island of Grande Terre aboard a pirate ship, and more than that shocking statement was the fact that she was the vessel's captain?

Her hesitation drew her tighter within Garrick's embrace as he tried without speaking to offer her his comfort and strength, allowing her to know that she could tell him anything. Even if she said that she did come to the island with Alex Blackthorn, he would not condemn her—how could he when he loved her so much!

Drawing a deep, tentative breath, Katelin knew that if their relationship were to have any kind of chance, she had to tell him the truth, and she had to tell him everything! "I came to Grande Terre aboard the ship called the *Kat's Eye*, Garrick."

Garrick's arms, which were wrapped around her, automatically stiffened. "The *Kat's Eye*?" Over the course of the last couple of months he as well as everyone else in the Caribbean had heard of the infamous pirate ship called the *Kat's Eye*. "Why on earth would you be aboard such a ship?" Had she traveled to the island with Alex Blackthorn aboard a pirate ship? He was more than a little confused at the moment as he rose up somewhat on the pillows to have a better look at her face.

"Let me tell you all, Garrick, before you say anything," Katelin begged, finding it hard to go on after being interrupted by his surprised questions. Slowly his hands relaxed their pressure and once again their touch was gentle. "I was not able to tell you this before but my father's plantation, Coral Rose, was in dire straits when I arrived in Saint Kitts. My brother was

324

about to lose his inheritance."

"What has this to do with the *Kat's Eye*?"

"Please, Garrick, I will tell you everything."

He realized he was being impatient, and not wishing her to close him out, he quickly kissed her on the lips. "I'm sorry, sweet, I won't do that again."

Katelin could not hold back the small smile that settled over her lips. "As I was saying, Coral Rose was in a state of financial ruin. My father had left absolutely no money and the people on the plantation had not been working the crops, or in fact had they been doing much of anything before I arrived." Here she drew in a nervous, ragged breath.

"I had to do something to save my brother from becoming destitute! That is why I agreed at first to marry Alex Blackthorn." Here she could sense that Garrick was going to speak out once again, and she quickly placed a finger over his lips.

"It was not long after that that Joshua took me to a secret cove that housed a smuggling ship, which I learned my brother and I were the owners of. The band of smugglers that my father was in business with also lived in the cove." Now she worried that he would think ill not only of her, but of her entire family. Having a father who was a smuggler did not reflect well on a family of supposedly good character. There was no help for it though, Katelin told herself. She had started this story and Garrick was going to hear her out. With the finish, he could judge for himself if he believed her and her family too tainted of reputation for him to associate with.

"Because Joshua and I owned the ship now that my father was no longer alive, the crew decided that they should change their occupation from smuggling to piracy. After refitting the ship, they also renamed her, the *Kat's Eye*."

After a slight pause, she went on, "I am the captain of the *Kat's Eye*, Garrick. They named the ship after me. I am the Kat who everyone is talking about."

Twenty-one

Silence hung within the ship's cabin for well over an entire minute. Katelin's heartbeat dashed madly against the wall of her chest as she awaited the words that Garrick would speak, which would either sound their condemnation of the life she had been leading since she had come to the Caribbean, or express their understanding, that she had no other choice.

When his response came, Katelin was somewhat thrown off. "For God's sake, Kat, why didn't you come to me if you needed money to keep Coral Rose going? You certainly did not have to agree to wed Blackthorn because of your finances! I hope you have effectively put a halt to all that nonsense!"

Katelin tried to make out his features in the dark room, but unable to, she wondered that he said nothing about her being a lady pirate. He seemed only to have heard what she had told him had been her reasons for agreeing to wed Alex Blackthorn. "I don't know why I didn't come to you, Garrick." She knew this was not the truth even as the words left her mouth. Her pride had kept her from making an appeal to this man. Her pride, and yes, her damnable stubbornness! "I was so confused, and I didn't know which way to turn. I thought at the time that you only cared for . . ." She could not complete the sentence.

He finished it for her. "You thought that I only desired your lovely body, did you?" There was a touch of humor in his voice, and Katelin felt her features explode in flame.

"There is that, I must admit." His hand swept over her naked length in a warm caress. "You do have the most tempting little body. But there is so much more. I would do anything within my power to see you happy, and if that means rescuing your brother's inheritance, I would be more than willing to do so."

"But I didn't know any of this! I felt so all alone, and when Alex began to pay me visits at Coral Rose, I thought I would do as most young women do, and wed for mutually satisfactory purposes. I could not go through with the engagement, though, once I had gained enough gold aboard the *Kat's Eye*. In truth, Garrick, I doubt if I would have ever been able to go through with marrying Alex, even if I had not become the captain of the *Kat's Eye*. There is something darkly mysterious about him that is not to my liking. The day I went to Shadow Mere to break off the engagement, he acted so strangely." Katelin felt a shiver course over her length with the remembrance. "He frightened me so terribly. I admit I behaved rather badly, and could not tell him the reason I had gone to his plantation."

Garrick felt the trembling that had taken hold of her, and tightening his arms around her, he assured,

"You don't have to go to Shadow Mere alone ever again, sweet. I will go there with you and we will finish this engagement once and for all." His words were a promise of protection and strength. "Now tell me, Kat, is it true that you fight with a sword as well as any man, and that you wear male attire?"

Once again Katelin heard the humor in his voice, and inwardly she marveled at such a man. Any other would feel threatened by her declaration that she was the captain of a notorious pirate vessel. "I took fencing lessons in London, and the clothes I wear while on the *Kat's Eye* were made by the wives of my crew."

"I am not surprised in the least," he declared. "Actually, my dear, nothing would surprise me where you are concerned. That night you were caught in Rose Bishop's establishment disguised as a young boy should have warned me what I was getting myself into." His husky laughter filled her ears.

"You mean that you hold no objections to my being the captain of the *Kat's Eye?*"

"Oh no, my love, I did not say that it was all right with me for the woman I love to risk her life upon the high seas in such a manner, but I admit that I understand how you could have been pulled along by the promise of adventure and a pirate's treasure."

He could understand her feelings? How could she not have seen this side of Garrick Steele in the past? How could she have let herself be so blinded by her misguided impressions of him, which had so totally allowed her to misjudge him? "This is to be the last trip that I will make aboard the *Kat's Eye*, Garrick. I plan to turn her over to the crew and they can do with her as they will. I am sure that Joshua will agree."

"That is a very wise decision, for in the future I plan to keep you so busy you won't have time to go pirating, or any other such foolishness." Garrick had made up his mind. He was allowing himself only another few weeks to try and capture Bristol Jack. Hopefully before this week was out he would have the outlaw pirate in the hold of the *Sea Witch* in irons, but if not, he would report back to London and explain that he had put in enough time for the British Navy. No one would be able to fault him, for he had given over three years of his life to Commodore Quinn's undertaking of trying to keep some law and order throughout the Caribbean.

"Busy how?" Katelin purred, right before Garrick's lips settled over her own. And as they lifted, she sighed, "Mmm, I might enjoy being kept so entertained, but I am not so sure that you will not grow bored after a time." That nagging fear of being deserted once again crept into her thoughts, and even though her words were spoken in jest, there was still that underlying moment of fear that her thoughts might not be so very far from the truth.

"Bored? With you, my beauty? Never!" He pushed her down upon the bed and rose up over her, capturing her beneath the strength of his large body. "Throughout this life and all eternity, I pledge to you, I will never grow bored with you, Kat."

"Do you mean it, Garrick?" she breathed softly, her heart hammering wildly against her chest.

"I will love you, Kat, from now until the stars fall from the heavens, until the ocean draws back its tide, until my body no longer holds breath." The

330

tender flame of his tongue streaked over her lips and sent spasms of sheer delight racing over her entire length.

She wanted to believe him. Oh how she longed to relax her guard and to be able to freely love and be loved in return. All those tender feelings she had held for him in the past, which she had forced herself to hide now came boldly to the surface. Some small voice in the back of her mind whispered, *You can trust him, Katelin. Take the chance for there may not be another.* This night aboard the *Sea Witch*, as the vessel rested upon the blue-green sea beneath a pirate moon, was magical, and Katelin was not lost to the potent arousal of her senses as she wound her arms around her lover's shoulders and drew him even closer.

With his own heartbeat pulsating against her breasts and his mouth plundering hers, Garrick held back nothing as for the first time he was given her full trust. He thought only of pleasing this woman who had somehow stolen into the very depths of his heart. Her soft, yielding body was like a temple of love, quenching his thirst with its heady liquid and setting his very soul afire with its passion.

Katelin was lost to a world of bittersweet passion as Garrick huskily whispered words of love and praise of her beauty into her ear. At this moment it mattered not at all about the tomorrows which would come. Only Garrick mattered! Only the sensations that he was evoking held any meaning. Caught within the raging power of such ecstasy, a spark quickened throughout her body and sent her mindlessly spiraling toward the brink of rapturous fulfillment.

Garrick's mouth slanted against hers and continued to skillfully conquer her over and over again. Lovingly he rained kisses down her slender throat, capturing a taut breast, his tongue circling the rose-tipped morsel with a warm wetness that drove Katelin mindless with desire. His hands roamed over her body at will, sliding gently over her shapely hips and lingering seductively at the crest of her woman's passion. His fondling continued until he brought her to such heights of rapture that she, with a deep-throated moan, thrust her lower body upward against his probing fingers, her body undulating and writhing with an unquenchable need for fulfillment. And just as she thought she could take no more of his searing torture, Garrick slid down the bed, and with a movement parted her legs and came between them, his enormous love tool filling her with a completeness that left her gasping aloud and clutching him tighter.

Their movements were totally encasing, leaving no room for thought as he moved atop her and she responded fully to every pulsating, rhythmic stirring within her depths. She was borne toward a goal of shattering wonder, his strong body atop hers filling her with passion's total saturation.

Wrapping her legs higher about his hips, she allowed Garrick to fill her even further, Katelin matching him need for need, movement for movement. Together they rode the trembling flow of ecstasy's rapture, gliding upon the wings of creation's bliss and sweeping high overhead toward the starry velvet heavens in the arms of seductive wonder. They were one, their heated murmurings of love sealing their oneness. As Garrick plunged deeply, a shattering chord caught and held within the center of Katelin's body and her length trembled from head to foot. She called out her lover's name, her body spinning into a vortex of shattering fulfillment.

As Garrick looked down into the passion-laced wonder upon Katelin's features, he also rushed over the zenith of rapture's brink, his large body quaking as his life-giving seed was pulled forth and spilled within the womb of the woman of his heart.

"Say that you will never leave me. Say that you will be mine and will become my bride," Garrick said as he clutched her tightly to him, not willing at this moment to release her even to draw a breath. At last he had brought her to that place wherein he sensed that she was giving herself over to him. Her heart, her thoughts, her very soul were united in their desire and need for him as his own need and desires were placed within her keeping, and he was not willing to chance that, with the light of the morning dawn, she would change her mind toward him once again. He had broken down that shell she used to ward off the world and her feelings for him, and he was not about to allow her time to build it up once again. He needed the commitment made by her own lips to keep him through the hours when she would not be at his side, and right then he swore to himself that there would be as few of those hours as possible.

"Become your bride?" Katelin gasped aloud as she tried to regain her breathing and also fought for some command of her senses. For a moment her thoughts were confused with the remembrance of Alex Blackthorn, her responsibilities at Coral Rose, and even her position as captain of the *Kat's Eye*, but the fact that Garrick wished her to become his bride stood out above all else! "You truly wish for me to be your wife?" she questioned with uncertainty as though fearing she had heard him incorrectly.

"I wish it with all my heart. I want you to be my wife, the mother of my children. The lovely face I look upon each morning when I awake." He declared all without a moment's second thought, then sealed the vow with a tender, all-consuming kiss that held the power to leave Katelin moaning softly against his broad chest.

"I need but a short time to finish up my business here in the Caribbean, and then we will be able to return to London."

"London?" Katelin's dark head rose from the comfortable position she had on his chest, her green gaze trying to glimpse his features.

"I have a home a few hours' ride outside of the city." He did not tell her it was a large estate with many servants; he would tell her the details at another time. "But if you prefer, there is a well-staffed brownstone not far from the palace."

"You have acquired all of this through your privateering?" Katelin questioned with some amazement. Perhaps she had not given his occupation enough consideration, she told herself.

Garrick's deep-throated laughter filled her ears. "My father was of some consequence in England and was a favorite of King George's. Though my stepmother would have willed it otherwise, his properties upon his death went to his only son."

Katelin digested this slowly. For some reason she had not thought such wealth to be at Garrick's disposal. He was so different from the many men she

334

had known in London who were of a habit of bragging about their wealth and flashing their jewels and peacock clothes. "My brother, Joshua, is only twelve years old. I am responsible for him until he comes of age." She knew that she was giving him one more reason to back out now while he was still able.

Garrick pulled her back upon his chest and lightly kissed the top of her head. "All the more reason for you to consent to becoming my wife. The boy will surely need me to teach him those things that only a man can." Feeling her beginning to squirm over his words, he amended, "We will both teach your brother what is needful for him to become a wise and generous-hearted young man."

That was more like it, Katelin thought, and settled herself in his arms once again. "You are sure that you are up to this, Garrick? I warn you, Joshua is not like other children his own age. He is very venturesome and mischievous." She wanted him to know what he was getting himself into right from the start.

"Much like his sister, hmm?" he joked. "I am up to any form of penance thrown before my path, to have you at my side always."

Katelin liked this answer and more of her insecurities were swept away. Garrick would be a wonderful example for Joshua to emulate, she told herself. Forgotten now was her earlier belief of his being a womanizing cad.

"Then it is settled?" Garrick questioned softly. "Tomorrow you will sail back to Saint Kitts and await me at Coral Rose. I want us to be married without delay."

"But what about Alex? I will need time to explain

to him that I cannot marry him. And Coral Rose? I will have to hire an overseer to stay on at the plantation to ensure that everything is run well in my absence. And there is also the *Kat's Eye*."

Garrick stilled her words with a kiss. "I will help you with everything once I return to Saint Kitts. And do not forget, you are not again to go to Shadow Mere alone. We will explain to Blackthorn together that regrettably for him you will not be able to wed him." Garrick was adamant about her not going back to Shadow Mere. He had felt the slight shiver that had coursed over her body when she had told him earlier about her visit to Blackthorn's plantation, and he would not have her put through such an ordeal again.

Grown accustomed to making her own decisions since arriving in the Caribbean, Katelin felt somewhat uncomfortable with his words. "Perhaps I will wait for your return to Saint Kitts to speak to Alex, but I will decide what to do with the *Kat's Eye*, and I will also choose an overseer for Coral Rose." She was not about to let just anyone take charge of the plantation and the people she had grown to love, and she was not about to willingly allow anyone to take over her life. The type of marriage she had in mind would be fifty-fifty—no man, not even Garrick Steele, would ever rule her!

As he had said jokingly earlier, his Kat was unlike most women, and once again her very words were pricking him with the truth of this fact. Well, at least she did concede on one point—not to go to Shadow Mere alone. "I guess I should take you back to the *Kat's Eye* now," he said reluctantly, and as she snuggled against the firmness of his large body, he told himself he would be counting the hours until they would no longer have to part.

Katelin knew that he was right and she should be returning to the *Kat's Eye*. For all she knew, at this very moment her crew was turning the island of Grande Terre upside down looking for her. The last she had seen of Tad and Slade, they had been in the company of Sonja, but that did not mean they had not turned around and searched for her and the handsome sultan who had been at her side. "I guess you're right. I should return to the *Kat's Eye*. I would not wish for Joshua and my men to worry needlessly." Her silken arms lightly brushed against his upper body as they wound around his neck, the fullness of her breasts pressing against his broad chest and forcing Garrick to claim an inward breath as her soft kiss-bruised lips coveted his own.

This was the first time she had boldly kissed him in such a manner and the act went straight to Garrick's heart, his tongue streaking across her lips. "If possible, I would wish us never to again part," he whispered below her mouth. "I would have you day and night within my arms and never grow tired of the temptation of your satin flesh."

Katelin's giggle touched his ears as her sweet breath mingled with his. "Day and night, my lord? Surely you have an overlarge appetite. But then I do admit that you are quite an overlarge man," she stated, and before he could say anything, her hand slowly wound its way over his chest and past his ribs to settle in a featherlike caress upon his manhood.

Instantly that large serpentlike shaft raised its marble head and filled her palm. "Like I said, quite large indeed!"

337

* * *

In the early hours of predawn, Garrick himself rowed Katelin in the small boat from the *Sea Witch* to the *Kat's Eye*. With a last parting kiss that bespoke the torture it would be for the couple to be separated, he at last released her and watched as she climbed the rope ladder to the deck of her ship. For a lingering minute he watched as she waved down to him from the railing of the *Kat's Eye*. He carried her smiling beauty in his mind as he rowed back to the *Sea Witch*.

It was just as Katclin left the deck and started down the companionway that a dark garbed figure ran past her and all but set her on her backside. Regaining her balance, she stared after the man, believing it one of her own crew. "He must have a hot wench awaiting him on the island!" she mumbled to herself as she continued on her way to her cabin.

Reaching her cabin, she found the door standing open. Perhaps Joshua had sought her out after he had returned from carnival. There was a lot she had to tell her brother when next she saw him. She knew that he would like Garrick as a better choice of a husband for her than Alex Blackthorn — or Old Cold Eyes, as he was more apt to call him.

Lighting the candle that sat in its holder near the bedstead, Katelin began to pull off the red flamenco outfit. Lord, she was tired, and perhaps she would even sleep late in the morning. Her men would probably welcome more time to spend on the island, she told herself, hoping they would not be too disappointed that they cut their stay on Grande Terre short by a day.

As she threw the dress across the bed, a slip of paper caught her eye as she reached to pull the lacings of her petticoats. Placing the rest of her underclothes with the gown, her hand reached out for the paper, noticing absently the manner in which the parchment had been ink-splattered and wrinkled.

Even as she read the brief message, Katelin shook her head, trying to clear it of her slow response. Her hours spent in Garrick's arms seemed to have dulled her wits. Stepping over to the candlelight, she studied the note.

If you value the life of your brother, do exactly as you are instructed. First — you are to tell no one at all that I hold your brother prisoner. Set sail with the morning tide for the island of Barbados. You will receive further instructions at Sal's tavern in Bridgetown. Do not tarry if you wish ever to see Joshua again.

The signature was a scrawl which she could just make out:

Bristol Jack.

Twenty-two

Katelin felt her knees beginning to buckle and slowly she slipped to a sitting position on the bed. Staring at the note in her hand, she murmured her brother's name aloud to the empty cabin. "Joshua." It was a soft cry of disbelief and agony. Still it was hard for her to fully take in the meaning of the words in the note: *Kidnapped . . . kidnapped . . . kidnapped!* It kept repeating itself over and over in her mind.

Crumbling the parchment up in her small fist, she hurriedly pulled on her blouse and breeches. Who had left this note on her bed? Her mind at last began to function. How did she know this was not some kind of hoax and Joshua was not at this moment in his hammock sleeping peacefully as he should be at this hour in the morning? Surely this Bristol Jack, this brigand pirate, had not stolen aboard the *Kat's Eye* and left her this message to follow him to Barbados! Suddenly she recalled the dark, hurrying figure that had almost toppled her in the companionway, and her fear for her brother instantly intensified.

Not bothering with her boots, she hurried from her cabin, and going down the companionway, past the galley, she entered the hold of the ship where the crew had their sleeping quarters. Katelin usually avoided this area of the ship in the early hours of the morning when the men were just rising and during the evenings while they readied themselves, between shifts, for sleep. But at this moment she had no thoughts of impropriety or a crewman's modesty. All her thoughts were centered on finding Joshua safe and sleeping soundly aboard the *Kat's Eye*.

It was dark as pitch down here in the bowels of the ship, and coming to the first hammock swinging freely between two thick ship's beams, she lightly called, "Joshua." She hated waking her men unnecessarily but there was no help for it, she told herself when she received no response and once again she called her brother's name, but this time somewhat louder.

"That be you, Captain? Be there something wrong?" Groggily, fair-haired Thomas pulled himself upright in the hammock she was standing near.

"I need to find my brother, Thomas. Can you point me to his hammock?" The desperation in her voice was not lost upon the man.

"I will do the deed for you, Captain. Why don't you wait out in the companionway?" Thomas was not a man to order his own captain about but he knew that most of the crew of the *Kat's Eye* wore little or nothing to sleep at night, and at this moment he himself was clutching a seldom-used woolen blanket over his naked loins. "I'll send the lad on out to you, Captain." He waited for her to leave the side of his hammock before jumping to his feet, and with his blanket wrapped around his midsection, he made his way to where Joshua slept.

Katelin was more than willing to make her way out of the hold and allow Thomas to search for her brother. She was as conscious as he of her surroundings, but once again she told herself that this could not be helped, as she felt the parchment still held tightly in her fist. She had to see for herself that her brother was safe.

A few minutes passed as Katelin silently paced outside in the companionway. The second that Thomas stepped out of the entrance of the hold, her worst fears took hold.

"The lad ain't in his bed, Captain. He must have stayed on the island for the night, 'cause Simon and Pete's hammocks are empty, too." Thomas had taken the time to pull on his baggy white pants and was hurriedly buttoning his shirt as he stood before his captain.

Katelin's features had visibly paled beneath the lantern light that filtered down the companionway. "Thomas, wake Tad, Dirk, and Slade and send them to my cabin."

Thomas plainly realized that something was very wrong. "I'm afraid that they ain't aboard ship either, ma'am." Seeing her distress, he forgot for the moment that she was his captain, and only saw her as a frightened woman. "Can I be helping you?" Like the rest of the crew aboard the *Kat's Eye* Thomas would do anything for his captain, and if she gave the word he would leave the ship this moment to go in search of her little brother and his fellow crewmen on the island.

"Wake the rest of the crew, Thomas, and send some of the men to the island to search for my brother as well as Simon and Pete! Make ready the *Kat's Eye* to set sail the minute Tad, Dirk, and Slade return to the ship." Katelin still prayed that the note was only a hoax and that her brother had indeed stayed the night on Grande Terre, but she could not take any chances, and time could mean her brother's life if this outlaw pirate Bristol Jack really had him aboard his ship.

Thomas did not question her, but quickly set out to do as instructed. As she turned and made her way back to her own cabin, he entered the hold and roused the men. He sent a group of four to the island to make the search for Joshua, Pete, and Simon, and two men he instructed to comb the taverns and ale houses for Slade, Dirk, and Tad. He was not sure what was going on, but by the look that had come across the captain's face when he had told her that her brother was not aboard ship, he knew something very serious had upset her.

In the captain's cabin Katelin found herself going over the note again and again. The thought came to her to send a message to Garrick and seek his help, but as quickly she discarded the notion. The note had said that she was to tell no one that her brother had been taken, and until she found out for sure that he was not sleeping peaceably somewhere on the island, she did not want to stir up any more trouble than she already had. And even if she found that her brother had been kidnapped, she knew that she could not tell anyone about his abduction. She would have to do as instructed and go to Barbados and to the tavern in Bridgetown, to find out what this Bristol Jack wanted in exchange for her brother.

The men who Thomas had designated to search out the island departed the *Kat's Eye* in one of the small boats and had not reached shore before Tad and Dirk were climbing the rope ladder on the side of the vessel. The activity aboard ship at this early hour startled them at first, but after speaking to Thomas and learning that the captain had come to the hold in search of her brother and, upon not finding him in his hammock, had given out instructions to ready the ship to set sail, both men hurried off to the captain's cabin.

They found Katelin at her desk with maps strewn across the top. Upon hearing the cabin door opening without a knock, Katelin gazed upward with hope that it was Joshua. Disappointment filled her features as she glimpsed Tad and Dirk, but some hope came back as she realized that these two men were more than her crewmen — they had become her friends, and she could turn to them in this hour of need.

"Thomas told us that the lad did not return to the ship. I see no reason to worry so soon, lass. More than likely Pete and Simon kept him hopping most of the evening and they found themselves a room on the island." Tad instantly tried to reassure her as he glimpsed the fear in the green eyes that were turned upon him.

"I hope you're right."

"Why would you think otherwise?" Dirk stepped closer to the desk and wondered why she would be poring over maps at this time of the morning. And remembering Thomas's words, and knowing, as all aboard the *Kat's Eye,* that they planned to remain on Grande Terre for one more day, he gazed at her questioningly.

"Look at this." She held out the crumpled piece of parchment for their inspection.

Both men peered at the piece of paper beneath the lantern light that burned brightly upon the desk. It was Tad who spoke up first. "Where did you get this note, lass?"

"It was lying on my bed when I returned to the *Kat's Eye* last night." She did not explain that she had returned to the ship only an hour or so ago.

"Did you see anyone? Did you question the crew? Who was posted to the deck watch?"

"You two are the first that I have shown the message to. I was hoping that someone was trying to play some kind of not so humorous game on me, and that Joshua would turn up soon."

"He still might, lass," Tad volunteered, but at the same time as his glance went over the signature on the message one last time, he held some very serious doubts.

"Why do you think this Bristol Jack would wish for me to go to Barbados? Do either of you have any idea what he could want from me or the *Kat's Eye?*" Katelin had been going over this question in her mind for the past hour, and hoped that some-

345

how one of these two faithful men would be able to supply her with the answer.

Dirk and Tad looked at each other before glancing back at her. "We haven't a clue, lass. This Bristol Jack is a real bad sort, but the *Kat's Eye* hasn't had a run-in with him or any member of his crew that I be knowing about."

"Perhaps it's the competition. I heard tell as he was looking for that Spanish galleon that we set upon sometime back," Dirk supplied.

"He and every other pirate ship in the Caribbean," Katelin mumbled as she remembered Sonja stating the same thing about the Spanish vessel at their first meeting.

"Perhaps it's the captain of the *Kat's Eye* herself that Bristol Jack has a desire to meet," Tad wondered but his words were stated softly aloud.

"That crossed my mind, but why would he not just approach me here on the island during carnival like everyone else we have met since we have been anchored off Grande Terre?"

"There be no telling with the likes of such a man, lass. The best thing that we can do for now is to wait for the search party to return, and then make our plans. The lad might well be on the island, and this could all be some ill-thought-up joke."

"I hope so." Katelin heard her own voice crack somewhat as she thought of the terror her brother would be feeling if he had been really taken hostage by this Bristol Jack. She knew that Joshua tried to appear brave at all times, but she also knew that much of his bravado in the face of fear

346

was an act. He was only a little boy, and as the minutes slowly passed, her own worry and fear increased. "Where is Slade? I thought he would be with you two." She tried to divert the conversation away from her brother for the time being before she fell to pieces right in front of these two men. "Did you both stay on the island last night?" And then remembering that Slade had been in their small group as they had roamed about Grande Terre last night, and that Dirk had not, she looked skeptically at the pair.

"It's more than likely that Slade got himself a room at Sammy Bates's tavern last night," Dirk volunteered, and with Katelin's green gaze still holding him, he squirmed under that questioning look. "Me and Slade sort of exchanged places as the night drew on. He stayed at the tavern and I went on with Tad here and Sonja."

Katelin's eyes widened. Did he mean that he had also gone aboard that fiery-haired woman's ship and been entertained in her cabin?

It was Tad who broke the moment with a hearty chuckle. "Now, lass, the truth of the telling is, that a woman with fire in her hair sometimes has a lot of loving to offer. Me and Dirk here just try to accommodate!"

Katelin knew that she should be shocked by such talk and in fact a few months ago she would have been. However, the crew of the *Kat's Eye* had showed her a life that was entirely different from her old one, and their coarse speech and manners were all a part of that new life. All she replied was, "Well, I hope that Slade is found before we

347

pull anchor."

"He'll be here, lass, don't you worry," Tad assured, still wearing his large grin.

And as though conjured up by those words, Slade stepped into the cabin after knocking once on the door. By the look he cast about the room, everyone knew that Joshua had not as yet been found. "John and Ben found me at the tavern. They told me that a search was going on for the boy and Simon and Pete. They haven't been found and the search party is gathering back on the beach. They will be returning to the *Kat's Eye* as soon as the small boat is rowed back to shore for them."

"Take a look at this," said Katelin. Slade was given the note lying on the desk, and as Katelin drew deep breaths to try and steady her emotions, the large man silently read the instructions that had been left for his captain. His gaze rose from the paper and across the desk to settle upon the pale features of the woman he knew as Kat, and then as quickly his gaze went to Tad and Dirk standing beside him. "What do you think?"

"We're not sure why Jack wants the *Kat's Eye* to go to Barbados, but I think we are all in agreement now: he has the boy and more than likely has shanghaied Pete and Simon."

"Bristol Jack has no rules to guide him; that's why he is so feared. We might better find us some help. Should we go to the *Sea Witch?*" Slade's gaze again held his captain.

Katelin felt her face beginning to flush with his questioning gaze.

348

It was Tad, though, who spoke up. "What would we go to the *Sea Witch* for? The captain of the *Lynx* would be more than willing to throw in her lot with the *Kat's Eye.*"

"I met the first mate of the *Sea Witch* last eve. He's known as Lucas Bennett. We had ourselves a long, friendly talk, and he appeared a nice enough sort." Still Slade stared across the desk at Katelin as though he was waiting for her to make some sort of statement that would confirm the information the first mate had given him, that the sultan from last night was in fact Garrick Steele, the captain of the *Sea Witch* and his captain had months ago been aboard his ship.

"We cannot get help from either ship!" Katelin declared, and rose to her feet. Leaving the desk, she tried to avoid Slade's questioning look. "The note states that we are to keep this to ourselves. Joshua's life could be in danger if it were found out that we sought help!" Bright tears filled her eyes as she thought of her brother being held prisoner.

"You're right, lass." Tad went to her, and placing a strong arm around her shoulders, he offered with as much confidence in his tone as he could muster, "We'll go to Barbados if we have to and we'll get the lad back ourselves!"

It was not until late that evening when Katelin retired to her lonely bed that her thoughts went to Garrick. Of course he would know that the *Kat's Eye* had pulled anchor and left Grande Terre, and he would assume that Katelin was returning to Saint Kitts and Coral Rose, to await his return to claim her as his bride. He would never have imagined that she was on her way to Barbados to meet the infamous blackguard, Bristol Jack. Katelin brushed away a lone tear with the back of her wrist as she recalled the brief time spent in Garrick's arms and how secure she had felt.

If only she could have done as Slade had suggested and sought Garrick's help in finding her brother. If only she were able to confide in the man who claimed to love her and allow him to help her shoulder this ordeal that had been forced upon her. But Katelin knew that she could not take the chance that someone would report back to the outlaw pirate that she had told someone about her brother's abduction. She could not risk Joshua's life, because she knew without being told that Garrick Steele would have rushed to her aid, and in so doing might have endangered the very one she sought to save.

More tears fell as Katelin's fear for her brother's life set her body to trembling beneath the silken covers. Some dark premonition lurked within the shadows of her mind, warning that the time spent aboard the *Sea Witch* last night with Garrick might well be the last time she would ever know true love. To at last have found the one man in all the world she could love and who in return loved her, only to have that love so quickly taken from her, left an ache in her heart that was more than she could bear.

* * *

At the time that Katelin was trying to find rest, Sonja was being rowed out to the *Sea Witch*. Boarding the privateer vessel, she was immediately shown to the captain's cabin.

After the first mate, Lucas Bennett, silently closed the cabin door, Sonja flashed her blue eyes at Garrick behind his desk, her walk seductively ensnaring as she began to make her way to him, and her hands brushed back the strands of bright copper curls hanging over her breasts. Her huskily alluring laugh filled the space of the cabin as she glimpsed the sparkle that ignited within the silver-blue eyes.

"What are you doing here, Sonja? I thought we had a meeting at Sammy Bates's tavern later tonight." Garrick's words were casually spoken as he closed his ship's ledger and leaned back in his chair.

"I thought to save you the trip." Her words were as seductive as her laugh, and gaining the desk she stepped around it, her pale, slender fingers reaching out and trailing the length of Garrick's muscular arm where his shirtsleeve had been rolled up.

Garrick picked up her meaning, but appearing not to have noticed her attentions, he easily stood to his full height. "Let me pour us a glass of wine." He circled the desk to get the decanter and glasses. "I thought you had set up the meeting with Bristol Jack for this evening. Won't he be waiting at the tavern?"

Sonja's long, shapely legs followed his steps, and by the time he finished pouring, she was standing close to his side, her full breasts brushing his forearm as he handed her a glass of the amber wine. "You and the little flamenco dancer disappeared last night all too quickly, Garrick. I thought it best not to take such a chance this evening." She took a sip of the brew, wishing it was something stronger.

"But what about Bristol Jack?" Garrick didn't want to have to turn her down point blank, he had hoped that he would be able to avoid her attentions this evening during the meeting she had promised to set up with Jack. He was a bit confused as to what had happened to their earlier plans, but he wanted to act interested enough in her till at least he was introduced to Bristol Jack.

Sonja threw her titian head back, her eyes caressing the expanse of throat and chest that was exposed where Garrick's top buttons were undone. "And what about Jack?" she murmured, her hand reaching out to fondle the flesh that her gaze was consuming.

Again Garrick avoided her touch by a movement—picking up his own glass of wine, he stepped away from the desk. "You told me last night that you had set up a meeting between Bristol Jack and me." He drank down the contents of his glass.

"That was last night. Tonight it is just you and I, alone here in your cabin." Sonja advanced, her full hips swaying in a provocative fashion that no man could misunderstand.

This was definitely not going at all well, Garrick thought to himself when once again Sonja's amorous figure was pressed up against his length. "Listen, Sonja, I think there is something I should explain," he at last said when both of her hands snaked out and firmly wrapped around his shoulders, her abundant curves boldly leaning into his body.

"Why don't you kiss me first? We can talk later . . . much, much later."

Having to use some strength because Sonja was a full-figured woman who had her mind set upon pressing her lush lips against his, Garrick used both hands to unclamp himself from her grip around his neck. "I think we should talk now, not later," he stated. "It's about Kat."

"Oh, her." Sonja pouted, and downing the wine in her glass, she stepped to the desk and refilled it. "Well, get on with whatever it is you want to say, so we can enjoy the rest of the evening. I guess you discovered who the flamenco dancer was after all."

Garrick nodded his head in agreement. "I knew who she was the minute she walked into the tavern."

"You knew who she was? Why, the little bitch never told me that she knew you!" Sonja laughed loudly. "I guess she thought she was fooling you with the mask." Her smile remained on her lips as she believed that the joke had been on the other woman.

"Kat and I met sometime back, and the truth is that we are going to be married." There, he had said the words that he knew would more than likely ruin his chance of gaining that meeting with Bristol Jack, but he told himself that some things

353

just could not be helped. He was not a man who could fall into bed with a woman when his heart belonged to another, no matter the price.

"Drat it all, I ain't never seen a woman who has such a hold over men!" Sonja declared and downed the wine in a single gulp. She had planned to find out just what kind of man the captain of the *Sea Witch* was this night. By the size of him, she had imagined a wild, lust-filled time to be shared upon his bed, but instead he was claiming that he was heartsick over another woman, and a woman who was definitely beginning to get under Sonja's skin!

"What do you mean by that? What men does Kat have a hold over beside myself?" Instantly Garrick's jealousy flared to the surface with her statement.

"Her crew for one. I had myself one hell of a good time with Tad and Dirk last night when we returned to the *Lynx*. But both men when they speak about their captain sound as though they're talking about some precious goddess or something!"

Garrick could well imagine that she had had a good time, and the two men also, and her statement about the manner in which they spoke of their captain did not strike him as anything but respectful.

"Bristol Jack for another!"

"Bristol Jack? What has he to do with Kat?"

"By what I was told by one of my crewmen, she's off chasing after him. Why do you think he didn't show for the meeting I had set up?"

"Kat is chasing after Bristol Jack?" Garrick couldn't believe what Sonja was saying. Why on earth would Kat be pursuing the outlaw pirate? She was supposed to be returning to Saint Kitts!

"Lonny, that's my helmsman, he has a friend who is a crewman aboard the *Black Dragon,* Jack's ship. Last night he met up with him in an ale house on the island, and he told Lonny that they were setting sail before morning. Said something about Jack stealing that brat kid that Kat drags around with her. Said as how Jack was planning to have the Kat follow him to Barbados, but he wasn't sure why."

"That's why the *Kat's Eye* left so early this morning," Garrick mumbled aloud, feeling as though the very wind had been knocked out of him. *Bristol Jack had Joshua and Kat was going after him!* But why had she not come to him?

"Yeah, I heard tell today on the island that she sent in a crew to search for the kid. He wasn't found, and neither were the two men who had been with him the night before. The *Kat's Eye* pulled anchor when the crew returned, and with the vessel went Tad and Dirk, some of the best sport I've had in some time." Sonja seemed unconcerned about Kat and Joshua; her only thoughts appeared to be on the two crewmen who had sailed away on the *Kat's Eye*, and her own disappointment that she would be deprived of their company.

Garrick had little time to stand and talk to Sonja. "I have to catch her!" He started toward the cabin door without giving his company a second thought.

"Hey, wait just a minute. If you're going to

chase down the *Kat's Eye*, I'm coming along, too!"

"You?" Garrick turned back into the room. He had not thought that Sonja cared that much about Kat.

"Yeah, the *Lynx* will be ready within the hour. I was going to ask Tad this evening to become my first mate aboard the *Lynx*. I ain't taking no more chances where men are concerned. Like I said, I ain't had such sport as I've had in the last couple of days, in some time!"

Garrick at the moment didn't give a damn what her reason was for going along with him to Barbados. All he cared about was making sure that Kat remained unharmed and that her brother was rescued. Staring at the bold and brassy woman a full moment, he finally nodded his dark head. "I set sail in an hour, no longer. Any crewmen who are still on the island after that get left!" He might well be in need of her and her crew when they arrived in Barbados, he told himself.

"An hour then." Sonja grinned widely. "I never did like Jack to begin with," she murmured when she stepped past him and through the cabin door.

Twenty-three

"I am your captain, and I'm telling all three of you that I will go into Bridgetown alone," Katelin heatedly declared. Since the *Kat's Eye* had docked at Bridgetown, she had been in her cabin arguing with Slade, Tad, and Dirk.

"But lass, you are being foolhardy. Who's to say Bristol Jack won't just take you like he did the boy? Then where will you both be? You won't be able to do the lad a bit of good alone." Tad tried again to appeal to her to allow them to go along with her to Sal's tavern.

Katelin had already reviewed everything that Bristol Jack had said in the note, but she could not take the chance that this pirate would become angry and not tell her where her brother was being held. She had to do it the way she had been instructed—it might be the only way she would ever see Joshua again! Shaking her head stubbornly, she flashed her green eyes over each of the men. "You know that I can take care of myself; I don't need your help in this." She tucked the dagger into its sheath at her hip.

"All right, Captain. I guess there ain't nothing we

357

can say to sway your mind," Dirk conceded, but the two men at his side turned on him.

"You know she can't be going alone!" Tad heatedly shouted.

"She'll not be leaving the *Kat's Eye* without me at her side," Slade added just as heatedly.

"She's good and well able to care for herself." Dirk directed a look upon the two that told them to settle down for the time being; he had a plan.

Though Tad and Slade still mumbled softly their disagreement, they no longer voiced their intention of going along with Katelin to Sal's tavern to meet whoever it was that Bristol Jack would have waiting for her.

"I would hope that this won't take too long. Whatever it is that Bristol Jack wants in exchange for Joshua, I'll give him. Keep the crew aboard ship. As soon as this thing is settled and I have Joshua at my side, we'll set sail." She wanted to put as much distance between the *Kat's Eye* and the crew of the *Black Dragon* as possible.

"The crew will be here waiting for you, Captain." Again it was Dirk who spoke up.

Strapping her sword belt to her side, Katelin nodded her dark head toward her men before she started toward the cabin door. The only thing at the moment that she had on her mind was meeting this Bristol Jack and finding out why he had kidnapped her brother.

The minute she was out the door, Tad and Slade turned their attention fully upon Dirk. "This had best be good, man. We should not have let her go alone." Tad's dark look held upon his friend.

"We'll just let her think that she's going at this

358

lone. We'll give her time to leave ship and then we'll
ollow. It's better than arguing with her."

The idea was simple enough and positive enough
or all three men to nod their heads in agreement.

"We had best go and fetch our weapons then,
oyos." Tad started to the cabin door, not watching to
ee who followed him. He for one would not be far
rom Katelin if she were to find herself in trouble.

It was early evening and Sal's tavern was along the
eedy portion of the wharf area. Katelin, with her
hand resting lightly upon the hilt of her jewel-en-
rusted dagger, made her way along the waterfront
and through the swinging double doors of the tavern.

The interior was much like all the other taverns
and ale houses that Katelin had been in over the past
few months, but Sal's seemed a shade more threatening. Silence hung heavily in the air as the patrons
wearily glanced in her direction. She noticed that
several men standing along the bar bent their heads
ow as her gaze went over them, and the two men at
the end of the bar turned their backs completely.
Those sitting at the tables appeared just as traitorous
and secretive, and as several pairs of eyes touched
her, Katelin felt her skin beginning to crawl.

There were no women whom she could see in the
tavern, not even a serving girl for her to approach.
With tentative steps she moved toward the end of the
bar, and looking down the length at the fat tavern
keeper, she nodded her head in his direction.

With a noticeable limp, the heavy man made his
way to the end of the bar. "What ya be needing?" His
beady black eyes went over her from head to foot in a
single long glance.

"I'm here to meet someone," Katelin nervously responded, keeping her voice low, as the tavern still appeared to hold its silence.

"You blokes go about your own business." The fat man's eyes traveled around the pub and instantly mugs were lifted and talk resumed. "Now spit it out Who you be wanting?"

At least Katelin did not have to fear that everyone was listening to her, but the bartender with his sharp beady eyes caused her knees to tremble and at the moment she prayed that it wasn't noticeable. It wouldn't do for whomever she was here to meet to believe her weak just because she was a woman. "Bristol Jack," she finally got out, but kept the name as low as possible, hoping that she would not draw attention to herself again.

The man seemed to study her for a long minute. "And who might you be?"

She noticed that his tone had lowered also. "I am known as the Kat."

The tavern owner did not appear surprised at her answer. "There's a table over there in the back corner. Have yourself a seat." He turned away from her, then waddled back down the length of the bar.

Looking over the dimly lit, smoke-filled interior, Katelin searched out the table that he had told her to take. There in the very back of the establishment was a small table near the door. Trying to keep her gaze on the table and not the men who appeared to find her even more interesting now that she was stepping into their midst, she at last reached her table. With a soft expelling of clutched breath and her hand still upon her dagger, Katelin sat with her back against the wall, her gaze traveling over the men who were now all looking in her direction.

It was one of the two men standing at the end of the bar who had turned their backs when she had first entered the tavern who now approached her table. "Sal said that you be the Kat?"

Katelin's green eyes rose from the mug of ale he set down on the table and peered up into his hard features. His dark eyes studied her with the same intense manner. The pale scar running from his right cheek to his chin stood out starkly against the darkly tanned face. Slowly her dark head with its red sash nodded. "I am the Kat. Who are you?" She wondered if this was Bristol Jack himself, for she had never met the pirate and would not recognize him. But she would not be surprised to find this man to be him, because he appeared dangerous and very cunning; it was apparent that he held all the markings of a killer, or an outlaw pirate.

"Don't ask questions. Drink your ale down, and we'll be off." His voice was harsh, leaving no room for argument.

At first Katelin thought to refuse the order, not given to a nature to easily comply to a strange man's demands, but quickly she nodded her head. She had no choice in the matter if she wanted to see her brother again. Lifting the mug to her lips, she tilted her head back and gulped down a measure of the bitter-tasting brew.

The man watched her silently for a minute before he nodded his head. Turning back around, he gazed around the tavern, and at the same time Katelin noticed that the man he had been standing with at the bar had disappeared.

As she waited for whatever it was the man appeared to be watching for, Katelin's hand went to her

361

head. Everything seemed to be swimming before her eyes in a hazy blur. "What is happening?" she got out, and still holding some of her senses, she realized that she had been drugged. She would have tried to leave the table, to escape this man who was looking at her so darkly, but a numbness had crept over her limbs; even her tongue felt thick in her mouth.

Without a word spoken, the man standing before her reached out and took hold of her arm, and in a matter of seconds, she was being pushed through the back door and into the arms of another man waiting in the alley behind the tavern.

Tad was the first to see Katelin being pulled by the tall man through the back door. From where the three men stood near the front swinging doors, he burst into the tavern with Slade and Dirk not far behind.

"You blokes be wanting something to drink?" The fat man behind the bar shouted as he watched the three large men run into the tavern and start toward the back door. Being ignored, he shouted louder, "Now that ain't any way to be acting. Men, I think these fellows need to be taught some manners!"

At this, every man within the tavern converged upon the three who had just entered. Tad was almost near the back door when the first punch landed upon his chin. Striking the man back with a beefy punch that sent him reeling into a small group, Tad took hold of the knob on the back door.

The door didn't budge, and even as Tad fought off his attackers, he realized that the door had been locked from without.

Slade and Dirk were in it up to their necks, their fists sailing through the air and connecting with a chin or an eye. It was not until they heard Tad shout that the door was barred, that the three of them began to fight their way toward the front door of the tavern. Slugging men out of their path, they at last reached the front swinging doors.

"Now you mates be coming on back to Sal's place any old time," the fat man behind the bar shouted out with some laughter in the tone as the three went through the front door, and a chorus of loud voices were called out in hearty agreement to the invitation.

"I'd like to be coming back with the entire crew of the *Kat's Eye!* We'd be showing these rowdy landlubbers a thing or two about fighting!" Slade declared angrily as he wiped away a splattering of blood from his mouth and hurriedly followed Tad and Dirk down the wharf until they came to the alley path that led to the back of Sal's tavern.

The alley was empty, but there was a lantern burning that had been hung on a beam on the back of the building, and tracks from a buggy could be seen in the dusty path at their feet.

"Damn their mangy hides to hell!" Tad swore loudly. "They've taken the lass! We'll have to get back to the *Kat's Eye* and get more help to search out the island!"

Shoved into the back of a buckboard wagon by the rough hands of the man who had been waiting in the alley, Katelin was powerless to resist as a moldy-smelling blanket was thrown over her prone figure and the two men climbed atop the open seat and called the pair of horses into motion.

She had not drunk enough of the tainted ale for it

to knock her out, but Katelin could not find the strength to push the blanket away and attempt to jump out of the wagon. She knew that her weapons had not even been taken from her, but reaching her hand down to the hilt of her sword or dagger also would be too much of an effort at this time. *God, why had she been so stupid as to go to Sal's tavern alone? If any one of her crew had been with her, this would never have happened. Now not only was Joshua a prisoner to this Bristol Jack, but she also was in his power!*

The wagon ride was a frantic careening excursion, down one street and up another. The man with the pale scar on his face, Katelin thought, must be the driver, for she could hear him shouting at the team as he directed them on a path that led out of Bridgetown and over a little used, bumpy path that circled the beach and came to a halt near a small bay.

The *Black Dragon* was anchored offshore, a few miles from Bridgetown, in order that the vessel could remain hidden from any other ship that might be searching for them. The two men wasted little time after the wagon came to a dashing stop. Jumping down from the seat, they hurriedly uncovered Katelin and pulled her to the ground between them.

"Did you have any trouble getting her?" one of the pair of men waiting near a small boat questioned, his busy gaze trying to make out her figure and features beneath the moonlight.

"It t'were as easy as taking candy from a baby. She came along all by herself just like Jack said he thought she would." With this answer, Katelin was put into the small boat by the two men who had taken her from the tavern, and the small boat was rowed out to the *Black Dragon*.

Katelin could see the dark shape of the large ship looming closer and closer to them; she could hear the rough talk of the sailors, and feel the heavy hand of those who held her. It was like a nightmare and she was powerless to do anything but be swept along with the force of the terror that was being played out around her.

As the small boat hit the larger vessel, strong hands drew Katelin against a hard chest, as she was carried up the rope ladder, then carried across the deck of the *Black Dragon*.

Scarface, as Katelin was now naming the man who had approached her in the tavern, knocked lightly upon a closed door, before stepping into the ship's cabin.

"Just dump her on the bed," a gruff voice ordered from across the room. "Let her sleep it off for a while and then you can bring in the boy for her to see. She might as well have the satisfaction of knowing that he's still alive."

The one talking must be Bristol Jack. And he must surely be talking about her brother! These were the last thoughts that came to Katelin as she was thrown upon a large bed and darkness descended upon her.

Some hours later, in the early morning, Katelin awoke to feel the motion of the ship. Slowly she regained some of her senses, her hand reaching to her waist for her dagger or sword. Finding both had been removed, she once again fell into exhausted slumber.

A groan filled Katelin's ears, and as she groggily pulled herself to her elbows, she realized the sound had come from her own lips. Fighting off the haze that seemed to linger over her mind, she shook her head to clear her thoughts.

Looking around, she knew that she was inside a ship's cabin, but by the discarded clothing lying around and the ill-kept condition of the cabin, she knew that it was not a ship she had ever been on before. She must be aboard the *Black Dragon*. The thought assaulted her, and with it she remembered Sal's tavern. She could remember little more after the man with the scar had approached her table and she had drunk the ale.

Pulling herself to the side of the bed, she quickly grabbed her head and another moan filled the cabin. For a minute everything seemed to be swimming around her. She stilled her movements in order to relax the heavy pounding in her skull.

The first thing she had to do was get out of this cabin and try to find Joshua, she told herself, but discovered quickly enough that every movement brought about the pounding once again.

Just as Katelin was about to put her feet on the wooden floor, the cabin door was thrown open and a large, frightening-looking man stepped into the room. He had a full, dark beard which covered much of his face, his hair was hanging long and tangled down his back, and a dangling hoop earring could be seen in one ear. As his dark eyes set beneath thick, bushy brows gazed upon her, Katelin felt herself beginning to cringe backward.

There was a greedy light in the passionless depths of the stare that Bristol Jack directed upon the woman in his bed. No wonder Blackthorn wanted the wench, he thought to himself, as he wondered if he had ever seen a more desirable creature in his life.

Even with her disheveled, drug-induced appearance, or perhaps because of it, she was beautiful. "You're the woman captain of the *Kat's Eye* and known as the Kat?" his gruff voice questioned, wanting to make sure for himself that no mistake had been made by his men. And with the thought, deep inside he hoped that she would deny the claim to the name, for in so doing he would not have to hand her over to Blackthorn; he would keep her for himself! Perhaps he would even take her along on his venture to the southern coast of Africa when he became a slaver. The nights with only his crew for company aboard the *Black Dragon* were lately becoming far too boring.

At that moment there was nothing Katelin would have liked better than to deny that she was the Kat, the woman he had lured to the island of Barbados, and whom he believed his men had kidnapped from Sal's tavern, but knowing that her brother's very life was at stake, she slowly nodded her head, the movement bringing another moan from her lips as her hands returned to that throbbing portion of her body.

A spark of disappointment filled the dark eyes that lingered upon her an added minute. Turning to his desk, Bristol Jack poured some liquid into a glass and approached the bed. "Here, drink this," he commanded as he held out the glass for her.

Katelin cringed even farther upon the bed with his nearness.

"Take it, it will clear your head."

The dark eyes held upon her, and as Katelin's slender hand reached for the glass, it was visibly shaking.

"By the tell of it from the boy, I would expect you to have more grit than that," Jack stated as he remembered all of the threats that had been heaped upon his head in expression of what the kid's big sister would do to him when she caught up with the *Black Dragon*.

"Is Joshua all right? You better not have harmed him!" This statement was almost laughable, Katelin knew as she looked upon the large, brutal-appearing man.

"Drink it!" he ordered once again, refusing to answer any questions until she did as told.

Katelin gazed down at the yellowish-looking liquid in the glass and remembered the last time she had drunk what she was told, she had been drugged. Feeling the dark eyes resting on her, she slowly drew the glass to her lips, and sipping a small portion, she found it not too distasteful. Seeing no way out, she tilted the glass back and finished the drink.

"In a few minutes your head should clear," the brute stated and turned away from the bed. Going to the washstand across the cabin, he peered into the mirror for a few seconds as though he wondered at the sight before him. Bending over the washbowl, he splashed some water over his face, and throwing his head back, he allowed the droplets to fly about the room. With his fingers, which he ran through his hair and beard, he calmed the wild mass somewhat. With the finish of this short toilet, he turned back to the bed, his dark eyes holding on his captive, and with the contact, he once again found himself reluctant to turn this woman over to Blackthorn.

Katelin did find the pounding in her head to be easing somewhat. Taking a deep breath as she stared at the large man across the cabin, she questioned, "What do you want in exchange for my brother?" She tried to make her voice sound steady, even though her heart was racing out of control.

"I want nothing in exchange. I have what I need."

"And what is that?"

"You!"

"Me?" Katelin gasped aloud. "But I thought you were holding my brother for some kind of ransom. Why would you want me?" Katelin tried to keep her wits about her. She had never met this Bristol Jack before in her life. She knew there had to be some reason why he would wish to abduct her.

Jack had been instructed early in his career never to divulge Blackthorn's name, so without doing so, he could only be evasive in his responses. "The ransom is the Kat, the captain of the *Kat's Eye!*"

"Will my brother be released then?" Katelin's breath seemed to hold as she awaited his answer, all her hope pinned on his answer being yes.

"That's not up to me to decide."

"Not up to you?" In the back of Katelin's mind she had wondered why this unkempt brute had not assaulted her here upon his bed, why he had been keeping a distance between them, and now she had her answer. He had abducted her and her brother for someone else!

Twenty-four

The *Sea Witch* and the *Lynx* also made good time arriving at Barbados. Docking in Bridgetown, Garrick was hard-pressed to stand silently along the railing of his ship to wait for his crew to secure the vessel along the dock. His first mate had pointed out the *Kat's Eye* as they were approaching the dock area, and Garrick desired little more at the moment than to leave his ship and find Katelin.

By the time the *Sea Witch* was tied off, and Garrick impatiently jumped the few feet from ship to the wooden wharf, the *Lynx* was also docking. Not waiting for the *Lynx*'s lady captain to accompany him, Garrick hurried toward the section of the docks where the *Kat's Eye* was secured.

Stepping quickly across the planking that was drawn from deck to wharf, Garrick's silver-blue gaze traveled over the space of the ship's deck, seeking out some sign that would lead him to Katelin.

"Ho, what say you be doing aboard the *Kat's Eye*, mate?" The call traveled across the deck of the ship and Garrick glimpsed the tall figure of a seaman approaching him.

"I need to speak with your captain."

"And who might be calling?" There was suspicion in the question, and as Slade came face to face with the large man who had stepped aboard the *Kat's Eye* without invitation, his hand rested upon the hilt of his large knife at his side.

"Tell her that the captain of the *Sea Witch* wishes to see her." Garrick was sure that Katelin would want to see him, even though the man before him seemed averse to allow him any farther aboard the vessel.

The crew of the *Kat's Eye* had searched the town over for some sign of their captain, and it had only been with the breaking of dawn that most of the crew had returned exhausted to the ship. Slade had remained awake to claim first watch while the rest of the crew had been allowed a few hours' rest. But before Tad and Dirk had retired to their hammocks in the hold, the three men had talked about the possibility that someone from Bristol Jack's crew would approach the *Kat's Eye* with a demand for ransom for both Joshua and their captain. As Slade eyed the large man before him, his fingers itched to pull the knife out of its sheath, but he forced himself not to act too hasty. If they were to find out where the outlaw pirate and his crew had taken his captain and her brother, he must first see if this man held the information they needed. "And how do I be knowing for sure that you're a ship's captain?" As far as he knew, the *Sea Witch* was anchored off the island of Grande Terre.

Garrick had not imagined that he would be faced with a sentry before he could make sure that Katelin was safe. His anger was beginning to mount as he declared, "I don't give a damn what you think, man. Go and tell your captain that Garrick Steele is waiting to speak with her."

The man appeared pretty intent upon seeing the Kat, and this fact alone is what stayed Slade's knife from leaving its sheath. "Wait here," he demanded. He would go and wake Tad and Dirk and let them decide what action to take.

Expecting the large man to go straight to Katelin and tell her of his presence on the *Kat's Eye*, Garrick was surprised when Slade returned with two more men. These two he recognized, though he knew that they would more than likely not recognize him without his sultan's costume. "Where is Kat?" he questioned in a hard voice as his worry increased. Why were these men stalling? he questioned himself. Had Kat already left the *Kat's Eye* to meet with Bristol Jack? And with this thought, his anxiety increased.

"Who be wanting to know?" There was something oddly familiar about this large man, but Tad for the moment was at a loss.

Garrick was not about to go all through this again with these two men. He was just about to push them aside, not caring that the three-to-one odds were in their favor, and go search for Katelin for himself. It was in that moment, though, that Sonja stepped across the gangplank that led to the deck of the *Kat's Eye*.

"Did you find her, Garrick?"

"Nay, these lugheads won't get out of the way!"

"Do you know this fellow, Sonja?" Slade questioned, more than a little surprised to find Sonja here in Bridgetown.

"What you be doing here, lass?" Tad asked the question that was on all their minds.

"Do you think that I would let you get away from me that easy, Tad?" Her blue eyes flashed as she threw back her red locks from her shoulder in a teasing manner. "The *Lynx* sailed from Grande Terre along with the *Sea Witch*, whose captain here wants a few words with the Kat," Sonja added on a more serious note, as she also wondered where Kat was at the moment.

Once again the men looked toward Garrick. "He claimed that he was a ship's captain," Slade confessed.

"You always did hold a suspicious nature, Slade." Sonja grinned. "But if he claimed it, you can believe him, or perhaps you would believe that he was also the sultan during carnival on Grande Terre." She glimpsed a light of recognition coming into his eyes. "Now where is Kat? My crewman was told that the *Kat's Eye* sailed to Barbados to meet up with Bristol Jack. He said something about the kid being stolen."

"You're right, lass. Yesterday evening she left the *Kat's Eye* and went to Sal's tavern to meet up with that good-for-nothing blackguard."

Before Tad could continue, Garrick had advanced upon him, his large hand reaching out and taking hold of the front of his shirt. "Where is she?" All of his anger and worry were combined in the words that came out in a deep growl.

Tad usually feared no man, but there was something in this man's eyes that told him he best be careful how he answered. There was no help for it, though, he realized — the truth was their captain had been stolen, too, and though they had searched high and low, they could find no sign of her or the *Black Dragon*. Taking a deep breath, he looked the man eye for eye. "They stole the lass, too."

"You mean you men allowed her to go alone?" Garrick's temper was at the boiling point as his fist tightened upon Tad's shirt, and his cold stare included Slade

373

and Dirk.

Tad jerked himself free of the angry man's grip. "It weren't like that, Captain. The lass insisted that no one go along. She feared Jack wouldn't take her to the lad if she went to Sal's tavern with any of her crew."

"And you men allowed it?" Garrick would have reached out again for the man and this time he would have throttled him right here on the deck of his own ship, except for Sonja grabbing hold of his arm.

"Hear him out, Garrick!" She, like the men, could feel the barely contained tension that filled the large man.

"That was what I was trying to say. We followed the lass to the tavern and stayed a distance outside the front door. A man standing near the bar approached her, and before we could get to the back of the tavern, he was pushing her through the back door."

Some of Garrick's anger began to slip away in disbelief. The woman whom he loved, his beautiful Kat, had been abducted!

"Every man in the tavern turned on us, Captain. We had to fight to get to the back door, and finding it barred from outside, we had to fight our way back out the front door. We found tracks made by a wagon out in the alley behind the tavern, but there was no sign of the lass."

"Have you had a search of the island?" It was Sonja who questioned.

"Aye, lass, but there is no sign that the *Black Dragon* ever came to Bridgetown. We searched the night through and returned only to catch a few hours' sleep, before we set out again."

"Are you men sure that it was Jack who abducted her?" Garrick's blood felt as though it were chilled within his veins.

"We watched her speak to the fat man behind the bar, who we later learned is called Sal and is as crooked as the worst sort of brigand. He sent her to a table in the back of the tavern near the door, then the man approached her with a mug of ale. It was plain that they had been waiting for her, Captain." It was Dirk who answered Garrick's question.

"Then we had best set our own crews to join in with the search," Sonja offered, knowing no other positive move to make at the moment, and winning a smile of gratitude from Tad and the other men.

"Has there been a search made along the coast?" Garrick questioned, knowing that the outlaw pirate may well have kept the *Black Dragon* out of sight.

Tad still felt somewhat uneasy in the presence of this man. He was reluctant to answer many more of his questions.

Sonja must have read Tad's thoughts by the way the Irish hunk, as she thought of him in her mind, did not answer his question right away. "Listen, Tad, Garrick here has as much at stake in trying to find your captain as any of you men. The night of carnival, as I already tried to tell you, he was dressed as the sultan and Kat disappeared with him, if you remember."

The three men turned their glances from Sonja to Garrick as though trying to discern for themselves if indeed he had been the large man dressed in the white sultan's costume. They must have believed Sonja, for slowly their heads began to nod with understanding. But glimpsing Tad still reluctant, she added, "The Kat is going to wed Garrick. That is if we can rescue her!"

All three men seemed more than surprised with this latest remark. Finally Dirk spoke up. "The captain never said anything about getting married. The boy once said something about a Blackthorn fellow."

"And did she have a habit of telling her crewmen everything?" Sonja was beginning to feel her own temper flaring. She didn't tell her crew anything that didn't concern them and she could well believe the Kat didn't either.

"We didn't think about searching the coastline, Captain," Tad said. If Sonja said that this Garrick Steele was truly concerned about their captain, then that was good enough for him. "I will set a few men to doing just that, right away."

"Let your men rest for now. We may need them later on. I will send a detail out on a search as soon as I return to the *Sea Witch*."

Just as Garrick would have turned away from the group, wanting to return to the *Sea Witch* and right away to start his own search, Thomas and two other crewmen stepped on deck.

"We found out where Bristol Jack is taking the captain," Thomas announced and at the same time his gaze included the large man and the woman captain whom he had seen before on the island of Grande Terre.

"Where, Thomas?" Tad quickly questioned, and let him know that he could speak freely before this group.

"Me and the boys were told by a certain little gal that wishes to remain quietly in the background that the first mate of the *Black Dragon* told her that Jack was going to be picking up a passenger and then they were to set sail on the early-evening tide last night, for Saint Kitts."

"Saint Kitts?" Tad and Slade both spoke at the same

376

time. "But why would Jack be taking the lass and her brother back to Saint Kitts?" Tad asked rather confused.

The whole ordeal of coming to Barbados must have been set up only to throw off any followers, Garrick quickly ascertained. Turning around and starting toward the gangplank, Garrick had already made up his mind. Just as quickly as he could return to the *Sea Witch* he would leave Bridgetown for Saint Kitts. The *Black Dragon* had at least a good twelve-hour start; he could not afford to waste any more time.

"Where are you going, Garrick?" Sonja called.

"To the *Sea Witch* and then to set sail for Saint Kitts." He did not bother to turn back toward the group on the deck of the *Kat's Eye* until he was on the dock. "Assign yourself a captain and set sail as soon as possible." Garrick spoke in a commanding voice to the three men who had first approached him on the ship. Without another word said, he turned and, with his long-legged stride, hurried away from the *Kat's Eye*'s berth.

"I would do as he says, men. Garrick Steele is not a man to be crossed." Standing next to Tad, the wanton redhead ran her hand over his chest. "I had hoped that when the *Lynx* set sail again, you would be at my side." A small sigh escaped her as she added, "I guess it will have to wait for a time. I know that you are needed aboard the *Kat's Eye* for now. But do not forget, my adorable man, Sonja does not wait long for any man. So let's find the Kat and get on with what we started in my cabin while we were anchored off of Grande Terre." With that, she took hold of his shirtfront much in the same manner that Garrick had earlier, but this time Tad's reward was different. Instead of Garrick's angry regard, he felt the heated stamp of Sonja's sweet mouth

377

over his own.

Instantly Tad's strong arms went around the bountiful figure of the lady pirate. When she pulled her lips away and her hand smoothed out his shirtfront, he would have drawn her to him once again, but feeling the hungry stare of the men encircling him, he released her and a large grin split his face. "The *Kat's Eye* will follow the *Lynx*, and you, sweet lass, straight into the bowels of hell if that's where you lead!"

Sonja laughed loudly at this. "I knew you were the man for me!" she declared as she also turned and hurriedly left the *Kat's Eye* and started down the wharf toward her own ship.

For an added minute Tad as well as the rest of the men around him stared after her winsome figure in the tightly molded breeches and silk shirt. "What a woman!" Dirk stated what was on all their minds.

The words seemed to break the moment and Tad turned toward the men. "Wake the entire crew and let's ready the *Kat's Eye* to set sail. Our captain's life can well depend upon our speed, so look lively now, lads, look lively!"

It was not until that afternoon that Joshua was brought to Bristol Jack's cabin and was once again reunited with his sister. Tears streamed down his boyish face as he ran into Katelin's open arms. "I didn't think you would ever come, sis." He wept openly, for the first time letting down his defenses and giving way to the tears he had forced to remain dry over the past days of his captivity.

"Are you all right, Joshua?" Katelin felt her own tears stinging the backs of her eyes, and at that moment would have lashed out at Bristol Jack for his cruelty in holding her little brother prisoner, except for the fact that he had left the cabin earlier and she and Joshua were now alone.

"I'm all right, sis. But I was awful scared. The crew on this ship are meaner than snakes!" He confessed his fear in a very descriptive manner.

"And how about Simon and Pete?"

"I guess they're all right, too. That mean man with the scar on his face made Simon go to the galley and help their cook, and Pete went along to help him. I was left in the hold until now."

Katelin lovingly brushed back the curling locks of hair around his face. "You have been very brave, Joshua. Now that I am here, you have nothing to fear." She hoped that her assurances were not given out falsely, but at the moment she could glimpse in his green eyes that her brother did, indeed, need her reassurances.

"What do you think they want with us, sis?" Joshua sniffled, trying to stem the flow of tears and appear brave once again.

"I have no idea," Katelin truthfully answered, and in fact she still held no idea why Bristol Jack had kidnapped her and her brother. All she knew was that he had been put up to the venture by someone else, but of course she could not tell Joshua this.

"I heard Scarface telling one of the crew that we were heading back to Saint Kitts."

"You did? Saint Kitts? Are you sure?" Katelin was at a loss as to why the *Black Dragon* would be going to Saint Kitts. Unless whoever it was Bristol Jack was working for was on Saint Kitts.

"Yeah, I'm sure, Kat. I was in the hold so long the

men got used to my being around. They talked as though I wasn't there. Do you think they're going to let us loose when we reach Saint Kitts? I sure hope so. I miss Lizzy's cooking something terrible! I can just taste her lemon tarts."

Katelin smiled but did not reveal her inner thoughts. Bristol Jack certainly was not taking them to Saint Kitts to let them go back to Coral Rose as though nothing had ever happened. He was taking them to the island for a reason, and that reason had to be the person whom he had taken his orders from to begin with; to kidnap them. A shiver of genuine fear traveled over her spine and once again she wished she had gone to Garrick when she had first found the note on her bed aboard the *Kat's Eye*. He would have known how to handle rescuing Joshua and her two crewmen. But now here she was aboard the *Black Dragon* with her brother, and as far as she knew, no one aboard the *Kat's Eye* even knew where she was. How could she have been so foolish as to go to Sal's tavern alone! And even more pressing was the worry of who it was on Saint Kitts that she and her brother were going to be handed over to!

Twenty-five

The balmy tropical, Caribbean breezes carried the *Black Dragon* to her destination without incident. Katelin and Joshua were kept within the captain's cabin throughout most of the voyage, and for the most part they were left to themselves. It was the man known to them as Scarface who brought them their meals, and Bristol Jack, of an evening, paid his captives a visit. At such times his attention was mostly that of silent brooding with his dark eyes centered upon the lovely vision of the woman known as the Kat. And with each visit, his regret was more heartfelt that he had to turn this woman over to Alex Blackthorn. He could only imagine what that cold-hearted man had in store for the lovely lady pirate, and though Jack himself held a reputation of infamy, he knew that what he had in mind for the Kat would be much preferable to what Blackthorn would force upon her.

This evening as Bristol Jack silently sat behind his desk, his pretext of studying maps long ago having been forgotten as he held his dark stare across the cabin at the brother and sister sitting on the edge of his bed, he spoke his first words since coming into the cabin over an hour ago. "Your time aboard the *Black Dragon* will come to an end this night."

Each appearance paid by the unsavory pirate brought about the same reaction from Katelin and Joshua. They sat close together on the cabin's bed, as though giving each other their support, and each remained stonily silent until his leave-taking. This evening, though, his words brought about a reaction from Katelin. "Are we nearing Basseterre then?" Believing their destination to be Saint Kitts, Katelin took a guess that the *Black Dragon* would dock in Basseterre. And with the guess was hope. The hope that somehow she and her brother would be able to escape their captors, or in some fashion bring about the help they needed for their release.

A dark bushy brow rose with her question, and a glimmer of a smile settled over Jack's full lips. The wench was smarter than he'd thought. How could she have figured out that they were going to Saint Kitts? She must have overheard one of his crewmen talking about their destination, he answered his own question. But he was wise to her desire for information. It was too bad it would do her no good. "The *Black Dragon* cannot dock in Basseterre. The governor will not allow it." His grin widened with this, for he didn't give a high-tail damn what Governor Langston allowed. It was Alex Blackthorn who gave him his orders and he did not wish the *Black Dragon* in port because he wanted none the wiser that Bristol Jack himself had any dealings with anyone on the island.

"Then you will be docking somewhere else?" Katelin needed confirmation that they were going to Saint Kitts. Perhaps at least Joshua could get away and go to Coral Rose to get help!

Again the grin settled over his lips. What harm to tell her they were indeed approaching Saint Kitts. Before she left the ship, she would be bound and tied—the boy also—so what harm could come of it? Slowly his head nodded. "Aye, we are approaching Saint Kitts, for all the good it will do you to know this."

Katelin said nothing else to their pirate captor; her mind was busily making plans. If possible, she would instruct Joshua to jump ship the moment they drew near enough to shore. He was a strong swimmer, and knowing the island well, he would know the best way to travel to get to Coral Rose. At last some small ray of hope filled her.

It was quickly dashed, though, with the entrance into the cabin of Scarface. "Here's the rope you wanted and the cloth for binding."

Bristol Jack nodded his dark head. "Set them on the desk. There's still a while before we drop anchor."

"That won't be necessary." Katelin spoke up, knowing without being told that the rope was for her and her brother. "We will give no resistance, the ropes are not needed," she boldly lied.

Bristol Jack's loud laughter filled the space of the cabin and Scarface's joined in. "Aye, Kat, we can take your word on that? You and the boy will just willingly walk straightaway to your undoing!"

Whatever fears Katelin had held before were nothing compared to his words. They confirmed the fact that whoever had set him upon the venture of abducting them had not done so for any good reason. She and her brother were in great peril, and if they did not try to escape, their fate would be sealed! While both men stood near the desk laughing over her request not to be tied, she whispered softly so that only Joshua could hear, "Run for the door, Joshua, get to the upper deck and go over the side. Bring back help!"

Joshua swallowed hard as he nodded his head, his own green gaze intently watching the two men and the pile of rope on the desk. Like Katelin, he knew that if they held any chance of escape, it would be before they were tied. Drawing a deep breath, he set his foot to the floor, and with a burst of pent-up energy, he lunged for the cabin door.

Taken by surprise, both men hesitated for a full minute. That minute allowed Joshua the needed time to get through the door and down the companionway.

"Get him back!" Bristol Jack shouted, and instantly Scarface was sprinting out of the cabin.

In the space of the next few minutes Katelin said nothing. She dared barely to breathe as she silently prayed that her brother would succeed in his attempt to escape.

Bristol Jack's glaring dark regard held her as he approached the bed. "Sims will catch him." That was all he said, as he, too, appeared to await Scarface's return to the captain's cabin.

Using all the cunning and litheness of foot that he had learned over the years while running wild over the island, Joshua zigzagged right and left across the upper deck as shouts were called and he heard the heavy pounding of footsteps not far behind him. Reaching the ship's railing, he did not wait an extra second, but dove headlong into the dark depths of the water surrounding the *Black Dragon*.

"Drop the small boat. You four men go after him and bring him back." Scarface was shouting out orders as he stood against the railing and peered over the side. He tried to glimpse some sight of the youth, but the moon was but a sliver in the clouds, and it did not aid him in his viewing. All he could see was dark water, the shoreline some distance, and without the aid of more light, he could not even make out the white beaches of the island.

There was much commotion as the crew aboard the *Black Dragon* hurriedly launched the small boat and began to row around the ship. Not finding sight of the boy, they began to row toward shore.

"Damn the brat's bloody hide to hell!" Scarface beat his fist upon the ship's railing. They would never find the kid in these dark waters! Turning back the way he had come, he soon was making his way into the captain's cabin to tell him the news.

Both Katelin and Scarface were more than a little surprised by Jack's reception to the news that the boy had made good his escape and the chances were slim that he would be found. They had expected anger and threats but not the slow smile that came over his full lips.

"The boy wasn't expected anyway. Now there's no

need to mention that we ever held him." Bristol Jack had been somewhat worried over Blackthorn's reaction to the kid being brought along. Usually Blackthorn wanted things nice and neat and none the wiser. He had made no mention of the Kat even having a brother tagging along with her, so the wisest thing to do now was just not bring up the subject of the kid. Anyway he would more than likely drown in these waters, or be eaten by a shark. He had seen some pretty big ones around the island.

Katelin's fear for her own safety increased with his mention that Joshua had not been expected by whoever it was he was working for.

"Tie her up, Sims. We don't want to take any more chances. Then you can go and give the order to drop anchor. As soon as the men return with the small boat, we go ashore." Bristol Jack stood back and watched as his man pulled the woman's hands in front of her and tied her tightly. He could not do the deed himself for he feared that just the touch of her skin would force him to change his mind and keep her for himself. And if indeed he did not fear Blackthorn as much as he did even at this late moment, he would take the woman and set his course for South Africa. But he knew better and told himself that the next port the *Black Dragon* made, he would find himself the fairest woman on the island and take her for his own.

Katelin's struggles were useless but she tried to fight off Scarface as he pushed her back upon the bed and, bending over her, bound both her hands together. With one tight jerk upon the rope, he stood to his feet and pulled her along with him.

"I'll get the small boat readied." Scarface turned away from Katelin and Bristol Jack and started out of the cabin.

Bristol Jack laughed aloud as he glimpsed the heated fury upon Katelin's features as she glared her hatred after the tall figure going through the cabin door. "Sims is a good man. As a captain, you should be able to appreciate that."

"I would more appreciate my sword or dagger and my hands untied. I would show you and your good man just how well a woman can defend herself if she is not drugged!" Katelin spat out.

"I am sure you would, Kat, and more's the pity that I won't be able to enjoy such a sight. But now if you are ready, we might just as well get this affair over with." Bristol Jack nodded his head toward the door as though she should proceed him.

Not on your life, Katelin told herself. If he wanted her out of this cabin, he would have to drag her from it!

Sims did exactly that. Still loath to touch her, Bristol Jack had called his man to bring the woman out on deck, and a few minutes later he was hefting her up and over his shoulder as he began to climb down the rope ladder.

Katelin was dropped in the bow of the small boat, Scarface having no inclination toward kindness where the opposite sex was concerned. With a whoof of breath escaping her, Katelin quickly tried to right herself to a sitting position.

The small boat was quickly rowed ashore and Scarface and another man who had come along pulled Katelin onto the damp sand as Bristol Jack climbed out of the boat. "Word has already been sent; there should be horses waiting along the path."

God, Katelin hoped that Joshua had made it to shore. It had seemed an awfully long way from ship to shore in the small boat. Maybe he had even found the horses that Bristol Jack was talking about and had chased them off.

Once again this was just wishful thinking on her part, Katelin soon realized after the small group on the beach made their way to the edge of the trees and foliage. Stepping onto a wide, cleared path, they quickly came across the horses that Jack had hoped to find.

Katelin was placed upon one of the beasts by Scarface, and the reins were taken by Jack, who led the group toward the inner portion of the island.

Katelin tried to make out some sign or landmark she could remember, but it was so dark she could not discern where on the island they were. For all she knew, they could be on the opposite side of Saint Kitts from Coral Rose, and it might take Joshua hours before he could find someone to bring help. By that time, Katelin knew it would be too late!

Joshua, gasping for breath and for a minute exhausted, lay not far from the path where Bristol Jack and his men were mounting the horses. Silently he pulled himself to his knees, and peered through the foliage. His eyes as sharp as a cat's, he made out the outline of the men and saw his sister sitting upon one of the horses.

For a few minutes longer he stayed still, not daring to make a sound that would draw attention. As the horses began to travel away from the beach, down the path, for a minute longer he watched their backs. They were heading toward the Blackthorn plantation, Shadow Mere. For a few minutes he wondered at this turn of events. Could Old Cold Eyes be the one who had set Bristol Jack on Kat's trail? But why? When they were supposed to be married, why would he want to abduct her? None of this made any sense to him, but knowing that time was of the essence if he was going to help his sister, he started off in the direction of Coral Rose.

Bristol Jack and his men might have horses, but Joshua knew every inch of this area along the coastline and around the adjoining plantations. He was sure he could make good time reaching Coral Rose, but he was not sure what he would do once he got there.

As he ran, sprinting over rocks and fallen trees, he tried to form some plan of action in his mind. He would get Rufuss—he had an old musket—and Kip—he could get the field hands. They could take the cotton wagon, but the horses were so slow. He worried that they would not arrive at Shadow Mere in time to help Kat, and even if they did, could he count on his people to stand up to a white man such as Alex Blackthorn?

Earlier that evening, but only about an hour or so before the *Black Dragon*, the *Sea Witch* along with the *Kat's Eye* and the *Lynx* had anchored off the same coastline as the *Black Dragon*. It had been Tad and the crew members of the *Kat's Eye* who were familiar with the area and who directed the other two ships to a stretch of beach that was on the Ashford property. The darkness of night helped to conceal them as the *Black Dragon* slipped silently past them.

Garrick had pushed his men unmercifully during this trip from Barbados to Saint Kitts, and he knew that the crews on the two ships following him had also strained their manpower to the limit. But Garrick had pushed himself the hardest. He was not able to sleep or even take a moment to eat; he could think only of Katelin and finding her safe. If there was a job that needed to be done aboard the *Sea Witch,* he did it himself, not asking another. He mended canvas sail, restrung cordage, and even relieved the helmsman, his pale eyes always directed across the ocean, in the direction of Saint Kitts. He had to arrive on Saint Kitts before Bristol Jack!

He held a sense of urgency, though at the same time he had no idea where the *Black Dragon* was taking Katelin and her brother. When the *Kat's Eye* bore away from the *Sea Witch* and the *Lynx* and indicated knowledge of a quicker route than going into dock at Basseterre, he steered the vessel himself along the coast, and was the first to jump in the small boat after anchoring.

"We can reach Coral Rose quicker this way," Slade shouted as the small boat from the *Kat's Eye* hit shore at the same time as the one Garrick was in.

There was only a moment's wait for Sonja and her crew, but in all of their minds was the hope that they had not made a mistake by coming this way instead of going first to Basseterre.

"Perhaps the captain and the lad were able to get away when the *Black Dragon* reached the island. They will be waiting for help at Coral Rose." Tad spoke aloud the only hope they now had as the crewmen of the *Kat's Eye* led the way from the beach to the plantation.

The house was dark and silent at this late hour, but Garrick boldly pounded on the front door.

Lizzy was the first to wake, and leaving her bedroom off the kitchen, she slowly opened the door and peered out into the night. "Lord's mercy," she cried aloud and began to make tracks backward as she saw the porch filling with a group of white men and a woman with bright, flaming hair.

Rufuss, hearing Lizzy's cry of alarm, hurried toward the front door with musket in hand. Right when he brought it down from his shoulder as though pointing it in the direction of the large man wearing a dark blue seaman's jacket, Garrick jerked the firearm out of his hand with a single motion and stepped into the house.

"Where is your mistress?" he demanded, his gaze circling the lower interior of the house and knowing already without being told that Katelin and her brother were not here.

"What you men be wanting?" Rufuss spoke up as he pulled Lizzy to his side.

"Kat, man. Have you heard word from her?"

"There ain't no Kat here, master. You done made a mistake." Rufuss with all his fear was still cautious of being respectful, particularly when the large man held his musket.

"Why, you old fool, the mistress called Kat. Master Joshua himself called her that." Lizzy was not one to remain silent, even though she felt her knees shaking.

"Have you seen or heard from her?" Garrick knew it was no use. If Katelin had been in the house, she would have surely left her bedchamber or any other hiding place by now. She had not gotten away from Bristol Jack as they had hoped, but was somewhere else on the island. The thought that the time lost coming to Coral Rose might well be disastrous assailed him and filled him with true terror.

"Not the mistress nor the master be here. Now what you all be wanting at this hour of the night?" Something in this large man's face spoke of worry, not meanness, and instantly Lizzy became alarmed. "Why you want the mistress? Is something wrong?" Her fear became genuine as she saw several heads beginning to nod and one man standing near the door spoke up. "Kat is the captain of the *Kat's Eye;* some of us men here are part of her crew. She and the boy were abducted by a pirate called Bristol Jack. He was bringing them back to Saint Kitts but we're not sure why or where they are taking them on the island." It was Slade who volunteered this much, hoping that if the old woman knew anything—perhaps a ransom note had been sent to the plantation—she would now feel free to speak.

Lizzy was well aware that her mistress was the captain of a pirate ship, and she in truth had been somewhat worried over the past few days when she and the young master had not returned to Coral Rose as promised. Now looking at the rough-appearing group standing on the porch and entering the front portion of the house, she knew this affair at being a pirate was far more dangerous than she had been led to believe by Miss Katelin. "Lordy mercy, what we going to do to save the mistress and master?" Her cry was directed at the large man with the silver-blue eyes. For some reason she assumed him to be in charge, and knew that she could place her trust in him.

Garrick ran his fingers through his thick dark hair in an agitated manner. He had not allowed himself to think any further than finding Katelin at Coral Rose. "First we should send some of the men into Basseterre and others can comb the island and try to find out any information that can tell us where the *Black Dragon* is anchored." This was the first course of action to come to Garrick. Before they could take measures to rescue Katelin and her brother, they would have to find out where they were being kept captive.

Sonja and Tad both nodded their heads in agreement, and turning toward their men, they began to give out orders when from the back of the group someone shouted, "It's the boy! It's young Joshua!"

Garrick was one of the first to push his way back out on the front porch, his eyes seeking out the figure of a child.

Weary from the night's ordeal, Joshua staggered into the group standing on the front porch of the plantation house, his green eyes going to Tad and Slade before his tears began to fall.

"Ah, there you be, lad. Don't be taking on so." Tad hurried to his side and placed a comforting arm around his shoulders.

"Where's Katelin?" Garrick questioned, his silver

393

gaze still glancing into the darkness from where the boy had come for some sign of the woman whom he loved.

Out of the mist of his tears, Joshua tried to make out the features of the man who was asking about his sister. He had never seen the man before, knowing that he would have remembered a fellow of such enormous size. "They took her. When the *Black Dragon* was anchoring, Kat told me to run for it and try to get some help." Looking at the man now standing in front of him, Joshua for the first time wondered why so many men were standing around and appearing to hang on his every word. He knew why the crew of the *Kat's Eye* was here, but looking up at Tad, he wondered how he had guessed that Bristol Jack had brought them to Saint Kitts. There was a lot he didn't understand, but the one thing he did know was that he had to help Kat!

"Did you see where Bristol Jack and his men were taking her?" Again it was the large man who was questioning him.

Brushing the tears away with the backs of his hands, Joshua nodded his head. "They were heading to Shadow Mere. There were horses left on the path leading to the plantation."

This was enough for Garrick. Turning to the men around him, he began shouting directions. "Go to the stables and hitch up the wagons. Saddle any horses that are available." If Bristol Jack was taking Katelin to Shadow Mere, he must be working for Alex Blackthorn. But why would Blackthorn want Katelin kidnapped? He couldn't figure it out, but at the moment he didn't have the time to try. Whatever reason Blackthorn had for forcing Katelin to be brought to Shadow Mere would not prove good enough! He would put an end to Bristol Jack's outlaw ways and Blackthorn's dark plans this very night, he swore as he mounted the horse that was brought to the front of the house for his use.

Twenty-six

What little moonlight there was did not reach through the trees, so it was left for the horses to find their way up the path that Bristol Jack and his group were traveling on and which they hoped would eventually lead them to their destination.

When the horses halted, Katelin was dragged off the back of the mount she was on, and standing between Jack and Scarface, she was shoved by the latter toward a small stone building that had been partially concealed by the dense underbrush and foliage in the area.

Unsure of what was going to happen, Katelin stumbled through the low doorway, and was soon followed by the two men. The other men who had accompanied them remained outside to stand watch.

"I don't know why the boss wanted us to bring her here. It would have been much easier to take her to the big house, instead of us having to wait out here in this decaying rubble," Jack complained as his dark glance took in the smelly, damp interior of the old rectory.

Katelin herself had not been able to suppress the

shudder that had swept over her as they entered the building. A single candle had been lit and the sparse furnishings and dankness of the place left her feeling more than a little ill at ease. "Where are we?" she questioned and felt the words sticking in her throat, even as she forced them out.

Both men ignored her question, for at that same moment, an immense form shadowed the doorway, then entered the room.

"Jubel!" Katelin gasped aloud when the man straightened and the candlelight caught his features. "What on earth is going on here? Where is Alex?" She would have said more except Scarface halted her words with a piece of cloth forced into her mouth and then another was tied tightly over her lips.

There was a penetrating gleam of wicked delight that came into the large man's eyes as he looked at the woman standing between the two men and watched as the man with the scarred face gagged her. He held no love for Katelin Ashford; in fact as he watched her struggling for her release, he regretted that her little brother was not also here in the old rectory. He would have taken immense pleasure in snuffing the life out of that little pest.

"You know the wench then?" Jack questioned the large man after Katelin had been secured with the gag that now silenced her. He had not been lost to the fact that the Kat had called out the man's name.

Holding out a bag of gold toward Bristol Jack, Jubel said in a tone that was more statement than question, "She is the woman known as the Kat. The one that the master desired."

Taking the offered bag of gold coins, Bristol Jack nodded his dark head in agreement to the other man's words. "Indeed she be the Kat."

"You men can leave now. The master will get in touch with you." Jubel moved farther into the room, his large hand curling around Katelin's forearm as he now took possession of the woman.

Jack turned at the door one last time, his glance going to Katelin. It was purely a rotten shame, he told himself as her wide green eyes seemed to look for him to halt what was soon to come. The large man was already dragging her across the chamber toward the table that made up the only furniture in the room.

Eye contact between Katelin and Jack was broken as Jubel pushed her upon the table, then Scarface and Jack left the building and started to remount their horses.

Katelin fought off the large man as best she could, but with her hands tied and her mouth now gagged, she was powerless to do much in her own defense.

It was when Jubel began to untie her hands that she thought perhaps she would have some kind of chance of getting away, but within seconds she knew otherwise. First one wrist and then the other was tied to the table, until Katelin was spread-eagle, ankles and wrists alike tied securely.

All the other women whom Jubel had brought to the rectory for Alex Blackthorn, he had stripped of their clothing, but wanting his master to have no doubt about who this woman was and not taking the chance that he would be fooled by her declarations that she was not the Kat, but Katelin Ashford, Jubel wanted him to see her in her pirate attire. With her mouth gagged, there would be no doubt in Blackthorn's mind that the woman on the table was the one he desired for the outlet of his mad rages!

Katelin could do naught but pull against her bonds, her head thrashing about as she tried to work the gag out of her mouth. All her efforts were futile; she was tied fast and the gag would not budge.

Some slight noise pulled her attention toward the doorway. Her green eyes enlarged as she watched Alex Blackthorn step into the chamber. His words sounded slurred as he spoke to Jubel, his dark eyes appearing glazed, and Katelin wondered if he had been drinking. He was not wearing one of the customary tailored outfits that she associated with him, but instead he wore only a dark silk shirt that was tucked into dark trousers.

"You have her ready?" Alex's dark eyes fell upon the table and the woman who was tied hand and foot, and Katelin shuddered as his glance settled upon her face.

She would have called to him to put a stop to this nonsense at once, reminded him that she was the same woman who he had asked to marry, and that whatever insanity was being played out here in this old rectory had to come to an end, but she could say none of this as he slowly advanced toward her and Jubel silently left the chamber.

Alex Blackthorn cunningly appraised his prey. "So you are the Kat," he murmured aloud. His regard of her took in the silk blouse tied beneath her swelling breasts and the dark breeches that lushly outlined every curve of her lower body. From his right hand flashed a knife, and as he heard the deep, indrawn breath from the woman lying before him, he felt the surging of dark power that always filled him as he faced a helpless victim. "Jubel should have relieved you of these." His words were spoken low and held a menacing tremor that set Katelin's body trembling. With a precise action, the knife sliced the knot of her silk blouse below her breasts and then ever so slowly the long, gleaming blade flicked at each tiny button, until the blouse fell away and exposed a measure of her full, perfect bosom.

At the moment Katelin wished herself to be of the frail constitution of other women and easily swoon away in order not to be forced to have knowledge of Alex Blackthorn's depravity, but she was not so lucky, and as she felt the slight pressure of cold steel against her flesh, her body quivered as she tried to pull away from the touch.

"Ah, Jasmine, you tremble as though a virgin, but we both know better." The blade went from her breasts to the waistline of her trousers, and with an easy motion of his wrist, he began to slice away the material.

Katelin bucked wildly, not caring of the danger that she was placing herself in as the wicked-looking knife finished cutting away the length of her pants on one side. Tears fell from her green eyes at the powerless position she was in and at the same time her head lolled from side to side as moans of desperation somehow found their way out of the gag.

"So you wish to plead with me? Have no fear, Mother, I would never disappoint you." And with this, the knife drew from her breeches where he had already freed one long, shapely leg, and with a deft movement, he cut the cloth that was tied over her lips. He desired her impotent pleadings for release to fill his ears. He wanted to hear the many promises that she would make to him now that she was powerless and in his keeping. To hear her agony and desperation made the moment so worthwhile. In the dark corners of his evil mind he was attaining all his childish dreams.

Katelin spat out the wad of material that had been forced into her mouth by Scarface. "No, Alex, no. You are making a mistake. I am Katelin Ashford; we are to be married!" Katelin held no doubts that the man standing over her was mad and somehow she prayed that she could reach into that part of him that could remember who she was.

"I always told you, Mother, that you were a witch. You know of my engagement to Katelin!" He had not thought she would be so clever, but slowly a sly gleam came into his glazed eyes. "Her cousin must have told you. Kat is the bad one. You two must have thought you could trick me, but I am not so easily deceived." He threw his dark head back and crazed laughter filled the space of the small chamber.

With his response, Katelin did feel some small dregs of darkness beginning to engulf her. This man was not only mad, he was totally depraved! A piercing scream swelled from within the center of her chest and soon erupted; another one followed, then another. She was entirely helpless and at this moment she knew that Alex Blackthorn was going to murder her!

Her screams brought him back to the madness of the moment, and as his laughter died in his throat, he voiced his welcome of her terror. "I remember your cries, Mother, but then they were of pleasure as you thrashed that seductive body of yours around and your flesh welcomed the many men whom you made pay to sample your evil charms. Go ahead and

401

scream all you want, I am the only one to hear, the only one who can give you the satisfaction you crave!"

Katelin's terror pulsed as though a viable thing within her breasts. She knew there was no release coming to her. Alex was violently deranged and he was going to kill her! She tried to block out his words, the feel of the cold, flat edge of the knife lying against her breasts and the pressure of his hand around her throat. She willed herself to think of Garrick and the all-consuming love she had known for such a short time, to think of her brother, who, thank all that was good in this world, had escaped the terrorizing ordeal which she was being forced to endure.

Alex, who fed off the fear of his victims, paused when Katelin's screams stopped. She held her eyes tightly shut as she tried to block out the madness of the moment, and thus his fury increased. "There is no escape from me, Jasmine," he harshly lashed out as his hand left her throat and jerked her chin in a hard grip.

The pressure upon her chin forced Katelin to cry out, her eyes opening with the pain and at that moment as she viewed the evil, insane lights within the black eyes so close to her face, a piercing scream left her throat and filled the chamber, circling the darkness outside—a scream that had no beginning and no end.

Joshua led the way from Coral Rose to Shadow Mere. Several crewmen held blazing torches high overhead to guide their way as they traversed the rough terrain that made up the inner portion of the island. The path they followed at one interval joined up with the path that led down to the beach — the same path that Bristol Jack and Scarface had used earlier.

It was just as they approached the path that Joshua signaled to Garrick. "That's the path up ahead. The one Bristol Jack took Kat up in order to reach Shadow Mere."

"Douse the torches," Garrick ordered in low tones and quickly his command was carried out. "You should go to the back of the group, Joshua." Garrick still spoke in low tones. He was not sure what kind of trouble they would meet head on now that they were so close to Shadow Mere, and he didn't want the boy harmed.

"The hell I will!" Joshua cried aloud. "They have my sister, and I'm going to be there to save her!" No one, not even this big brute, was going to send him to the back of the group!

No wonder Katelin had tried to warn him of her brother's unsocial manners, Garrick told himself as his silver eyes watched the boy holding his chin stubbornly straight. He was by no means lacking in spirit. With a quick nod of his dark head, he allowed the boy to have his way, agreeing that Joshua had a lot at stake in what was taking place and perhaps he even deserved to have a place at the head of the group. "You can stay here at the front but keep yourself out of harm's way. Your sister will have my hide if anything happens to you." With this, Garrick kicked the sides of his mount and started down the path.

Whoever this large man was, Joshua told himself,

he must be afraid of Kat. His childish thoughts bolstered his spirit, as without another word spoken, he stayed to the front of the group on his pony.

It was not long before voices could be heard from up ahead on the path. Garrick's heart skipped a beat as the thought crossed his mind that perhaps Bristol Jack had not delivered Kat to Blackthorn yet. Perhaps for some reason they had been delayed on the trail, and there was still time to save her from enduring whatever it was that Blackthorn had in mind for her. "Keep the men quiet," he instructed Tad, and he in turn whispered out the order. The only sound that was now heard coming from up the path was the soft creaking noise of the wagon, which Garrick prayed Bristol Jack and his group would not hear over the sound of their own voices.

Minutes passed, and as the sounds grew closer, Garrick realized that the group was coming toward his own. They must have already delivered Kat to Blackthorn, he told himself, and with the thought hot fury coursed over him. Quickly he dismounted, and with a motion of his hand, he instructed the crewmen behind him and Sonja to do likewise. Those with horses tied them a few steps off the path, but for the most part the men were in the wagon, and this vehicle they left in the path as the men jumped to the ground.

Bristol Jack, Scarface, and the two men with them did not realize that they were set upon until it was too late. As they easily bantered back and forth about Jack's next venture, that of being a slaver, they allowed their mounts to pick their way down the dark path. A warning cry was not heard until each man alike was pulled from the seat of his mount and amid punches and curses they were stripped of their weapons and their hands tied behind their backs.

"What the hell is the meaning of this?" Bristol Jack yelled as a large man pulled him to his feet with a jerk that set his teeth to shaking.

"You are under arrest in the name of the Royal Crown," Garrick stated as he tied his hands behind his back in not so easy a manner.

"And who the hell are you?"

"I'm the man who will see you hang!" Garrick supplied, his anger high as he demanded, "Where is she, Jack? Where is Kat?" He took hold of the back of his shirt and shook him as though a rag doll.

The rest of Jack's men were now all similarly tied and held in their tracks by one of the crewmen from the three ships. All watched on as the large man demanded answers to his questions.

"It be Blackthorn you're wanting, man. Me and my men didn't do no harm to the Kat. Ask the boy there." Jack looked toward Joshua for him to supply the information that would take the angry pair of hands off him.

"Leave the boy out of this. Where is she?" Garrick was not one to let up and again he shook his prisoner.

"Blackthorn has her!"

"For what? What was his purpose in having you capture her and bring her to him?"

"How am I to know that? All I do is as he orders me."

Garrick knew that this was all the information he would get out of the pirate. Releasing him, Garrick let Bristol Jack slump to his knees. "Tad, have some of your men take them back to the *Sea Witch*. Use the wagon; the men remaining can use their horses." Garrick was already turning to regain his mount and continue on to Shadow Mere.

Tad set out a few of his men to do as ordered, then hurried on after Garrick Steele and the rest of the crewmen.

Approaching the front of the dark house, Garrick sensed that all was too quiet. With a silent motion of his hand, he indicated that they should go around toward the stables. It was as they drew abreast of the Shadow Mere stables that Garrick heard a piercing scream. His blood chilled within his veins, his heart hammering heavily in his chest. Finding the path behind the stables too overgrown for a horse to traverse, Garrick quickly dismounted, his long strides taking him at a racing pace closer and closer to the terrifying screams.

Sonja was right behind Garrick, and Tad, Slade, Dirk, and Joshua were running behind her. The rest of the men followed as all heard the screams of a woman and raced against the heavy hand of time to find the place that the deathly sounds were coming from.

The hulking shape of Jubel standing guard outside the old rectory was the first sight that came to Garrick as he broke through a tangle of trees and underbrush. The screams coming from within the crumbled, decaying stone building enveloped Garrick in a piercing sound that seemed to go on forever in his brain. "Kat!" The name escaped his lips at the same time as the large man saw him running toward him and threw up his arms in a protective stance.

Jubel's efforts at defense did him little good. Garrick swung his mighty fist, connecting with the massive man's jawbone and sending him sprawling in the dust at Garrick's feet. As he dazedly tried to pull his huge body from the ground, he was punched again, then again, until he lay unconscious.

Having laid the large man out in the dirt before the rectory door, Garrick did not give him a second thought, but charged like a mad bull into the building. The sight that met his eyes instantly halted him there in his tracks.

Blackthorn held the serrated knife at Katelin's throat, her screams still filling the chamber as neither noticed his entrance into the room.

It was Sonja only steps behind Garrick, after leaping over the large form of Jubel in the doorway, who entered the rectory behind Garrick, and it was she who drew Alex's attention when she let out a large gasp of surprise. "Alex. Let her go!" she cried as the cold dark eyes went to the doorway and held upon her.

"Jasmine?" The name left Blackthorn's lips in disbelief. "How can you be standing over there?" he questioned in some confusion.

"It is I, Sonja, Alex." The lady pirate spoke out to the surprise of all standing near her. Even Katelin's screams had stilled in her throat as some small touch of reason returned to her when she heard the sound of another woman's voice, and the knife at her throat lessened its pressure.

In his madness Alex Blackthorn did not see the men standing around Sonja; he only saw the image of his mother. The long, flaming-red hair, the same blue eyes, and that creamy white flesh. "How can you be there? I killed you long ago and left your whore's body burning when I set fire to the whore-house you ran on Martinique. You cannot be here!"

Sonja's blue eyes filled with sadness as she looked upon the brother she had not seen in years. She had been told about their mother's death, but no one had suspected that her brother had been the cause. There had been little said about Alex the last time she had visited Martinique; like the rest of the people who had known her mother, Madeline Crofter, known as Jasmine to her customers, Sonja had believed that her brother had just disappeared to start a new life for himself. She would never have had a clue that he had taken on the name of Black-thorn and was the owner of Shadow Mere. "Alex, why don't you put the knife down and let me help you?" She knew by the gleam in his eyes that he was mad.

"Help me, Jasmine? When have you ever helped me?" Alex threw his head back and like the madman he was he howled with laughter. "Over and over I have killed you, trying to purge your vileness from my soul. Every whore has your smell about her. They all deserve to die!"

Garrick reached out and placed a hand on Sonja's arm, knowing with Blackthorn's statement that he was the villain who had been preying on and mur-dering the prostitutes on Saint Kitts.

"I can handle him," Sonja softly stated and surged off the hand that was offered in help. This was up to her. Sonja would have no other confront Alex Black-thorn. He was her brother, and though they had been separated when she had been only a child—her father, a pirate himself, had taken her away from

408

their mother — Sonja felt some obligation toward Alex. Her heart ached for what she had been told by friends that he had suffered at her mother's hand, but knowing that his evilness had to be stopped, she took a step toward him. "Come to me then, Alex. Come and at last have an ending to this madness that eats up your soul."

Alex Blackthorn did not glance down in Katelin's direction as he stepped away from the table where she was tied. His knife was held loosely in his hand as he approached the image that belonged to his mother. He could hear her tantalizing voice as she used to force him to lie next to her in bed and make him listen to all the seductive ploys she had used on her male customers, and in the telling leaving Alex sweating and aching with a desire that was unnatural for a son to have for his mother. He would still the words that ran rampant in his head, her high shrill laughter washing over him in a heated flood. Raising the knife above his head, he charged the woman he believed to be his mother.

Sonja was ready for the assault, and even as Tad stepped forward to protect her, her own knife instantly came to her hand. The black stare held her as she sprang forward, her free hand clutching the wrist that held the serrated knife, and at the same time, her own blade struck deeply into his chest.

Blackthorn stepped back away from Sonja as though caught by surprise; the lady pirate's knife pressed into his chest so near his heart. "I always loved you, Jasmine," he said right before he fell to the floor.

Garrick did not hesitate but quickly went to Katelin's side and within seconds had her free from her bonds and held her tightly against his chest.

"Oh, Garrick, it was so terrible." Katelin wept against his beating heart.

"It is over, my heart. I will never again allow you out of my sight. No more harm shall ever befall you." His words were a tender promise that went straight to Katelin's heart.

"Sis, sis, are you all right?" Joshua ran from the doorway the minute he was able to clear a path through the men who stood near the entrance.

By the time Joshua reached Katelin's side, Garrick had already covered her with his seaman's jacket, and opening her arms, her brother ran into them. "I am fine now." Katelin wiped away her tears, wanting to be brave for her brother.

"I was so afraid I wouldn't bring help in time," the boy confessed, and squeezing Katelin tightly, he sniffed back his own tears.

"You did fine, Joshua. You and Garrick are the bravest men I know, and I'm so thankful you're both mine." Her green eyes rose above the boy's head to Garrick and all the love she held for him was in the glance.

"You mean him, sis?" Joshua's dark head pulled away from her breast as he looked up at the large man standing at their side.

"Yes, little brother, I mean him." Katelin smiled as happiness filled her heart. She was alive and Garrick's arm was still wrapped around her shoulders as her brother was so close.

For a full minute Joshua appeared to study the large man who was looking down at his sister with adoring eyes. "Well, I guess he'll do, sis," he at last relented as though it took a special man to stand at his sister's side.

Garrick winked down at the boy. "Thanks, Joshua, I'm glad you approve. I love your sister and I plan to take care of her from this day forth."

Joshua opened his mouth to tell the large man that his sister was well able to take care of herself, but Katelin's fingers pressed over his lips, halting the words before they could be spoken. Slowly he nodded his dark head and, with a grin, stated when the hand moved away, "I guess Kat can love us both — she can do everything else!"

Epilogue

"Do you know what I love most about making love to you?" Garrick softly questioned as he ran his hand over Katelin's slender back.

Katelin arched toward him as though a favorite feline luxuriating in his attentions. Her breathing was still somewhat ragged from the heated bout of lovemaking they had just finished, and feeling blissfully content upon his captain's bed, she responded with a soft, "Hmm?"

"I love the little noises that come from your throat. As I fill you, they seem to spill from your lips and fill my ears until I want only to remain a part of you forever."

Lying against his broad chest, Katelin brushed her fingers against the crisp, dark matting of hair. "Do you think it will always be like this, Garrick?"

Wrapping his strong arms around her, he replied, "I will have it no other way, madam. No matter what comes before us, I will always keep you close to my heart."

"You may think otherwise after facing my aunt tomorrow and witnessing her wrath over our wedding on Saint Kitts and our not waiting until we returned to London, so she could be in attendance."

"I think when she meets young Joshua, her mind will be taken off all that." A chuckle rumbled deep within his chest.

Katelin playfully slapped at his chest. "She will love Joshua, just you wait and see." Katelin had her own doubts about this latest remark, but she would not let on to her husband that she feared that, within moments of meeting her brother, her aunt Elizabeth would be totally worn out. "I hope Sonja and Tad are doing all right on Saint Kitts."

Garrick sighed softly and placed a kiss upon her soft brow. He had definitely married a worrier, he told himself. "Tad and Sonja are very capable. Sonja will run Shadow Mere, and Tad will run Coral Rose, and their nights they shall spend together."

"I hope that Slade and Dirk and the people in the cove will be happy wherever they decide to go." Katelin had handed the *Kat's Eye* over to her crew, and the last time she had spoken to them, they had told her that they were going to move out of the secret cove and go to another island. She hoped that they would find happiness.

"We'll go back to Saint Kitts in a couple of years like I promised. After all, Joshua will be older then. But for now, enough talk of others. Do you know what's the first thing I am going to buy you when we reach London?"

Already forgotten were her thoughts of Saint Kitts and her friends, as she excitedly questioned, "What would you buy me, Garrick? I have everything I could ever want right here."

Garrick was pleased with her answer, and feeling

414

her silken limbs entwined with his own, he knew that she was all he would ever want. "I am going to purchase a black lace headdress to go with your flamenco outfit. I brought it along and thought you might wear it for me one evening."

Katelin remembered that the headdress had been discarded there on the streets of Grande Terre when they had taken a moment's shelter from the rain. She also remembered vividly the heated kiss they had shared. "Perhaps I will wear it with the next Pirate Moon."

Garrick's head swam with the image of his beautiful bride in her red flamenco outfit beneath a Pirate Moon. Bending his head to her right before his mouth covered hers, he whispered, "Yield to me, my love."

"Aye, forever!" she murmured in return.